SEASON
OF STORMS

ANDRZEJ SAPKOWSKI

Translated by David French

This paperback first published in Great Britain in 2020 by Gollancz
First published in Great Britain in 2018 by Gollancz
an imprint of The Orion Publishing Group Ltd
Carmelite House, 50 Victoria Embankment
London EC4Y 0DZ

An Hachette UK Company

1 3 5 7 9 10 8 6 4 2

Originally published in Polish as *Sezon Burz*
Published by arrangement with Literary Agency 'Agence de l'Est'

Original text Copyright © Andrzej Sapkowski 2013
English translation copyright © David French 2018
All rights reserved

A CIP catalogue record for this book is
available from the British Library.

ISBN (Mass Market Paperback) 978 1 473 23113 9
ISBN (eBook) 978 1 473 21809 3

Typeset by Input Data Services Ltd, Somerset
Printed in Great Britain by Clays Ltd, Elcograf S.p.A.

www.sapkowski.pl
www.gollancz.co.uk

Battle not with monsters, lest ye become a monster; for if you gaze into the abyss, the abyss gazes back into you.
Friedrich Nietzsche, *Beyond Good and Evil*

I consider gazing into the abyss utter foolishness. There are many things in the world much more worth gazing into.

Dandelion, *Half a Century of Poetry*

CHAPTER ONE

It lived only to kill.

It was lying on the sun-warmed sand.

It could sense the vibrations being transmitted through its hair-like feelers and bristles. Though the vibrations were still far off, the idr could feel them distinctly and precisely; it was thus able to determine not only its quarry's direction and speed of movement, but also its weight. As with most similar predators, the weight of the prey was of cardinal importance. Stalking, attacking and giving chase meant a loss of energy that had to be compensated by the calorific value of its food. Most predators similar to the idr would quit their attack if their prey was too small. But not the idr. The idr didn't exist to eat and sustain the species. It hadn't been created for that.

It lived to kill.

Moving its limbs cautiously, it exited the hollow, crawled over a rotten tree trunk, covered the clearing in three bounds, plunged into the fern-covered undergrowth and melted into the thicket. It moved swiftly and noiselessly, now running, now leaping like a huge grasshopper.

It sank into the thicket and pressed the segmented carapace of its abdomen to the ground. The vibrations in the ground became more and more distinct. The impulses from the idr's feelers and bristles formed themselves into an image. Into a plan. The idr now knew where to approach its victim from, where to cross its path, how to force it to flee, how to swoop on it from behind with a great leap, from what height to strike and lacerate with its razor-sharp mandibles. Within it the vibrations and impulses were already arousing the joy it would experience when its victim started struggling under its weight, arousing the euphoria that the taste of hot blood would induce in it. The ecstasy it would feel when the air was rent by a scream of pain. It trembled slightly,

1

opening and closing its pincers and pedipalps.

The vibrations in the ground were very distinct and had also diversified. The idr now knew there was more than one victim – probably three, or perhaps four. Two of them were shaking the ground in a normal way; the vibrations of the third suggested a small mass and weight. The fourth, meanwhile – provided there really was a fourth – was causing irregular, weak and hesitant vibrations. The idr stopped moving, tensed and extended its antennae above the grass, examining the movements of the air.

The vibrations in the ground finally signalled what the idr had been waiting for. Its quarry had separated. One of them, the smallest, had fallen behind. And the fourth – the vague one – had disappeared. It had been a fake signal, a false echo. The idr ignored it.

The smallest target moved even further away from the others. The trembling in the ground was more intense. And closer. The idr braced its rear limbs, pushed off and leaped.

*

The little girl gave an ear-splitting scream. Rather than running away, she had frozen to the spot. And was screaming unremittingly.

*

The Witcher darted towards her, drawing his sword mid-leap. And realised at once that something was wrong. That he'd been tricked.

The man pulling a handcart loaded with faggots screamed and shot six feet up into the air in front of Geralt's eyes, blood spraying copiously from him. He fell, only to immediately fly up again, this time in two pieces, each spurting blood. He'd stopped screaming. Now the woman was screaming piercingly and, like her daughter, was petrified and paralysed by fear.

Although he didn't believe he would, the Witcher managed to save her. He leaped and pushed hard, throwing the blood-spattered woman from the path into the forest, among the ferns. And realised at once that this time, too, it had been a trick. A ruse.

For the flat, grey, many-limbed and incredibly quick shape was now moving away from the handcart and its first victim. It was gliding towards the next one. Towards the still shrieking little girl. Geralt sped after the idr.

Had she remained where she was, he would have been too late. But the girl demonstrated presence of mind and bolted frantically. The grey monster, however, would easily have caught up with her, killed her and turned back to dispatch the woman, too. That's what would have happened had it not been for the Witcher.

He caught up with the monster and jumped, pinning down one of its rear limbs with his heel. If he hadn't jumped aside immediately he would have lost a leg – the grey creature twisted around with extraordinary agility, and its curved pincers snapped shut, missing him by a hair's breadth. Before the Witcher could regain his balance the monster sprang from the ground and attacked. Geralt defended himself instinctively with a broad and rather haphazard swing of his sword that pushed the monster away. He hadn't wounded it, but now he had the upper hand.

He sprang up and fell on the monster, slashing backhand, cleaving the carapace of the flat cephalothorax. Before the dazed creature came to its senses, a second blow hacked off its left mandible. The monster attacked, brandishing its limbs and trying to gore him with its remaining mandible like an aurochs. The Witcher hacked that one off too. He slashed one of the idr's pedipalps with a swift reverse cut. Then hacked at the cephalothorax again.

*

It finally dawned on the idr that it was in danger. That it must flee. Flee far from there, take cover, find a hiding place. It only lived to kill. In order to kill it must regenerate. It must flee . . . Flee . . .

*

The Witcher didn't let it. He caught up with it, stepped on the rear segment of the thorax and cut from above with a fierce blow. This time, the carapace gave way, and viscous, greenish fluid gushed and poured from the wound. The monster flailed around, its limbs thrashing the ground chaotically.

Geralt cut again with his sword, this time completely severing the flat head from the body.

He was breathing heavily.

It thundered in the distance. The growing wind and darkening sky heralded an approaching storm.

*

Right from their very first encounter, Albert Smulka, the newly appointed district reeve, reminded Geralt of a swede – he was stout, unwashed, thick-skinned and generally pretty dull. In other words, he didn't differ much from all the other district clerks Geralt had dealt with.

'Would seem to be true,' said the reeve. 'Nought like a witcher for dealing with troubles. Jonas, my predecessor, couldn't speak highly enough of you,' he continued a moment later, not waiting for any reaction from Geralt. 'To think, I considered him a liar. I mean that I didn't completely lend credence to him. I know how things can grow into fairy tales. Particularly among the common folk, with them there's always either a miracle or a marvel, or some witcher with superhuman powers. And here we are, turns out it's the honest truth. Uncounted people have died in that forest beyond the little river. And because it's a shortcut to the town the fools went that way . . . to their own doom. Heedless of warnings. These days it's better not to loiter in badlands or wander through forests. Monsters and man-eaters everywhere. A dreadful thing has just happened in the Tukaj Hills of Temeria – a sylvan ghoul killed fifteen people in a charcoal-burners' settlement. It's called Rogovizna. You must have heard. Haven't you? But it's the truth, cross my heart and hope to die. It's said even the wizardry have started an investigation in that there Rogovizna. Well, enough of stories. We're safe here in Ansegis now. Thanks to you.'

He took a coffer from a chest of drawers, spread out a sheet of paper on the table and dipped a quill in an inkwell.

'You promised you'd kill the monster,' he said, without raising his head. 'Seems you weren't having me on. You're a man of

4

your word, for a vagabond . . . And you saved those people's lives. That woman and the lass. Did they even thank you? Express their gratitude?'

No, they didn't. The Witcher clenched his jaw. *Because they haven't yet fully regained consciousness. And I'll be gone before they do. Before they realise I used them as bait, convinced in my conceited arrogance that I was capable of saving all three of them. I'll be gone before it dawns on the girl, before she understands I'm to blame for her becoming a half-orphan.*

He felt bad. No doubt because of the elixirs he'd taken before the fight. No doubt.

'That monster is a right abomination.' The reeve sprinkled some sand over the paper, and then shook it off onto the floor. 'I had a look at the carcass when they brought it here . . . What on earth was it?'

Geralt wasn't certain in that regard, but didn't intend to reveal his ignorance.

'An arachnomorph.'

Albert Smulka moved his lips, vainly trying to repeat the word.

'Ugh, meks no difference, when all's said and done. Did you dispatch it with that sword? With that blade? Can I take a look?'

'No, you can't.'

'Ha, because it's no doubt enchanted. And it must be dear . . . Quite something . . . Well, here we are jawing away and time's passing. The task's been executed, time for payment. But first the formalities. Make your mark on the bill. I mean, put a cross or some such.'

The Witcher took the bill from Smulka and held it up to the light.

'Look at 'im.' The reeve shook his head, grimacing. 'What's this, can he read?'

Geralt put the paper on the table and pushed it towards the official.

'A slight error has crept into the document,' he said, calmly and softly. 'We agreed on fifty crowns. This bill has been made out for eighty.'

Albert Smulka clasped his hands together and rested his chin on them.

5

'It isn't an error.' He also lowered his voice. 'Rather, a token of gratitude. You killed the monster and I'm sure it was an exacting job . . . So the sum won't astonish anyone . . .'

'I don't understand.'

'Pull the other one. Don't play the innocent. Trying to tell me that when Jonas was in charge he never made out bills like this? I swear I—'

'What do you swear?' Geralt interrupted. 'That he inflated bills? And went halves with me on the sum the royal purse was deprived of?'

'Went halves?' the reeve sneered. 'Don't be soft, witcher, don't be soft. Reckon you're that important? You'll get a third of the difference. Ten crowns. It's a decent bonus for you anyway. For I deserve more, if only owing to my function. State officials ought to be wealthy. The wealthier the official, the greater the prestige to the state. Besides, what would you know about it? This conversation's beginning to weary me. You signing it or what?'

The rain hammered on the roof. It was pouring down outside. But the thunder had stopped; the storm had moved away.

INTERLUDE

Two days later

'Do come closer, madam.' Belohun, King of Kerack, beckoned imperiously. 'Do come closer. Servants! A chair!'

The chamber's vaulting was decorated with a plafond of a fresco depicting a sailing ship at sea, amidst mermen, hippocampi and lobster-like creatures. The fresco on one of the walls, however, was a map of the world. An absolutely fanciful map, as Coral had long before realised, having little in common with the actual locations of lands and seas, but pleasing and tasteful.

Two pages lugged in and set down a heavy, carved curule seat. The sorceress sat down, resting her hands on the armrests so that her ruby-encrusted bracelets would be very conspicuous and not escape the king's attention. She had a small ruby tiara on her coiffed hair, and a ruby necklace in the plunging neckline of her dress. All especially for the royal audience. She wanted to make an impression. And had. King Belohun stared goggle-eyed: though it wasn't clear whether at the rubies or the cleavage.

Belohun, son of Osmyk, was, it could be said, a first-generation king. His father had made quite a considerable fortune from maritime trade, and probably also a little from buccaneering. Having finished off the competition and monopolised the region's cabotage, Osmyk named himself king. That act of self-anointed coronation had actually only formalised the status quo, and hence did not arouse significant quibbles nor provoke protests. Over the course of various private wars and skirmishes, Osmyk had smoothed over border disputes and jurisdictional squabbles with his neighbours, Verden and Cidaris. It was established where Kerack began, where it finished and who ruled there. And since he ruled, he was king – and deserved the title. By the natural order of things titles and power pass from father to son, so no one was surprised when

Belohun ascended his father's throne, following Osmyk's death. Osmyk admittedly had more sons – at least four of them – but they had all renounced their rights to the crown, one of them allegedly even of his own free will. Thus, Belohun had reigned in Kerack for over twenty years, deriving profits from shipbuilding, freight, fishery and piracy in keeping with family traditions.

And now King Belohun, seated on a raised throne, wearing a sable calpac and with a sceptre in one hand, was granting an audience. As majestic as a dung beetle on a cowpat.

'Our dear Madam Lytta Neyd,' he greeted her. 'Our favourite sorceress, Lytta Neyd. She has deigned to visit Kerack again. And surely for a long stay again?'

'The sea air's good for me.' Coral crossed her legs provocatively, displaying a bootee with fashionable cork heels. 'With the gracious permission of Your Royal Highness.'

The king glanced at his sons sitting beside him. Both were tall and slender, quite unlike their father, who was bony and sinewy, but of not very imposing height. Neither did they look like brothers. The older, Egmund, had raven-black hair, while Xander, who was a little younger, was almost albino blond. Both looked at Lytta with dislike. They were evidently annoyed by the privilege that permitted sorceresses to sit in the presence of kings, and that such seated audiences were granted to them. The privilege was well established, however, and could not be flouted by anyone wanting to be regarded as civilised. And Belohun's sons very much wanted to be regarded as civilised.

'We graciously grant our permission,' Belohun said slowly. 'With one proviso.'

Coral raised a hand and ostentatiously examined her fingernails. It was meant to signal that she couldn't give a shit about Belohun's proviso. The king didn't decode the signal. Or if he did he concealed it skilfully.

'It has reached our ears,' he puffed angrily, 'that the Honourable Madam Neyd makes magical concoctions available to womenfolk who don't want children. And helps those who are already pregnant to abort the foetus. We, here in Kerack, consider such a practice immoral.'

'What a woman has a natural right to,' replied Coral,

dryly, 'cannot – *ipso facto* – be immoral.'

'A woman—' the king straightened up his skinny frame on the throne '—has the right to expect only two gifts from a man: a child in the summer and thin bast slippers in the winter. Both the former and the latter gifts are intended to keep the woman at home, since the home is the proper place for a woman – ascribed to her by nature. A woman with a swollen belly and offspring clinging to her frock will not stray from the home and no foolish ideas will occur to her, which guarantees her man peace of mind. A man with peace of mind can labour hard for the purpose of increasing the wealth and prosperity of his king. Neither do any foolish ideas occur to a man confident of his marriage while toiling by the sweat of his brow and with his nose to the grindstone. But if someone tells a woman she can have a child when she wants and when she doesn't she mustn't, and when to cap it all someone offers a method and passes her a physick, then, Honourable Lady, then the social order begins to totter.'

'That's right,' interjected Prince Xander, who had been waiting for some time for a chance to interject. 'Precisely!'

'A woman who is averse to motherhood,' continued Belohun, 'a woman whose belly, the cradle and a host of brats don't imprison her in the homestead, soon yields to carnal urges. The matter is, indeed, obvious and inevitable. Then a man loses his inner calm and balanced state of mind, something suddenly goes out of kilter and stinks in his former harmony, nay, it turns out that there *is* no harmony or order. In particular, there is none of the order that justifies the daily grind. And the truth is I appropriate the results of that hard work. And from such thoughts it's but a single step to upheaval. To sedition, rebellion, revolt. Do you see, Neyd? Whoever gives womenfolk contraceptive agents or enables pregnancies to be terminated undermines the social order and incites riots and rebellion.'

'That is so,' interjected Xander. 'Absolutely!'

Lytta didn't care about Belohun's outer trappings of authority and imperiousness. She knew perfectly well that as a sorceress she was immune and that all the king could do was talk. However, she refrained from bluntly bringing to his attention that things had been out of kilter and stinking in his kingdom for ages, that there was next to no order in it, and that the only 'Harmony' known to his subjects was a harlot of the same name at the portside brothel. And mixing up in it women and motherhood – or aversion to motherhood – was evidence not only of misogyny, but also imbecility.

Instead of that she said the following: 'In your lengthy disquisition you keep stubbornly returning to the themes of increasing wealth and prosperity. I understand you perfectly, since my own prosperity is also extremely dear to me. And not for all the world would I give up anything that prosperity provides me with. I judge that a woman has the right to have children when she wants and not to have them when she doesn't, but I shall not enter into a debate in that regard; after all, everyone has the right to some opinion or other. I merely point out that I charge a fee for the medical help I give women. It's quite a significant source of my income. We have a free market economy, Your Majesty. Please don't interfere with the sources of my income. Because *my* income, as you well know, is also the income of the Chapter and the entire consorority. And the consorority reacts extremely badly to any attempts to diminish its income.'

'Are you trying to threaten me, Neyd?'

'The very thought! Not only am I not, but I declare my far-reaching help and collaboration. Know this, Belohun, that if – as a result of the exploitation and plunder you're engaged in – unrest occurs in Kerack, if – speaking grandiloquently – the fire of rebellion flares up, or if a rebellious rabble comes to drag you out by the balls, dethrone you and hang you forthwith from a dry branch . . . Then you'll be able to count on my consorority. And the sorcerers. We'll come to your aid. We shan't allow revolt or anarchy, because they don't suit us either. So keep on exploiting and increasing your wealth. Feel free. And don't interfere with others doing the same. That's my request and advice.'

'Advice?' fumed Xander, rising from his seat. 'You, advising? My father? My father is the king! Kings don't listen to advice – kings command!'

'Sit down and be quiet, son.' Belohun grimaced, 'And you, witch, listen carefully. I have something to say to you.'

'Yes?'

'I'm taking a new lady wife . . . Seventeen years old . . . A little cherry, I tell you. A cherry on a tart.'

'My congratulations.'

'I'm doing it for dynastic reasons. Out of concern for the succession and order in the land.'

Egmund, previously silent as the grave, jerked his head up.

'Succession?' he snarled, and the evil glint in his eyes didn't escape Lytta's notice. 'What succession? You have six sons and eight daughters, including bastards! What more do you want?'

'You can see for yourself.' Belohun waved a bony hand. 'You can see for yourself, Neyd. I have to look after the succession. Am I to leave the kingdom and the crown to someone who addresses his parent thus? Fortunately, I'm still alive and reigning. And I mean to reign for a long time. As I said, I'm wedding—'

'What of it?'

'Were she . . .' The king scratched behind an ear and glanced at Lytta from under half-closed eyelids. 'Were she . . . I mean my new, young wife . . . to ask you for those physics . . . I forbid you from giving them. Because I'm against physicks like that. Because they're immoral!'

'We can agree on that.' Coral smiled charmingly. 'If your little cherry asks I won't give her anything. I promise.'

'I understand.' Belohun brightened up. 'Why, how splendidly we've come to agreement. The crux is mutual understanding and respect. One must even differ with grace.'

'That's right,' interjected Xander. Egmund bristled and swore under his breath.

'In the spirit of respect and understanding—' Coral twisted a ginger ringlet around a finger and looked up at the plafond '—and also out of concern for harmony and order in your country . . . I have some information. Confidential information. I consider informants repellent; but fraudsters and thieves even more so. And this concerns impudent embezzlement, Your Majesty. People are trying to rob you.'

Belohun leaned forward from his throne, grimacing like a wolf.

'Who? I want names!'

11

Kerack, *a city in the northern kingdom of Cidaris, at the mouth of the River Adalatte. Once the capital of the independent kingdom of K., which, as the result of inept governments and the extinction of the royal line, fell into decline, lost its significance and became parcelled up by its neighbours and incorporated into them. It has a port, several factories, a lighthouse and roughly two thousand residents.*

Effenberg and Talbot,
Encyclopaedia Maxima Mundi, vol. VIII

CHAPTER TWO

The bay bristled with masts and filled with sails, some white, some many-coloured. The larger ships stood at anchor, protected by a headland and a breakwater. In the port itself, smaller and absolutely tiny vessels were moored alongside wooden jetties. Almost all of the free space on the beach was occupied by boats. Or the remains of boats.

A white-and-red-brick lighthouse, originally built by the elves and later renovated, stood tall at the end of the headland where it was being buffeted by white breakers.

The Witcher spurred his mare in her sides. Roach raised her head and flared her nostrils as though also enjoying the smell of the sea breeze. Urged on, she set off across the dunes. Towards the city, now nearby.

The city of Kerack, the chief metropolis of the kingdom bearing the same name, was divided into three separate, distinct zones straddling both banks at the mouth of the River Adalatte.

The port complex with docks and an industrial and commercial centre, including a shipyard and workshops as well as food-processing plants, warehouses and stores was located on the left bank of the Adalatte.

The river's right bank, an area called Palmyra, was occupied by the shacks and cottages of labourers and paupers, the houses and stalls of small traders, abattoirs and shambles, and numerous bars and dens that only livened up after nightfall, since Palmyra was also the district of entertainment and forbidden pleasures. It was also quite easy, as Geralt knew well, to lose one's purse or get a knife in the ribs there.

Kerack proper, an area consisting of narrow streets running between the houses of wealthy merchants and financiers, manufactories, banks, pawnbrokers, shoemakers' and tailors' shops, and large and small stores, was situated further away from the sea, on the left bank, behind a high palisade of robust stakes. Located there were also taverns, coffee houses and inns of superior category, including establishments offering, indeed, much the same as the port quarter of Palmyra, but at considerably higher prices. The centre of the district was a quadrangular town square featuring the town hall, the theatre, the courthouse, the customs office and the houses of the city's elite. A statue of the city's founder, King Osmyk, dreadfully spattered in bird droppings, stood on a plinth in the middle of the town square. It was a downright lie, as a seaside town had existed there long before Osmyk arrived from the devil knows where.

Higher up, on a hill, stood the castle and the royal palace, which were quite unusual in terms of form and shape. It had previously been a temple, which was abandoned by its priests embittered by the townspeople's total lack of interest and then modified and extended. The temple's campanile – or bell tower – and its bell had even survived, which the incumbent King Belohun ordered to be tolled every day at noon and – clearly just to spite his subjects – at midnight. The bell sounded as the Witcher began to ride between Palmyra's cottages.

Palmyra stank of fish, laundry and cheap restaurants, and the crush in the streets was dreadful, which cost the Witcher a great deal of time and patience to negotiate the streets. He breathed a sigh when he finally arrived at the bridge and crossed onto the Adalatte's left bank. The water smelled foul and bore scuds of dense foam – waste from the tannery located upstream. From that point it wasn't far to the road leading to the palisaded city.

Geralt left his horse in the stables outside the city centre, paying for two days in advance and giving the stableman some baksheesh in order to ensure that Roach was adequately cared for. He headed towards the watchtower. One could only enter Kerack through the watchtower, after undergoing a search and the rather unpleasant procedures accompanying it. This necessity somewhat angered the Witcher, but he understood its purpose – the fancier townspeople weren't especially overjoyed at the thought of visits by guests from dockside Palmyra, particularly in the form of mariners from foreign parts putting ashore there.

He entered the watchtower, a log building that he knew accommodated the guardhouse. He thought he knew what to expect. He was wrong.

He had visited numerous guardhouses in his life: small, medium and large, both nearby and in quite distant parts of the world, some in more and less civilised – and some quite uncivilised – regions. All the world's guardhouses stank of mould, sweat, leather and urine, as well as iron and the grease used to preserve it. It was no different in the Kerack guardhouse. Or it wouldn't have been, had the classic guardhouse smell not been drowned out by the heavy, choking, floor-to-ceiling odour of farts. There could be no doubt that leguminous plants – most likely peas and beans – prevailed in the diet of the guardhouse's crew.

And the garrison was wholly female. It consisted of six women currently sitting at a table and busy with their midday meal. They were all greedily slurping some morsels floating in a thin, paprika sauce from earthenware bowls.

The tallest guard, clearly the commandant, pushed her bowl away and stood up. Geralt, who always maintained there was no such thing as an ugly woman, suddenly felt compelled to revise this opinion.

'Weapons on the bench!'

The commandant's head like those of her comrades – was shaven. Her hair had managed to grow back a little, giving rise to patchy stubble on her bald head. The muscles of her midriff showed from beneath her unbuttoned waistcoat and gaping shirt, bringing to mind a netted pork roast. The guard's biceps – to remain on the subject of cooked meat – were the size of hams.

'Put your weapons on the bench!' she repeated. 'You deaf?'

One of her subordinates, still hunched over her bowl, raised herself a little and farted, loud and long. Her companions guffawed. Geralt fanned himself with a glove. The guard looked at his swords.

'Hey, girls! Get over here!'

The 'girls' stood up rather reluctantly, stretching. Their style of clothing, Geralt noticed, was quite informal, mainly intended to show off their musculature. One of them was wearing leather shorts with the legs split at the seams to accommodate her thighs.

Two belts crossing her chest were pretty much all she had on above the waist.

'A witcher,' she stated. 'Two swords. Steel and silver.'

Another – like all of them, tall and broad-shouldered – approached, tugged open Geralt's shirt unceremoniously and pulled out his medallion by the silver chain.

'He has a sign,' she stated. 'There's a wolf on it, fangs bared. Would seem to be a witcher. Do we let him through?'

'Rules don't prohibit it. He's handed over his swords . . .'

'That's correct,' Geralt joined the conversation in a calm voice. 'I have. They'll both remain, I presume, in safe deposit? To be reclaimed on production of a docket. Which you're about to give me?'

The guards surrounded him, grinning. One of them prodded him, apparently by accident. Another farted thunderously.

'That's your receipt,' she snorted.

'A witcher! A hired monster killer! And he gave up his swords! At once! Meek as a schoolboy!'

'Bet he'd turn his cock over as well, if we ordered him to.'

'Let's do it then! Eh, girls? Have him whip it out!'

'We'll see what witchers' cocks are like!'

'Here we go,' snapped the commandant. 'They're off now, the sluts. Gonschorek, get here! Gonschorek!'

A balding, elderly gentleman in a dun mantle and woollen beret emerged from the next room. Immediately he entered he had a coughing fit, took off his beret and began to fan himself with it. He took the swords wrapped in their belts and gestured for Geralt to follow him. The Witcher didn't linger. Intestinal gases had definitely begun to predominate in the noxious mixture of the guardhouse.

The room they entered was split down the middle by a sturdy iron grating. The large key the elderly gentleman opened it with grated in the lock. He hung the swords on a hook beside other sabres, claymores, broadswords and cutlasses. He opened a scruffy register, scrawled slowly and lengthily in it, coughing incessantly and struggling to catch his breath. He finally handed Geralt the completed receipt.

'Am I to understand that my swords are safe here? Locked away and under guard?'

The dun-clad elderly gentleman, puffing and panting heavily, locked the grating and showed him the key. It didn't convince Geralt. Any grating could be forced, and the noisy flatulence of the 'ladies' from the guardhouse was capable of drowning out any attempts at burglary. But there was no choice. He had to accomplish in Kerack what he had come to do. And leave the city as soon as he could.

*

The tavern – or, as the sign declared, the Natura Rerum osteria – was a small but tasteful building of cedar wood, with a steep roof and a chimney sticking up high out of it. The building's façade was decorated by a porch with steps leading to it, surrounded by spreading aloe plants in wooden tubs. The smell of cooking – mainly meat roasting on a gridiron – drifted from the tavern. The scents were so enticing that right away it seemed to the Witcher that Natura Rerum was an Eden, a garden of delights, an island of happiness, a retreat for the blessed flowing with milk and honey.

It soon turned out that this Eden – like every Eden – was guarded. It had its own Cerberus, a guard with a flaming sword. Geralt had the chance to see him in action. Before his very eyes, the guard, a short but powerfully built fellow, was driving a skinny young man from the garden of delights. The young man was protesting – shouting and gesticulating – which clearly annoyed the guard.

'You're barred, Muus. As well you know. So be off. I won't say it again.'

The young man moved away from the steps quickly enough to avoid being pushed. He was, Geralt noticed, prematurely balding, his long, thin hair only beginning somewhere in the region of his crown, which gave a generally rather unprepossessing impression.

'Fuck you and your ban!' yelled the young man from a safe distance. 'I don't need any favours! You aren't the only ones! I'll go to the competition! Big-heads! Upstarts! The sign may be gilded, but there's still dung on your boots. You mean as much to me as that dung. And shit will always be shit!'

Geralt was slightly worried. The balding young man, apart from

19

his unsightly looks, was dressed in quite a grand fashion, perhaps not too richly, but in any case, more elegantly than the Witcher. So, if elegance was the determining criterion . . .

'And where might you be going, may I ask?' The guard's icy voice interrupted his train of thought. And confirmed his fears.

'This is an exclusive tavern,' continued the Cerberus, blocking the stairs. 'Do you understand the meaning of the word? It's off limits, as it were. To some people.'

'Why to me?'

'Don't judge a book by its cover.' The guard looked down on the Witcher from two steps higher up. 'You are a foreigner, a walking illustration of that old folk saying. Your cover is nothing to write home about. Perhaps there are other objects hidden in its pages, but I shan't pry. I repeat, this is an exclusive tavern. We don't tolerate people dressed like ruffians here. Or armed.'

'I'm not armed.'

'But you look like you are. So kindly take yourself off somewhere else.'

'Control yourself, Tarp.'

A swarthy man in a short velvet jacket appeared in the doorway of the tavern. His eyebrows were bushy, his gaze piercing and his nose aquiline. And large.

'You clearly don't know who you're dealing with,' the aquiline nose informed the guard. 'You don't know who has come to visit.'

The guard's lengthening silence showed he indeed did not.

'Geralt of Rivia. The Witcher. Known for protecting people and saving their lives. As he did a week ago, here, in our region, in Ansegis, when he saved a mother and her child. And several months earlier, he famously killed a man-eating leucrote in Cizmar, suffering wounds in so doing. How could you bar entry to my tavern to somebody who plies such an honest trade? On the contrary, I'm very happy to see a guest like him. And I consider it an honour that he desires to visit me. Master Geralt, the Natura Rerum osteria warmly welcomes you. I'm Febus Ravenga, the owner of this humble house.'

The table that the head waiter sat him at had a tablecloth. All the tables in the Natura Rerum – most of which were occupied – had tablecloths. Geralt couldn't recall the last time he'd seen any in a tavern.

Although curious, he didn't look around, not wanting to appear provincial and uncouth. However, a cautious glance revealed modest – though elegant and tasteful – decor. The clientele, whom he judged to be mainly merchants and craftsmen, were also elegantly – although not always tastefully – attired. There were ships' captains, weather-beaten and bearded. And there was no shortage of garishly dressed noblemen. It smelled nice and elegant: of roast meat, garlic, caraway and big money.

He felt eyes on him. His witcher senses immediately signalled whenever he was being observed. He had a quick, discreet look around.

A young woman with fox-red hair was observing him, also very discreetly, and to an ordinary mortal imperceptibly. She was pretending to be completely absorbed in her meal – something tasty looking and temptingly fragrant even from a distance. Her style and body language left no doubt. Not to a witcher. He would have bet anything she was a sorceress.

The head waiter shook him out of his contemplation and sudden nostalgia.

'Today,' he announced ceremonially and not without pride, 'we propose veal shank stewed in vegetables with mushrooms and beans. Saddle of lamb roast with aubergines. Bacon in beer served with glazed plums. Roast shoulder of boar, served with stewed apples. Fried duck breasts, served with red cabbage and cranberries. Squid stuffed with chicory in a white sauce served with grapes. Grilled monkfish in a cream sauce, served with stewed pears. Or as usual, our speciality: goose legs in white wine, with a choice of baked fruit, and turbot in caramelised cuttlefish ink, served with crayfish necks.'

'If you have a liking for fish,' Febus Ravenga suddenly appeared at the table out of the blue, 'I heartily recommend the turbot. From the morning catch, it goes without saying. The pride and boast of our head chef.'

'The turbot in ink then.' The Witcher fought against an irrational desire to order several dishes in one go, aware it would have been in bad taste. 'Thank you for the suggestion. I'd begun to suffer the agony of choice.'

'Which wine,' the head waiter asked, 'would sir like to order?'

'Please choose something suitable. I'm not very au fait with wines.'

'Few are,' smiled Febus Ravenga. 'And very few admit it. Never fear, *we* shall choose the type and vintage, master witcher. I'll leave you in peace, bon appétit.'

That wish was not to come true. Neither did Geralt have the opportunity to find out what wine they would choose. The taste of turbot in cuttlefish ink was also to remain a mystery to him that day.

The red-haired woman suddenly abandoned discretion, as her eyes found his. She smiled. Spitefully, he couldn't help feeling. He felt a quiver run through him.

'The Witcher called Geralt of Rivia?' The question was asked by one of three characters dressed in black who had noiselessly approached the table.

'It is I.'

'You are arrested in the name of the law.'

What judgment shall I dread, doing no wrong?

William Shakespeare, *The Merchant of Venice*

CHAPTER THREE

Geralt's court-appointed barrister avoided eye contact. She flicked
through the portfolio of documents with a persistence worthy of a
better cause. There were very few papers in it. Two, to be precise.
His lawyer had probably learned them by heart. To dazzle them
with her speech for the defence, he hoped. But that was, he suspected, a forlorn hope.

'You assaulted two of your cellmates while under arrest.' His
lawyer finally raised her eyes. 'Ought I perhaps to know the
reason?'

'*Primo*, I rejected their sexual advances. They didn't want to
understand that "no" means "no". *Secundo*, I like beating people
up. *Tertio*, it's a falsehood. They self-inflicted their wounds. By
banging themselves against the wall. To slander me.'

He spoke slowly and carelessly. After a week spent in prison he
had become utterly indifferent.

His barrister closed the portfolio. Only to open it again straight
away. Then she tidied her elaborate coiffure.

'The victims aren't pressing charges, it transpires.' She sighed.
'Let us focus on the prosecutor's charge. The tribunal assessor is
accusing you of a grave crime, punishable by a severe penalty.'

How could it be otherwise? he thought, contemplating the lawyer's
features. He wondered how old she had been when she entered the
school for sorcerers. And how old she was when she left.

The two schools for sorcerers – Ban Ard School for boys and
Aretuza School for girls, both on the Isle of Thanedd – apart from
male and female graduates, also produced rejects. In spite of the
strict selection procedure of their entry examinations, which was
supposed to facilitate the winnowing out and discarding of hopeless
cases, it was only the first semesters that really found and revealed
the ones who had managed to remain hidden. The ones for whom
thinking turned out to be a disagreeable and hazardous experience.

Latent idiots, sluggards and intellectual slackers of both sexes, who had no place in schools of magic. The difficulty was that they were usually the offspring of wealthy people or considered important for other reasons. After being expelled from school it was necessary to do something with these difficult youngsters. There was no problem for the boys rejected by Ban Ard – they joined the diplomatic service, the army, navy or police while politics was left for the stupidest. Magical rejects in the shape of the fairer sex seemed to be more difficult to place. Although expelled, the young ladies had nonetheless crossed the threshold of a school of magic and had tasted magic to some degree or other. And the influence of sorceresses on monarchs, and on all areas of political and economic life, was too powerful for the young ladies to be left in the lurch. They were provided with a safe haven. They joined the judiciary. They became lawyers.

The defence counsel closed the portfolio. Then opened it.

'I recommend an admission of guilt,' she said. 'Then we can expect a more lenient punishment—'

'Admit to what?' interrupted the Witcher.

'When the judge asks if you plead guilty you are to reply in the affirmative. An admission of guilt will be regarded as a mitigating circumstance.'

'How do you mean to defend me, then?'

The lawyer closed the portfolio. As though it were a coffin lid.

'Let's go. The judge is waiting.'

The judge was waiting. For right then the previous miscreant was being escorted from the courtroom. *He looks none too cheerful*, thought Geralt.

A shield flecked with flies bearing the emblem of Kerack, a blue dolphin *naiant*, hung on the wall. Under the coat of arms was the bench, with three people sitting behind it. A scrawny scribe. A faded subjudge. And the judge, a woman of equable appearance and countenance.

The bench on the judges' right was occupied by the tribunal assessor, acting as prosecutor. He looked serious. Serious enough to avoid an encounter with him in a dark alley.

On the other side, on the judges' left, was the dock. The place assigned to Geralt.

Things moved quickly after that.

'Geralt, called Geralt of Rivia, a witcher by profession, is accused of embezzlement, of the seizure and misappropriation of Crown property. Acting in league with other persons whom he corrupted, the accused inflated the fees on the bills issued for his services with the intention of arrogating those surpluses. Which resulted in losses to the state treasury. The proof is a report, *notitia criminis*, that the prosecution has enclosed in the file. That report . . .'

The judge's weary expression and absent gaze clearly showed that this respectable lady was miles away. And that quite other matters and problems were distressing her: the laundry, the children, the colour of the curtains, preparing the dough for a poppy-seed cake and the stretch marks on her large behind auguring a marital crisis. The Witcher humbly accepted the fact that he was less important. That he could not compete with anything of that kind.

'The crime committed by the accused,' the prosecutor continued without emotion, 'not only damages the country, but also undermines the social order and spreads dissent. The law demands—'

'The report included in the file,' interrupted the judge, 'has to be treated by the court as *probatio de relato*, evidence supplied by a third party. Can the prosecution supply any other proof?'

'There is no other evidence . . . For the moment . . . The accused is, as has been pointed out, a witcher. He is a mutant, beyond the margins of human society, flouting human laws and placing himself above them. In his criminogenic and antisocial profession, he communes with criminals, as well as non-humans, including races traditionally hostile to humanity. Law-breaking is part of a witcher's nihilistic nature. In the case of *this* witcher, Your Honour, the lack of evidence is the best proof . . . It proves perfidy and—'

'Does the accused . . .' The judge was clearly uninterested in whatever the lack of evidence proved. 'Does the accused plead guilty?'

'He does not.' Geralt ignored his lawyer's desperate signals. 'I am innocent; I haven't committed any crime.'

He had some skill, he had dealt with the law. He had also familiarised himself with the literature on the subject.

'I am accused on the basis of prejudice—'

'Objection!' yelled the assessor. 'The accused is making a speech!'

'Objection dismissed.'

'—as a result of prejudice against my person and my profession, i.e. as a result of *praeiudicium*. *Praeiudicium* implies, in advance, a falsehood. Furthermore, I stand accused on the grounds of an anonymous denunciation, and only one. *Testimonium unius non valet. Testis unus, testis nullus. Ergo*, it is not an accusation, but conjecture, i.e. *praesumptio*. And conjecture leaves doubt.'

'*In dubio pro reo!*' the defence counsel roused herself. '*In dubio pro reo*, Your Honour!'

'The court has decided to set bail of five hundred Novigradian crowns.' The judge struck her gavel on the bench, waking up the faded subjudge.

Geralt sighed. He wondered if both his cellmates had come around and drawn any kind of lesson from the matter. Or whether he would have to give them another hiding.

What is the city but the people?

William Shakespeare, *Coriolanus*

CHAPTER FOUR

A stall carelessly nailed together from planks, manned by an old dear in a straw hat and as plump and ruddy-faced as a good witch from a fairy tale, stood at the very edge of the crowded market place. The sign above the old dear read: *Come to me for joy and happiness. Gherkin complimentary.* Geralt stopped and dug some copper pennies from his pocket.

'Pour me a gill of happiness, Granny,' he demanded gloomily.

He took a deep breath, downed it in one, and breathed out. He wiped away the tears that the hooch brought to his eyes.

He was at liberty. And angry.

He had learned that he was free, interestingly, from a person he knew. By sight. It was the same prematurely bald young man who he had observed being driven from the steps of the Natura Rerum osteria. And who, it turned out, was the court scribe.

'You're free,' the bald young man had told him, locking and unlocking his thin, ink-stained fingers. 'Someone came up with the bail.'

'Who?'

The information turned out to be confidential – the bald scribbler refused to give it. He also refused – rather bluntly – the return of Geralt's confiscated purse. Which contained cash and bank cheques among other things. The Witcher's personal property – he declared not without spitefulness – had been treated by the authorities as a *cautio pro expensis*, a down payment against court costs and expected penalties.

There was no point or purpose in arguing. On release, Geralt had to content himself with what he had in his pockets when he was arrested. Personal trifles and petty cash. So petty no one had bothered to steal it.

He counted the remaining copper pennies and smiled at the old dear.

'And a gill of joy, please. I'll decline the gherkin.'

After the old dear's hooch, the world took on a more beautiful hue. Geralt knew it would quickly pass so he quickened his step. He had things to do.

Roach, his mare, had fortunately escaped the attentions of the court and wasn't included in the cost of the *cautio pro expensis*. She was where he'd left her, in the stable stall, well-groomed and fed. The Witcher couldn't accept something like that without a reward, irrespective of his own assets. The stableman received at once a few of the handful of silver coins that had survived in a hiding place sewn into the saddle. Geralt's generosity took the man's breath away.

The horizon over the sea was darkening. It seemed to Geralt that he could see flashes of lightning there.

Before entering the guardhouse, he prudently filled his lungs with fresh air. It didn't help. The guardswomen must have eaten more beans than usual that day. Many, many more beans. Who knew, perhaps it was Sunday.

Some of them were eating, as usual. Others were busy playing dice. They stood up from the table upon seeing him. And surrounded him.

'The Witcher, just look,' said the commandant, standing very close. ''e's up and come here.'

'I'm leaving the city. I've come to collect my property.'

'If we lets you.' Another guard prodded him with an elbow, apparently by accident. 'What will 'e give us for it? You'll have to buy yourself out, sonny, buy yourself out! Eh, lasses? What'll we make him do?'

'Kiss all our bare arses!'

'With a lick! And a dick!'

'Nothing of the kind! He might infect us with something.'

'But he'll 'ave to give some pleasure, won't 'e?' Another one pushed her rock-hard bust onto him.

'He can sing us an air.' Another one farted thunderously. 'And fit the tune to my pitch!'

'Or mine!' Yet another one farted even louder. 'Mine's more full-blooded!'

The other women laughed so much they clasped their sides.

Geralt made his way through, trying hard not to use excessive force. At that moment, the door to the deposit opened and an elderly gentleman in a grey mantle and beret appeared. The attendant, Gonschorek. On seeing the Witcher he opened his mouth wide.

'You, sir?' he mumbled. 'How so? Your swords . . .'

'Indeed. My swords. May I have them?'

'But . . . But . . .' Gonschorek choked and clutched his chest, struggling to catch his breath. 'But I don't have the swords!'

'I beg your pardon?'

'I don't have them . . .' Gonschorek's face flushed. And contorted as though in a paroxysm of pain. 'Them bin took—'

'What?' Geralt felt cold fury gripping him.

'Bin . . . took . . .'

'What do you mean, taken?' He grabbed the attendant by the lapels. 'Taken by whom, dammit? What the bloody hell is this about?'

'The docket . . .'

'Exactly!' He felt an iron grip on his arm. The commandant of the guard shoved him away from the choking Gonschorek.

'Exactly! Show us the docket!'

The Witcher did not have the docket. The docket from the weapon store had been in his purse. The purse the court had confiscated. Against the costs and the expected punishments.

'The docket!'

'I don't have it. But—'

'No docket, no deposit.' The commandant didn't let him finish. 'Swords bin took, didn't you 'ear? You probably took 'em. And now you're putting on this pantomime? Want to con something out of us? Nothing doing. Get out of here.'

'I'm not leaving until . . .'

The commandant, without loosening her grasp, dragged Geralt away and turned him around. To face the door.

'Fuck off.'

Geralt shied away from hitting women. He didn't, however, have any reluctance when it came to somebody who had the shoulders of a wrestler, a belly like a netted pork roast and calves like a discus thrower, and on top of that who farted like a mule. He pushed the commandant away and smashed her hard in the jaw. With his favourite right hook.

The others froze, but only for a second. Even before the commandant had tumbled onto the table, splashing beans and paprika sauce around, they were on him. He smashed one of them in the nose without thinking, and hit another so hard her teeth made a cracking noise. He treated two to the Aard Sign. They flew like rag dolls into a stand of halberds, knocking them all over with an indescribable crash and clatter.

He got hit in the ear by the commandant, who was dripping sauce. The other guard, the one with the rock-hard bust, seized him from behind in a bear hug. He elbowed her so hard she howled. He pushed the commandant onto the table again, and whacked her with a haymaker. He thumped the one with the smashed nose in the solar plexus and knocked her to the ground, where she vomited audibly. Another, struck in the temple, slammed her head against a post and went limp, her eyes immediately misting over.

But four of them were still on their feet. That marked the end of his advantage. He was hit in the back of the head and then in the ear. And after that in the lower back. One of them tripped him up and when he fell down two dropped on him, pinning him down and pounding him with their fists. The other two weighed in with kicks.

A head-butt in the face took out one of the women lying on him, but the other immediately pressed him down. The commandant – he recognised her by the sauce dripping from her. She smacked him from above in the teeth. He spat blood right in her eyes.

'A knife!' she yelled, thrashing her shaven head around. 'Give me a knife! I'll cut his balls off!'

'Why a knife?' yelled another. 'I'll bite them off!'

'Stop! Attention! What is the meaning of this? Attention, I said!'

A stentorian voice, commanding respect, tore through the hubbub of the fracas, pacifying the guards. They released Geralt from their grasp. He got up with difficulty, somewhat sore. The sight of the battlefield improved his humour a little. He observed his accomplishments with some satisfaction. The guard lying by the wall had opened her eyes, but was still unable even to sit upright. Another, bent over, was spitting blood and feeling her teeth with a finger. Yet another, the one with the smashed nose, was trying hard to stand, but kept falling over, slipping in a puddle of her own beany vomit. Only three of the six could keep their balance. So he could be satisfied with the result. Despite the fact that had it not been for the intervention he would have suffered more serious injuries and might not have been able to get up unaided.

The person who had intervened, however, was an elegantly attired man with noble features, emanating authority. Geralt didn't know who he was. But he knew perfectly well who the noble-looking man's companion was. A dandy in a fanciful hat with an egret feather stuck into it, with shoulder-length blond hair curled with irons. Wearing a doublet the colour of red wine and a shirt with a lace ruffle. Along with his ever-present lute and with that ever-present insolent smile on his lips.

'Greetings, Witcher! What *do* you look like? With that smashed-up fizzog! I'll split my sides laughing!'

'Greetings, Dandelion. I'm pleased to see you too.'

'What's going on here?' The man with the noble looks stood with arms akimbo. 'Well? What are you up to? Standard report! This moment!'

'It was him!' The commandant shook the last of the sauce from her ears and pointed accusingly at Geralt. 'He's guilty, Honourable Instigator. He lost his temper and stirred up a row, and then began brawling. And all because of some swords in the deposit, what he hasn't got a docket for. Gonschorek will confirm . . . Hey, Gonschorek, what are you doing curled up in the corner? Shat yourself? Move your arse, get up, tell the Honourable Instigator . . . Hey! Gonschorek? What ails you?'

A close look was enough to guess what ailed him. There was no need to check his pulse, it sufficed to look at his chalky white face. Gonschorek was dead. He was, quite simply, deceased.

*

'We will institute an investigation, Lord Rivia,' said Ferrant de Lettenhove, instigator of the Royal Tribunal. 'Since you are lodging a formal complaint and appeal we must institute one – the law so decrees. We shall interrogate everyone who during your arrest and trial had access to your effects. We shall arrest any suspects.'

'The usual ones?'

'I beg your pardon?'

'Nothing, nothing.'

'Indeed. The matter will certainly be explained, and those guilty of the theft of the swords will be brought to justice. If a theft was really committed. I promise that we shall solve the mystery and the truth will out. Sooner or later.'

'I'd rather it were sooner.' The Witcher didn't care too much for the instigator's tone of voice. 'My swords are my existence; I can't do my job without them. I know my profession is adversely perceived by many and that I suffer as a result of this negative portrayal caused by prejudice, superstition and xenophobia. I hope that fact won't influence the investigation.'

'It won't,' replied Ferrant de Lettenhove dryly, 'since law and order prevail here.'

After the servants had carried Gonschorek's body out, the instigator ordered a search of the weapon store and the entire cubbyhole. Predictably, there wasn't a trace of the Witcher's swords. And the commandant of the guard – still annoyed with Geralt – pointed out to them a filing spike where the deceased had kept the completed deposit slips. The Witcher's was soon found among them. The commandant searched through the stack, thrusting it under his nose a moment later.

'There you go.' She pointed triumphantly. 'It's here in black and white. Signed *Gerland of Ryblia*. Told yer the witcher had bin here and took his swords away. And now 'e's lying, no doubt to claim damages. Gonschorek turned 'is toes up thanks to 'im! His gall bladder ruptured from the worry and 'is heart gev out.'

But neither she, nor any of the other guards, elected to testify that any of them had actually seen Geralt collect his weapons. The explanation was that 'there's always someone 'anging around 'ere' and they had been busy eating.

Seagulls circled over the roof of the court, uttering ear-splitting screeches. The wind had blown the storm cloud southwards over the sea. The sun was out.

'May I warn you in advance,' said Geralt, 'that my swords are protected by powerful spells. Only witchers can touch them;

others will have their vitality drained away. It mainly manifests in the loss of male potency. I'm talking about sexual enfeeblement. Absolute and permanent.'

'We shall bear that in mind.' The instigator nodded. 'For the moment, though, I would ask you not to leave the city. I'm inclined to turn a blind eye to the brawl in the guardhouse – in any case, they occur there regularly. The guards are pretty volatile. And because Julian – I mean Lord Dandelion – vouches for you, I'm certain that your case will be satisfactorily solved in court.'

'My case—' the Witcher squinted his eyes '—is nothing but harassment. Intimidation resulting from prejudice and hatred—'

'The evidence will be examined—' the instigator cut him off '—and measures taken based on it. That is what law and order decrees. The same law and order that granted you your liberty. On bail, and thus conditionally. You ought, Lord Rivia, to respect those caveats.'

'Who paid the bail?'

Ferrant de Lettenhove coldly declined to reveal the identity of the Witcher's benefactor, bade farewell and headed towards the entrance to the court, accompanied by his servants. It was just what Dandelion had been waiting for. Scarcely had they exited the town square and entered a narrow street than he revealed everything he knew.

'It's a genuine catalogue of unfortunate coincidences, Geralt, my dear. And unlucky incidents. And as far as the bail is concerned, it was paid for you by a certain Lytta Neyd, known to her friends as Coral, from the colour of the lipstick she uses. She's a sorceress who works for Belohun, the local kinglet. Everybody's racking their brains wondering why she did it. Because it was none other than she who sent you down.'

'What?'

'Listen, will you? It was Coral who informed on you. That actually didn't surprise anyone, it's widely known that sorcerers have it in for you. And then a bolt from the blue: the sorceress suddenly pays your bail and gets you out of the dungeon where you'd been thrown because of her. The whole city—'

'Widely known? The whole city? What are you saying, Dandelion?'

'I'm using metaphors and circumlocution. Don't pretend you don't know, you know me well enough. Naturally not the "whole city", and only certain well-informed people among those close to the crown.'

'And you're one of them, I presume?'

'Correct. Ferrant is my cousin – the son of my father's brother. I dropped in to visit him, as you would a relative. And I found out about your imbroglio. I immediately interceded for you, you can't possibly doubt that. I vouched for your honesty. I talked about Yennefer . . .'

'Thank you very much.'

'Drop the sarcasm. I had to talk about her to help my cousin realise that the local witch is maligning and slandering you out of jealousy and envy. That the entire accusation is false, that you never stoop to swindle people. As a result of my intercession, Ferrant de Lettenhove, the royal instigator, a high-ranking legal executive, is now convinced of your innocence—'

'I didn't get that impression,' said Geralt. 'Quite the opposite. I felt he didn't believe me. Neither in the case of the alleged embezzlement, nor in the case of the vanished swords. Did you hear what he said about evidence? Evidence is a fetish to him. The denunciation will thus be evidence of the fraud and Gerland of Ryblia's signature on the docket is proof of the hoax involving the theft of the swords. Not to mention his expression when he was warning me against leaving the city . . .'

'You're being too hard on him,' pronounced Dandelion. 'I know him better than you. That fact that I'm vouching for you is worth more than a dozen inflated pieces of evidence. And he was right to warn you. Why do you think both he and I headed to the guardhouse? To stop you from doing anything foolish. Someone, you say, is framing you, fabricating phoney evidence? Then don't hand that someone irrefutable proof. Which is what fleeing would be.'

'Perhaps you're right,' agreed Geralt. 'But my instinct tells me otherwise. I ought to do a runner before they utterly corner me. First arrest, then bail, and then right after that the swords . . . What next? Dammit, without a sword I feel like . . . like a snail without a shell.'

'I think you worry too much. And anyway, the place is full of shops. Forget about those swords and buy some more.'

'And if someone were to steal your lute? Which was acquired, as I recall, in quite dramatic circumstances? Wouldn't *you* worry? Would you let it slide? And buy another in the shop around the corner?'

Dandelion involuntarily tightened his grip on his lute and his eyes swept around anxiously. However, none of the passers-by looked like a potential robber, nor displayed an unhealthy interest in his unique instrument.

'Well, yes,' he sighed. 'I understand. Like my lute, your swords are also unique and irreplaceable. And what's more . . . What were you saying? Enchanted? Triggering magical impotence . . Dammit, Geralt! Now you tell me. I mean, I've often spent time in your company, I've had those swords at arm's length! And sometimes closer! Now everything's clear, now I get it . . . I've been having certain difficulties lately, dammit . . .'

'Relax. That impotence thing was nonsense. I made it up on the spot, hoping the rumour would spread. That the thief would take fright . . .'

'If he takes fright he's liable to bury the swords in a muck heap,' the bard noted, still slightly pale. 'And you'll never get them back. Better to count on my cousin Ferrant. He's been instigator for years, and has a whole army of sheriffs, agents and narks. They'll find the thief in no time, you'll see.'

'If the thief's still here.' The Witcher ground his teeth. 'He might have run for it while I was in the slammer. What did you say was the name of that sorceress who landed me in this?'

'Lytta Neyd, nicknamed Coral. I can guess what you're planning, my friend. But I don't think it's a good idea. She's a sorceress. An enchantress and a woman in one; in a word, an alien species that doesn't submit to rational understanding, and functions according to mechanisms and principles incomprehensible to ordinary men. Why am I telling you this, anyway? You know it very well. You have, indeed, very rich experience in this matter . . . What's that racket?'

Aimlessly wandering through the streets, they had ended up in the vicinity of a small square resounding with the ceaseless banging of hammers. There was a large cooper's workshop there, it turned out. Cords of seasoned planks were piled up evenly beneath an awning by the street. From there, the planks were carried by bare-foot youngsters to tables where they were attached to special trestles and shaped using drawknives. The carved staves went to other craftsmen, who finished them on long planing benches, standing astride them up to their ankles in shavings. The completed staves ended up in the hands of the coopers, who assembled them. Geralt watched for a while as the shape of the barrel emerged under the pressure of ingenious vices and clamps tightened by screws. Metal hoops hammered onto the staves then created the form of the barrel. Vapour from the large coppers where the barrels were being steamed belched right out into the street. The smell of wood being toasted in a fire – the barrels were being hardened before the next stage in the process – drifted from the courtyard into the workshop.

'Whenever I see a barrel,' Dandelion declared, 'I feel like a beer. Let's go around the corner. I know a pleasant inn.'

'Go by yourself. I'm visiting the sorceress. I think I know which one she is; I've already seen her. Where will I find her? Don't make faces, Dandelion. She, it would seem, is the original source and cause of my troubles. I'm not going to wait for things to develop, I'll go and ask her directly. I can't hang around in this town. If only for the reason that I'm rather skint.'

'We shall find a remedy for that,' the troubadour said proudly. 'I shall support you financially . . . Geralt? What's going on?'

'Go back to the coopers and bring me a stave.'

'What?'

'Fetch me a stave. Quickly.'

The street had been barred by three powerful-looking bruisers with ugly, unshaven and unwashed mugs. One of them, so broad-shouldered he was almost square, held a metal-tipped club, as thick as a capstan bar. The second, in a sheepskin coat with the fur on the outside, was holding a cleaver and had a boarding axe in his belt. The third, as swarthy as a mariner, was armed with a long, hideous-looking knife.

'Hey, you there, Rivian bastard!' began the square-shaped man.

40

'How do you feel without any swords on your back? Bare-arsed in the wind, eh?'

Geralt didn't join in the discourse. He waited. He heard Dandelion arguing with a cooper about a stave.

'You're toothless now, you freak, you venomous witcher toad,' continued the square-shaped man, clearly the most expert of the three in the oratory arts. 'No one's afraid of a reptile without fangs! For it's nothing but a worm or a slimy lamprey. We put filth like that under our boots and crush it to a pulp so it won't dare to come into our towns among decent people no more. You won't foul our streets with your slime, you reptile. Have at him, boys!'

'Geralt! Catch!'

He caught the stave Dandelion threw to him, dodged a blow from the club, smashed the square-shaped man in the side of the head, spun around and slammed it into the elbow of the thug in the sheepskin, who yelled and dropped the cleaver. The Witcher hit him behind the knees, knocking him down, and then, in passing, struck him on the temple with the stave. Without waiting until the thug fell down, or interrupting his own movement, he ducked under the square-shaped man's club and slammed him over the fingers clenched around it. The square-shaped man howled in pain and dropped the club, and Geralt struck him in turn on the right ear, the ribs and the left ear. And then kicked him hard in the crotch. The square-shaped man fell over and rolled into a ball, cringing and curling up, his forehead touching the ground.

The swarthy one, the most agile and quickest of the three, danced around the Witcher. Deftly tossing his knife from hand to hand, he attacked on bent legs, slashing diagonally. Geralt easily avoided the blows, stepped back and waited for him to lengthen his strides. And when that happened he knocked the knife away with a sweeping blow of the stave, circled the assailant with a pirouette and slammed him in the back of the head. The knifeman fell to his knees and the Witcher whacked him in the right kidney. The man howled and tensed up and the Witcher bashed him with the stave below the ear, striking a nerve. One known to physicians as the parotid plexus.

'Oh, dear,' said Geralt, standing over the man, who was curled up, retching and choking on his screams. 'That must have hurt.'

The thug in the sheepskin coat drew the axe from his belt, but didn't get up from his knees, uncertain what to do. Geralt dispelled his doubts, smashing him over the back of the neck with the stave.

The fellows from the town guard came running along the street, jostling the gathering crowd of onlookers. Dandelion pacified them, citing his connections, frantically explaining who had been the assailant and who had acted in self-defence. The Witcher gestured the bard over.

'See that the bastards are tied up. Persuade your cousin the instigator to give them a hard time. They either had a hand in stealing the swords themselves or somebody hired them. They knew I was unarmed, which is why they dared to attack. Give the coopers back their stave.'

'I had to buy it,' admitted Dandelion. 'And I think I did the right thing. You wield a mean plank, I can see. You should pack one all the time.'

'I'm going to the sorceress. To pay her a visit. Should I take the stave?'

'Something heavier would come in useful with a sorceress.' The bard grimaced. 'A fence post, for example. A philosopher acquaintance of mine used to say: when visiting a woman, never forget to take a—'

'Dandelion.'

'Very well, very well, I'll give you directions to the witch. But first, if I might advise . . .'

'Yes?'

'Visit a bathhouse. And a barber.'

Guard against disappointments, because appearances can deceive. Things that are really as they seem are rare. And a woman is never as she seems.

Dandelion, *Half a Century of Poetry*

CHAPTER FIVE

The water in the fountain swirled and boiled, spraying small golden drops around. Lytta Neyd, known as Coral, a sorceress, held out her hand and chanted a stabilising charm. The water became as smooth as though oil had been poured over it and pulsated with glimmers of light. The image, at first vague and nebulous, became sharper and stopped shimmering, and, although slightly distorted by the movement of the water, was distinct and clear. Coral leaned over. She saw the Spice Market, the city's main street, in the water. And a white-haired man crossing it. The sorceress stared. Observed. Searched for clues. Some kind of details. Details that would enable her to make the appropriate evaluation. And allow her to predict what would happen.

Lytta had a tried and tested opinion, formed by years of experience, of what constituted a real man. She knew how to recognise a real man in a flock of more-or-less successful imitations. In order to do that she did not have to resort to physical contact, a method of testing manhood she considered like the majority of sorceresses, not just trivial, but also misleading and liable to lead one astray. Savouring them directly, as her attempts had proven, was perhaps some kind of indication of taste, but all too often left a bitter aftertaste. Indigestion. And heartburn. And even vomiting.

Lytta was able to recognise a real man even at a distance, on the basis of trifling and apparently insignificant criteria. A real man, the sorceress knew from experience, is an enthusiastic angler, but only using a fly. He collects military figures, erotic prints and models of sailing ships he builds himself, including the kind in bottles, and there is never a shortage of empty bottles of expensive alcoholic drinks in his home. He is an excellent cook, able to conjure up veritable culinary masterpieces. And well – when all's said and done – the very sight of him is enough to make one desirous.

The Witcher Geralt, about whom the sorceress had heard a

great deal, about whom she had acquired much information, and whom she was right then observing in the fountain, met but one of the above conditions, it appeared.

'Mozaïk!'

'Yes, madam.'

'We're going to have a guest. Everything is to be suitably prepared and elegant. But first bring me a gown.'

'The tea rose? Or the aquamarine?'

'The white one. He dresses in black, we'll treat him to yin and yang. And sandals, select something matching, make sure they have at least four-inch heels. I can't let him look down on me too much.'

'Madam . . . That white gown . . .'

'Yes?'

'It's, well . . .'

'Modest? Without any ornamentation or furbelows? Oh, Mozaïk, Mozaïk. Will you ever learn?'

*

He was met in the doorway by a burly and pot-bellied bruiser with a broken nose and little piggy eyes, who searched Geralt from head to toe and then once again the other way. Then he stood back, giving a sign for the Witcher to pass.

A girl with smoothly combed – almost slicked-down – hair was waiting in the anteroom. She invited him in with a gesture, without uttering a single word.

He entered straight onto a patio dotted with flowers and a splashing fountain in the centre. In the middle of the fountain stood a small marble statue portraying a naked, dancing girl. Apart from the fact that it was sculpted by a master, the statue was conspicuous for another detail – it was attached to the plinth at a single point: the big toe of one foot. In no way, judged the Witcher, could the construction be stable without the help of magic.

'Geralt of Rivia. Welcome. Do come in.'

The sorceress Lytta Neyd was too sharp-featured to be considered classically beautiful. The warm peach shade of rouge on her cheekbones softened the sharpness but couldn't hide it. Her lips

– highlighted by coral-red lipstick – were so perfectly shaped as to be too perfect. But that wasn't what mattered.

Lytta Neyd was a redhead. A classic, natural redhead. Her hair's mellow, light russet evoked associations with a fox's summer coat. If one were to catch a red fox and place it alongside her – Geralt was quite convinced about this – the two of them would prove to be identically coloured and indistinguishable from each other. And when the sorceress moved her head, lighter, yellowish accents lit up among the red, identical to a fox's fur. That type of red hair was usually accompanied by freckles – usually in excess. That wasn't the case with Lytta.

Geralt felt an anxiety, forgotten and dormant, suddenly awaking somewhere deep inside him. He had a strange and inexplicable inclination towards redheads in his nature, and several times that particular colouring had made him do stupid things. Thus he ought to be on his guard, and the Witcher made a firm resolution in that regard. His task was actually made easier. It was almost a year since he'd stopped being tempted by that kind of stupid mistake.

Erotically alluring red hair wasn't the sorceress's only attractive attribute. Her snow-white dress was modest and utterly without effects, which was the aim, the intended aim, and without the slightest doubt deliberate. Its simplicity didn't distract the attention of the observer, but focused it on her attractive figure. And the plunging cleavage. To put it concisely, Lytta Neyd could easily have posed for an engraving accompanying the chapter 'Impure Desire' in the illustrated edition of the prophet Lebioda's *Good Book*.

To put it even more concisely, Lytta Neyd was a woman whom only a complete idiot would have wanted to have relations with for longer than two days. It was curious that women like that were usually pursued by hordes of men inclined to stay for much longer.

She smelled of freesias and apricots.

Geralt bowed and then pretended the statue in the fountain was more interesting than her figure and cleavage.

'Come in,' repeated Lytta, pointing at a malachite-topped table and two wicker armchairs. She waited for him to sit down, then as she was taking her place showed off a shapely calf and a lizard skin sandal. The Witcher pretended his entire attention was absorbed by the carafes and fruit bowl.

'Wine? It's Nuragus from Toussaint, in my opinion more compelling than the overrated Est Est. There is also Côte-de-Blessure, if you prefer red. Pour please, Mozaïk.'

'Thank you.' He took a goblet from the girl with the slicked-down hair and smiled at her. 'Mozaïk. Pretty name.'

He saw terror in her eyes.

Lytta Neyd placed her goblet on the table. With a bang, meant to focus his attention.

'What brings the celebrated Geralt of Rivia to my humble abode?' She tossed her shock of red curls. 'I'm dying to find out.'

'You bought me out,' he said, deliberately coolly. 'Paid my bail, I mean. I was released from gaol thanks to your munificence. Where I also ended up because of you. Right? Is it because of you I spent a week in a cell?'

'Four days.'

'Four days. I'd like to learn, if possible, the motives behind those actions. Both of them.'

'Both?' She raised her eyebrows and her goblet. 'There's one. And only one.'

'Oh.' He pretended to be devoting all his attention to Mozaïk, who was busying herself on the other side of the patio. 'So you informed on me and got me thrown into the clink, and then got me out for the same reason?'

'Bravo.'

'So, I ask: why?'

'To show you I can.'

He took a sip of wine. Which was indeed very good.

'You proved that you can,' he nodded. 'In principle, you could have simply told me that, by meeting me in the street, for instance. I would've believed it. You preferred to do it differently. And forcibly. So, I ask: what now?'

'I'm wondering myself.' She looked at him rapaciously from under her eyelashes. 'But let's leave things to take their own course. In the meantime, let's say I'm acting on behalf of several of my confraters. Sorcerers who have certain plans regarding you. These

48

sorcerers, who are familiar with my diplomatic talents, chose me as the right person to inform you about their plans. For the moment that is all I can disclose to you.'

'That's very little.'

'You're right. But for the moment, I'm ashamed to admit, I don't know any more myself. I didn't expect you to show up so quickly, didn't expect you to discover so quickly who paid your bail. Which was, they assured me, to have remained a secret. When I know more I shall reveal more. Be patient.'

'And the matter of my swords? Is that part of the game? Of the plans of those mysterious sorcerers? Or is that further proof of your capabilities?'

'I don't know anything about the matter of your swords, whatever it might mean or concern.'

He wasn't entirely convinced. But he didn't delve further into the subject.

'Your confrater sorcerers have recently been trying to outdo each other in showing me antipathy and hostility,' he said. 'They're falling over one another to antagonise me and make my life difficult. I expect to find their interfering fingerprints in every misadventure that befalls me. It's a catalogue of unfortunate coincidences. They throw me into gaol, then release me, then communicate that they have plans for me. What will your confraters dream up this time? I'm afraid even to speculate. And you order me to be patient, most diplomatically, I admit. But I don't have a choice. After all, I have to wait until the case triggered by that tip-off comes before the court.'

'But meanwhile,' the sorceress smiled, 'you can take full advantage of your liberty and enjoy its benefits. You have been released pending trial. If the case comes before the court at all, which isn't by any means certain. And even if it does, you don't have any reason to be anxious, believe me. Trust me.'

'Trust may come a bit harder,' he retorted, with a smile. 'The actions of your confraters in recent times have severely taxed my trust. But I shall try hard. And now I shall be on my way. To trust and wait patiently. Good day.'

'Don't go yet. Stay a while longer. Mozaïk, wine.'

She changed her position on the chair. The Witcher continued to stubbornly pretend he couldn't see her knee and thigh in the split of her skirt.

'Oh well,' she said a moment later. 'There's no point beating about the bush. Witchers have never been highly thought of in our circles, so it sufficed to ignore you. At least up to a certain moment.'

'Until—' he'd had enough of fudging '—I embarked on a romance with Yennefer.'

'No, no, you're mistaken.' She fixed eyes the colour of jade on him. 'Twice over, actually. *Primo*, you didn't embark on a romance with Yennefer, but she with you. *Secundo*, the liaison didn't shock many of us, we're no strangers to excesses of that kind. The turning point was your parting. When did it happen? A year ago? Oh, how time flies . . .'

She made a dramatic pause, counting on a reaction from him.

'Exactly a year ago,' she continued, when it became clear there would be no reaction. 'Some members of our community – not many, but influential – deigned to notice you. No one was clear what precisely occurred between you. Some of us thought that Yennefer, after coming to her senses, broke off with you and kicked you out. Others dared to suppose that you, after seeing through her, ditched her and took to your heels. Consequently, as I mentioned, you became the object of interest. And, as you correctly guessed, antipathy. Why, there were those who wanted you punished in some way. Fortunately for you the majority thought it not worth the trouble.'

'What about you? What part of the community do you belong to?'

'Those whom your love affair merely entertained, if you can imagine.' Lytta twisted her coral lips. 'And occasionally amused. And occasionally supplied with true sporting thrills. I personally have to thank you for a significant influx of cash, Witcher. Bets were laid about how long you'd last with Yennefer – the stakes were high. My wager, as it turned out, was the most accurate. And I scooped up the pot.'

'In that case, it'd be better if I went. I oughtn't to visit you, we oughtn't to be seen together. People are liable to think we fixed the bet.'

'Does it bother you what they're liable to think?'

'Not a lot. And I'm delighted with your win. I'd planned to refund you the five hundred crowns you put up as bail. But since you scooped up the pot betting on me, I no longer feel obliged. Let's call it quits.'

'I hope the mention of refunding the bail doesn't betray a plan to escape and flee? Without waiting for the court case?' An evil gleam appeared in Lytta Neyd's green eyes. 'No, no, you don't have any such intention; you can't have. You know, I'm sure, that it would send you back into the slammer. You *do* know that, don't you?'

'You don't have to prove to me you can do it.'

'I'd prefer not to have to. I mean that most sincerely.'

She placed her hand on her cleavage, with the clear intention of drawing his gaze there. He pretended not to notice and shifted his eyes towards Mozaïk again. Lytta cleared her throat.

'With regard to settling up or sharing out the winnings from the wager,' she said, 'you're actually right. You deserve it. I wouldn't dare to offer you money . . . But what would you say to unlimited credit at the Natura Rerum? For the time of your stay here? Because of me, your last visit ended before it began, so now—'

'No thank you. I appreciate your willingness and good intentions. But no, thank you.'

'Are you sure? Why, you must be. I needlessly mentioned . . . sending you to the slammer. You provoked me. And beguiled me. Your eyes, those strange, mutated eyes, so apparently sincere, endlessly wander . . . and beguile. You aren't sincere, not at all. I know, I know, that's a compliment, coming from a sorceress. You were about to say so, weren't you?'

'Touché.'

'And would you be capable of sincerity? If I demanded it of you?'

'If you were to ask for it.'

'Oh. Let it be. So, I ask you. Why Yennefer? Why her and no one else? Could you explain it? Name it?'

'If this is another wager—'

'It's not. Why exactly Yennefer of Vengerberg?'

Mozaïk appeared like a wraith. With a fresh carafe. And biscuits.

51

Geralt looked her in the eyes. She turned her head away at once.

'Why Yennefer?' he repeated, staring at Mozaïk. 'Why her, precisely? I'll answer frankly: I don't know myself. There are certain women . . . One look is enough . . .'

Mozaïk opened her mouth and shook her head gently. In terror. She knew. And was begging him to stop. But he'd already gone too far into the game.

'Some women attract you like a magnet,' he said, his eyes continuing to wander over the girl's figure. 'You can't take your eyes off them . . .'

'Leave us, Mozaïk.' The sound of pack ice grating against iron could be heard in Lytta's voice. 'And to you, Geralt of Rivia, my thanks. For the visit. For your patience. And for your sincerity.'

A witcher sword (fig. 40) distinguishes itself by being, as it were, an amalgam of other swords, the fifth essence of what is best in other weapons. The first-rate steel and manner of forging typical of dwarven foundries and smithies lend the blade lightness, but also extraordinary resilience. A witcher sword is also sharpened in the dwarven fashion, a secret fashion, may we add, and one that shall remain secret forever, for the mountain dwarves guard their arts jealously. For a sword whetted by dwarves can cut in two a silken scarf thrown into the air. We know from the accounts of eyewitnesses that witchers were able to accomplish the same trick with their swords.

Pandolfo Forteguerra, *A Treatise on Edged Weapons*

CHAPTER SIX

A fleeting morning rainstorm freshened the air for a short time, after which the stench of refuse, burnt fat and rotting fish borne on the breeze from Palmyra once again became noisome.

Dandelion put Geralt up at the inn. The room the bard was occupying was cosy. In the literal sense – they had to cosy up to pass each other. Fortunately, the bed was big enough for two and was serviceable, although it creaked dreadfully and the paillasse had been compacted by travelling merchants, well-known enthusiasts of ardent extramarital sex.

Geralt – God knew why – dreamed of Lytta Neyd during the night.

They went to break their fast at the nearby market hall, where the bard had previously discovered that excellent sardines were to be had. Dandelion was treating him. Which didn't inconvenience Geralt. After all, it had quite often been the other way around, with Dandelion taking advantage of Geralt's generosity when he was skint.

So they sat at a roughly planed table and got down to crisply fried sardines, brought to them on a wooden platter as large as a barrow wheel. Dandelion looked around fearfully from time to time, the Witcher observed. And froze when it seemed to him that some passer-by was scrutinising them too persistently.

'You ought, think I, to get yourself some sort of weapon,' Dandelion finally muttered. 'And carry it in plain sight. It's worth learning from yesterday's incident, don't you think? Oh, look, do you see those shields and mail shirts on display? That's an armourer's. They're bound to have swords there, too.'

'Weapons are prohibited in this town.' Geralt picked a sardine's spine clean and spat out a fin. 'Visitors' weapons are confiscated. It looks as though only bandits can stroll around here armed.'

'Perhaps they can.' The bard nodded towards a passing ruffian with a long battleaxe on his shoulder. 'But in Kerack the prohibitions are issued, enforced and punished for contravention by Ferrant de Lettenhove, who is, as you know, my cousin. And since the oldboy network is a sacred law of nature, we can make light of the local prohibitions. We are, I hereby state, entitled to possess and carry arms. Let's finish breakfasting and go and buy you a blade. Good mistress! These fish are excellent! Please fry another dozen!'

'As I eat these sardines, I realise that the loss of the swords was nothing but a punishment for my greed and snobbism.' Geralt threw away a well-chewed sardine skeleton. 'For wanting a little luxury. Work came up in the vicinity, so I decided to drop into Kerack and feast at the Natura Rerum tavern, the talk of the town. While there were places I could have eaten tripe, cabbage and peas, or fish soup . . .'

'Incidentally—' Dandelion licked his fingers '—the Natura Rerum, although justly famous for its board, is only one of many. There are restaurants where the food is no worse, and possibly even better. For instance, the Saffron and Pepper in Gors Velen or the Hen Cerbin in Novigrad, which has its own brewery. Or alternatively the nearby Sonatina in Cidaris, with the best seafood on the entire coast. The Rivoli in Maribor and their *capercaillie à la Brokilon*, heavily larded with pork fat – heavenly. The Fer de Moline in Aldersberg and their celebrated saddle of hare with morels à la King Videmont. The Hofmeier in Hirundum. Oh, to pay a call there in the autumn, after Samhain, for roast goose in pear sauce . . . Or the Two Weatherfish, a few miles outside Ard Carraigh, an ordinary tavern on the crossroads, serving the best pork knuckle I've ever eaten . . . Why! Look who's come to see us. Talk of the devil! Greetings, Ferrant . . . I mean, hmm . . . my lord instigator . . .'

Ferrant de Lettenhove approached alone, gesturing to his servants to remain in the street.

'Julian. Lord Rivia. I come with tidings.'

'I don't deny that I'm getting impatient,' responded Geralt. 'How did the criminals testify? The ones who attacked me yesterday, exploiting the fact that I was unarmed? They spoke of it quite loudly and openly. It's proof they had a hand in the theft of my swords.'

'There is no evidence of that, unfortunately.' The instigator shrugged. 'The three prisoners are typical rapscallions and on top of that, slow-witted. They carried out the assault, it's true, emboldened by your not having a weapon. Rumours about the theft spread incredibly swiftly, thanks, it would seem, to the ladies from the guardhouse. And at once there were willing people . . . Which is actually not too surprising. You aren't especially liked . . . Nor do you seek to be liked or popular. When in custody, you committed an assault on your fellow prisoners . . .'

'That's right.' The Witcher nodded. 'It's all my fault. Yesterday's assailants also sustained injuries. Didn't they complain? Didn't ask for compensation?'

Dandelion laughed, but fell silent at once.

'The witnesses to yesterday's incident,' said Ferrant de Lettenhove tartly, 'testified that the three men were thrashed with a cooper's stave. And beaten extremely severely. So severely that one of them . . . soiled himself.'

'Probably from excitement.'

'They were beaten even after being incapacitated and no longer posing a threat.' The instigator's expression didn't change. 'Meaning that the limits of necessary defence were exceeded.'

'I'm not worried. I have a good lawyer.'

'A sardine, perhaps?' Dandelion interrupted the heavy silence.

'I inform you that the investigation is under way,' the instigator finally said. 'The men arrested yesterday are not mixed up in the theft of the swords. Several people who may have participated in the crime have been questioned, but no evidence has been found. Informers were unable to indicate any leads. It is known though – and this is the main reason I am here – that the rumour about the swords has stirred up a commotion in the local underworld. Even strangers have appeared, keen to square up to a witcher, particularly an unarmed one. I thus recommend vigilance. I cannot exclude further incidents. I'm also certain, Julian, that in this situation to accompany the Lord Rivia—'

'I have accompanied Geralt in much more hazardous places; in predicaments that the local hoodlums could not imagine,' the troubadour interrupted combatively. 'Provide us with an armed escort, cousin, if you regard it as appropriate. Let it act as a deterrent. Otherwise, when Geralt and I give the next bunch of dregs a good hiding, they'll be bellyaching about the limits of the necessary defence being overstepped.'

'If they are indeed dregs and not paid hitmen, hired by someone,' said Geralt. 'Is the investigation also paying attention to that?'

'All eventualities are being taken into consideration.' Ferrant de Lettenhove cut him off. 'The investigation will continue. I shall assign an escort.'

'We're grateful.'

'Farewell. I wish you good luck.'

Seagulls screeched above the city's rooftops.

*

They might just as well not have bothered with the visit to the armourer. All Geralt needed was a glance over the swords on offer. When, though, he found out the prices he shrugged and exited the shop without a word.

'I thought we understood each other.' Dandelion joined him in the street. 'You were supposed to buy any old thing, so as not to look unarmed!'

'I won't throw away money on any old thing. Even if it's your money. That was junk, Dandelion. Primitive, mass-produced swords. And little decorative rapiers for courtiers, fit for a masked ball, if you mean to dress up as a swordsman. And priced to make you burst out in insane laughter.'

'We'll find another shop! Or workshop!'

'It'll be the same everywhere. There's a market for cheap, poor-quality weapons that are meant to serve in one decent brawl. And not to serve the victors, either, for when they're collected from the battlefield they're already useless. And there's a market for shiny ornaments that dandies can parade with. And which you can't even slice a sausage with. Unless it's liver sausage.'

'You're exaggerating, as usual.'

'Coming from you that's a compliment.'

'It wasn't intended! So where, pray tell me, do we get a good sword? No worse than the ones that were stolen? Or better?'

'There exist, to be sure, masters of the swordsmith's art. Perhaps one of them might even have a decent blade in stock. But I have to have a sword that's fitted to my hand. Forged and finished to order. And that takes a few months or even a year. I don't have that much time.'

'But you have to get yourself some sort of sword,' the bard observed soberly. 'And pretty urgently, I'd say. What's left? Perhaps . . .'

He lowered his voice and looked around.

'Perhaps . . . Perhaps Kaer Morhen? There are sure to be—'

'Certainly,' Geralt interrupted, clenching his jaw. 'To be sure. There are still enough blades, a wide choice, including silver ones. But it's too far away, and barely a day goes by without a storm and a downpour. The rivers are swollen and the roads softened. The ride would take me a month. Apart from that—'

He angrily kicked a tattered punnet someone had thrown away.

'I was robbed, Dandelion, outwitted and robbed like a complete sucker. Vesemir would mock me mercilessly. My comrades – if I happened upon them in the Keep – would also have fun, they'd rib me for years. No. It's out of the bloody question. I have to sort this out some other way. And by myself.'

They heard a pipe and a drum. They entered a small square, where the vegetable market was taking place and a group of goliards were performing. It was the morning repertoire, meaning primitively stupid and not at all amusing. Dandelion walked among the stalls, where with admirable – and astonishing – expertise he immediately took up the assessment and tasting of the cucumbers, beetroots and apples displayed on the counters, all the while bantering and flirting with the market traders.

'Sauerkraut!' he declared, scooping some from a barrel using wooden tongs. 'Try it, Geralt. Excellent, isn't it? It's a tasty and salutary thing, cabbage like this. In winter, when vitamins are lacking, it protects one from scurvy. It is, furthermore, a splendid antidepressant.'

'How so?'

'You eat a big pot of sauerkraut, drink a jug of sour milk . . . and soon afterwards depression becomes the least of your worries. You

59

forget about depression. Sometimes for a long time. Who are you staring at? Who's that girl?'

'An acquaintance. Wait here. I'll have a brief word with her and I'll be back.'

The girl he'd spotted was Mozaïk, whom he'd met at Lytta Neyd's. The sorceress's shy pupil with the slicked-down hair in a modest, though elegant dress the colour of rosewood. And cork wedge-heeled shoes in which she moved quite gracefully, bearing in mind the slippery vegetable scraps covering the uneven cobbled street.

He approached, surprising her by a stall of tomatoes as she filled a basket hanging from the crook of her arm.

'Greetings.'

She blanched slightly on seeing him, despite her already pale complexion. And had it not been for the stall she would have taken a step or two back. She made a movement as though trying to hide the basket behind her back. No, not the basket. Her hand. She was hiding her forearm and hand, which were tightly wrapped up in a silk scarf. He noticed her behaviour and an inexplicable impulse made him take action. He grabbed the girl's hand.

'Let go,' she whispered, trying to break free.

'Show me. I insist.'

'Not here . . .'

She let him lead her away from the market to somewhere they could be alone. He unwound the scarf. And couldn't contain himself. He swore. Crudely, and at great length.

The girl's left hand was turned over. Twisted at the wrist. The thumb stuck out to the left, the back of her hand was facing downwards. And the palm upwards. A long, regular life-line, he noticed involuntarily. The heart-line was distinct, but dotted and broken.

'Who did that to you? Did she?'

'You did.'

'What?'

'You did!' She jerked her hand away. 'You used me to make a fool of her. She doesn't let something like that slide.'

'I couldn't—'

'—have predicted it?' She looked him in the eyes. He had misjudged her – she was neither timid, nor anxious. 'You could and should have. But you preferred to play with fire. Was it worth it, though? Did it give you satisfaction, make you feel better? Give you something to boast about to your friends in the tavern?'

He didn't answer. He couldn't find the words. But Mozaïk, to his astonishment, suddenly smiled.

'I don't bear a grudge,' she said easily. 'Your game amused me and I'd have laughed if I hadn't been afraid. Give me back the basket, I'm in a hurry. I still have shopping to do. And I've got an appointment at the alchemist's—'

'Wait. You can't leave it like that.'

'Please.' Mozaïk's voice changed slightly. 'Don't get involved. You'll only make it worse . . . I got away with it, anyway,' she added a moment later. 'She treated me leniently.'

'Leniently?'

'She might have turned both my hands over. She might have twisted my foot around, heel facing forward. She might have swapped my feet over, left to right and vice versa. I've seen her do that to somebody.'

'Did it—?'

'—hurt? Briefly. Because I passed out almost at once. Why are you staring like that? That's how it was. I hope it'll be the same when she twists my hand back again. In a few days, after she's enjoyed her revenge.'

'I'm going to see her. Right away.'

'Bad idea. You can't—'

He interrupted her with a rapid gesture. He heard the crowd buzzing and saw it disperse. The goliards had stopped playing. He saw Dandelion at a distance, giving him sudden and desperate signals.

'You! Witcher filth! I challenge you to a duel! We shall fight!'

'Dammit. Move aside, Mozaïk.'

A short and stocky character in a leather mask and a cuirass of boiled oxhide stepped out of the crowd. The character shook the trident he was holding and with a sudden movement of his left hand unfurled a fishing net in the air, flourished and shook it.

'I am Tonton Zroga, known as the Retiarius! I challenge you to a fight, wi—'

Geralt raised his hand and struck him with the Aard Sign, putting as much power into it as he could. The crowd yelled. Tonton Zroga, known as the Retiarius, flew into the air and – entangled in his own net and kicking his legs – wiped out a bagel stall, crashed heavily onto the ground and, with a loud clank, slammed his head against a small cast-iron statue of a squatting gnome, which for no apparent reason stood in front of a shop offering haberdashery. The goliards rewarded the flight with thunderous applause. The Retiarius lay on the ground, alive, but displaying fairly feeble signs of consciousness. Geralt, not hurrying, walked over and kicked him hard in the region of the liver. Someone seized him by the sleeve. It was Mozaïk.

'No. Please. Please, don't. You can't do that.'

Geralt would have continued kicking the net-fighter, because he knew quite well what you can't do, what you can, and what you must do. And he wasn't in the habit of heeding anyone in such matters. Especially people who had never been beaten up.

'Please,' Mozaïk repeated. 'Don't take it out on him. For me. Because of her. And because you've mixed everything up.'

He did as she asked. Then took her by the arms. And looked her in the eyes.

'I'm going to see your mistress,' he declared firmly.

'That's not good.' She shook her head. 'There'll be consequences.'

'For you?'

'No. Not for me.'

Wild nights! Wild nights!
Were I with thee,
Wild nights should be
Our luxury!

Emily Dickinson

CHAPTER SEVEN

The sorceress's hip was graced by an intricate tattoo with fabulously colourful details, depicting a fish with coloured stripes.

Nil admirari, thought the Witcher. *Nil admirari*.

*

'I don't believe my eyes,' said Lytta Neyd.

He – and he alone – was to blame for what happened and for it happening as it happened. On the way to the sorceress's villa he passed a garden and couldn't resist the temptation of picking a freesia from a flower bed. He remembered it being the predominant scent of her perfume.

'I don't believe my eyes,' said Lytta Neyd. She greeted him in person; the burly porter wasn't there. Perhaps it was his day off.

'You've come, I guess, to give me a dressing down for Mozaïk's hand. And you've brought me a flower. A white freesia. Come in before there's a sensation and the city explodes with rumours. A man on my threshold with a flower! This never happens.'

She was wearing a loose-fitting black dress, a combination of silk and chiffon, very sheer, and rippling with every movement of the air. The Witcher stood, staring, the freesia still in his outstretched hand, wanting to smile and not for all the world able to. *Nil admirari*. He repeated in his head the maxim he remembered from a cartouche over the entrance to the Philosophy Faculty of the University of Oxenfurt. He had been repeating it all the way to Lytta's villa.

'Don't shout at me.' She snatched the freesia from his fingers. 'I'll fix the girl's hand as soon as she appears. Painlessly. I'll possibly even apologise to her. I apologise to you. Just don't shout at me.'

He shook his head, trying not to smile again. Unsuccessfully.

'I wonder—' she brought the freesia up to her face and fixed her jade-coloured eyes on it '—if you know the symbolism of flowers? And their secret language? Do you know what this freesia is saying, and therefore you're communicating it to me quite consciously? Or perhaps the flower is purely accidental, and the message . . . subconscious?'

Nil admirari.

'But it's meaningless anyway.' She came up to him, very close. 'For either you're openly, consciously and calculatingly signalling to me what you desire . . . Or you're concealing the desire your subconscious is betraying. In both cases I owe you thanks. For the flower. And for what it says. Thank you. And I'll return the favour. I'll also present you with something. There, that drawstring. Pull it. Don't be shy.'

That's what I do best, he thought as he pulled. The woven drawstring slid smoothly from embroidered holes. All the way. And then the silk and chiffon dress flowed from Lytta like water, gathering itself around her ankles ever so softly. He closed his eyes for a moment, her nakedness dazzling him like a sudden flash of light. *What am I doing?* he thought, putting his arm around her neck. *What am I doing?* he thought, tasting the coral-red lipstick on his mouth. *What I'm doing is completely senseless*, he thought, gently leading her towards a bureau by the patio and placing her on the malachite top.

She smelled of freesias and apricots. And something else. Tangerines, perhaps. Lemon grass, perhaps.

It lasted some time and towards the end, the bureau was rocking quite violently. Coral, although she was gripping him tight, didn't once release the freesia from her fingers. The flower's fragrance didn't suppress hers.

'Your enthusiasm is flattering.' She pulled her mouth away from his and opened her eyes. 'And very complimentary. But I do have a bed, you know.'

*

Indeed, she did have a bed. An enormous one. As large as the deck of a frigate. She led him there, and he followed her, unable to take his eyes off her. She didn't look back. She had no doubt that he was following her. That he would go without hesitation where she led him. Without ever taking his eyes off her.

The bed was huge and had a canopy. The bed linen was of silk and the sheets of satin.

It's no exaggeration to say they made use of the entire bed, of every single inch. Every inch of the bed linen. And every fold of the sheets.

*

'Lytta . . .'

'You may call me Coral. But for the time being don't say anything.'

Nil admirari. The scent of freesias and apricots. Her red hair strewn across the pillow.

*

'Lytta . . .'

'You may call me Coral. And you may do that to me again.'

*

The sorceress's hip was graced by an intricate tattoo with fabulously colourful details, depicting a fish with coloured stripes, its large fins giving it a triangular shape. Fish like that – called angelfish – were usually kept in aquariums and basins by wealthy people and the snobbish *nouveaux riches*. So Geralt – and he wasn't the only one – had always associated them with snobbism and pretentious ostentation. Thus, it astonished him that Coral had chosen that particular tattoo. The astonishment lasted a moment and the explanation came quickly. Lytta Neyd both looked and seemed quite young. But the tattoo dated back to the years of her real youth. From the times when angelfish brought from abroad were indeed a rare attraction, when there were few wealthy people, when the *nouveaux riches* were still making their fortunes and few could afford an aquarium. *So her tattoo is like a birth certificate,* thought Geralt, caressing the angelfish with his fingertips. *It's a wonder Lytta still has it, rather than magically removing it.* Why, he thought, shifting his caresses to regions some distance from the fish, *a memory from one's youth is a lovely thing. It's not easy to get rid of such a memento. Even if now it's passé and pompously banal.*

He raised himself on an elbow and took a closer look, searching her body for other – equally nostalgic – mementos. He didn't find any. He didn't expect to; he simply wanted to look. Coral sighed. Clearly bored by the abstract – and not very purposeful – peregrinations of his hand, she seized it and decisively directed it to a specific place; in her opinion the only suitable one. *Good for you,* thought Geralt, pulling the sorceress towards him and burying his face in her hair. Fiddlesticks to stripy fish. As though there weren't more vital things worth devoting one's attention to. Or worth thinking about.

*

Perhaps model sailing ships too, thought Coral chaotically, trying hard to control her rapid breathing. *Perhaps military figures too, perhaps fly-fishing. But what counts . . . What really counts . . . Is the way he holds me.*

Geralt embraced her. As though she were all the world to him.

*

They didn't get much sleep the first night. And even when Lytta dropped off, the Witcher found it difficult. Her arm was girdling his waist so tightly he found it hard to breathe and her leg was thrown across his thighs.

The second night she was less possessive. She didn't hold him or hug him as tightly as before. By then she'd stopped fearing he'd run away before dawn.

*

'You're pensive. You have a gloomy, male expression. The reason?'

'I'm wondering about the ... hmm ... naturalism of our relationship.'

'What do you mean?'

'As I said. Naturalism.'

'It seems you used the word "relationship"? The semantic capacity of that concept is indeed astonishing. Furthermore, I hear post-coital tristesse intruding on you. A natural state, indeed, it affects all the higher creatures. A strange little tear has come to my eye too, Witcher ... Cheer up, cheer up. I'm joking.'

'You lured me ... As a buck is lured.'

'What?'

'You lured me. Like an insect. With magical freesia-and-apricot pheromones.'

'Are you serious?'

'Don't get cross. Please, Coral.'

'I'm not. Quite the opposite. On second thoughts, I have to admit you're right. Yes, it's naturalism in its purest form. Except it's utterly the reverse. It was you who beguiled and seduced me. At first sight. You naturalistically and animalistically treated me to a male courtship display. You hopped, stamped and fluffed up your tail—'

'That's not true.'

'—fluffed up your tail and flapped your wings like a blackcock. You crowed and clucked—'

'No, I didn't.'

'Yes, you did.'

'Didn't.'

'Did. Embrace me.'

*

'Coral?'

'What?'

'Lytta Neyd ... That isn't your real name, is it?'

'My real one was troublesome.'

'Why so?'

'Try saying quickly: Astrid Lyttneyd Ásgeirrfinnbjornsdottir.'

'I get it.'

'I doubt you do.'

*

'Coral?'

'Uh-huh?'

'And Mozaïk? Where did she get her nickname?'

'Know what I don't like, Witcher? Questions about other women. And particularly when the enquirer is lying in bed with me. And asks a lot of questions, instead of concentrating on the matter in hand. You wouldn't dare doing anything like that if you were in bed with Yennefer.'

'And *I* don't like certain names being mentioned either. Especially when—'

'Shall I stop?'

'I didn't say that.'

Coral kissed his arm.

'When she arrived at school her given name was Aïk. I don't remember her family name. Not only did she have a strange name, but she suffered from loss of skin pigment. Her cheeks were dotted with pale spots, she indeed looked like a mosaic. She was cured, naturally, after the first semester, for a sorceress cannot have any blemishes. But the spiteful nickname stuck. And quickly stopped being spiteful. She grew to like it herself. But enough of her. Talk to me and about me. Go on, right now.'

'What, right now?'

'Talk about me. What I'm like. Beautiful, aren't I? Go on, say it!'

'Beautiful. Red-haired. And freckled.'

'I'm not freckled. I magically removed them.'

'Not all. You forgot about some of them. But I found them.'

'Where are . . . Oh. Well, all right. True. So, I'm freckled. And what else am I?'

'Sweet.'

'I beg your pardon?'

'Sweet. As a honey wafer.'

'You aren't making fun of me, are you?'

70

'Look at me. Into my eyes. Do you see even the slightest insincerity in them?'

'No. And that's what worries me most.'

*

'Sit down on the edge of the bed.'

'Or else?'

'I want to get my own back.'

'I beg your pardon?'

'For the freckles you found where you found them. For your efforts and the thorough . . . exploration. I want to get my own back and repay you. May I?'

'By all means.'

*

The sorceress's villa, like almost all the villas in that part of the city, had a terrace with a view of the sea stretching out below. Lytta liked to sit there and spend hours observing the ships riding at anchor, using a telescope of hefty proportions on a tripod. Geralt didn't really share her fascination with the sea and what sailed on it, but liked to accompany her on the terrace. He sat close, right behind her, with his face beside her red curls, enjoying the scent of freesias and apricots.

'That galleon, casting its anchor, look—' Coral pointed '—with the blue cross on its flag. That's the *Pride of Cintra*. It's probably sailing to Kovir. And that cog is *Alke* from Cidaris, probably taking on a cargo of hides. And over there, that's *Tetyda*, a hulk from here, four hundred tons' capacity, a freighter, plying between Kerack and Nastróg. And there, see, the Novigradian schooner *Pandora Parvi* sailing to anchor right now. It's a beautiful, beautiful ship. Look into the eyepiece. You'll see it . . .'

'I can see without a telescope. I'm a mutant.'

'Oh, true. I'd forgotten. And over there is the galley *Fuchsia*, thirty-two oars, it can take a cargo of eight hundred tons. And that elegant three-mast galleon is *Vertigo*; it sailed from Lan Exeter. And there, in the distance, with the amaranth flag, is the Redanian galleon

71

Albatross. Three masts, a hundred and twenty feet in the beam . . . There, look, look, the post clipper *Echo* is setting sail and putting out to sea. I know the captain, he eats at Ravenga's when he anchors here. There again, look, a galleon from Poviss under full sail . . .'

The Witcher brushed Lytta's hair from her back. Slowly, one by one, he unfastened the hooks and eyes and slid the dress from the sorceress's shoulders. After that he utterly devoted his hands and attention to a pair of galleons under full sail. Galleons one would search for in vain on all the maritime routes, harbours, ports and registers of the admiralty.

Lytta didn't protest. And didn't take her eyes away from the telescope's eyepiece.

'You're behaving like a fifteen-year-old,' she said at one point. 'As if you've never seen breasts before.'

'It's always the first time for me,' he reluctantly confessed. 'And I never really was fifteen.'

*

'I come from Skellige,' she told him later, in bed. 'The sea's in my blood. And I love it.'

'I dream of sailing away one day,' she continued, when he remained silent. 'All alone. Set sail and put out to sea . . . Far, far away. All the way to the horizon. Only water and sky all around. The salt foam splashes me, the wind tugs my hair in an utterly male caress. And I'm alone, completely alone, endlessly alone among the strange and hostile elements. Solitude amid a sea of strangeness. Don't you dream of that?'

No, I don't, he thought. *I have it every day.*

*

The summer solstice arrived, and after it a magical night, the shortest of the year, when the flower of the fern bloomed in the forest and naked girls, rubbed with adder's-tongue fern, danced in dew-sprinkled clearings.

A night as short as the blink of an eye.

A wild night, bright from lightning.

He awoke alone in the morning after the solstice. Breakfast was waiting for him in the kitchen. And not just breakfast.

'Good morning, Mozaïk. Beautiful weather, isn't it? Where's Lytta?'

'You have a day off,' she replied without looking at him. 'My unparalleled mistress will be busy. Until late. During the time she devoted to . . . pleasure, the list of patients grew.'

'Patients?'

'She treats infertility. And other women's disorders. Didn't you know? Well, now you do. Good day.'

'Don't go out yet. I'd like to—'

'I don't know what you'd like to do,' she interrupted. 'But it's probably a bad idea. It'd be better if you didn't talk to me. Pretend I wasn't here at all.'

'Coral won't harm you any more, I give my word. In any case, she's not here, she can't see us.'

'She sees everything she wants to see; all she needs is a few spells and an artefact. And don't kid yourself that you have any influence on her. That requires more than . . .' She nodded towards the bedroom. 'Please, don't mention my name in her presence. Not even casually. Because she won't let me forget it. Even if it takes a year, she'll remind me.'

'Since she treats you like that . . . can't you simply go?'

'Go where?' she said crossly. 'To a weaving manufactory? To serve time with a seamstress. Or head at once to a brothel? I don't have anyone. I'm a nobody. And I'll always be a nobody. Only she can change that. I can endure it all . . . But please don't make it any worse.

'I met your pal in town.' She glanced at him a moment later. 'That poet, Dandelion. He asked about you. He was anxious.'

'Did you calm him down? Explain I was safe? In no danger?'

'Why should I lie?'

'I beg your pardon?'

'You aren't safe here. You're here with her out of sorrow for the other one. Even when you're close to her you only think about the other one. She knows it. But she plays along, because it pleases

73

her, and you dissemble splendidly; you're awfully convincing. Have you thought about what will happen when you give yourself away?'

*

'Are you staying with her tonight, too?'

'Yes,' Geralt confirmed.

'That'll be a week, did you know?'

'Four days.'

Dandelion strummed the strings of his lute with a dramatic glissando. He looked around the tavern. He swigged from his mug and wiped the froth from his nose.

'I know it's not my business,' he said, for him unusually emphatically and forcefully. 'I know I shouldn't meddle. I know you don't like it when anyone meddles. But certain things, Geralt, my friend, ought not to be left unsaid. Coral, if you want to know my opinion, is one of those women who ought to always wear a conspicuous warning sign. One proclaiming "Look but don't touch". In menageries, they put things like that in terrariums containing rattlesnakes.'

'I know.'

'She's playing with you and toying with you.'

'I know.'

'You, meanwhile, are simply filling the void after Yennefer, whom you can't forget about.'

'I know.'

'So why—?'

'I don't know.'

*

They would go out in the evening. Sometimes to the park, sometimes to the hill overlooking the port. Sometimes they simply walked around the Spice Market.

They visited the Natura Rerum osteria together. Several times. Febus Ravenga was beside himself with joy. On his orders, the waiters danced attendance on them. Geralt finally experienced the taste of turbot in cuttlefish ink. And then goose legs in white wine and veal shank with vegetables. Only at first – and briefly – did the intrusive and ostentatious interest of the other guests bother him. Then he followed Lytta's example and ignored them. The wine from the local cellar helped greatly.

Then they returned to the villa. Coral shed her dress in the anterooms and led him – quite naked – to the bedroom.

He followed her. His eyes never left her. He adored looking at her.

*

'Coral?'

'What?'

'Rumour has it you can always see what you want to see. All you need is a few spells and an artefact.'

'I think I'll have to twist another of that rumour's joints again.' She lifted herself up on an elbow and looked him in the eyes. 'That ought to teach it not to gossip.'

'Please—'

'I was joking.' She cut him off. There wasn't a trace of merriment in her voice.

'And what would you like to see?' she continued, after he had fallen silent, 'Or have prophesied? How long you're going to live? When and how you'll die? What horse will win the Grand Tretorian? Who the electoral college will elect as the Hierarch of Novigrad? Who Yennefer is with now?'

'Lytta.'

'What's bothering you, if I may ask?'

He told her about the theft of the swords.

*

There was a flash of lightning. And a moment later, a peal of thunder.

The fountain splashed very softly. The basin smelt of wet stone. The marble girl was petrified, wet and shining, in her dancing position.

'The statue and the fountain,' Coral hurried to explain, 'aren't there to satisfy my love for pretentious kitsch, nor are they an expression of subservience to snobbish fashions. They serve more concrete ends. The statue portrays me. In miniature. When I was fifteen.'

'Who would have supposed then that you would develop so prettily?'

'It's a magical artefact powerfully linked to me. While the fountain, or more precisely the water, serves for divination. You know, I think, what divination is?'

'Vaguely.'

'The theft of your weapons took place around ten days ago. Oneiromancy is the best and most certain way of interpreting and analysing past events, even very distant ones, but the rare talent of dream-reading, which I don't possess, is necessary for that. Sortilege, or cleromancy, won't really help us; likewise, pyromancy and aeromancy, which are more effective in the case of foretelling people's fates, on condition that one has something belonging to those people . . . hair, fingernails, a fragment of clothing or something similar. They can't be used with objects – in our case, swords.

'And so all that remains to us is divination.' Lytta brushed a red lock from her forehead. 'That, as you probably know, lets one see and predict future events. The elements will assist us, for a truly stormy season has set in. We shall combine divination with ceraunoscopy. Come closer. Grasp my hand and don't release it. Lean over and look into the water, but don't touch it under any circumstances. Concentrate. Think about your swords! Think hard about them!'

He heard her chanting a spell. The water in the basin reacted, foaming and rippling more powerfully with every sentence of the formula being uttered. Large bubbles began to rise from the bottom.

The water became smooth and cloudy. And then completely clear.

Dark, violet eyes look out from the depths. Raven-black locks fall onto shoulders in cascades, gleam, reflect light like a peacock's feathers, writhing and rippling with every movement . . .

'The swords,' Coral reminded him, quietly and scathingly. 'You were supposed to be thinking about the swords.'

The water swirled, the black-haired, violet-eyed woman disappeared in the vortex. Geralt sighed softly.

'Think about the swords,' hissed Lytta. 'Not her!'

She chanted a spell in another flash of lightning. The statue in the fountain lit up milkily, and the water again calmed and became transparent. And then he saw.

His sword. Hands touching it. Rings on fingers.

. . . made from a meteorite. The superb balance, the weight of the blade precisely equal to the weight of the hilt . . .

The other sword. Silver. The same hands.

. . . a steel tang edged with silver . . . Runic characters along the entire length . . .

'I can see them,' he whispered aloud, squeezing Lytta's hand. 'I can see my swords . . . Really—'

'Quiet.' She responded with an even stronger grip. 'Be quiet and concentrate.'

The swords vanish. Instead of them he sees a black forest. An expanse of stones. Rocks. One of the rocks is immense, towering, tall and slender . . . Carved into a bizarre shape by strong winds. . .

The water foamed briefly.

A grizzled man with noble features, in a black velvet jacket and a gold-brocaded waistcoat, both hands resting on a mahogany lectern. Lot number ten, he declares loudly. An absolute curio, an exceptional find, two witcher swords . . .

A large, black cat turns around on the spot, trying hard with its paw to reach the medallion on a chain swinging above it. Enamel on the medallion's golden oval, a blue dolphin naiant.

A river flows among trees, beneath a canopy of branches and boughs hanging over the water. A woman in a long, close-fitting dress stands motionless on one of the boughs.

The water foams briefly and almost immediately becomes calm again.

He saw a sea of grass: a boundless plain reaching to the horizon. He saw it from above, as though from a bird's-eye view . . . Or from the top of a hill. A hill, down whose slopes descend a row of vague shapes. When they turned their heads, he saw unmoving faces, unseeing, dead eyes. *They're dead*, he suddenly realised. *It's a cortège of the dead . . .*

Lytta's fingers squeezed his hand again. With the strength of pliers.

A flash of lightning. A sudden gust of wind tugged at their hair. The water in the basin churned up, seethed, surged with foam, rose in a wave as high as the wall. And tumbled straight down on them. They both leaped back from the fountain. Coral stumbled and he held her up. Thunder boomed.

The sorceress screamed a spell and waved an arm. Lights came on throughout the house.

The water in the basin, a moment earlier a seething maelstrom, was smooth, calm, only being moved by the languidly trickling stream of the fountain. Even though a moment earlier a veritable tidal wave had poured over them, there wasn't a single drop of water to be seen.

Geralt breathed out heavily. And stood up.

'Right at the end . . .' he muttered, helping the sorceress to stand up. 'That last image . . . The hill and that procession . . . of people . . . I didn't recognise it . . . I've no idea what it could be . . .'

'Neither do I,' she answered in an uneasy voice. 'But it wasn't your vision. That image was meant for me. I have no idea what it could mean either. But I have a strange feeling there's nothing good in it.'

The thunder fell silent. The storm moved away. Inland.

*

'Charlatanism, all that divination of hers,' repeated Dandelion, adjusting the pegs on his lute. 'Fraudulent visions for the naive. The power of suggestion, nothing more. You were thinking about swords, so you saw swords. What else do you think you saw? A march of corpses? A terrible wave? A rock with a bizarre shape? Meaning what?'

'Something like a huge key.' The Witcher pondered. 'Or a two-and-a-half heraldic cross . . .'

The troubadour fell into pensive mood. And then dipped his

finger into his beer. And drew something on the table top.

'Similar to that?'

'Oh. Very similar.'

'Damn!' Dandelion plucked the strings, attracting the attention of the entire tavern. 'And blast! Ha-ha, Geralt, my friend! How many times have you got me out of trouble? How many times have you helped me? Rendered me a favour? Without even counting them! Well, now it's my turn. Perhaps I'll help you recover your famed weapons.'

'Eh?'

Dandelion stood up.

'Madam Lytta Neyd, your newest conquest, unto whom I hereby return her honour as an outstanding diviner and unrivalled clairvoyant, has indicated – in her divination – a place I know. In an obvious, clear way, leaving no room for doubt. We're going to see Ferrant. At once. He'll have to arrange an audience for us, using his shadowy connections. And issue you with a pass to leave the city, by the official gate, in order to avoid a confrontation with those harpies from the guardhouse. We're going on a little outing. And actually not too far from here.'

'Where to?'

'I recognised the rock in your vision. Something experts call a mogote. And local residents the "Gryphon". A distinctive point, simply a signpost leading to the home of the person who may in fact know something about your swords. The place we're heading for bears the name Ravelin. Does that ring a bell?'

It is not only the execution and the excellence of the craft that determine the quality of a witcher's sword. As with mysterious elven or gnomish blades, whose secret has been lost, the mysterious power of a witcher's sword is bound to the hand and skill of the witcher wielding it. And, forsooth, owing to that magic's mysteries it is greatly potent against the Dark Powers.

Pandolfo Forteguerra, *A Treatise on Edged Weapons*

I shall reveal one secret to you. About witcher swords. It's poppycock that they have some kind of secret power. And that they are supposedly wonderful weapons. That there are no better ones. It's all fiction, invented for the sake of appearances. I know this from a quite certain source.

Dandelion, *Half a Century of Poetry*

CHAPTER EIGHT

They recognised the rock called the Gryphon at once. It was visible a long way off.

*

The place they were aiming for was located more or less halfway along the route from Kerack to Cidaris, some way from the road linking the two cities which wound among forests and rocky wildernesses. The journey took them some time; time they killed with idle chatter. Mainly contributed by Dandelion.

'Common knowledge claims that swords used by witchers have magical properties,' said the poet. 'Passing over the fabrications about sexual impotence, there must be some truth in it. Your swords aren't ordinary. Would you like to comment?'

Geralt reined in his mare. Bored by the protracted stay in the stables, Roach's urge to gallop was growing.

'Yes, I would. Our swords aren't ordinary swords.'

'It's claimed that the magical power of your witcher weaponry, fatal to the monsters you fight, resides in the steel from which they are forged,' said Dandelion, pretending not to hear the mockery. 'From the very metal, that is the ores found in meteorites fallen from the sky. How so? Meteorites aren't magical, after all, they're a natural phenomenon, accounted for by science. Where's that magic to come from?'

Geralt looked at the sky darkening from the north. It looked like another storm was gathering. And that they could expect a soaking.

'As far as I recall,' he said, answering a question with a question, 'you have studied all seven liberal arts?'

'And I graduated *summa cum laude.*'

'You attended the lectures of Professor Lindenbrog as part of the astronomy course within the Quadrivium?'

'Old Lindenbrog, known as Fiddle-Faddle?' laughed Dandelion. 'Why of course! I can still see him scratching his backside and tapping his pointer on maps and globes, wittering on monotonously. *De sphaera mundi*, errr, *subdividitur* into four Elementary Parts. The Earthly Part, the Aqueous, the Aerial and the Igneous. Earth and Water form the globe, which is surrounded on all sides, errr, by Air, or *Aer*. Over the Air, errr, stretches the *Aether*, Fiery Air or Fire. Above the Fire, meanwhile, are the Subtle Sidereal Heavens, known as the *Firmamentum*, which is spherical in character. On that is located the *Errant Siderea*, or wandering stars, and *Fixa Siderea*, or fixed stars . . .'

'I don't know what to admire more; your talent for mimicry or your memory,' Geralt snorted. 'Returning, meanwhile, to the issue of interest to us: meteorites, which our good Fiddle-Faddle termed falling stars, *Siderea Cadens*, or something like that, break off from the firmament and fall downwards, to burrow into our good old earth. Along the way, meanwhile, they penetrate all the other planes, that is the elemental planes, as well as the para-elemental planes, for such are also said to exist. The elements and para-elements are imbued, as is known, with powerful energy, the source of all magic and supernatural force, and the meteorite penetrating them absorbs and retains that energy. Steel smelted from a meteorite – and also blades forged from such steel – contains a great deal of such elements. It's magical. The entire sword is magical. *Quod erat demonstrandum*. Do you understand?'

'Certainly.'

'So forget it. Because it's poppycock.'

'What?'

'Poppycock. Fabrication. You don't find meteorites under every bush. More than half the swords used by witchers were made from steel from magnetic ores. I used them myself. They are as good as the ones that fell from the sky when it comes to the siderites penetrating the elements. There is absolutely no difference. But keep it to yourself, Dandelion, please. Don't tell anyone.'

'What? I'm to stay silent? You can't demand that! What's the point of knowing something if you can't show off the knowledge?'

'Please. I'd prefer to be thought of as a supernatural creature armed with a supernatural weapon. They hire me to be that and pay me to be that. Normality, meanwhile, is the same as banality, and banality is cheap. So I ask you to keep your trap shut. Promise?'

'Have it your way. I promise.'

*

They recognised the rock called the Gryphon at once; it was visible a long way off.

Indeed, with a little imagination, it could be interpreted as a gryphon's head set on a long neck. However – as Dandelion observed – it more resembled the fingerboard of a lute or another stringed instrument.

The Gryphon, as it turned out, was an inselberg dominating a gigantic crater. The crater – Geralt recalled the story – was called the Elven Fortress, because of its fairly regular shape, which suggested the ruins of an ancient building, with walls, towers, bastions and all the rest. There had never been any fortress there, elven or other. The shapes of the crater were a work of nature – a fascinating work, admittedly.

'Down there.' Dandelion pointed, standing up in his stirrups. 'Do you see? That's our destination. Ravelin.'

And the name was particularly apt, as the inselberg described the astonishingly regular shape of a large triangle, extending out from the Elven Fortress like a bastion. A building resembling a fort rose up inside the triangle. Surrounded by something like a walled, fortified camp.

Geralt recalled the rumours circulating about Ravelin. And about the person who dwelt there.

They turned off the road.

There were several entrances beyond the first wall, all guarded by sentries armed to the teeth, easily identifiable as mercenaries by their multicoloured and diverse apparel. They were stopped at the first guard post. Although Dandelion loudly referred to a previously arranged audience and emphatically stressed his good relations with the commanders, they were ordered to dismount and wait. For quite a long time. Geralt was becoming somewhat impatient, when finally a bruiser resembling a galley slave appeared and told them to follow him. It soon turned out that he was leading them by a circuitous route to the back of the complex, from the centre of which they could hear a hubbub and the sound of music.

They crossed a drawbridge. Just beyond it lay a man, semi-conscious and groping around himself. His face was bloodied and so puffy that his eyes were almost completely hidden beneath the swelling. He was breathing heavily and each breath blew bloody bubbles from his smashed nose. The bruiser leading them didn't pay any attention to the man on the ground, so Geralt and Dandelion pretended not to see anything either. They were in a place where it didn't behove them to display excess curiosity. It was recommended not to stick one's nose into Ravelin's affairs. In Ravelin, so the story went, a nose thus stuck usually parted company with its owner and remained where it had been stuck.

The bruiser led them through a kitchen, where cooks were bustling around hectically. Cauldrons bubbled and Geralt noticed crabs, lobsters and crayfishes cooking in them. Conger eels squirmed in vats, and clams and mussels simmered in large pots. Meat sizzled in huge frying pans. Servants seized trays and bowls full of cooked food to carry them away down corridors.

The next rooms were filled – for a change – with the scent of women's perfume and cosmetics. Over a dozen women in various stages of *déshabillé*, including total undress, were touching up their make-up before a row of mirrors, jabbering away ceaselessly. Here, also, Geralt and Dandelion maintained inscrutable expressions and didn't let their eyes wander inordinately.

In the next room, they were subjected to a thorough body search. The characters carrying this out were severe of appearance, professional of manner and resolute of action. A dagger was confiscated from Geralt. Dandelion, who never carried any weapons, was relieved of a comb and a corkscrew. But – after a moment's thought – he was allowed to keep his lute.

'There are chairs in front of His Excellency,' they were finally instructed. 'Sit down on them. Sit down and do not stand up until His Excellency commands. His Excellency is not to be interrupted when he speaks. You are not to speak until His Excellency gives a sign that you may. And now enter. Through this door.'

'His Excellency?' muttered Geralt.

'He was once a priest,' the poet muttered back. 'But don't worry, he never assumed much of a priestly manner. His subordinates have to address him somehow, and he can't bear to be called "boss". We don't have to use his title.'

When they entered, their way was immediately barred by something. That something was as big as a mountain and smelled strongly of musk.

'Wotcha, Mikita,' Dandelion greeted the mountain.

The giant addressed as Mikita, clearly the bodyguard of His Excellency the boss, was a half-breed, the result of a cross between an ogre and a dwarf. The result was a bald dwarf with a height of well over seven feet, quite without a neck, sporting a curly beard, with teeth protruding like a wild boar's and arms reaching down to his knees. It was rare to see such a cross: the two species, as could be observed, were quite at variance genetically; something like Mikita couldn't have arisen naturally. It couldn't have happened without the help of extremely powerful magic. Forbidden magic, incidentally. Rumour had it that plenty of sorcerers ignored the ban. Proof of those rumours' veracity was standing before Geralt.

They sat down on two wicker chairs, in accordance with the prevailing protocol. Geralt looked around. Two scantily dressed young women were pleasuring each other on a large chaise longue in the furthest corner of the chamber. Watching them, while feeding a dog at the same time, was a small, inconspicuous, hunched and unremarkable man in a loose, flowery embroidered robe and a fez with a tassel. Having fed the dog the last piece of lobster, the man wiped his hands and turned around.

'Greetings, Dandelion,' he said, sitting down in front of them on something deceptively similar to a throne, though it was made of wicker. 'Good day, Master Geralt of Rivia.'

His Excellency, Pyral Pratt, considered – not without reason – the head of organised crime in the entire region, looked like a retired silk merchant. He wouldn't have looked out of place at a retired silk merchants' picnic and wouldn't have been singled out as an imposter. At least not from a distance. A closer look would have revealed in Pyral Pratt what other silk merchants didn't have. An old, faded scar on his cheekbone: a mark left by a knife. The ugly and ominous grimace of his thin mouth. A pair of bright, yellowish eyes, as unmoving as a python's.

No one broke the silence for a long time. Music drifted in from somewhere outside, and a hubbub could be heard.

'I'm very pleased to see you and greet you both,' Pyral Pratt said finally. An old and unquenched love for cheap, crudely distilled alcohol could clearly be heard in his voice.

'I'm particularly glad to welcome you, singer.' His Excellency smiled at Dandelion. 'We haven't seen you since my granddaughter's wedding, which you graced with a performance. And I was just thinking about you, because my next granddaughter is in a hurry to get married. I trust that this time you won't refuse again, for old time's sake. Well? Will you sing at the wedding? I won't have to keep asking you like last time? I won't be forced to . . . convince you?'

'I'll sing, I'll sing,' Dandelion, blanching slightly, hurried to assure him.

'And today you dropped in to ask about my health, I imagine?' continued Pratt. 'Well, it's shitty, this health of mine.'

Dandelion and Geralt made no comment. The ogre-dwarf reeked of musk. Pyral Pratt sighed heavily.

'I've gone down with stomach ulcers and food phobia,' he announced, 'so the delights of the table aren't for me now. I've been diagnosed with a sick liver and ordered not to drink. I've got a herniated disc, which affects in equal measure both my cervical and lumbar vertebrae and has ruled out hunting and other extreme sports from my pastimes. Medicaments and treatments eat up a great deal of my money, which I formerly used to spend on gambling. My john thomas, admittedly, let's say, still rises but how much effort it takes to keep it up! The whole thing bores me before it gives me pleasure . . . So what's left? Eh?'

'Politics?'

Pyral Pratt laughed so much the tassel on his fez shook.

'Well done, Dandelion. Apt, as ever. Politics, oh yes, that's something for me now. At first I wasn't favourably disposed to the matter. I thought rather to earn a living from harlotry and invest in bawdy houses. I moved among politicians and came to know countless of them. And became convinced it'd be better to give up on whores, for whores at least have their honour and some sort of principles. On the other hand, though, it's better to govern from the town hall than from a brothel. And one would like to run, if not the country, as they say, then at least the county. The old adage goes, if you can't beat 'em, join 'em . . .'

He broke off and glanced at the chaise longue, craning his neck. 'Don't sham, girls!' he yelled. 'Don't put it on! More gusto! Hmm . . . Where was I?'

'Politics.'

'Ah yes. But leaving politics aside, you, Witcher, have had your famous swords stolen. Isn't it owing to that matter that I have the honour of welcoming you?'

'For that matter, indeed.'

'Someone stole your swords.' Pratt nodded. 'A painful loss, methinks? Painful, no doubt. And irretrievable. Ha, I've always said that Kerack's crawling with thieves. Give the people there one chance and they'll swipe anything that isn't nailed down, it's well known. And they always carry a crowbar with them in case they chance on anything nailed down.

'The investigation, I trust, continues?' he went on a moment later. 'Ferrant de Lettenhove taking action? Stare truth in the eyes, though, gentlemen. You can't expect miracles from Ferrant. No offence, Dandelion, but your relative would be a better account- ant than an investigator. With him it's nothing but books, legal codes, articles, rules. Well, that and evidence, evidence and once again that evidence of his. Like that story about the goat and the cabbage. Know it? They once locked a goat in a barn with a head of cabbage. In the morning, there wasn't a trace of it and the goat was shitting green. But there was no evidence or witnesses, so they dismissed the case, *causa finita*. I wouldn't like to be a prophet of doom, Witcher Geralt, but the case of your swords' theft may end up likewise.'

Geralt didn't comment this time, either.

'The first sword is steel.' Pyral Pratt rubbed his chin with a beringed hand. 'Siderite steel, iron ore from a meteorite. Forged in Mahakam, in the dwarven hammer works. Total length forty and a half inches, the blade alone twenty-seven and one quarter. Splendid balance, the weight of the blade is precisely equal to the weight of the hilt, the entire weapon certainly weighs less than forty ounces. The execution of the hilt and cross guard is simple, but elegant.

'And the second sword, of a similar length and weight, is silver. Partially, of course. A steel tang fitted with silver, also the edges are steel, since pure silver is too soft to be sharpened effectively. On the cross guard and along the entire length of the blade there are runic signs and glyphs considered by my experts indecipherable, but undoubtedly magical.'

'A precise description.' Geralt was stony-faced. 'As though you'd seen the swords.'

'I have indeed. They were brought to me and I was invited to buy them. The broker representing the interests of the current owner, a person of impeccable reputation and known to me personally, pledged that the swords were acquired legally, that they came from a find in Fen Carn, an ancient necropolis in Sodden. Endless treasures and artefacts have been unearthed in Fen Carn, hence in principle there were no grounds to question the source's veracity. I had my doubts, though. And didn't buy the swords. Are you listening to me, Witcher?'

'I'm hanging on your every word. Waiting for the conclusion. And the details.'

'The conclusion is as follows: you scratch my back . . . Details cost money. Information has a price tag.'

'Come on,' Dandelion said irritably. 'Our old friendship brought me here, along with a friend in need—'

'Business is business,' Pyral Pratt interrupted him. 'I said, the information I possess has its price. If you want to find something out about the fate of your swords, Witcher from Rivia, you have to pay.'

'What's the price on the tag?'

Pratt took out a large gold coin from under his robe and handed it to the ogre-dwarf, who without visible effort snapped it in his fingers, as though it were a biscuit. Geralt shook his head.

'A pantomime cliché,' he drawled. 'You hand me half a coin and someone, someday, perhaps even in a few years, shows up with the other half. And demands that I fulfil his wish. Which I will have to fulfil unconditionally. Nothing doing. If that's supposed to be the price, no deal. *Causa finita*. Let's go, Dandelion.'

'Don't you care about regaining your swords?'

'Not *that* much.'

'I suspected so. But it doesn't harm to try. I'll make another offer. This time one you won't refuse.'

'Let's go, Dandelion.'

'You can leave, but through another door.' Pratt indicated with his head. 'That one. After first getting undressed. You leave in naught but your long johns.'

Geralt thought he was controlling his facial expression. He must have been mistaken, because the ogre-dwarf suddenly yelled in warning and moved towards him, raising a hand and stinking twice as much as before.

'This is some kind of joke,' Dandelion pronounced loudly, as usual bold and mouthy at the Witcher's side. 'You're mocking us, Pyral. Which is why we will now say farewell and leave. And by the same door we came in through. Don't forget who I am! I'm leaving!'

'I don't think so.' Pyral Pratt shook his head. 'You once proved you aren't that clever. But you're too clever to try to leave now.'

In order to emphasise the weight of his boss's words, the ogre-dwarf brandished a clenched fist the size of a watermelon. Geralt said nothing. He'd been observing the giant for a long time, searching for a place sensitive to a kick. Because it looked like a kicking was inevitable.

'Very well.' Pratt appeased his bodyguard with a gesture. 'I'll yield a little, I'll demonstrate goodwill and a desire for compromise. The entire local industrial and commercial elite, financiers, politicians, nobility, clergy, and even an incognito prince, are gathered here. I promised them a show the like of which they've never seen before, and they've certainly never seen a witcher in his smalls. But let it be, I'll yield a tad: you'll go out naked to the waist. In exchange, you'll receive the promised information, right away. Furthermore, as a bonus . . .'

Pyral Pratt picked up a small sheet of paper from the table.

'. . . as a bonus, two hundred Novigradian crowns. For the witcher's pension fund. Here you are, a bearer cheque, on the Giancardis' bank, to be cashed at any branch. What do you say to that?'

'Why do you ask?' Geralt squinted his eyes. 'You made it clear, I understood, that I can't refuse.'

'You understood right. I said it was an offer you can't refuse. But mutually beneficial, methinks.'

'Take the cheque, Dandelion.' Geralt unbuttoned his jacket and took it off. 'Speak, Pratt.'

'Don't do it.' Dandelion blanched even more. 'Unless you know what's on the other side of the door?'

'Speak, Pratt.'

'As I mentioned.' His Excellency lounged on his throne. 'I declined to purchase the swords from the broker. But because it was, as I've already said, a person who is well known to me and trusted, I suggested another, more profitable way of selling them. I advised that their present owner put them up for auction. At the Borsody brothers' auction house in Novigrad. It's the biggest and most renowned collectors' fair. Lovers of rarities, antiques, recherché works of art, unique objects and all kinds of curiosities descend on it from all over the world. In order to come into possession of some kind of marvel for their collections, those cranks bid like madmen. Various exotic peculiarities often go for titanic sums at the Borsody brothers'. Nowhere else are things sold so dearly.'

'Speak, Pratt.' The Witcher took off his shirt. 'I'm listening.'

'The auction at the Borsodys' occurs once a quarter. The next one will be held in July, on the fifteenth. The thief will undoubtedly appear there with your swords. With a bit of luck, you'll manage to get them off him before he puts them up for auction.'

'And is that all?'

'That's plenty.'

'The identity of the thief? Or the broker—?'

'I don't know the thief's identity,' Pratt interjected. 'And I won't reveal the broker's. This is business; laws, rules and – no less important than that – customs apply. I'd lose face. I revealed something to you, big enough for what I demand from you. Lead him out into the arena, Mikita. And you come with me, Dandelion, we can watch. What are you waiting for, Witcher?'

'I'm to go out without a weapon, I understand? Not just bare to the waist, but barehanded too?'

'I promised my guests something they'd never seen before,'

explained Pratt, slowly, as though to a child. 'They've seen a witcher with a weapon.'

'Of course.'

He found himself in an arena, on sand, in a circle marked out by posts sunk into the ground, flooded by the flickering light of numerous lanterns hung on iron bars. He could hear shouts, cheers, applause and whistles. He saw faces, open mouths and excited eyes above the arena.

Something moved opposite him, at the very edge of the arena. And jumped.

Geralt barely managed to arrange his forearms into the Heliotrope Sign. The spell thrust back the attacking beast. The crowd yelled as one.

The two-legged lizard resembled a wyvern, but was smaller, the size of a large Great Dane. Its head, though, was considerably larger than a wyvern's. And it had a much toothier maw. And a much longer tail, tapering to a thin point. The lizard brandished it vigorously, sweeping the sand and lashing the posts. Lowering its head, it leaped at the Witcher again.

Geralt was ready, struck with the Aard Sign and repelled it. But the lizard managed to lash him with the end of its tail. The crowd yelled again. Women squealed. The Witcher felt a ridge as thick as a sausage growing and swelling on his naked shoulder. He knew now why he had been ordered to strip. He also recognised his opponent. It was a vigilosaur, a specially bred, magically mutated lizard, used for guarding and protection. Things looked pretty bad. The vigilosaur treated the arena as though it were its lair. Geralt was thus an intruder to be overpowered. And, if necessary, eliminated.

The vigilosaur circled the arena, rubbing itself against the posts, hissing furiously. And attacked again, swiftly, leaving no time for a Sign. The Witcher dodged nimbly out of range of the toothy jaws, but couldn't avoid being lashed by the tail. He felt another ridge swelling beside the first.

The Heliotrope Sign again blocked the charging vigilosaur. The lizard's tail whistled as it whirled around. Geralt's ear caught a change in the note, hearing it a second before the end of the tail struck him across the back. The pain was blinding and blood ran down his skin. The crowd went crazy.

The Signs weakened. The vigilosaur circled him so fast that the Witcher could barely keep up. He managed to elude two lashes of the tail, but not the third, and was struck again with the sharp edge on the shoulder blade. The blood was now pouring down his back.

The crowd roared; the spectators were bellowing and leaping up and down. One of them leaned far over the balustrade to get a better view, resting on an iron bar holding a lantern. The bar broke and tumbled down with the lantern onto the arena. It stuck into the sand and the lantern struck the vigilosaur's head, bursting into flames. The lizard threw it off, spraying a cascade of sparks around and hissed, rubbing its head against the piles of the arena. Geralt saw his chance at once. He tore the bar out of the sand, took a short run-up and jumped, thrusting the spike hard into the lizard's skull. It passed straight through. The vigilosaur struggled and, clumsily flapping its forepaws, fought to rid itself of the iron rod penetrating its brain. Hopping unco-ordinatedly, it finally lurched into the posts and sank its teeth into the wood. It thrashed around convulsively for some time, churning the sand with its claws and lashing with its tail. Eventually it stopped moving.

The walls shook with cheers and applause.

Geralt climbed out of the arena up a rope ladder somebody had lowered. The excited spectators crowded around him. A man slapped him on his swollen shoulder, and Geralt barely refrained himself from punching him in the face. A young woman kissed him on the cheek. Another, even younger, wiped the blood from his back with a cambric handkerchief which she immediately unfolded and displayed triumphantly to her friends. Another, much older woman, took a necklace from her wrinkled neck and tried to give it to him. His expression sent her scuttling back into the crowd.

There was a reek of musk and the ogre-dwarf Mikita forced his way through the crowd, like a ship through seaweed. He shielded the Witcher and led him out.

A physician was summoned, who dressed Geralt and stitched up his wounds. Dandelion was very pale. Pyral Pratt was calm. As though nothing had happened. But the Witcher's face must have spoken volumes, as he hurried to explain.

'Incidentally, that bar, previously filed through and sharpened, ended up in the arena on my orders.'

'Thanks for hurrying it up.'

'My guests were in seventh heaven. Even Mayor Coppenrath was so pleased he was beaming, and it's hard to satisfy that whoreson. He sniffs at everything, gloomy as a brothel on a Monday morning. I have the position of councillor in my pocket, ha. And maybe I'll rise higher, if . . . Would you perform in a week, Geralt? With a similar show?'

'Only if you're in the arena instead of a vigilosaur, Pratt.' The Witcher wriggled his sore shoulder furiously.

'That's good, ha, ha. Hear what a jester he is, Dandelion?'

'I heard,' confirmed the poet, looking at Geralt's back and clenching his teeth. 'But it wasn't a joke, it was quite serious. I also, equally solemnly, declare that I shan't be gracing your granddaughter's nuptial ceremony with a performance. You can forget it after the way you've treated Geralt. And that applies to any other occasions, including christenings and funerals. Yours included.'

Pyral Pratt shot him a glance, and something lit up in his reptilian eyes.

'You aren't showing me respect, singer,' he drawled. 'You aren't showing me respect again. You're asking to be taught a lesson in this regard. One you won't forget . . .'

Geralt went closer and stood in front of him. Mikita panted, raised a fist and there was a reek of musk. Pyral Pratt gestured him to calm down.

'You're losing face, Pratt,' said the Witcher slowly. 'You've done a deal, classically, according to rules and, no less important than them, customs. Your guests are satisfied with the spectacle; you've gained prestige and the prospect of a position on the town council. I've gained the necessary information. You scratch my back. Both parties are content, so now we should part without remorse or anger. Instead of that you're resorting to threats. You're losing face. Let's go, Dandelion.'

Pyral Pratt blanched slightly. Then turned his back on them.

'I was planning to treat you to supper,' he tossed over his shoulder. 'But it looks like you're in a hurry. Farewell then. But think yourself lucky I'm letting you both leave Ravelin scot-free. I usually punish a lack of respect. But I'm not stopping you.'

'Quite right.'

Pratt turned around.

'What did you say?'

Geralt looked him in the eyes. 'You aren't especially clever, though you like to think otherwise. But you're too clever to try to stop me.'

*

Scarcely had they passed the hillock and arrived at the first road-side poplars than Geralt reined in his horse and listened.

'They're following us.'

'Dammit!' Dandelion's teeth chattered. 'Who? Pratt's thugs?'

'It doesn't matter who. Go on, ride as fast as you can to Kerack. Hide at your cousin's. First thing tomorrow take that cheque to the bank. Then we'll meet at The Crab and Garfish.'

'What about you?'

'Don't worry about me.'

'Geralt—'

'Be quiet and spur on your horse. Ride. Fly!'

Dandelion obeyed, leaned forward in the saddle and spurred his horse to a gallop. Geralt turned back, waiting calmly.

Riders emerged from the gloom. Six riders.

'The Witcher Geralt?'

'It is I.'

'You're coming with us,' the nearest one croaked, reaching for Geralt's horse. 'But no foolishness, d'you hear?'

'Let go of my reins, or I'll hurt you.'

'No foolishness!' The rider withdrew his hand. 'And don't be hasty. We be legal and lawful. We ain't no cutpurses. We're on the orders of the prince.'

'What prince?'

'You'll find out. Follow us.'

They set off. Geralt recalled Pratt had claimed some sort of prince was staying in Ravelin, incognito. Things were not look-ing good. Contacts with princes were rarely pleasant. And almost never ended well.

They didn't go far. Only to a tavern at a crossroads smelling of smoke, with lights twinkling. They entered the main chamber, which was almost empty, not counting a few merchants eating a late supper. The entrance to the private chambers was guarded by two armed men wearing blue cloaks, identical in colour and cut to the ones Geralt's escort were wearing. They went in.

'Your Princely Grace—'

'Get out. And you sit down, Witcher.'

The man sitting at the table wore a cloak similar to that of his men, but more richly embroidered. His face was obscured by a hood. There was no need. The cresset on the table only illumin-ated Geralt; the mysterious prince was hidden in the shadows.

'I saw you in Pratt's arena,' he said. 'An impressive display indeed. That leap and blow from above, augmented by your entire body weight . . . The weapon, although just a bar, passed through the dragon's skull like a knife through butter. I think that had it been, let's say, a bear spear or a pike it would have passed through a mail shirt, or even plate armour . . . What do you think?'

'It's getting late. It's hard to think when you're feeling drowsy.'

The man in the shadows snorted.

'We shan't dally then. And let's get to the matter in hand. I need you. You, Witcher. To do a witcher's job. And it somehow appears that you also need me. Perhaps even more.

'I'm Prince Xander of Kerack. I desire, desire overwhelmingly, to be King Xander the First of Kerack. At the moment, to my regret and the detriment of the country, the King of Kerack is my father, Belohun. The old buffer is still sound in mind and body, and may reign for twenty more bloody years. I don't have either the time or the desire to wait that long. Why, even if I waited, I couldn't be certain of the succession, since the old fossil may name another successor at any moment; he has an abundant collection of offspring. And is presently applying himself to begetting another; he has planned his royal nuptials with pomp and splendour for the feast of Lughnasadh, which the country can ill afford. He – a miser who goes to the park to relieve himself to spare the enamel on his chamber pot – is spending a mountain of gold on the wedding feast. Ruining the treasury. I'll be a better king. The crux is that

I want to be king at once. As soon as possible. And I need you to achieve that.'

'The services I offer don't include carrying out palace revolutions. Or regicide. And that is probably what Your Grace has in mind.'

'I want to be king. And in order to ascend the throne my father has to stop being king. And my brothers must be eliminated from the succession.'

'Regicide plus fratricide. No, Your Highness. I have to decline. I regret.'

'Not true,' the prince snapped from the shadows. 'You haven't regretted it yet. Not yet. But you will, I promise you.'

'Your Royal Highness will deign to take note that threatening me with death defeats the purpose.'

'Who's talking about death? I'm a prince, not a murderer. I'm talking about a choice. Either my favour or my disfavour. You'll do what I demand and you'll enjoy my favour. And you absolutely *do* need it, believe me. Now, with a trial and sentence for a financial swindle awaiting you, it looks as though you'll be spending the next few years at an oar aboard a galley. You thought you'd wriggled out of it, it appears. That your case has already been dismissed, that the witch Neyd, who lets you bed her on a whim, will withdraw her accusation and it'll be over in a trice. You're mistaken. Albert Smulka, the reeve of Ansegis, has testified. That testimony incriminates you.'

'The testimony is false.'

'It will be difficult to prove that.'

'Guilt has to be proved. Not innocence.'

'Good joke. Amusing indeed. But I wouldn't be laughing, in your shoes. Take a look at these. They're documents.' The prince tossed a sheaf of papers on the table. 'Certified testimonies, witness statements. The town of Cizmar, a hired witcher, a leucrote dispatched. Seventy crowns on the invoice, in actuality fifty-five paid, the difference split with a local pen-pusher. The settlement of Sotonin, a giant spider. Killed, according to the bill, for ninety, actually, according to the alderman's testimony, for sixty-five. A harpy killed in Tiberghien, invoiced for a hundred crowns, seventy paid in actuality. And your earlier exploits and rackets;

a vampire in Petrelsteyn Castle which didn't exist at all and cost the burgrave a cool thousand orens. A werewolf from Guaamez had the spell taken from it and was magically de-werewolfed for an alleged hundred crowns. A very dubious affair, because it's a bit too cheap for that kind of spell removal. An echinops, or rather something you brought to the alderman in Martindelcampo and called an echinops. Some ghouls from a cemetery near the town of Zgraggen, which cost the community eighty crowns, although no one saw any bodies, because they were devoured by, ha-ha, other ghouls. What do you say to that, Witcher? This is proof.'

'Your Highness continues to err,' Geralt countered. 'It isn't proof. They are fabricated slanders, ineptly fabricated, to boot. I've never been employed in Tiberghien. I haven't even heard of the settlement of Sotonin. Any bills from there are thus blatant counterfeits; it won't be hard to prove it. And the ghouls I killed in Zgraggen were, indeed, devoured by, ha-ha, other ghouls, because such are the habits of ghouls. And the corpses buried in that cemetery from then on are decomposing peacefully, because the surviving ghouls have moved out. I don't even want to comment on the rest of the nonsense contained in those documents.'

'A suit will be brought against you on the basis of those documents.' The prince placed a hand on them. 'It will last a long time. Will the evidence turn out to be genuine? Who can say? What verdict will finally be reached? Who cares? It's meaningless. The important thing is the stink that will spread around. And which will trail after you to the end of your days.

'Some people found you disgusting, but tolerated you out of necessity, as a lesser evil, as the killer of the monsters that threaten them,' he continued. 'Some couldn't bear you as a mutant, felt repulsion and abomination as though to an inhuman creature. Others were terribly afraid of you and hated themselves for their own fear. All that will sink into oblivion. The renown of an effective killer and the reputation of an evil sorcerer will evaporate like feathers in the wind, the disgust and fear will be forgotten. They will remember you only as an avaricious thief and charlatan. He who yesterday feared you and your spells, who looked away, who spat at the sight of you or reached for an amulet, will tomorrow guffaw and elbow his companion: "Look, here comes the Witcher

Geralt, that lousy fraudster and swindler!" If you don't undertake the task I'm commissioning you with, I'll destroy you, Witcher. I'll ruin your reputation. Unless you serve me. Decide. Yes or no?'

'No.'

'Let it not seem to you that your connections – Ferrant de Lettenhove or your red-headed sorceress lover – will help you with anything. The instigator won't risk his own career, and the Chapter will forbid the witch from getting involved in a criminal case. No one will help you when the judicial machine entangles you in its gears. I've commanded you to decide. Yes or no?'

'No. Definitively no, Your Highness. The man hidden in the bedchamber can come out now.'

The prince, to Geralt's astonishment, snorted with laughter. And slapped a hand on the table. The door creaked and a figure emerged from the adjoining bedchamber. A familiar figure, in spite of the gloom.

'You've won the wager, Ferrant,' said the prince. 'Report to my secretary tomorrow for your winnings.'

'Thank you, Your Princely Grace,' Ferrant de Lettenhove, the royal instigator, replied with a slight bow. 'But I treated the wager purely in symbolic terms. To emphasise just how certain I was of being right. I was by no means concerned about the money—'

'The money you won,' the prince interrupted, 'is also a symbol to me, just like the emblem of the Novigradian mint and the profile of the reigning monarch stamped on it. Know also, both of you, that I have also won. I have regained something I thought was irretrievably lost. Namely, faith in people. Geralt of Rivia, Ferrant was absolutely certain of your reaction. I, however, admit that I thought him naive. I was convinced you would yield.'

'Everybody's won something,' Geralt stated sourly. 'And I?'

'You too.' The prince became grave. 'Tell him, Ferrant. Enlighten him as to what's at stake here.'

'His Grace Prince Egmund, here present,' explained the instigator, 'deigned for a moment to impersonate Xander, his younger brother. And also, symbolically, his other brothers, the pretenders to the throne. The prince suspected that Xander or another of his brothers would want to make use of this convenient witcher with the aim of seizing the throne. So we decided to stage this . . .

100

spectacle. And now we know that if it were in fact to occur . . . Should someone indeed make a proposition, you wouldn't be lured into princely favour. Or be daunted by threats or blackmail.'

'Quite.' The Witcher nodded. 'And I acknowledge your talent. Your Majesty entered the role splendidly. I didn't detect any artifice in what you deigned to say about me, in the opinion you had of me. On the contrary. I sensed pure frankness—'

'The masquerade had its objective.' Egmund interrupted the awkward silence. 'I achieved it and don't intend to account for myself before you. And you will benefit. Financially. For I indeed mean to engage you. And reward your services amply. Tell him, Ferrant.'

'Prince Egmund,' said the instigator, 'fears an attempt on the life of his father, King Belohun, which may happen during the nuptials planned for the feast of Lughnasadh. The prince would feel better if at that time somebody . . . like a witcher . . . could be responsible for the king's safety. Yes, yes, don't interrupt, we know witchers aren't bodyguards, that their *raison d'être* is to defend people from dangerous magical, supernatural and unnatural monsters—'

'That's how it is in books,' the prince interrupted impatiently. 'In life it's not so simple. Witchers have been employed to defend caravans, trekking through wildernesses and backwoods teeming with monsters. It has happened, however, that instead of monsters, the merchants were attacked by ordinary robbers, and the witcher's role was not at all to assault their persons, and yet he did. I have grounds to fear that during the nuptials the king may be attacked by . . . basilisks. Would you undertake to defend him from basilisks?'

'That depends.'

'On what?'

'On whether this is still a set-up. And whether I'm the object of another entrapment. From one of the other brothers, for instance. A talent for impersonation is not, I wager, a rarity in your family.'

Ferrant bristled with rage. Egmund banged a fist on the table.

'Watch your step,' he snapped. 'And don't forget yourself. I asked you if you would undertake it. Answer!'

'I might undertake the defence of the king from hypothetical basilisks.' Geralt nodded. 'Unfortunately, my swords were stolen from me in Kerack. The royal services have still not managed to pick up the thief's trail and are probably doing little in that regard. I'm unable to defend anyone without my swords. I must therefore decline for practical reasons.'

'If it is merely a matter of your swords, there's no problem. We shall recover them. Shan't we, Lord Instigator?'

'Absolutely.'

'You see. The royal instigator confirms absolutely. Well?'

'Let them first recover the swords. Absolutely.'

'You're a stubborn character. But let it be. I stress that you will receive payment for your services and I assure you that you won't find me parsimonious. Regarding other benefits, however, some of them you will gain at once, as an advance, as proof of my good-will, if you like. You may consider your court case dismissed. The formalities must be carried out, and bureaucracy doesn't recognise the concept of haste, but you may now consider yourself a person free of suspicion, with freedom of movement.'

'I am inordinately grateful. And the testimonies and invoices? The leucrote from Cizmar, the werewolf from Guaamez? What about the documents? The ones Your Royal Highness deigned to use as . . . theatrical properties?'

'The documents will remain with me.' Egmund looked him in the eye. 'In a safe place. An absolutely safe place.'

*

King Belohun's bell was just striking midnight when he returned.

Coral, it ought to be acknowledged, kept calm and reserved. She knew how to control herself. Even her voice didn't change. Well, almost.

'Who did that to you?'

'A vigilosaur. A kind of lizard . . .'

'A lizard put in those stitches? You let a lizard stitch you up?'

'The stitches were put in by a physician. And the lizard—'

'To hell with the lizard! Mozaïk! A scalpel, scissors and tweezers. A needle and catgut. Elixir of woundwort. Decoction of aloes. *Unguentum ortolani.* A compress and sterile dressing. And prepare

102

a mustard seed and honey poultice. Move, girl!'

Mozaïk made short work of it. Lytta set about the procedure. The Witcher sat and suffered in silence.

'Physicians who don't know magic ought to be banned from practising,' drawled the sorceress, putting in the stitches. 'Lecture at universities, why not? Sew up corpses after post-mortems, by all means. But they shouldn't be allowed to touch living patients. But I probably won't live to see it, everything's going the opposite way.'

'Not only magic heals,' Geralt risked an opinion. 'And physicians are necessary. There's only a handful of specialised healing mages, and ordinary sorcerers don't want to treat the sick. They either don't have time or they don't think it worth it.'

'They think right. The results of overpopulation may be disastrous. What's that? That thing you're fiddling with?'

'The vigilosaur was tagged with it. It had it permanently attached to its hide.'

'You tore it from it as a trophy deserving of the victor?'

'I tore it off to show you.'

Coral examined the brass oval plate the size of a child's hand. And the signs embossed on it.

'A curious coincidence,' she said, applying the mustard poultice to his back, 'bearing in mind the fact that you're heading that way.'

'Am I? Oh, yes, true, I'd forgotten. Your confraters and their plans concerning me. Have the plans taken shape, perhaps?'

'That's right. I've received news. You've been asked to go to Rissberg Castle.'

'Been asked? What an honour. To Rissberg. The seat of the renowned Ortolan. A request, I presume, I cannot decline.'

'I wouldn't advise it. You're asked to go forthwith. Bearing in mind your injuries, when will you be able to set off?'

'Bearing in mind my injuries, you tell me. Physician.'

'I shall tell you. Later . . . But now . . . You won't be around for some time and I shall miss you . . . How do you feel now? Will you be able . . . That'll be all, Mozaïk. Go to your room and don't disturb us. What's the meaning of that smirk? Am I to freeze it permanently to your mouth?'

INTERLUDE

Dandelion, *Half a Century of Poetry*
  (a passage of a rough draft never officially published)

Verily, the Witcher was greatly in my debt. More and more every day.

The visit to Pyral Pratt in Ravelin, which ended, as you know, turbulently and bloodily, brought certain benefits, however. Geralt had picked up the sword thief's trail. It was to my credit, in a way, for it was I, using my cunning, who led Geralt to Ravelin. And the following day it was I, and no other, who fitted Geralt out with a new weapon. I couldn't bear to see him unarmed. You'll say that a witcher is never unarmed? That he is a mutant well-versed in every form of combat, twice as strong as a normal fellow and ten times as fast? Who can fell three armed thugs with a cooper's oaken stave in no time? That to cap it all he can work magic using his Signs, which are no mean weapon? True. But a sword is a sword. He repeated relentlessly that he felt naked without a sword. So, I fitted him out with one.

Pratt, as you now know, rewarded the Witcher and I financially, none too generously, but I mustn't grumble. The next day, as Geralt had instructed me, I hurried with the cheque to the Giancardi branch and cashed it. I'm standing there, looking around. And I see that somebody is observing me intently. A lady, not too old, but also not in the first flush of youth, tastefully and elegantly attired. I am no stranger to a lady's delighted look; plenty of women find my manly and wolfish features irresistible.

The lady suddenly walks over, introduces herself as Etna Asider and claims to know me. Huh, what a thing! Everybody knows me, my fame precedes me, wherever I go.

'News has reached me, m'lord poet,' she says, 'about the unfortunate accident that befell your comrade, the Witcher, Geralt of Rivia. I know he has lost his weapons and is in urgent need of new ones. I am also aware that a good sword is hard to find. It so happens that I possess one. Left by my deceased husband, may the Gods have mercy upon his soul. At this very moment, I've come to the bank to sell the sword; for what could a widow want with a sword? The bank has valued it and wants to take it on a commission basis. While I, nonetheless, am in urgent need of ready coin, for I needs must pay the debts of the deceased, otherwise my creditors will torment me. Thus . . .'

Upon which the lady picks up a roll of damask and unwraps a sword from it. A marvel, let me tell you. Light as a feather. The scabbard tasteful and elegant, the hilt of lizard's skin, the cross guard gilt, with a jasper the size of a pigeon's egg in the pommel. I draw it and can't believe my eyes. A punch in the shape of the sun on the blade, just above the cross guard. And just beyond it the inscription: *Draw me not without reason; sheath me not without honour*. Meaning the blade was wrought in the Nilfgaardian city of Viroleda, a place famous throughout the world for its armourers' forges. I touch the blade with the tip of my thumb – razor-sharp, I swear.

Since I'm nobody's fool, I betray nothing, I look on indifferently as the bank clerks bustle around and some poor old woman polishes the brass doorknobs.

'The Giancardis' bank,' quoth the little widow, 'valued the sword at two hundred crowns. For official sale. But for cash in hand I'll part with it for a hundred and fifty.'

'Ho, ho,' I reply. 'A hundred and fifty is a deal of money. You can buy a house for that. A small one. In the suburbs.'

'Oh, Lord Dandelion.' The woman wrings her hands, shedding a tear. 'You're mocking me. You are a cruel fellow, sir, to take advantage of a widow so. Since I am trapped, so be it: a hundred.'

And thus, my dears, I solved the Witcher's problem.

I scurry off to The Crab and Garfish, Geralt is already sitting there over his bacon and scrambled eggs, ha, no doubt there was white cheese and chives for breakfast at the red-headed witch's. I stride up and – clang! – I slam the sword down on the table. Dumbfounding him. He drops his spoon, draws the weapon from the scabbard and examines it. His countenance stony. But I am accustomed to his mutant state and know that emotions have no effect on him. No matter how delighted or happy he might be, he doesn't betray it.

'How much did you give for it?'

I wished to answer that it wasn't his business, but I recalled in time that I had paid with his money. So I confessed. He squeezed my arm, didn't say a word, the expression on his face unchanged. That is him all over. Simple, but sincere.

And he told me he was setting off. Alone.

'I'd like you to stay in Kerack.' He anticipated my protests. 'And keep your eyes and ears open.'

He told me what had happened the previous day, about his evening conversation with Prince Egmund. And fidgeted with the Viroledian sword the whole time, like a child with a new toy.

'I don't mean to serve the duke,' he recapitulated. 'Nor participate in the royal nuptials in August in the role of bodyguard. Egmund and your cousin are certain they will seize the sword thief forthwith. I don't share their optimism. And that actually suits me. With my swords, Egmund would have an advantage over me. I prefer to catch the thief myself, in Novigrad in July, before the auction at the Borsodys'. I'd get my swords back and I wouldn't show my face in Kerack again. And you, Dandelion, keep your mouth shut. No one can know what Pratt told us. No one. Including your cousin the instigator.'

I promised to be as silent as the grave. While he looked at me strangely. Quite as though he didn't trust me.

'And because anything might happen,' he continued, 'I must have an alternative plan. I'd like to know as much as possible about Egmund and his siblings, about all the possible pretenders to the throne, about the king himself, about the whole, dear royal family. I'd like to know what they're planning and plotting. Who's in with whom, what factions are active here and so on. Is that clear?'

'You don't want to involve Lytta Neyd in this, I gather,' I responded. 'And rightly so, I think. The red-haired beauty certainly has perfect insight into the matters interesting you, but the local monarchy binds her too much for her to consider double loyalty, for one thing. And for another, don't let on that you'll soon flee and won't be showing up again. Because her reaction may be violent.

Sorceresses, as you've found out directly, don't like it when people disappear.

'As regards the rest,' I promised, 'you can count on me. I shall have my ears and eyes in readiness and directed at where they're needed. And I've become acquainted with the dear, local royal family and heard enough gossip. Our Gracious King Belohun has produced numerous offspring. He has changed his wife quite often. Whenever he spots a new one, the old one conveniently bids farewell to this world, by an unfortunate twist of fate, suddenly falling into infirmity, in the face of which medicine turns out to be impotent. In this way, the king has four legal sons today, each one with a different mother. Not counting his innumerable daughters, as they can't pretend to the throne. Or bastards. It's worth mentioning, however, that all the significant positions and offices in Kerack are filled by his daughters' husbands – my cousin Ferrant is an exception. And his illegitimate sons manage commerce and industry.'

The Witcher, I heed, is listening attentively.

'The four legitimate sons,' I go on, 'are, in order of seniority, the firstborn, whose name I don't know; it's forbidden to mention his name at court. After a quarrel with his father he went away and disappeared without trace, no one has seen him since. The second, Elmer, is a deranged drunk kept under lock and key. It's supposedly a state secret, but in Kerack it's common knowledge. Egmund and Xander are the real pretenders. They detest each other, and Belohun exploits it cunningly, keeping both of them in a state of permanent uncertainty. In matters of the succession he is also often capable of ostentatiously favouring one of the bastards, and tantalising him with promises. Whereas now it's whispered in dark corners that he has promised the crown to the son to be borne by his new wife, the one he's officially marrying at Lughnasadh.

'Cousin Ferrant and I think, however, that they are but fine words,' I continue, 'used by the old prick with the intention of stirring the young thing to sexual fervour, since Egmund and Xander are the only true heirs to the throne. And if it comes to a *coup d'état* it'll be carried out by one of the two. I've met them both, through my cousin. They are both – I had the impression – as slippery as turds in mayonnaise. If you know what I mean.'

Geralt confirmed he knew and that he had the same impression when he spoke to Egmund, only he was unable to express it in such beautiful words. Then he pondered deeply.

'I'll return soon,' he finally said. 'And you, don't sit around, and keep an eye on things.'

'Before we say farewell,' I responded, 'be a good chap and tell me something about your witch's pupil. The one with the slicked-down hair. She's a true rosebud, all she needs is a little work and she'll bloom wonderfully. So I've decided that I'll devote myself—'

Geralt's face, however, changed. Without warning he slammed his fist down on the table, making the mugs jump.

'Keep your paws well away from Mozaïk, busker,' he started on me without a trace of respect. 'Knock that idea out of your head. Don't you know that sorceresses' pupils are strictly prohibited from even the most innocent flirting? For the smallest offence of that kind Coral will decide she's not worth teaching and send her back to the school, which is an awful embarrassment and loss of face for a pupil. I've heard of suicides caused by that. And there's no fooling around with Coral. She doesn't have a sense of humour.'

I felt like advising him to try tickling her with a hen's feather in her intergluteal cleft. For such a measure can cheer up even the greatest of sourpusses. But I said nothing, for I know him. He can't bear anyone to talk tactlessly about his women. Even brief dalliances. Thus, I swore on my honour that I would strike the slicked-down novice's chastity from the agenda and not even woo her.

'If that stings you so much,' he said brightly as he was leaving, 'then know that I met a lady lawyer in the local court. She looked willing. Pursue her instead.'

Not on your life. What, does he expect me to bed the judiciary? Although, on the other hand . . .

INTERLUDE

Highly Honourable Madam
Lytta Neyd
Kerack, Upper Town
Villa Cyclamen
Rissberg Castle, 1 July 1245 p. R.

Dear Coral,

I trust my letter finds you in good health and mood. And that
everything is as you would wish.

I hasten to inform you that the Witcher – called Geralt of Rivia
– finally deigned to put in an appearance at our castle. Immediately
after arriving, in less than an hour, he showed himself to be an-
noyingly unbearable and managed to alienate absolutely everyone,
including the Reverend Ortolan, a person who could be regarded
as kindness personified, and favourably disposed to everyone. The
opinions circulating about that individual aren't, as it turns out,
exaggerated in even the tiniest respect, and the antipathy and hostility that he encounters everywhere have their own deep-seated
grounds. But, however, insomuch as esteem should be paid him
I shall be the first to do so *sine ira et studio*. The fellow is every
inch the professional and totally trustworthy as regards his trade.
There can be no doubt that he executes whatever he attempts or
falls trying to achieve it.

We may thus consider the goal of our enterprise accomplished,
mainly thanks to you, dear Coral. We express our thanks to you
for your efforts, and you shall find us – as always – grateful. You,
meanwhile, have my especial gratitude. As your old friend, mind-
ful of what we have shared, I – more than the others – understand
your sacrifice. I realise how you must have suffered the proximity
of that individual, who is, indeed, an amalgam of the vices you
cannot bear. Cynicism derived from a profound complex, with a

pompous and introvert nature, an insincere character, a primitive mind, mediocre intelligence and great arrogance. I pass over the fact that he has ugly hands and chipped fingernails, in order not to irritate you, dear Coral; after all, I know you detest such things. But, as it's been said before, an end has come to your suffering, troubles and distress. Nothing now stands in the way of your breaking off relations with that individual and ceasing all contact with him. In the process, definitively putting an end to and making a stand against the false slander spread by unfriendly tongues, that have brazenly tried to turn your – let's be honest – simulated and feigned kindness to the Witcher into a vulgar affair. But enough of that, it's not worth belabouring the point.

I'd be the happiest of people, my dear Coral, if you were to visit me in Rissberg. I don't have to add that one word of yours, one gesture, one smile is enough for me to hasten to you as quickly as I might.

Yours with heartfelt respect,

Pinety

P.S. The unfriendly tongues I mentioned posit that your favour towards the Witcher comes from a desire to annoy our consoror Yennefer, who is still said to be interested in the Witcher. The naivety and ignorance of those schemers is indeed pitiful. Since it is widely known that Yennefer is in an ardent relationship with a certain young entrepreneur from the jewellery trade, and she cares as much about the Witcher and his transient love affairs as she does about last year's snow.

INTERLUDE

The Highly Honourable
Lord Algernon Guincamp
Rissberg Castle
Ex urbe Kerack,
die 5 mens. Jul. anno 1245 p. R.

My dear Pinety,

Thanks for the letter, you haven't written to me in ages. Why, there clearly has been nothing to write about or any reason to do so.

Your concern about my health and mood is endearing, also about whether things go as I would wish. I inform you with satisfaction that everything is turning out as it ought, and I'm sparing no effort in that regard. Every man, as you know, steers his own ship. Please note that I steer my ship with a sure hand through squalls and reefs, holding my head high, whenever the storm rages around.

As far as my health is concerned, everything is in order, as a matter of fact. Not only physically, but psychologically too, for some little time, since I've had what I'd long been lacking. I only realised how much I was missing it when I stopped missing it.

I'm glad the enterprise requiring the Witcher's participation is heading towards success; my modest contribution in the enterprise fills me with pride. Your sorrow is needless, my dear Pinety, if you think it involved suffering, sacrifices and difficulties. It wasn't quite so bad. Geralt is indeed a veritable conglomeration of vices. I nevertheless also uncovered in him – *sine ira et studio* – virtues. Considerable ones, at that. I vouch that many a man, were he to know, would worry. And many would envy.

We have become accustomed to the gossip, rumours, tall tales and intrigues of which you write, my dear Pinety, we know how to cope with them. And the method is simple: ignore them. I'm sure you recall the gossip about you and Sabrina Glevissig when it was rumoured there was something between us? I ignored it. I advise you to do the same now.

Bene vale,

Coral

P.S. I'm extremely busy. A potential rendezvous seems impossible for the foreseeable future.

They wander through various lands, and their tastes and moods demand that they be sans all dependencies. That means they recognise not any authority – human or divine. They respect not any laws or principles. They believe themselves innocent of and uncontaminated by any obedience. Being fraudsters by nature, they live by divinations with which they deceive simple folk, serve as spies, distribute counterfeit amulets, fraudulent medicaments, stimulants and narcotics, also dabble in harlotry; that is, they supply paying customers with lewd maidens for filthy pleasures. When they know poverty, they are not ashamed to beg or commit common theft, but they prefer swindles and fraud. They delude the naive that they supposedly protect people, that supposedly they kill monsters for the sake of folk's safety, but that is a lie. Long ago was it proven that they do it for their own amusement, for killing is a first-rate diversion to them. In preparing for their work, they make certain magic spells, howbeit it is but to delude the eyes of observers. Devout priests at once uncovered the falsity and jiggery-pokery to the confusion of those devil's servants who call themselves witchers.

Anonymous, *Monstrum, or a description of witchers*

CHAPTER NINE

Rissberg looked neither menacing nor impressive. There it was, a small castle like many others, of average size, elegantly built into the mountain's steep sides, hugging a cliff, its bright wall contrasting with the evergreen of a spruce forest, the tiles of two quadrangular towers – one tall, the other lower – overlooking the treetops. The wall surrounding the castle wasn't – as it transpired from close up – too tall and wasn't topped by battlements, while the small towers positioned at the corners and over the gatehouse were more decorative than defensive.

The road meandering around the hill bore the signs of intensive use. For it was used, and used intensively. The Witcher was soon overtaking carts, carriages, lone riders and pedestrians. Plenty of travellers were also moving in the opposite direction, away from the castle. Geralt guessed at the destination of these pilgrimages. Which was proved correct, it turned out, after he'd only just left the forest.

The flat hilltop beneath the curtain of the wall was occupied by a small town built of timber, reeds and straw; an entire complex of large and small buildings and roofs surrounded by a fence and enclosures for horses and livestock. There was a hubbub and people moved around briskly, like at a market or a fair. For it was indeed a fair, a bazaar, an open market; except neither poultry, fish nor vegetables were traded there. The goods on sale below the castle were magic – amulets, talismans, elixirs, opiates, philtres, decocts, extracts, distillates, concoctions, incense, syrups, scents, powders and ointments, as well as various practical, enchanted objects, tools, domestic equipment, decorations, and even children's toys. The whole assortment attracted purchasers in great numbers. There was demand, there was supply – and business was clearly flourishing.

The road divided. The Witcher headed along the path leading

towards the castle gate, considerably less rutted than the other, which led the buyers towards the marketplace. He rode across the cobbled area in front of the gatehouse, along an avenue of menhirs specially set there, mostly considerably taller than him on his horse. He was soon greeted by a gate, more suited to a palace than a castle, decorated with pilasters and a pediment. The Witcher's medallion vibrated powerfully. Roach neighed, her horseshoes clattering on the cobbles, and stopped abruptly.

'Identity and purpose of visit.'

He raised his head. A rasping and echoing voice, undoubtedly female, seemed to emerge from the wide-open mouth of the harpy's head depicted on the tympanum. His medallion quivered and the mare snorted. Geralt felt a strange tightness at the temples.

'Identity and purpose of visit,' came the voice from the hole in the relief. A little louder than before.

'Geralt of Rivia, witcher. I'm expected.'

The harpy's head uttered a sound resembling a trumpet call. The magic blocking the portal vanished, the pressure at his temples stopped at once, and the mare set off without being urged. Her hooves clattered on the stones.

He rode from the portal into a cul-de-sac ringed by a cloister. Two servants – boys in practical brown and grey attire – ran over to him at once. One attended to the horse and the other served as a guide.

'This way, sire.'

'Is it always like this here? Such a commotion? Down there in the suburbs?'

'No, sire.' The servant threw a frightened glance at him. 'Nobbut on Wednesdays. Wednesday's market day.'

On the arcaded finial of the next portal was a cartouche bearing another relief, undoubtedly also magical, depicting an amphisbaena's maw. The portal was closed off by an ornate, solid-looking grille, which, however, opened easily and smoothly when the servant pushed against it.

The next courtyard was significantly larger. And the castle could only be properly admired from there. The view from a distance, it turned out, was very deceptive.

Rissberg was much larger than it appeared to be. A complex of severe and unsightly buildings – seldom encountered in castle architecture – extended deep into the mountain wall. The buildings looked like factories and probably were. For there were chimneys and ventilation pipes protruding from them. The smell of burning, sulphur and ammonia was in the air and the ground trembled slightly, proof that some kind of subterranean machinery was in operation.

A cough from the servant drew Geralt's attention away from the industrial complex. For they were supposed to be going the other way, towards the lower of the two towers rising above the buildings with more classical architecture, befitting a palace. The interior also turned out to be typical of a palace: it smelled of dust, wood, wax and old junk. It was bright: magic balls veiled in haloes of light – the standard illumination of sorcerers' dwelling places – floated beneath the ceiling, as languid as fish in an aquarium.

'Welcome, Witcher.'

The welcome party turned out to be two sorcerers. He knew them both, although not personally. Yennefer had once pointed out Harlan Tzara to him, and Geralt remembered him because he was probably the only mage to cultivate a completely shaven head. He remembered the other, Algernon Guincamp, called Pinety, from the academy in Oxenfurt.

'Welcome to Rissberg,' Pinety greeted him. 'We're glad you agreed to come.'

'Are you mocking me? I'm not here of my own will. In order to force me to come, Lytta Neyd shoved me in the clink—'

'But, she extracted you later,' interrupted Tzara, 'and rewarded you amply. She made good your discomfort with great, hmm, devotion. Word has it that you've been enjoying her . . . company for at least a week.'

Geralt fought the overwhelming urge to punch him in the face. Pinety must have noticed it.

'*Pax*.' He raised a hand. '*Pax*, Harlan. Let's end these squabbles. Let's give this battle of snide remarks and acerbities a miss. We know Geralt has something against us, it's audible in every word he utters. We know why that is, we know how the affair with Yennefer saddened him. And the reaction of the wizarding

119

community to the affair. We shan't change that. But Geralt is a professional, he will know how to rise above it.'

'He will,' Geralt admitted caustically. 'But the question is whether he'll want to. Can we finally get to the point? Why am I here?'

'We need you,' said Tzara dryly. 'You in particular.'

'Me in particular. Ought I to feel honoured? Or to start feeling afraid?'

'You are celebrated, Geralt of Rivia,' said Pinety. 'Your deeds and exploits are indeed regarded by general consensus as spectacular and admirable. You may not especially count on *our* admiration, as you conclude. We aren't so inclined to show our esteem, particularly to someone like you. But we're able to acknowledge professionalism and respect experience. The facts speak for themselves. You are, I dare say, an outstanding . . . hmm—'

'Yes?'

'—eliminator.' Pinety found the word without difficulty; he had clearly prepared it in advance. 'Someone who eliminates monsters and beasts that endanger people.'

Geralt made no comment. He waited.

'Our aim, the aim of all sorcerers, is also people's prosperity and safety. Thus, we may talk of a community of interests. Occasional misunderstandings ought not to obscure that. The lord of this castle gave us to understand that not long ago. He is aware of you and would like to meet you personally. That is his wish.'

'Ortolan.'

'Grandmaster Ortolan. And his closest collaborators. You will be introduced. Later. The servants will show you to your quarters. You may refresh yourself after your journey. Rest. We'll send for you soon.'

*

Geralt pondered. He recalled everything he had ever heard about Grandmaster Ortolan. Who was – as general consensus had it – a living legend.

*

Ortolan was a living legend, a person who had rendered extraordinary service to the magic arts.

His obsession was the popularisation of magic. Unlike the majority of sorcerers, he thought that the benefits and advantages deriving from supernatural powers ought to be a common good and serve to strengthen universal prosperity, comfort and general bliss. It was Ortolan's dream that everybody ought to have guaranteed free access to magical elixirs and medicaments. Magical amulets, talismans and every kind of artefact ought to be universally and freely available. Telepathy, telekinesis, teleportation and telecommunication ought to be the privilege of every citizen. In order to achieve that, Ortolan was endlessly coming up with things. Meaning inventions. Some just as legendary as he himself.

Reality painfully challenged the venerable sorcerer's fantasies. None of his inventions – intended to popularise and democratise magic – moved beyond the prototype phase. Everything that Ortolan thought up – and what in principle ought to have been simple – turned out to be horrendously complicated. Everything that was meant to be mass-produced turned out to be devilishly expensive. But Ortolan didn't lose heart and, instead of discouraging him, the fiascos aroused him to greater efforts. Leading to further fiascos.

It was suspected although, naturally, this never dawned on Ortolan himself – that the cause of the inventor's failures was often sheer sabotage. It wasn't caused by – well, not *just* – by the simple envy of the sorcerers' brotherhood, the reluctance to popularise the art of magic, which sorcerers and sorceresses preferred to see in the hands of the elite – i.e. their own. The fears were more about inventions of a military and lethal nature.

And the fears were justified. Like every inventor, Ortolan had phases of fascination with explosive and flammable materials, siege catapults, armoured chariots, crude firearms, sticks that hit by themselves and poison gases. Universal peace among nations is a condition of prosperity, the old man tried to prove, and peace is achieved by arming oneself. The most certain method of preventing wars is to have a terrible weapon as a deterrent: the more terrible it is, the more enduring and certain the peace. Because Ortolan wasn't accustomed to listening to arguments, saboteurs who torpedoed his dangerous inventions were hidden among his inventing team. Almost none of the inventions saw the light of day. An exception was the notorious missile-hurler, the subject of numerous anecdotes. It was a kind of telekinetic arbalest with a large container for lead missiles. This missile-hurler – as the name suggested – was meant to throw missiles at a target, in whole series. The prototype made it out of Rissberg's walls – astonishingly – and it was even tested in some skirmish or other. With pitiful results, however. The artilleryman using the invention, when asked about the weapon's usefulness, apparently said that the missile-hurler was like his mother-in-law. Heavy, ugly, totally useless and only fit to be taken and thrown in a river. The old sorcerer wasn't upset when this was relayed to him. The weapon was a toy – he was said to have declared – and he already had many more advanced projects on his drawing board capable of mass destruction. He, Ortolan, would give humanity the benefit of peace, even if it would first be necessary to destroy half of it.

*

The wall of the chamber where he was led was graced by a huge tapestry, a masterpiece of weaving, of Arcadian verdure. The tapestry was marred by a stain, somewhat resembling a large squid, that hadn't been completely washed off. *Someone*, thought the Witcher, *must have puked up on the masterpiece not long before.*

Seven people were seated at a long table occupying the centre of the chamber.

'Master Ortolan.' Pinety bowed slightly. 'Let me introduce to you Geralt of Rivia. The Witcher.'

Ortolan's appearance didn't surprise Geralt. It was believed he was the world's oldest living sorcerer. Perhaps that was really true, perhaps not, but the fact remained that Ortolan was the oldest-*looking* sorcerer. This was strange, in so far as Ortolan was the inventor of a celebrated mandrake decoction, an elixir used by sorcerers in order to arrest the ageing process. Ortolan himself, when he had finally developed a reliably acting formula for the magical liquid, didn't gain much benefit from it, because by then he was quite advanced in age. The elixir prevented ageing, but by no means rejuvenated. For which reason Ortolan too, although he had used the remedy for a long time, continued to look like an old codger – particularly when compared to his confraters: venerable sorcerers, who resembled men in the prime of life, and his consorors: world-weary sorceresses, who looked like maids. The sorceresses bursting with youth and charm and the slightly grey-haired sorcerers, whose real dates of birth had vanished in the mists of time, jealously guarded the secrets of Ortolan's elixir, and sometimes quite simply even denied its existence. Meanwhile, they kept Ortolan convinced that the elixir was generally available, owing to which humanity was practically immortal and – consequently – absolutely happy.

'Geralt of Rivia,' repeated Ortolan, crushing a tuft of his grey beard in his hand. 'Indeed, indeed, we have heard. The Witcher. A defender, they say, a guardian, protecting people from Evil. A prophylactic agent and esteemed antidote to all fearsome Evil.'

Geralt assumed a modest expression and bowed.

'Indeed, indeed . . .' continued the mage, tugging at his beard. 'We know, we know. According to all testimony you spare not your strength to defend folk, my boy, you spare it not. And your practice is verily estimable, your craft is estimable. We welcome you to our castle, content that the fates brought you here. For though you may not know it yourself, you have returned like a bird to its nest . . . Verily, like a bird. We are glad to see you and trust that you also are glad to see us. Eh?'

Geralt was undecided about how to address Ortolan. Sorcerers didn't recognise polite forms and didn't expect them from others. But he didn't know if that was acceptable with regard to a grey-haired and grey-bearded old man, and a living legend to boot. Instead of speaking, he bowed again.

Pinety introduced the sorcerers seated at the table in turn. Geralt had heard of some of them.

The forehead and cheeks of Axel Esparza, more widely known as Pockmarked Axel, were indeed covered with pitted scars. He hadn't removed them, so went the rumour, out of sheer contrariness. The slightly grizzled Myles Trethevey and slightly more grizzled Stucco Zangenis examined the Witcher with moderate interest. The interest of Biruta Icarti, a moderately attractive blonde, seemed a little greater. Tarvix Sandoval, broad-shouldered, with a physique more befitting a knight than a sorcerer, looked to one side, at the tapestry, as though he was also admiring the stain and was wondering where it came from and who was responsible for it.

The seat nearest Ortolan was occupied by Sorel Degerlund, apparently the youngest of those present, whose long hair lent him a slightly effeminate look.

'We, too, welcome the famous Witcher, the defender of folk,' said Biruta Icarti. 'We are glad to welcome you, since we also toil in this castle under the auspices of Grandmaster Ortolan, in order that thanks to progress we will make people's lives safer and easier. People's best interests are our overriding goal, too. The grandmaster's age doesn't permit us overly to prolong the audience. Thus, I shall ask what is appropriate: do you have any wishes, Geralt of Rivia? Is there something we can do for you?'

'I thank you, Grandmaster Ortolan.' Geralt bowed again. 'And you, distinguished sorcerers. And since you embolden me with the question . . . Yes, there is something you can do for me. You could enlighten me . . . about this. This thing. I tore it from a vigilosaur I killed.'

He placed on the table the oval plate the size of a child's hand. With characters embossed in it.

'*RISS PSREP Mk IV/002 025*,' Pockmarked Axel read aloud. And passed the plate to Sandoval.

'It's a mutation, created here, by us, at Rissberg,' Sandoval stated bluntly. 'In the pseudoreptile section. It's a guard lizard. Mark four, series two, specimen twenty-five. Obsolete, we've been manufacturing an improved model for a long time. What else needs explaining?'

'He says he killed the vigilosaur.' Stucco Zangenis grimaced. 'So, it's not about an explanation, but a claim. We only accept and look into complaints, Witcher, from legal buyers, and only on the basis of proof of purchase. We only service and remove defects on the basis of proof of purchase . . .'

'That model's guarantee expired long ago,' added Myles Trethevey. 'And anyway, no guarantee covers defects resulting from inappropriate use of the product or in breach of the operating instructions. If the product was used inappropriately, Rissberg doesn't take responsibility. Of any kind.'

'And do you take responsibility for this?' Geralt took another plate from his pocket and threw it down on the table.

The other plate was similar in shape and size to the previous one, but darkened and tarnished. Dirt had become embedded and fused into the grooves. But the characters were still legible:

IDR UL Ex IX 0012 BETA.

A long silence fell.

'Idarran of Ulivo,' Pinety said at last, surprisingly quietly and surprisingly hesitantly. 'One of Alzur's students. I never expected . . .'

'Where did you get it, Witcher?' Pockmarked Axel leaned across the table. 'How did you come by it?'

'You ask as though you didn't know,' retorted Geralt. 'I dug it out of the carapace of a creature I killed. One that had murdered at least twenty people in the district. At least twenty – for I think it was many more. I think it had been killing for years.'

'Idarran . . .' muttered Tarvix Sandoval. 'And before him Malaspina and Alzur . . .'

'But it wasn't us,' said Zangenis. 'It wasn't us. Not Rissberg.'

'Experimental model nine,' added Biruta Icarti pensively. 'Beta version. Specimen twelve . . .'

'Specimen twelve,' Geralt chimed in, not without spitefulness. 'And how many were there all together? How many were manufactured? I won't be getting an answer to my question about responsibility, that's clear, because it wasn't you, it wasn't Rissberg, you're clean and you want me to believe that. But at least tell me, because you surely know how many of them there are wandering around in forests, murdering people. How many of them will have to be found? And hacked to death? I meant to say: eliminated.'

'What is it, what is it?' Ortolan suddenly became animated. 'What do you have there? Show me! Ah . . .'

Sorel Degerlund leaned over towards the old man's ear, and whispered for a long time. Myles Trethevey, showing him the plate, whispered from the other side. Ortolan tugged at his beard.

'Killed it?' he suddenly shouted in a high, thin voice. 'The Witcher? Destroyed Idarran's work of genius? Killed it? Unthinkingly destroyed it?'

The Witcher couldn't control himself. He snorted. His respect for advanced age and grey hair suddenly abandoned him altogether. He snorted again. And then laughed. Heartily and relentlessly.

The stony faces of the sorcerers sitting at the table, rather than restraining him, made him even more amused. *By the devil*, he thought, *I don't remember when I last laughed so heartily. Probably in Kaer Morhen*, he recalled, *yes, in Kaer Morhen. When that rotten plank broke underneath Vesemir in the privy.*

'He's still laughing, the pup,' cried out Ortolan. 'He's neighing like an ass! Doltish whippersnapper! To think I came to your defence when others vilified you! *So what if he has become enamoured of little Yennefer?* I said. *And what if little Yennefer dotes on him? The heart is no servant*, I said, *leave them both in peace!*'

Geralt stopped laughing.

'And what have you done, most stupid of assassins?' the old man yelled. 'What did you do? Do you comprehend what a work of art, what a miracle of genetics you have ruined? No, no, you cannot conceive of that with your shallow mind, layman! You cannot comprehend the ideas of brilliant people! Such as Idarran and Alzur, his teacher, who were graced with genius and extraordinary talent! Who invented and created great works, meant to serve humanity, without taking profit, nor taking base mammon into account, not recreation nor diversion, but solely progress and the commonweal! But what can you apprehend of such things? You apprehend nothing, nothing, nothing, not a scrap!

'And indeed, I tell you further,' Ortolan panted, 'that you have dishonoured the work of your own fathers with this imprudent murder. For it was Cosimo Malaspina, and after him his student Alzur, yes, Alzur, who created the witchers. They invented the mutation owing to which men like you were bred. Owing to which you exist, owing to which you walk upon this earth, ungrateful one. You ought to esteem Alzur, his successors and their works, and not destroy them! Oh dear . . . Oh dear . . .'

The old sorcerer suddenly fell silent, rolled his eyes and groaned heavily.

'I needs must to the stool,' he announced plaintively. 'I needs must quickly to the stool! Sorel! My dear boy!'

Degerlund and Trethevey leaped up from their seats, helped the old man stand up and led him out of the chamber.

A short while after, Biruta Icarti stood up. She threw the Witcher a very expressive glance, then exited without a word. Sandoval and Zangenis headed out after her, not even looking at Geralt at all. Pockmarked Axel stood up and crossed his arms on his chest. He looked at Geralt for a long time. Lengthily and rather unpleasantly.

'It was a mistake to invite you,' he said finally. 'I knew it. But I deluded myself in thinking you'd muster up even a semblance of good manners.'

'It was a mistake to accept your invitation,' Geralt replied coldly. 'I also knew it. But I deluded myself in thinking I would receive answers to my questions. How many numbered masterpieces are still at large? How many similar masterworks did Malaspina, Alzur and Idarran manufacture? And the esteemed Ortolan? How many more monsters bearing your plates will I have to kill? I, a witcher, prophylactic agent and antidote? I didn't receive an answer and I well apprehend why not. Regarding good manners, however: fuck off, Esparza.'

Esparza the Pockmarked slammed the door as he went out. So hard that plaster fell from the ceiling.

'I don't think I made a good impression,' concluded the Witcher. 'But I didn't expect to, hence there is no disappointment. But that probably isn't everything, is it? So much trouble to get me here . . . And that would be all? Why, if it's like that . . . Will I find a tavern selling alcohol in the suburbs? Can I toddle along now?'

'No,' replied Harlan Tzara. 'No, you can't.'

'Because it's by no means all,' added Pinety.

*

The chamber he was led to wasn't typical of the rooms where sorcerers usually received applicants. Usually – Geralt was well acquainted with the custom – mages gave audiences in large rooms with very formal, often severe and cheerless décor. It was practically unthinkable for a sorcerer to receive anybody in a private, personal room, a room able to provide information about the disposition, tastes and predilections of a mage – particularly about the type and specific character of the magic they made.

This time it was totally different. The chamber's walls were decorated with numerous prints and watercolours, every last one of them of erotic or downright pornographic character. Models of sailing ships were displayed on shelves, delighting the eye with the precision of their details. Miniature sails proudly billowed out on tiny ships in bottles. There were numerous display cases of various sizes full of toy soldiers: cavalry and infantry, in all sorts of formations. Opposite the entrance, also behind glass, hung a stuffed and mounted brown trout. Of considerable size, for a trout.

'Be seated, Witcher.' Pinety, it became clear at once, was in charge.

Geralt sat down, scrutinising the stuffed trout. The fish must have weighed a good fifteen pounds alive. Assuming it wasn't a plaster imitation.

'Magic protects us from being eavesdropped upon.' Pinety swept a hand through the air. 'We shall thus be able finally to speak freely about the real reasons for your being brought here, Geralt of Rivia. The trout which so interests you was caught on a fly in the River Ribbon and weighed fourteen pounds nine ounces. It was released alive, and the display case contains a magically created copy. And now please concentrate. On what I'm about to tell you.'

'I'm ready. For anything.'

'We're curious to know what experience you have with demons.'

Geralt raised his eyebrows. He hadn't been expecting that. And a short time before, he had thought that nothing would surprise him.

'And what is a demon? In your opinion?'

Harlan Tzara grimaced and shifted suddenly. Pinety appeased him with a look.

'There is a department of supernatural phenomena at the Academy of Oxenfurt,' he said. 'Masters of magic give guest lectures there. Some of which concern the subject of demons and demonism, in the many aspects of that phenomenon, including the physical, metaphysical, philosophical and moral. But I think I'm telling you about it needlessly, for you attended those lectures, after all. I remember you, even though as a visiting student you would usually sit in the back row of the lecture theatre. I therefore repeat the question regarding your experience of demons. Be good enough to answer. Without being a smart aleck, if you please. Or feigning astonishment.'

'There isn't a scrap of pretence in my astonishment,' Geralt replied dryly. 'It's so sincere it pains me. How can it not astonish me when I, a simple witcher, a simple prophylactic agent and even more simple antidote, am asked about my experience with demons? And the questions are being asked by masters of magic, who lecture about demonism and its aspects at the university.'

'Answer the question.'

'I'm a witcher, not a sorcerer. Which means my experience comes nowhere near yours regarding demons. I attended your lectures at Oxenfurt, Guincamp. Anything important reached the back row of the lecture theatre. Demons are creatures from different worlds than ours. Elemental planes . . . dimensions, spacetimes or whatever they're called. In order to have any kind of experience with a demon you have to invoke it, meaning forcibly extract it from its plane. It can only be accomplished using magic—'

'Not magic, but goetia,' interrupted Pinety. 'There's a fundamental difference. And don't tell us what we already know. Answer the question that was asked. I request it for the third time, amazed by my own patience.'

'I'll answer the question: yes, I have dealt with demons. I was hired twice in order to . . . eliminate them. I've dealt with two demons. With one that entered a wolf. And another that possessed a human being.'

'You "dealt" with them.'

'Yes, I did. It wasn't easy—'

'But it was feasible,' interjected Tzara. 'In spite of what's claimed. And it's claimed that it's impossible to destroy a demon.'

'I didn't claim I ever destroyed a demon. I killed a wolf and a human being. Do the details interest you?'

'Very much.'

'I acted alongside a priest in the case of the wolf that had, in broad daylight, killed and ripped eleven people to pieces. Magic and sword triumphed side by side. When, after a hard fight, I finally killed the wolf, the demon possessing it broke free in the form of a large glowing ball. And devastated a fair stretch of forest, scattering the trees all around. It didn't pay any attention to me or the priest, but cleared the forest in the opposite direction. And then it disappeared, probably returning to its dimension. The priest insisted he deserved the credit, that his exorcisms had dispatched the demon to the beyond. Although I think the demon went away because he was simply bored.'

'And the other case—?'

'—was more interesting.

'I killed a possessed man,' he continued without being pressed. 'And that was it. No spectacular side effects. No ball lightning, auroras, thunderbolts or whirlwinds; not even a foul smell. I've no idea what happened to the demon. Some priests and mages – your confraters – examined the dead man. They didn't find or discover anything. The body was cremated, because the process of decay proceeded quite normally, and the weather was very hot—'

He broke off. The sorcerers looked at each other. Their faces were inscrutable.

'That would be, as I understand it, the only proper way of dealing with a demon,' Harlan Tzara finally said. 'To kill, to destroy the energumen, meaning the possessed person. The person, I stress. They must be killed at once, without waiting or deliberating. They should be chopped up with a sword. And that's it. Is that the witcher method? The witcher technique?'

'You're doing poorly, Tzara. That's not how it's done. In order to insult someone properly, you need more than overwhelming desire, enthusiasm and fervour. You need technique.'

'*Pax, pax.*' Pinety headed off an argument again. 'We're simply establishing the facts. You told us that you killed a man, those were your very words. Your witcher code is meant to preclude killing people. You claim to have killed an energumen, a person who'd been possessed by a demon. After that fact, i.e. the execution of a person, "no spectacular effects were observed", to quote you again. Where, then, is your certainty that it wasn't—'

'Enough,' Geralt interrupted. 'Enough of that, Guincamp, these allusions are going nowhere. You want facts? By all means, they are as follows. I killed him, because it was necessary. I killed him to save the lives of other people. And I received a dispensation from the law to do it. It was granted to me in haste, albeit in quite high-sounding words. "A state of absolute necessity, a circumstance precluding the lawlessness of a forbidden deed, sacrificing one good in order to save another one, a real, direct threat." It was, indeed, real and direct. You ought to regret you didn't see the possessed man in action, what he did, what he was capable of. I know little of the philosophical and metaphysical aspects of demons, but their physical aspect is truly spectacular. It can be astonishing, take my word for it.'

'We believe you,' confirmed Pinety, exchanging glances with Tzara again. 'Of course, we believe you. Because we've also seen a thing or two.'

'I don't doubt it.' The Witcher grimaced. 'And I didn't doubt that during your lectures at Oxenfurt. It was apparent you knew what you were talking about. The theoretical underpinning really came in handy with that wolf and that man. I knew what it was about. The two cases had an identical basis. What did you call it, Tzara? A method? A technique? And thus, it was a magical method and the technique was also magical. Some sorcerer summoned a demon using spells, extracted it forcibly from its plane, with the obvious intention of exploiting it for their own magical goals. That's the basis of demonic magic—'

'—goetia.'

'—That's the basis of goetia: invoking a demon, using it, and then releasing it. In theory. Because in practice it happens that the sorcerer, instead of freeing the demon after using it, imprisons it magically in a body. That of a wolf, for example. Or a human being. For a sorcerer – as Alzur and Idarran have shown us – likes to experiment. Likes observing what a demon does in someone else's skin when it's set free. For a sorcerer – like Alzur – is a sick pervert, who enjoys and is entertained by watching the killing wrought by a demon. That has occurred, hasn't it?'

'Various things have occurred,' said Harlan Tzara in a slow, drawling voice. 'It's stupid to generalise, and low to reproach. And to remind you of witchers who didn't shrink from robbery. Who didn't hesitate to work as hired assassins. Am I to remind you of the psychopaths who wore medallions with a cat's head, and who were also amused by the killing being wrought around them?'

'Gentlemen.' Pinety raised a hand, silencing the Witcher, who was preparing to make a rejoinder. 'This isn't a session of the town council, so don't try to outdo one another in vices and pathologies. It's probably more judicious to admit that no one is perfect, everyone has their vices, and even celestial creatures are no strangers to pathologies. Apparently. Let's concentrate on the problem before us and which demands a solution.'

'Goetia is prohibited,' Pinety began after a long silence, 'because it's an extremely dangerous practice. Sadly, the simple evocation of a demon doesn't demand great knowledge, nor great magical abilities. It's enough to possess a necromantic grimoire, and there are plenty of them on the black market. It is, however, difficult to control a demon once invoked without knowledge or skills. A self-taught goetic practitioner can think himself lucky if the invoked demon simply breaks away, frees itself and flees. Many of them end up torn to shreds. Thus, invoking demons or any other creatures from elemental planes and para-elements was prohibited and had the threat of severe punishments imposed on it. There exists a system of control that guarantees the observance of the prohibition. However, there is a place that was excluded from that control.'

'Rissberg Castle. Of course.'

'Of course. Rissberg cannot be controlled. For the system of goetia control I was talking about was created here, after all. As a result of experiments carried out here. Thanks to tests carried out here the system is still being perfected. Other research is being conducted here, and other experiments. Of a wide variety. Various things and phenomena are studied here, Witcher. Various things are done here. Not always legal and not always moral. The end justifies the means. That slogan could hang over the gate to Rissberg.'

'And beneath that slogan ought to be added: "What happens at Rissberg stays at Rissberg",' added Tzara. 'Experiments are carried out here under supervision. Everything is monitored.'

'Clearly not everything,' Geralt stated sourly. 'Because something escaped.'

'Something escaped.' Pinety was theatrically calm. 'There are currently eighteen masters working at the castle. And on top of that, well over four score apprentices and novices. Most of the

132

latter are only a few formalities away from the title of "master". We fear . . . We have reason to suppose before that someone from that large group wanted to play at goetia.'

'Don't you know who?'

'We do not,' Harlan Tzara replied without batting an eye. But the Witcher knew he was lying.

'In May and at the beginning of June, three large-scale crimes were committed in the vicinity.' The sorcerer didn't wait for further questions. 'In the vicinity, meaning here, on the Hill, between twelve and twenty miles from Rissberg. Each time, forest settlements, the homesteads of foresters and other forest workers, were targeted. All the residents were murdered in the settlements, no one was left alive. Post-mortem examinations confirmed that the crimes must have been committed by a demon. Or more precisely, an energumen, someone possessed by a demon. A demon that was invoked here, at the castle.'

'We have a problem, Geralt of Rivia. We have to solve it. And we hope you'll help us with it.'

Sending matter is an elaborate, sophisticated and subtle thing, hence before setting about teleporting, one must without fail defecate and empty the bladder.

Geoffrey Monck,
The Theory and Practice of Using Teleportals

CHAPTER TEN

As usual, Roach snorted and protested on seeing the blanket, and fear and protest could be heard in her snorting. She didn't like it when the Witcher covered her head. She liked even less what occurred right after it was covered. Geralt wasn't in the least surprised at the mare. Because he didn't like it either. Naturally, it didn't behove him to snort or splutter, but it didn't stop him expressing his disapproval in another form.

'Your aversion to teleportation is truly surprising,' said Harlan Tzara, showing his astonishment for the umpteenth time.

The Witcher didn't join in the discussion. Tzara hadn't expected him to.

'We've been transporting you for over a week,' he continued, 'and each time you put on the look of a condemned man being led to the scaffold. Ordinary people, I can understand. For them matter transfer remains a dreadful, unimaginable thing. But I thought that you, a witcher, had more experience in matters of magic. These aren't the times of Geoffrey Monck's first portals! Today teleportation is a common and absolutely safe thing. Teleportals are safe. And teleportals opened by me are absolutely safe.'

The Witcher sighed. He'd happened to observe the effects of the safe functioning teleportals more than once and he'd also helped sorting the remains of people who'd used teleportals. Which was why he knew that declarations about their safety could be classified along with such statements as: 'my little dog doesn't bite', 'my son's a good boy', 'this stew's fresh', 'I'll give you the money back the day after tomorrow at the latest', 'he was only getting something out of my eye', 'the good of the fatherland comes before everything', and 'just answer a few questions and you're free to go'.

There wasn't a choice or an alternative, however. In accordance with the plan adopted at Rissberg, Geralt's daily task was to patrol a selected region of the Hills and the settlements, colonies and homesteads there. Places where Pinety and Tzara feared another attack by the energumen. Settlements like that were spread over the entire Hills; sometimes quite far from each other. Geralt had to admit and accept the fact that effective patrolling wouldn't have been possible without the help of teleportational magic.

To maintain secrecy, Pinety and Tzara had constructed the portals at the end of the Rissberg complex, in a large, empty, musty room in need of refurbishment, where cobwebs stuck to your face, and shrivelled up mouse droppings crunched under your boots. A spell was activated on a wall covered in damp patches and slimy marks and then the brightly shining outline of a door – or rather a gateway – appeared, beyond which whirled an opaque, iridescent glow. Geralt walked the blindfolded mare into the glow – and then things became unpleasant. There was a flash and he stopped seeing, hearing or feeling anything – apart from cold. Cold was the only thing felt inside the black nothingness, amid silence, amorphousness and timelessness, because the teleport dulled and extinguished all the other senses. Fortunately, only for a split second. The moment passed, the real world flared up, and the horse, snorting with terror, clattered its horseshoes on the hard ground of reality.

'The horse taking fright is understandable,' Tzara stated again. 'While your anxiety, Witcher, is utterly irrational.'

Anxiety is never irrational, Geralt thought to himself. *Aside from psychological disturbances. It was one of the first things novice witchers were taught. It's good to feel fear. If you feel fear it means there's something to be feared, so be vigilant. Fear doesn't have to be overcome. Just don't yield to it. And you can learn from it.*

'Where to today?' asked Tzara, opening the lacquer box in which he kept his wand. 'What region?'

'Dry Rocks.'

'Try to get to Maple Grove before sundown. Pinety or I will pick you up from there. Ready?'

'For anything.'

Tzara waved his hand and wand in the air as though conducting an orchestra and Geralt thought he could even hear music. The sorcerer melodiously chanted a long spell that sounded like a poem being recited. Flaming lines flared up on the wall, then linked up to form a shining, rectangular outline. The Witcher swore under his breath, calmed his pulsating medallion, jabbed the mare with his heels and rode her into the milky nothingness.

*

Blackness, silence, amorphousness, timelessness. Cold. And suddenly a flash and a shock, the thud of hooves on hard ground.

*

The crimes of which the sorcerers suspected the energumen, the person possessed by a demon, were carried out in the vicinity of Rissberg, in an uninhabited area called the Tukaj Hills, a chain of upland covered in ancient woodland, separating Temeria from Brugge. The hills owed their name – some people insisted – to a legendary hero called Tukaj, or to something completely different, as others claimed. Since there weren't any other hills in the region it became common to simply say 'the Hills', and that shortened name also appeared on many maps.

The Hills stretched in a wide belt about a hundred miles long and twenty to thirty miles wide. The western part, in particular, was worked intensively by foresters. Large-scale felling had been carried out and industries and crafts linked to felling and forestry had developed. Large, medium, small and quite tiny, permanent and makeshift, tolerably and poorly built settlements, colonies, homesteads and camps of the people earning their living by forest crafts had been established in the wilderness. The sorcerers estimated that around four dozen such settlements existed throughout the Hills.

Massacres – from whom no one escaped with their life – had occurred in three of them.

*

Dry Rocks, a complex of low limestone hills surrounded by dense forests, formed the westernmost edge of the Hills, the western border of the patrol region. Geralt had been there before; he knew the area. A lime kiln – used for burning limestone – had been built in a clearing at the edge of the forest. The end product of this burning was quicklime. Pinety, when they were there together, explained what the lime was for, but Geralt had listened inattentively and forgot it. Lime – of any kind – lay quite far beyond his sphere of interests. But a colony of people had sprung up by the kiln who made a living from said lime. He had been entrusted with their protection. And only that mattered.

The lime burners recognised him, one of them waved his hat at him. Geralt returned the greeting. *I'm doing my job*, he thought. *I'm doing my duty. Doing what they pay me for.*

He guided Roach towards the forest. He had about a half-hour ride along a forest track ahead of him. Nearly a mile separated him from the next settlement. It was called Pointer's Clearing.

*

The Witcher covered a distance of from seven to ten miles over the course of a day. Depending on the region, that meant visiting anything from a handful to more than a dozen homesteads and then reaching an agreed-upon location, from where one of the sorcerers would teleport him back to the castle before sundown. The pattern was repeated the following day, when another region of the Hills was patrolled. Geralt chose the regions at random, wary of routines and patterns that might easily be decoded. Despite that, the task turned out to be quite monotonous. The Witcher, however, wasn't bothered by monotony, he was accustomed to it in his profession: in most cases, only patience, perseverance and determination guaranteed a successful kill. Actually, never before – and this was pertinent – had anyone ever been willing to pay for his patience, perseverance and determination as generously as the sorcerers of Rissberg. So he couldn't complain, he just had to do his job.

Without believing overly in the success of the enterprise.

*

'You presented me to Ortolan and all the high-ranking mages immediately after my arrival at Rissberg,' he pointed out to the sorcerers. 'Even if one assumes that the person guilty of the goetia and the massacres wasn't among them, news of a witcher at the castle must have spread. Your wrongdoer, assuming he exists, will understand in no time what's afoot, so will go into hiding and abandon his activities. Entirely. Or will wait until I leave and then begin again.'

'We can stage your departure,' replied Pinety. 'And your continued stay at the castle will be a secret. Fear not, magic exists to guarantee the confidentiality of what must remain a secret. Believe us, we can work that kind of magic.'

'So you believe my daily patrols make sense?'

'They do. Do your job, Witcher. And don't worry about the rest.'

Geralt solemnly promised not to worry. Although he had his doubts. And didn't entirely trust the sorcerers. He had his suspicions.

But had no intention of divulging them.

*

Axes banged and saws rasped briskly in Pointer's Clearing, and there was a smell of fresh timber and resin. The relentless felling of the forest was being carried out by the woodcutter Pointer and his large family. The older members of the family chopped and sawed, the younger ones stripped the branches from the trunks and the youngest carried brushwood. Pointer saw Geralt, sank his axe into a trunk and wiped his forehead.

'Greetings.' The Witcher rode closer. 'How are things? Everything in order?'

Pointer looked at him long and sombrely.

'Things are bad,' he said at last.

'Why?'

141

Pointer said nothing for a long time.

'Someone stole a saw,' he finally snarled. 'Stole a saw! How can it be, eh? Why do you patrol the clearings, sire, eh? And Torquil roams the forests with his men, eh? Guarding us, are you? And saws going missing!'

'I'll look into it,' Geralt lied easily. 'I'll look into the matter. Farewell.'

Pointer spat.

*

In the next clearing, this time Dudek's, everything was in order, no one was threatening Dudek and probably no one had stolen anything. Geralt didn't even stop. He headed towards the next settlement. Called Ash Burner.

*

Forest tracks, furrowed by wagon wheels, eased his movement between the settlements. Geralt often happened upon carts, some loaded with forestry products and others unladen, on their way to be loaded up. He also met groups of pedestrian wayfarers; there was an astonishing amount of traffic. Even deep in the forest it was seldom completely deserted. Occasionally, the large rump of a woman on all fours gathering berries or other forest fruits emerged above the ferns like the back of a narwhal from the ocean waves. Sometimes, something with a stiff gait and the posture and expression of a zombie mooned about among the trees, turning out to be an old geezer looking for mushrooms. From time to time, something snapped the brushwood with a frenzied yell – it was children, the offspring of the woodsmen and charcoal burners, armed with bows made of sticks and string. It was astonishing how much damage the children were capable of causing in the forest using such primitive weapons. It was horrifying to think that one day these youngsters would grow up and make use of professional equipment.

*

Ash Burner settlement – where it was also peaceful, with nothing disturbing the work or threatening the workers – took its name, very originally, from the production of potash, a valued agent in the glassmaking and soap-making industries. Potash, the sorcerers explained to Geralt, was obtained from the ash of the charcoal which was burned in the locality. Geralt had already visited – and planned to visit again that day – the neighbouring charcoal burners' settlement. The nearest one was called Oak Grove and the way there indeed led beside a huge stand of immense oaks several hundred years old. A murky shadow always lay beneath the oaks, even at noon, even in full sun and under a cloudless sky.

It was there by the oaks, less than a week before, that Geralt had first encountered Constable Torquil and his squad.

*

When men in green camouflage outfits with longbows on their backs galloped out of the oaks and surrounded him from all sides, Geralt first took them for Foresters, members of the notorious volunteer paramilitary unit, who called themselves the Guardians of the Forest, and whose mission was to hunt non-humans – elves and dryads in particular – and murder them in elaborate ways. It sometimes happened that people travelling through the forests were accused by the Foresters of supporting the non-humans or trading with them. They punished the former and the latter by lynching and it was difficult to prove one's innocence. The encounter by the oaks thus promised to be extremely violent – so Geralt sighed with relief when the green-coated horsemen turned out to be law enforcers carrying out their duties. Their commander, a swarthy character with a piercing gaze, having introduced himself as a constable in the service of the bailiff of Gors Velen, bluntly and brusquely demanded that Geralt reveal his identity, and when he was given it, demanded to see his witcher's emblem. The medallion with the snarling wolf was not only considered satisfactory proof, but aroused the evident admiration of the guardian of the law. The esteem, so it seemed, also extended to Geralt himself. The constable dismounted, asked the Witcher to do the same, and invited him for a short conversation.

'I am Frans Torquil.' The constable dropped the pretence of a brusque martinet, revealing himself to be a calm, businesslike man. 'You, indeed, are the Witcher Geralt of Rivia. The same Geralt of Rivia who saved a woman and child from death in Ansegis a month ago, by killing a man-eating monster.'

Geralt pursed his lips. He had happily already forgotten about Ansegis, about the monster with the plate and the man of whose death he was guilty. He had fretted over that a long time, had finally managed to convince himself that he'd done as much as he could, that he'd saved the other two, and that the monster wouldn't kill anyone else. Now it all came back.

Frans Torquil could not have noticed the clouds that passed over the Witcher's brow following his words. And if he had he wasn't bothered.

'It would appear, Witcher, that we're patrolling these thickets for the same reasons,' he continued. 'Bad things began to happen in the Tukaj Hills after the spring, very unpleasant events have occurred here. And it's time to put an end to them. After the slaughter in Arches I advised the sorcerers from Rissberg to hire a witcher. They took it to heart, I see, although they don't like doing as they're told.'

The constable took off his hat and brushed needles and seeds from it. His headgear was of identical cut to Dandelion's, only made of poorer quality felt. And instead of an egret's feather it was decorated with a pheasant's tail feather.

'I've been guarding law and order in the Hills for a long time,' he continued, looking Geralt in the eyes. 'Without wishing to boast, I've captured many a villain and bedecked many a tall tree with them. But what's been going on lately . . . That requires an additional person; somebody like you. Somebody who is well-versed in spells and knows about monsters, who isn't scared of a beast or a ghost or a dragon. And so, right well, we shall guard and protect folk together. I for my meagre salary, you for the sorcerers' purse. I wonder if they pay you well for this work?'

Five hundred Novigradian crowns, transferred in advance to my bank account. Geralt had no intention of revealing that. *The sorcerers of Rissberg bought my services and my time for that sum. Fifteen days of my time. And when fifteen days have passed, irrespective of what happens, the same amount will be transferred again. A handsome sum. More than satisfactory.*

'Aye, they're surely paying a good deal.' Frans Torquil quickly realised he wouldn't be receiving an answer. 'They can afford to. And I'll tell you this: no money here is too much. For this is a hideous matter, Witcher. Hideous, dark and unnatural. The evil that raged here came from Rissberg, I swear. As sure as anything, something's gone awry in the wizards' magic. Because that magic of theirs is like a sack of vipers: no matter how tightly it's tied up, something venomous will always crawl out.'

The constable glanced at Geralt. That glance was enough for him to understand that the Witcher would tell him nothing, no details of his agreement with the sorcerers.

'Did they acquaint you with the details? Did they tell you what happened in Yew Trees, Arches and Rogovizna?'

'More or less.'

'More or less,' Torquil repeated. 'Three days after Beltane, the Yew Trees settlement, nine woodcutters killed. Middle of May, a sawyers' homestead in Arches, twelve killed. Beginning of June, Rogovizna, a colony of charcoal burners. Fifteen victims. That's the state of affairs, more or less, for today, Witcher. For that's not the end. I give my word that it's not the end.'

Yew Trees, Arches, Rogovizna. Three mass crimes. And thus not an accident, not a demon who broke free and fled, whom a bungling goetic practitioner was unable to control. It was premeditated, it has all been planned. Someone has thrice imprisoned a demon in a host and sent it out thrice to murder.

'I've seen plenty.' The constable's jaw muscles worked powerfully. 'Plenty of battlefields, plenty of corpses. Robberies, pillages, bandits' raids, savage family revenge and forays, even one wedding that six corpses were carried out of, including the groom. But slitting tendons to then butcher the lame? Scalping? Biting out throats? Tearing apart someone alive, dragging their guts out of their bellies? And finally building pyramids from the heads of the slaughtered? What are we facing here, I ask? Didn't the wizards tell you that? Didn't they explain why they need a witcher?'

What do sorcerers from Rissberg need a witcher for? So much so that he needs to be forced by blackmail to co-operate? For the sorcerers could have coped admirably with any demon or any host themselves, without any great difficulty. Fulmen sphaericus *or* Sagitta aurea – *the first two spells of many that spring to mind – could have been used on an energumen at a distance of a hundred paces and it's doubtful if it would survive the treatment. But no, the sorcerers prefer a witcher. Why? The answer's simple: a sorcerer, confrater or comrade has become an energumen. One of their colleagues invokes demons and lets them enter him and runs around killing. He's already done it three times. But the sorcerers can't exactly shoot ball lightning at a comrade or run him through with a golden arrowhead. They need a witcher to deal with a comrade.*

There was something Geralt couldn't and didn't want to tell Torquil. He couldn't and didn't want to tell him what he'd told the sorcerers in Rissberg. And which they had shrugged off. As you would something inconsequential.

*

'You're still doing it. You're still playing at this, as you call it, goetia. You invoke these creatures, summon them from their planes, behind closed doors. With the same tired old story: we'll control them, master them, force them to be obedient, we'll set them to work. With the same inevitable justification: we'll learn their secrets, force them to reveal their mysteries and arcana, and thus we'll redouble the power of our own magic, we'll heal and cure, we'll eliminate illness and natural disasters, we'll make the world a better place and make people happier. And it inevitably turns out that it's a lie, that all you care about is power and control.'

Tzara, it was obvious, was spoiling to retaliate, but Pinety held him back.

'Regarding creatures from behind closed doors,' Geralt continued, 'creatures we are calling – for convenience – "demons", you certainly know the same as we witchers do. Which we found out

146

a long time ago, which is written about in witcher registers and chronicles. Demons will never, ever reveal any secrets or arcana to you. They will never let themselves be put to work. They let themselves be invoked and brought to our world for just one reason: they want to kill. Because they enjoy it. And you know that. But you allow them in.'

'Perhaps we'll pass from theory to practice,' said Pinety after a very long silence. 'I think something like that has also been written about in witcher registers and chronicles. And it is not moral treatises, but rather practical solutions we expect from you, Witcher.'

*

'Glad to have met you.' Frans Torquil shook Geralt's hand. 'And now to work, patrolling. To guard, to protect folk. That's what we're here for.'

'We are.'

Once in the saddle, the constable leaned over.

'I'll bet,' he said softly, 'that you're most aware of what I'm about to tell you. But I'll say it anyway. Beware, Witcher. Be heedful. You don't want to talk, but I know what I know. The wizards sure as anything hired you to fix what they spoiled themselves, to clear up the mess they made. But if something doesn't go right, they'll be looking for a scapegoat. And you have all the makings of one.'

*

The sky over the forest began to darken. A sudden wind blew up in the branches of the trees. Distant thunder rumbled.

*

'If it's not storms, it's downpours,' said Frans Torquil when they next met. 'There's thunder and rain every other day. And the result is that when you go looking for tracks they're all washed away by the rain. Convenient, isn't it? As though it's been ordered. It too

147

stinks of sorcery – Rissberg sorcery, to be precise. It's said that wizards can charm the weather. Raise up a magical wind, or enchant a natural one to blow whichever way they want. Chase away clouds, stir up rain or hail, and unleash a storm, too, as if on cue. When it suits them. In order, for example, to cover their tracks. What say you to that, Geralt?'

'Sorcerers, indeed, can do much,' he replied. 'They've always controlled the weather, from the First Landing, when apparently only Jan Bekker's spells averted disaster. But to blame mages for all adversities and disasters is probably an exaggeration. You're talking about natural phenomena, after all, Frans. It's simply that kind of season. A season of storms.'

*

He spurred on his mare. The day was already drawing to a close, and he intended to patrol a few more settlements before dusk. First, the nearest colony of charcoal burners, located in a clearing called Rogovizna. Pinety had been with him the first time he was there.

*

To the Witcher's amazement, instead of the site of the massacre being a gloomy, godforsaken wilderness, it turned out to be a place of intense work, full of people. The charcoal burners – who called themselves 'smokers' – were labouring on the building site of a new kiln used for burning charcoal. The charcoal kiln was a dome of wood, not some random heap by any means, but a meticulously and evenly arranged mound. When Geralt and Pinety arrived at the clearing they found the charcoal burners covering the mound with moss and carefully topping it with soil. Another charcoal kiln, built earlier, was already in operation, meaning it was smoking copiously. The entire clearing was enveloped in eye-stinging smoke and an acrid resinous smell attacked the nostrils.

'How long ago . . .' the Witcher coughed. 'How long ago, did you say, was—?'

148

'Exactly a month ago.'

'And people are working here as if nothing happened?'

'There's great demand for charcoal,' explained Pinety. 'Charcoal is the only fuel that can achieve a high enough temperature for smelting. The furnaces near Dorian and Gors Velen couldn't function without it, and smelting is the most important and most promising branch of industry. Because of demand, charcoal burning is a lucrative job, and economics, Witcher, is like nature and abhors a vacuum. The massacred smokers were buried over there, do you see the graves? The sand is still a fresh yellow colour. And new workers replaced them. The charcoal kiln's smoking, and life goes on.'

They dismounted. The smokers were too busy to pay them any attention. If anyone was showing them interest it was the women and children, a few of whom were running among the shacks.

'Indeed.' Pinety guessed the question before the Witcher could ask it. 'There are also children among those under the burial mound. Three. And three women. And nine men and youths. Follow me.'

They walked between cords of seasoning timber.

'Several men were killed on the spot, their heads smashed in,' the sorcerer said. 'The rest of them were incapacitated and immobilised, the heel cords of their feet severed with a sharp instrument. Many of them, including all the children, had their arms additionally broken. The captives were then murdered. Their throats were torn apart, they were eviscerated and their chests ripped open. Their backs were flayed and they were scalped. One of the women—'

'Enough.' The Witcher looked at the black patches of blood, still visible on the birch trunks. 'That's enough, Pinety.'

'You ought to know who – what – you're dealing with.'

'I already do.'

'And so just the final details. Some of the bodies were missing. All the dead were decapitated. And the heads arranged in a pyramid, right here. There were fifteen heads and thirteen bodies. Two bodies disappeared.

'The dwellers of two other settlements, Yew Trees and Arches, were murdered in almost identical fashion,' the sorcerer continued after a short pause. 'Nine people were killed in Yew Trees and twelve in Arches. I'll take you there tomorrow. We still have to drop in at New Tarworks today, it's not far. You'll see what the manufacture of pitch and wood tar looks like. The next time you have to rub wood tar onto something you'll know where it came from.'

'I have a question.'

'Yes?'

'Did you really have to resort to blackmail? Didn't you believe I'd come to Rissberg of my own free will?'

'Opinions were divided.'

'Whose idea was it to throw me into a dungeon in Kerack, then release me, but still threaten me with the court? Who came up with the idea? It was Coral, wasn't it?'

Pinety looked at him. For a long time.

'Yes,' he finally admitted. 'It was her idea. And her plan. To imprison, release and threaten you. And then finally have the case dismissed. She sorted it out immediately after you left, your file in Kerack is now as clean as a whistle. Any other questions? No? Let's ride to New Tarworks then, and have a look at the wood tar. Then I'll open the teleportal and we'll return to Rissberg. In the evening, I'd like to pop out for a spot of fly-fishing. The mayflies are swarming, the trout will be feeding . . . Have you ever angled, Witcher? Does hunting attract you?'

'I hunt when I have an urge for a fish. I always carry a line with me.'

Pinety was silent for a long time.

'A line,' he finally uttered in a strange tone. 'A line, with a lead weight. With many little hooks. On which you skewer worms?'

'Yes. Why?'

'Nothing. It was a needless question.'

*

He was heading towards Pinetops, the next charcoal burner settlement, when the forest suddenly fell silent. The jays were dumbstruck, the cries of magpies went silent all of an instant, the drumming of a woodpecker suddenly broke off. The forest had frozen in terror.

Geralt spurred his mare to a gallop.

CHAPTER ELEVEN

The charcoal kiln in Pinetops was close to a logging site, as the charcoal burners used woody debris left over after felling. The burning had begun a short time before and foul-smelling, yellowish smoke was streaming from the top of the dome, as though from a volcano's crater. The smell couldn't mask the odour of death hanging over the clearing.

Geralt dismounted. And drew his sword.

He saw the first corpse, without head or feet, just beside the charcoal kiln; blood spurting over the soil covering the mound. Not far away lay three more bodies, unrecognisably mutilated. Blood had soaked into the absorbent forest sand, leaving darkening patches.

Two more cadavers – those of a man and a woman – were lying nearer to the centre of the clearing and the campfire encircled by stones. The man's throat had been torn out so savagely his cervical vertebrae were visible. The upper part of the woman's body was lying in the embers of the fire, smeared in groats from an upturned cooking pot.

A little further away, by a woodpile, lay a child; a little boy, of perhaps five years old. He had been rent in two. Somebody – or rather something – had seized him by both legs and torn them apart.

Geralt saw another body; this one had been disembowelled and its guts pulled out. To their full length, or about two yards of the large bowel and over six of the small. The guts were stretched in a straight, shiny, greyish-pink line all the way to a shack of pine branches into which they vanished.

Inside the shelter, a slim man was lying on his back on a primitive pallet. It was clear at once that he was quite out of place there. His ornate clothing was completely covered in blood, soaked through. But the Witcher noticed it wasn't squirting, gushing or dripping from any of the main blood vessels.

Geralt recognised him despite his face being covered in drying blood. It was that long-haired, slim, somewhat effeminate fop, Sorel Degerlund, introduced to him during the audience with Ortolan. At that time, he had also been wearing the same braided cloak and embroidered doublet as the other sorcerers, had been sitting among them and like the others had been observing the Witcher with barely concealed aversion. And now he was lying, unconscious, in a charcoal burner's shack, covered in blood, with a human intestine coiled around his right wrist. Pulled from the belly of a corpse lying not ten paces away.

The Witcher swallowed. *Shall I hack him to death*, he thought, *while he's unconscious? Are Pinety and Tzara expecting that? Shall I kill the energumen? Eliminate the goetic practitioner who amuses himself by evoking demons?*

A groan shook him out of his reflections. Sorel Degerlund, it appeared, was coming around. He jerked his head up, moaned, and then slumped back onto the pallet. He lifted himself up, looking vacantly around him. He saw the Witcher and opened his mouth, looked at his blood-spattered stomach and raised a hand. To see what he was holding. And began to scream.

Geralt looked at his sword, Dandelion's purchase with the gilt cross guard. He looked at the sorcerer's thin neck. At the swollen vein on it.

Sorel Degerlund unpeeled and stripped the intestine from his hand. He stopped screaming and just groaned, shaking. He got up, first onto his hands and knees and then onto his feet. He lurched out of the shelter, looked about him, shrieked and made to bolt. The Witcher grabbed him by the collar, set him in one place and pushed him down to his knees.

'What . . . has . . .' Degerlund mumbled, still shaking. 'What . . . . what happened . . . here?'

'I think you know.'

The sorcerer swallowed loudly.

'How . . . How did I end up here? Nothing . . . I don't remember anything . . . I don't remember anything. Nothing!'

'I don't actually believe you.'

'The invocation . . .' Degerlund seized his face in his hands. 'I invoked it . . . And it appeared. In the pentagram, in the chalk

154

circle . . . And entered . . . Entered me.'

'Not for the first time, I imagine, eh?'

Degerlund sobbed. Somewhat theatrically, Geralt couldn't help thinking. He regretted that he hadn't surprised the energumen before the demon had abandoned him. His regret, he realised, wasn't very rational, he was aware how dangerous a confrontation with a demon could be, and he should have been glad he'd avoided it. But he wasn't glad. Because at least he would have known what to do.

It just had to happen to me, he thought. *And not Frans Torquil and his troop. The constable wouldn't have had any qualms or scruples. Bloodied, caught with the entrails of his victim in his fist, the sorcerer would have had a noose around his neck at once and would have been dangling from the handiest bough. Neither hesitations nor doubts would have held Torquil back. It wouldn't have bothered Torquil that the effeminate and scrawny sorcerer was absolutely incapable of slaughtering so many people in such a short time that his blood-soaked clothing hasn't managed to dry out or stiffen. And wouldn't have been able to tear a child apart with his bare hands. No, Torquil wouldn't have had any qualms.*

But I do.

Pinety and Tzara were sure I wouldn't.

'Don't kill me . . .' Degerlund whined. 'Don't kill me, Witcher . . . I will never . . . Never more—'

'Shut up.'

'I swear I'll never—'

'Shut up. Are you conscious enough to use magic? To summon the sorcerers from Rissberg here?'

'I have a sigil . . . I can . . . I can teleport myself to Rissberg.'

'Not alone. With me. And no tricks. Don't try to stand up, stay on your knees.'

'I must stand up. And you . . . If the teleportation is to work, you must stand close to me. Very close.'

'Why exactly? Come on, what are you waiting for? Get that amulet out.'

'It's not an amulet. I said, it's a sigil.'

Degerlund undid his blood-soaked doublet and shirt. He had a tattoo on his skinny chest, two overlapping circles. The circles were dotted with points of various sizes. It looked a little like the diagram of the planets' orbits that Geralt had once admired at the academy in Oxenfurt.

The sorcerer uttered a melodious spell. The circles shone blue, the points red. And began to rotate.

'Now. Stand close.'

'Close?'

'Still closer. Cling to me.'

'What?'

'Get in close and hug me.'

Degerlund's voice had changed. His eyes, a moment before tearful, now lit up hideously and his lips contorted repugnantly.

'Yes, that's right. Firmly and tenderly. As though I were your Yennefer.'

Geralt understood what was on the cards. But he didn't manage to push Degerlund away, strike him with the pommel of his sword, or slash him across the neck with the blade. He was simply too slow.

An iridescent glow flashed in Geralt's eyes. In a split second, he plunged into black nothingness. Into bitter cold, silence, amorphousness and timelessness.

*

They landed with a thud, the stone slabs of the floor seemingly leaping up to meet them. The impact threw them apart. Geralt was unable even to look around properly. An intense stench reached his nostrils, the odour of filth mixed with musk. Two sets of immense, mighty hands caught him under the arms and behind his head, fat fingers closed easily over his biceps, steely thumbs dug painfully into his nerves, into the brachial plexus. He went totally numb and his sword slipped from his inert hand.

He saw before him a hunchback with a hideous face covered in sores, his head dotted with sparse tufts of stiff hair. The hunchback, standing with his crooked legs wide apart, was pointing a large crossbow at him, or actually an arbalest with two steel bows one above the other. The two four-cornered bolts aimed at Geralt were a good two inches wide and razor-sharp.

Sorel Degerlund was standing in front of him.

'As you've probably realised,' he said, 'you haven't ended up at Rissberg. You're in my asylum and lair. A place – about which the people at Rissberg know nothing – where I conduct experiments with my master. I am, as you probably know, Sorel Albert Amador Degerlund, *magister magicus*. I am, which you don't know yet, he who will inflict pain and death on you.'

The feigned terror and simulated panic, all appearances, vanished as though blown away by the wind. Everything in the charcoal burners' clearing had been feigned. A quite different Sorel Degerlund was standing before Geralt as he hung in the paralysing grip of those gnarled hands. A triumphant Sorel Degerlund, bursting with arrogance and hubris. Sorel Degerlund grinning a vicious smile. A smile calling to mind centipedes squeezing through gaps under doors. Disturbed graves. White maggots squirming in carrion. Fat horseflies wriggling their legs in a bowl of broth.

The sorcerer came closer. He was holding a steel syringe with a long needle.

'I deceived you like a child in the clearing,' he hissed. 'You turned out to be as naive as a child. The Witcher Geralt of Rivia! Although his instinct didn't mislead him he didn't kill, because he wasn't certain. For he's a good witcher and a good man. Shall I tell you, good witcher, what good people are? They're people whom fate hasn't blessed with the chance of profiting from the benefits of being evil. Or alternatively people who were given a chance but were too stupid to take advantage of it. It doesn't matter which group you belong to. You let yourself be tricked, you fell into a trap, and I guarantee that you won't get out of it alive.'

He lifted the syringe. Geralt felt a prick and immediately acute pain. A stabbing pain that darkened his eyes, tensed his entire body, a pain so dreadful that only the greatest effort stopped him from screaming. His heart began to beat frantically and, compared to his usual pulse – four times slower than that of a normal person – it was an extremely unpleasant sensation. Everything went black, the world spun around, blurred and dissolved.

He was dragged away in the glow of magical balls dancing over the bare walls and ceilings. One of the walls he passed was covered in patches of blood and was hung with weapons. He saw broad, curved scimitars, huge sickles, gisarmes, battleaxes and morning stars. They were all streaked with blood. *They were used in Yew Trees, Arches and Rogovizna*, he thought lucidly. They were used to massacre the charcoal burners in Pinetops.

He had gone quite numb, had stopped feeling anything, he couldn't even feel the crushing grip of the hands holding him.

'Buueh-hhhrrr-eeeehhh-bueeeeh! Bueeh-heeh!'

He didn't realise at once that what he could hear was merry chuckling. Whoever was dragging him was clearly enjoying the situation.

The hunchback walking in front with the crossbow was whistling.

Geralt had almost lost consciousness.

He was shoved down roughly into an upright chair. He could finally see who was dragging him, crushing his armpits with their huge hands.

He remembered the giant ogre-dwarf Mikita, Pyral Pratt's bodyguard. These two resembled him a little, they could just about have passed for close relatives. They were of similar height to Mikita, reeked similarly, like him had no neck, and like him their teeth protruded from their lower lips like wild boars' tusks. Mikita was bald and bearded, however, while these two didn't have beards. Their simian faces were covered in bristles and the tops of their egg-shaped heads were adorned with something like tousled oakum. Their eyes were small and bloodshot, their ears large, pointed and horribly hairy.

Their garb bore streaks of blood. And their breath stank as though they'd eaten nothing but garlic, shit and dead fish for many days.

'Bueeeeh! Bueeh-heeh-heeh!'

'Bue, Bang, enough laughter, get to work, both of you. Get out, Pastor. But stay close.'

The two giants went out, their great feet slapping. The hunchback addressed as 'Pastor' hurried after them.

Sorel Degerlund appeared in the Witcher's field of view. Scrubbed, hair combed, in fresh clothes and looking effeminate. He slid a chair closer, sat down, with a table piled with weighty tomes and grimoires behind him. He looked at the Witcher, grinning malevolently. At the same time he was playing with and swinging a medallion on a gold chain, which he was winding around a finger.

'I treated you to extract of white scorpion's venom,' he said detachedly. 'Nasty, isn't it? Can't move a hand, a leg; not even a finger? Can't wink or even swallow? But that's nothing. Uncontrollable movements of your eyeballs and disturbances to your sight will soon follow. Then you'll feel cramps, really powerful cramps, they'll probably strain your intercostal muscles. You won't be able to control the grinding of your teeth, you're certain to break a few. Then excessive salivation will occur and finally breathing difficulties. If I don't give you the antidote, you'll suffocate. But don't worry, I shall. You'll live, for now. But I think you'll soon regret that you've survived. I'll explain what it's all about. We have time. But first I'd like to watch you turning blue.

'I was observing you on the last day of June, during the audience,' he continued a moment later. 'You flaunted your arrogance before us. Before *us*, people a hundredfold your betters, people you're no match for. Playing with fire amused and excited you, I saw that. It was then that I determined to prove to you that playing with fire will get you burnt, and interfering in matters of magic and mages has equally painful consequences. You'll soon find out for yourself.'

Geralt tried to move, but couldn't. His limbs and entire body were paralysed and insensitive. He felt an unpleasant tingling in his fingers and toes, his face was completely numb and his lips felt like they were laced together. His vision was deteriorating, his eyes were misting over and a cloudy mucus was gluing them together.

Degerlund crossed his legs and swung the medallion. There was a symbol on it, an emblem, in blue enamel. Geralt didn't recognise it. His eyesight was getting worse. The sorcerer hadn't lied, the disturbance to his sight was intensifying.

'The thing is, you see, that I plan to go far in the sorcerers' hierarchy,' Degerlund continued casually. 'In my designs and plans I'm relying on Ortolan, who's known to you from your visit to Rissberg and the memorable audience.'

Geralt had the sensation that his tongue was swelling and filling his entire mouth. He was afraid it wasn't just a sensation. The venom of the white scorpion was lethal. He'd never previously been exposed to its action and didn't know how it might affect his witcher's body. He was seriously worried, desperately fighting the toxin that was destroying him. The situation didn't look good. It appeared he couldn't expect help from anywhere.

'A few years ago,' said Sorel Degerlund, still delighting in the sound of his own voice, 'I became Ortolan's assistant. The Chapter assigned me to the post, and the Rissberg research team approved it. I was, like my predecessors, to spy on Ortolan and sabotage his more dangerous ideas. I didn't owe my assignment merely to my magical talent, but also to my looks and personal charm. For the Chapter would supply the old man with the kind of assistants he was fond of.

'You may not know, but during the times of Ortolan's youth, misogyny and the fashion for male friendship, which very often turned into something more – or even something *much* more – were rife among sorcerers. Thus it happened that a young pupil or novice didn't have a choice, had to be obedient to his seniors in this regard, as with all others. Some of them didn't like it very much, but had to take it as it came. And some acquired a liking for it. As you've probably guessed, Ortolan belonged to the latter. The boy, whose avian nickname fitted him then, became, after the experiences with his preceptor, a lifelong enthusiast and champion of noble male friendship and love – as poets would have it. It would be defined in prose more bluntly and crudely, as you know.'

A large black cat, with its tail fluffed up like a brush and purring loudly, rubbed itself against the sorcerer's calf. Degerlund leaned over, stroked it and swung the medallion in front of it. The cat swatted the medallion casually with its paw. It turned away, signalling that the game was boring it, and set about licking the fur on its chest.

'As you've doubtless observed,' continued the sorcerer, 'I have exceptional looks and women have been known to call me an ephebe. I'm fond of women, indeed, but in principle I didn't and don't have anything against homosexuality. Under one condition: if it is to be, it must help me to advance my career.

'My physical intimacy with Ortolan didn't demand excessive

160

sacrifices, the old man had long passed both the age limit for capability and desire. But I did my best for people to think otherwise and believe he'd utterly fallen for me. Believe there was nothing he would refuse his gorgeous lover. Believe that I knew his codes, that I had access to his secret books and notes. That he was giving me artefacts and talismans he hadn't previously revealed to anyone. And that he was teaching me forbidden spells. Including goetia. And if previously the great men and women of Rissberg had disdained me, now they suddenly began to esteem me. I had grown in their eyes. They believed I was doing what they themselves dreamed of. And that I was achieving success.

'Do you know what transhumanism is? What kind of specialisation it is? Radiation speciation? Introgression? No? There's nothing to be ashamed of. I don't really either. But everybody thinks I know a great deal. That under the tutelage and auspices of Ortolan I'm conducting research into perfecting the human race. With the lofty goal of refining and improving it. To improve the human condition, to eliminate illness and disability, to banish the ageing process, blah, blah, blah. For that is the goal and task of magic. To follow the path of the great masters: Malaspina, Alzur and Idarran. The masters of hybridisation, mutation and genetic modification.'

Announcing its arrival by meowing, the black cat appeared again. It jumped into the sorcerer's lap, stretched and purred. Degerlund stroked it rhythmically. The cat purred even louder, extending claws of truly tiger-like proportions.

'You surely know what hybridisation is, for it's another word for cross-breeding. The process of obtaining cross-breeds, hybrids, bastards – it's all the same. They actively experiment with that at Rissberg, they've produced endless peculiarities, monsters and sports. Some find wide practical applications, like, for example, para-zeugles cleaning municipal dust heaps, para-woodpeckers keeping down tree parasites and mutated gambezis feeding on the larvae of malarial mosquitos. Or vigilosaurs, guard lizards the killing of which you bragged about during the audience. But they consider them trifles, by-products. What really interests them is the hybridisation and mutation of people and humanoids. That is forbidden, but Rissberg disregards prohibitions. And the Chapter turns a blind eye to it. Or, which is more likely, it remains immersed in blissful, dull ignorance.

'Malaspina, Alzur and Idarran, it has been proved, took small, ordinary creatures to their workshops to create giants from them, like those centipedes, spiders, koshcheys and the devils know what else. What then, they asked, stands in the way of taking an ordinary little man and transforming him into a titan, into somebody stronger, able to work twenty hours a day, who's unaffected by illness, who can live fully fit to a hundred? It's known that they wanted to do it. Apparently, they managed to, apparently they were successful. But they took the secret of their hybrids to the grave. Even Ortolan, who has devoted his life to studying their works, has achieved little. Bue and Bang, who dragged you here, have you observed them? They're hybrids, magical crosses of ogres and trolls. The marksman Pastor? No, in fact he is, so to speak, in the likeness and image, the completely natural result of a cross between a hideous woman and an ugly man. But Bue and Bang, ha, they came straight out of Ortolan's test tubes. You may ask: why the hell would anyone want such hideous creatures, what the hell would you create something like that for? Ha, I didn't know that myself until quite recently. Until I saw how they ripped the woodcutters and charcoal burners apart. Bue is capable of wresting someone's head from their shoulders with one tug, and Bang can tear a child apart like a roast chicken. And if you give them some sharp tools, ha! Then they can achieve a rip-roaring bloodbath. When you ask Ortolan he says that hybridisation is meant to be a way of eliminating hereditary illnesses, and witters on about increasing immunity to infectious diseases, or some such old fogey's nonsense. I know better! And you do too. Specimens like Bue and Bang, and the thing you tore Idarran's plate off, are only fit for one thing: killing. And that's good, because what I needed were killing tools. I wasn't certain about my own skills and capabilities in that regard. Unjustly, as a matter of fact, as it later transpired.

'But the sorcerers of Rissberg go on cross-breeding, mutating and genetically modifying, from dawn to dusk. And they've had numerous successes, they've produced so many hybrids it takes your breath away. They think all of them are useful, meant to make people's lives easier and more pleasant. Indeed, they're one step away from creating a woman with a perfectly flat back, so you can fuck her from behind and have somewhere to put a glass of champagne and play solitaire at the same time.

'But let's return *ad rem*, that is to my scientific career. Not having any tangible successes to boast of, I had to create semblances of those successes. It was easy.

'Do you know that other worlds, different from ours, exist, which the Conjunction of the Spheres cut off access to? Universes, called elemental and para-elemental planes. Inhabited by creatures called demons? The accomplishments of Alzur *et consortes* were excused by saying they had gained access to those planes and creatures. That they'd managed to invoke and tame such creatures, that they'd wrested from them and gained possession of their secrets and knowledge. I think that's all nonsense and fabrication, but everybody believes it. And what can one do when faith is so strong? In order for people to believe I was close to discovering the secrets of the old masters, I had to convince Rissberg that I know how to invoke demons. Ortolan, who'd once successfully carried out goetia, didn't want to teach me that art. He had an insultingly low opinion of my magical abilities and made me remember where my place was. Why, for the good of my career I'll remember that. They'll see!'

The black cat, weary of being stroked, hopped off the sorcerer's lap. He swept a cold glance of his golden, wide-open eyes over the Witcher. And walked away, tail held aloft.

Geralt was having more and more difficulty breathing and felt shivers shooting through his body which he couldn't control at all. The situation looked grave and only two circumstances augured well, giving him reason to hope. Firstly, he was still alive, *and where there's life there's hope*, as his preceptor in Kaer Morhen, Vesemir, used to say.

The second circumstance that augured well was Degerlund's swollen ego and conceitedness. It seemed the sorcerer had fallen in love with his own words as a young man and they were clearly the love of his life.

'Unable, thus, to become a goetic practitioner,' the sorcerer went on, twisting the medallion and endlessly delighting in his own voice, 'I had to pretend to be one. Pretend. It's known that a demon invoked by a goetic practitioner often breaks free and wreaks destruction. So, I did just that. Several times. I slaughtered several settlements. And they believed it was a demon.

'You'd be astonished how gullible they are. I once decapitated a peasant I had caught and sewed the head of a large goat onto his neck using biodegradable catgut, disguising the stitches with plaster and paint. After that I displayed it to my learned colleagues as a baphomet, the result of an extremely difficult experiment in the field of creating humans with animal heads. Only a partly successful one, because the end result didn't survive. They believed me, just imagine. I rose even higher in their esteem. They're still waiting for me to create something that will survive. I confirm their belief in this by constantly sewing some head or other onto a decapitated corpse.

'But that was a digression. Where was I? Aha, the massacred settlements. As I expected, the masters of Rissberg took them as acts of demons or energumens possessed by them. But I made a mistake, I went too far. No one would have bothered with one settlement of woodcutters, but we slaughtered several. Bue and Bang did most of the work, but I also contributed as much as I could.

'In the first colony, Yew Trees, or some such, I didn't exactly distinguish myself. When I saw what Bue and Bang were doing I vomited, puking all over my cloak. It was only fit to be thrown away. A cloak of the best wool, trimmed with silver mink, it cost almost a hundred crowns. But then I did better and better. Firstly, I attired myself suitably, like a labourer. Secondly, I grew fond of those expeditions. It turned out there can be great pleasure in chopping off somebody's legs and watching the blood spurting from the stump. Or gouging out somebody's eye. Or tugging a handful of steaming guts from a mutilated belly . . . I shall be brief. Along with today's haul it comes to almost two score and ten persons of both sexes of various ages.

'Rissberg decided that I must be stopped. But how? They still believed in my power as a goetic practitioner and feared my demons. And feared infuriating Ortolan, who was enamoured of me. You were meant to be the solution. The Witcher.'

Geralt was breathing shallowly. And growing in optimism. His eyesight was much better and the shivers were abating. He was immune to most known toxins, and the venom of the white scorpion – fatal to an ordinary mortal – was no exception, as it was fortunately turning out. The symptoms – which were dangerous at first – were weakening and fading with time, and it was turning out that the Witcher's body was capable of neutralising the poison quite quickly. Degerlund didn't know that, or in his conceitedness was underestimating it.

'I found out they planned to send you to get me. I got slightly cold feet, I don't deny it, since I'd heard this and that about witchers, and about you in particular. I ran to Ortolan as quickly as I could, crying *save me, my beloved master*. My beloved master first told me off and muttered something about killing woodcutters being very naughty, that it wasn't nice and that it was to be the last time. But then he advised me how to trick you and lure you into a trap. How to capture you, using a teleportational sigil that I had tattooed on my manly chest a few years ago. He forbade me, however, from killing you. Don't think that it's out of kindness. He needs your eyes. To be precise: the *tapetum lucidum*, the layer of tissue lining the inside of your eyeballs, a tissue that reflects and intensifies the light directed at the photoreceptor cells, thanks to which you can see at night and in the dark like a cat. Ortolan's newest *idée fixe* is to equip the whole of humanity with the ability to see like cats. As part of the preparations for such a lofty goal he intends to graft your *tapetum lucidum* onto some other mutation he's creating and the tissue for the implant must be taken from a live donor.'

Geralt cautiously moved his fingers and hand.

'Ortolan, an ethical and merciful mage, intends – in his boundless goodness – to spare your life after removing your eyeballs. He thinks that it's better to be blind than deceased, furthermore he hesitates at the thought of causing pain to your lover, Yennefer of Vengerberg, for whom he feels a great and – in his case, strange – affection. On top of that, he, Ortolan, is now close to completing a magical regenerational formula. In several years you'll be able to report to him and he'll restore your eyesight. Are you pleased? No? And rightly. What? Do you want to say something? Please speak.'

Geralt pretended to be having difficulty moving his lips. Actually, he didn't have to pretend at all. Degerlund raised himself from his chair and leaned over him.

'I can't understand anything.' He grimaced. 'In any case, what you have to say doesn't interest me much. Whereas I, indeed, still have something to announce to you. So, know that clairvoyance is among my numerous talents. I can see quite clearly that when Ortolan restores your freedom to you as a blind man, Bue and Bang will be waiting for you. And you will land up in my laboratory, definitively this time. I shall vivisect you. Mainly for pleasure, although I'm also a little curious as to what's inside you. When I finish, however, I shall – to use the terminology of the abattoir – portion you up. I shall send your remains piece by piece to Rissberg, as a warning of what befalls my foes. Let them see.'

Geralt gathered all his strength. There wasn't much of it.

'But where Yennefer is concerned—' the sorcerer leaned over even closer, the Witcher could smell his minty breath '—unlike Ortolan, the thought of causing her suffering pleases me inordinately. Thus, I shall cut off the part she valued most in you; I shall send it to her in Vengerb—'

Geralt placed his fingers in a Sign and touched the sorcerer's face. Sorel Degerlund choked and drooped on the chair. He snorted. His eyes had sunk deep into his skull, his head lolled on his shoulder. The medallion chain slipped from his limp fingers.

Geralt leaped to his feet – or rather tried to. The only thing he managed to do was to fall from the chair onto the floor, his head right in front of Degerlund's shoe. The sorcerer's medallion was in front of his nose. With a blue enamel dolphin *naiant* on a golden oval. The emblem of Kerack. He didn't have time either to be surprised or to think about it. Degerlund began to wheeze loudly, it was apparent he was about to awaken. The Somne Sign had been effective, but faint and fleeting – the Witcher was too weakened by the effect of the venom.

He stood up, holding on to the table, knocking the books and scrolls from it.

Pastor burst into the room. Geralt didn't even try to use a Sign. He grabbed a leather and brass-bound grimoire from the table and struck the hunchback in the throat with it. Pastor sat down heavily

166

on the floor, dropping the arbalest. The Witcher hit him one more time. And would have repeated it, but the incunable slipped from his numb fingers. He seized a carafe standing on the books and shattered it on Pastor's forehead. The hunchback, although covered in blood and red wine, didn't yield. He rushed at Geralt, not even brushing the slivers of crystal from his eyelids.

'Bueee!' he yelled, grabbing the Witcher by the knees. 'Baaang! Get to me! Get to—'

Geralt seized another grimoire from the table. It was heavy, with a binding encrusted with fragments of a human skull. He slammed the hunchback with it, sending bone splinters flying in all directions.

Degerlund spluttered, fighting to raise a hand. Geralt realised he was trying to cast a spell. The growing thud of heavy feet indicated that Bue and Bang were approaching. Pastor scrambled up from the floor, fumbling around, searching for the crossbow.

Geralt saw his sword on the table and seized it. He staggered, almost falling over. He grasped Degerlund by the collar and pressed the blade against his throat.

'Your sigil!' he screamed into his ear. 'Teleport us out of here!'

Bue and Bang, armed with scimitars, collided with each other in the doorway and got caught there, jammed solid. Neither of them thought of letting the other one through. The door frame creaked.

'Teleport us!' Geralt grabbed Degerlund by the hair, bending his head backwards. 'Now! Or I'll slit your throat.'

Bue and Bang tumbled out of the doorway, taking the frame with them. Pastor found the crossbow and raised it.

Degerlund opened his shirt with a trembling hand and shrieked out a spell, but before the darkness engulfed them he broke free of the Witcher and pushed him away. Geralt caught him by a lace cuff and tried to pull the sorcerer towards him, but at that moment the portal was activated and all his senses, including touch, vanished. He felt an elemental force sucking him in, jerking him and spinning him as though in a whirlpool. The cold was numbing. For a split second. One of the longer and more ghastly split seconds of his life.

He thudded against the ground. On his back.

He opened his eyes. Black gloom, impenetrable darkness, was

167

all around him. *I've gone blind*, he thought. *Have I lost my sight?*

He hadn't. It was simply a very dark night. His *tapetum lucidum* – as Degerlund had eruditely named it – had started working, picking up all the light there was in those conditions. A moment later he recognised around him the outlines of some tree trunks, bushes or undergrowth.

And above his head, when the clouds parted, he saw stars.

INTERLUDE

The following day

You had to hand it to them: the builders of Findetann knew their trade and hadn't been idle. In spite of having seen them in action several times, Shevlov watched in fascination as they assembled the piledriver again. The three connected timbers formed a tripod at the top of which a pulley was hung. A rope was tossed over the pulley and a heavy metal-edged block – called a ram in the builders' jargon – was fastened to it. Shouting rhythmically, the builders tugged on the line, lifting the ram right to the top of the tripod, then quickly released it. The ram fell heavily onto a post positioned in the hole, forcing it deep into the ground. It took three, at most four, blows of the ram for the pile to be standing securely. The builders swiftly dismantled the tripod and loaded the parts onto a wagon, during which time one of them climbed up a ladder and nailed an enamel plaque with the Redanian coat of arms – a silver eagle on a red field – to the post.

Thanks to Shevlov and his free company – and also to the piledrivers and their operation – the province of Riverside, part of the Kingdom of Redania, had increased in area that day. Quite significantly.

The foreman walked over, wiping his forehead with his cap. He was in a sweat, although he hadn't done anything, unless you count effing and blinding. Shevlov knew what the foreman would ask, because he did so each time.

'Where's the next one going? Commander?'

'I'll show you.' Shevlov reined his horse around. 'Follow me.'

The carters lashed the oxen and the builders' vehicles moved sluggishly along the ridge, along ground somewhat softened by the recent storm. They soon found themselves by the next post, which was decorated with a black plaque painted with lilies. The post was lying on the ground, having been previously rolled into the bushes; Shevlov's crew had made sure of that.

Here's how progress triumphs, thought Shevlov. *Here's how technical thought triumphs.* The hand-sunk Temerian posts could be torn out and tossed down in a trice. The Redanian post driven in by a piledriver couldn't be pulled out of the ground so easily.

He waved a hand, indicating the direction to the builders. A few furlongs south. Beyond the village.

The residents of the village – insofar as a handful of shacks and huts could be called a village – had already been driven onto the green by Shevlov's riders, and were scurrying around, raising dust, being pushed back by the horses. The always hot-headed Escayrac wasn't sparing them the bullwhip. Others spurred their horses around the homesteads. Dogs barked, women wailed and children bawled.

Three riders trotted over to Shevlov. Yan Malkin, as skinny as a rake and nicknamed Poker. Prospero Basti, better known as Sperry. And Aileach Mor-Dhu, nicknamed Fryga, on a grey mare.

'They're gathered together, as you ordered,' said Fryga, pushing back a lynx-fur calpac. 'The entire hamlet.'

'Silence them.'

The crowd were quietened, not without the help of knouts and staves. Shevlov went closer.

'What do you call this dump?'

'Woodend.'

'Woodend, again? These peasants don't have a scrap of imagination. Lead the builders on, Sperry. Show them where they're to drive in the post, because they'll get the place wrong again.'

Sperry whistled, reining his horse around. Shevlov rode over to the huddled villagers. Fryga and Poker flanked him.

'Dwellers of Woodend!' Shevlov stood up in the stirrups. 'Heed what I say! By the will and order of His Majesty by grace here reigning King Vizimir, I inform you that this day the land up to the border posts belongs to the Kingdom of Redania, and His Majesty King Vizimir is your lord and monarch! You owe him honour, obedience and levies. And you're behind with your rent and taxes!

By order of the king you are to settle your debts immediately. Into this here bailiff's coffer.'

'How so?' yelled a man in the crowd. 'What do you mean pay? We'm paid!'

'You've already fleeced us for levies!'

'Temerian bailiffs fleeced you. And illegally, for this is not Temeria, but Redania. Look where the posts are.'

'But yesterday it was still Temeria!' howled one of the settlers, 'How can it be? We paid as they ordered . . .'

'You have no right!'

'Who?' roared Shevlov. 'Who said that? It is my right! I have a royal decree! We are royal troops! I said whoever wants to stay on their farm must pay the levies to the last penny! Any who resist will be banished! You paid Temeria? So you clearly think yourselves Temerians! Then scram, get over the border! But only with what you can carry, because your farms and livestock belong to Redania!'

'Robbery! That's robbery and plunder!' yelled a large peasant with a shock of hair, stepping forward. 'And you aren't the king's man but a brigand! You have no r—'

Escayrac rode over and lashed the loudmouth with a bullwhip. The loudmouth fell. Others were quelled with pikestaffs. Shevlov's company knew how to cope with peasants. They had been moving the border for a week and had pacified plenty of settlements.

'Someone's approaching at speed.' Fryga indicated with her scourge. 'Will it be Fysh?'

'And none other.' Shevlov shielded his eyes. 'Have that freak taken from the wagon and hand her over. And you take a few of the boys and ride around the place. Various odd settlers remain dotted throughout the clearings and logging sites, you need to inform them as well to whom they're now paying rent. Should anyone offer resistance, you know what to do.'

Fryga smiled evilly, flashing her teeth. Shevlov sympathised with the settlers she'd be visiting. Although their fate didn't bother him much.

He glanced up at the sun. *We must hurry*, he thought. *It'd be worth knocking down a few Temerian posts before noon. And driving in a few of ours.*

'You, Poker, follow me. Let's ride out to meet our guests.'

There were two guests. One was wearing a straw hat, had prominent jawbones and a jutting out chin, and his whole face was blue with several days' beard. The second was powerfully built, a veritable giant.

'Fysh.'

'Sergeant.'

That annoyed Shevlov. Javil Fysh – not without reason – had brought up their old friendship, the times when they had served together in the regular army. Shevlov didn't like to be reminded of those days. He didn't want to be reminded about Fysh, about serving, or about his non-commissioned officer's pay.

'Free company.' Fysh nodded towards the village, from where yells and crying reached them. 'Busy, I see. Punitive expedition, is it? Will you be doing some burning?'

'That's my business.'

I won't be, he thought. With regret, because he liked burning down villages, and the company did too. But he had no orders to do so. The orders were to redraw the border and collect levies from the settlers. Drive away insubordinate individuals, but not touch goods or property. For they would serve the new settlers who would be brought there. From the North, where it was crowded even on barren land.

'I caught the freak and am holding her,' he declared. 'As ordered. Tied up. It wasn't easy. Had I known I would have asked for more. But we agreed on five hundred, so I'm due five hundred.'

Fysh nodded and the giant rode up and gave Shevlov two plump purses. He had a viper curled around a dagger blade tattooed on his forearm. Shevlov knew that tattoo.

A horseman from the company appeared with the captive. The freak had a sack over her head reaching her knees, with a cord restraining her arms. Bare legs, as thin as rakes, protruded from the sack.

'What's this?' Fysh pointed at the captive. 'My dear sergeant? Five hundred Novigradian crowns? Bit steep for a pig in a poke.'

'The sack comes free,' replied Shevlov coldly. 'Like this good advice. Don't untie her and don't look inside.'

'Why?'

'It's risky. She bites. And might cast a spell.'

The giant slung the captive across his saddle. The freak, until then calm, struggled, kicked and howled in the sack. It was very little use, as the sack was holding her fast.

'How do I know it is what I'm paying for?' asked Fysh, 'and not some chance maid? Like from this here village?'

'Are you accusing me of lying?'

'Not in the least,' Fysh appeased him, helped by the sight of Poker stroking the shaft of a battleaxe hanging from his saddle. 'I believe you, Shevlov. I know I can count on you. I mean we're mates, aren't we? From the good old days—'

'I'm in a hurry, Fysh. Duty calls.'

'Farewell, sergeant.'

'I wonder,' said Poker, watching them riding away. 'I wonder what they want of her. That freak. You didn't ask.'

'I didn't,' Shevlov confessed coldly. 'Because you don't ask about things like that.'

He pitied the freak a little. But he wasn't too bothered about her fate. He guessed it would be miserable.

CHAPTER TWELVE

A signpost stood at the crossroads, a post with planks nailed to it, indicating the four points of the compass.

*

Dawn found him where he had landed, tossed out of the portal, on the dew-soaked grass, in a thicket beside a swamp or small lake, teeming with birds, whose gaggling and quacking roused him from his sound and exhausting sleep. He had drunk a witcher's elixir during the night. He always made sure to keep some on him, in a silver tube in a hiding place sewn into his belt. The elixir, called Golden Oriole, was used as a panacea which was particularly effect-ive against every kind of poisoning, infections and the action of all kinds of venoms and toxins. Golden Oriole had saved Geralt more often than he could remember, but drinking the elixir had never caused the effects it had that night. For an hour after drinking it he had fought cramps and extremely powerful vomiting reflexes, aware that he couldn't let himself be sick. As a result, although he had won the battle, he fell wearily into a deep sleep. Which may also have been a consequence of the combination of the scorpion's venom, the elixir and the teleportational journey.

As far as the journey was concerned, he wasn't certain what had happened, how and why the portal opened by Degerlund had spat him out here, onto the boggy wilderness. He doubted whether the sorcerer had done that deliberately; more likely it was simply a teleportational failure, something he had been afraid of for a week. Something he had heard about many times and had witnessed several times, when a portal, instead of sending the traveller where they were meant to go, threw them out somewhere else, in a totally unexpected place.

When he came to his senses, he was holding his sword in his

right hand and in his clenched left hand he had a shred of material, which he identified in the morning light as a shirt sleeve. The material was cut through cleanly as though by a knife. It didn't bear the marks of blood, however, so the teleportal hadn't cut off the sorcerer's hand, but only his shirt, Geralt realised with regret.

The worst portal failure Geralt had witnessed – which had forever discouraged him from teleportation – had occurred at the beginning of his witcher career. At that time, a fashion for being transported from place to place had prevailed among the *nouveaux riches*, wealthy lordlings and gilded youth, and some sorcerers offered such entertainment for astronomical sums. One day – the Witcher happened to have been there – a teleportation enthusiast had appeared in a portal bisected precisely down the middle. He looked like an open double bass case. Then everything flopped out of him and poured down. Fascination with teleportals decreased perceptibly after that accident.

Compared to something like that, he thought, *landing on a marsh was quite simply a luxury.*

He still hadn't fully regained his strength, was still experiencing dizziness and nausea. But there was no time to rest. He knew that portals left tracks and sorcerers had ways of tracking the path of the teleportal. Although if, as he suspected, there was a flaw in the portal, tracking his flight would be virtually impossible. But in any case, remaining for too long in the proximity of the landing place wouldn't be prudent.

He set off at a brisk pace to get warm and loosen up. *It began with the swords,* he thought, splashing through a puddle. *How had Dandelion expressed it? It's a streak of bad luck and unlucky incidents. First, I lost the swords. It's barely three weeks later, and now I've lost my mount. Roach, who I left in Pinetops, is sure to be eaten by wolves, presuming somebody doesn't find and steal her. The swords, the horse. What next? I dread to think.*

After an hour of traipsing through the marsh, he emerged onto drier ground, and after another hour happened upon a tramped down highway. And reached the crossroads after half an hour's march along it.

A signpost stood at the crossroads, a post with planks nailed to it, indicating the four points of the compass. They had all been shat on by birds of passage and copiously dotted by crossbow bolt holes. It appeared that every traveller felt duty bound to shoot at the signpost. In order, then, to decipher the words, one had to approach quite close.

The Witcher went over. And decoded the directions. The plank pointing westwards – according to the position of the sun – bore the name of Chippira, and the opposite one pointed to Tegmond. The third plank indicated the way to Findetann, while the fourth God knew where, because someone had covered the lettering in pitch. In spite of that, Geralt already more or less knew where he was.

The teleport had tossed him out on the marsh created by two branches of the River Pontar. The southern branch, owing to its size, had even been given its own name by cartographers – and thus appeared on many maps as the Embla. The land lying between the branches – or rather the scrap of land – was called Emblonia. At least it had been once. And quite a long time ago had stopped being called anything. The Kingdom of Emblonia had ceased to exist around half a century before. And there were reasons for that.

In most kingdoms, duchies and other forms of government and social communities in the lands Geralt knew, things were in order and in fairly good shape – it would be reasonable to state. Admittedly, the system faltered occasionally, but it functioned. In the vast majority of the social communities the ruling class ruled, rather than just stealing and organising by turns gambling and prostitution. Only a small percentage of the social elite consisted of people who thought that 'Hygiene' was a prostitute and 'gonorrhoea' a member of the lark family. Only a small number of the labouring and farming folk were morons who lived solely for today and today's vodka, incapable of comprehending with their vestigial intellects something as incomprehensible as tomorrow and tomorrow's vodka. Most of the priests didn't corrupt minors or swindle money out of the people, but dwelt in temples, devoting themselves wholly to attempts at fathoming the insoluble mysteries of their faith. Psychopaths, freaks, oddballs, and dullards kept away from politics and important positions in the government and administration, busying themselves instead with the ruination of their own personal lives. Village idiots hunkered down behind barns and didn't try to act as tribunes of the people. Thus it was in most states.

But the Kingdom of Emblonia wasn't part of the majority. It was a minority in all the above-mentioned respects. And in many others.

Hence, it fell into decline. And finally disappeared. So its powerful neighbours, Temeria and Redania, fought over it. Emblonia, though a politically inept creation, possessed certain wealth. For it lay in the alluvial valley of the River Pontar, which for centuries had deposited silt there, carried by floods. Fen soil – an extremely fertile and agriculturally high-yield variety – was formed from the silt. Under the rule of Emblonia's kings, the fen soil began to turn into a swampy wasteland, on which little could be grown – much less harvested. Meanwhile, Temeria and Redania were recording considerable increases in population, and agricultural production had become a matter of vital importance. Emblonia's fen soil tempted. So, the two kingdoms, divided by the River Pontar, carved up Emblonia between themselves without further ado and struck its name from the map. The part annexed by Temeria was called Pontaria and what fell to Redania became Riverside. Hordes of settlers were brought in to work the soil. Under the gaze of able stewards and owing to judicious agriculture and drainage, the region, though small, soon became a veritable agrarian Horn of Plenty.

Disputes also quickly sprang up, becoming more heated the more abundant became the harvests yielded by the Pontarian fen soil. The treaty demarcating the border between Temeria and Redania contained clauses permitting all sorts of interpretations, and the maps appended to the treaty were useless because the cartographers botched their work. The river itself also played a part – after periods of heavy rain it would alter and move its course by two or even three miles. And so the Horn of Plenty turned into a bone of contention. The plans for dynastic marriages and alliances came to naught, and diplomatic notes, tariff wars and trade embargos began. The border conflicts grew stronger and blood-shed seemed inevitable. Then finally occurred. And continued to occur regularly.

In his wanderings in search of work, Geralt usually avoided places beset by armed clashes, because it was difficult to find a job. Having experienced regular armies, mercenaries and marauders once or twice, the farmers became convinced that werewolves, strigas, trolls under bridges and barrow wights were actually trifling problems and minor threats and that by and large hiring a witcher was a waste of money. And that there were more urgent matters like, say, rebuilding a cottage burned down by the army and buying new hens to replace the ones the soldiers had stolen and devoured. For these reasons, Geralt was unfamiliar with the lands of Emblonia – or Pontaria and Riverside, according to more recent maps. He didn't especially have any idea which of the places named on the signpost were closer and where he ought to head from the crossroads in order to bid farewell to the wilderness as quickly as possible and greet any kind of civilisation again.

Geralt decided on Findetann, which meant heading north. For more or less in that direction lay Novigrad, where he had to get to if he was to recover his swords, and by the fifteenth of July at that.

After around an hour of brisk marching he walked right into what he had so wanted to avoid.

*

There was a thatched peasant homestead and several shacks close to the logging site. The fact that something was occurring there was being announced by the loud barking of a dog and the furious clucking of poultry. The screaming of a child and the crying of a woman. And swearing.

He approached, cursing under his breath both his ill luck and his scruples.

Feathers were flying and an armed man was tying a fowl to his saddle. Another was thrashing a peasant cringing on the ground with a scourge. Another was struggling with a woman in torn clothing and the child hanging on to her.

He walked up and without thinking twice or speaking, seized the raised hand holding the scourge and twisted. The armed man howled. Geralt shoved him against the wall of a hen house. He hauled the other one away from the woman by the collar and pushed him up against the fence.

'Begone,' he stated curtly. 'This minute.'

He quickly drew his sword as a sign for them to treat him in accordance with the gravity of the situation. And remind them emphatically of the possible consequences of wrong-headed behaviour.

One of the armed men laughed loudly. The other joined in, taking hold of his sword hilt.

'Who are you assaulting, vagabond? Do you seek death?'

'Begone, I said.'

The armed soldier tying on the fowl turned around from the horse. And was revealed to be a woman. A pretty one, in spite of her unpleasantly narrowed eyes.

'Had enough of life?' It turned out the woman was able to contort her lips even more grotesquely. 'Or perhaps you're retarded? Perhaps you can't count? I'll help you. There's only one of you, there are three of us. Meaning you're outnumbered. Meaning you ought to turn around and sod off as fast as your legs can carry you. While you still have any.'

'Begone. I won't say it again.'

'Aha. Three people are a piece of cake to you. And a dozen?'

The sound of hooves thudding. The Witcher looked around. Nine armed riders. Pikes and bear spears were pointed at him.

'You! Good-for-nothing! Drop your sword!'

He ignored the instruction and dodged towards the hen house to have some protection at his back.

'What's going on, Fryga?'

'This settler is resisting,' snorted the woman addressed as Fryga. 'Claiming that he won't pay the levy because he's already paid it, blah, blah, blah. So, we decided to teach the oaf some sense, and then suddenly this grey-haired fellow sprang up from nowhere. A knight, it turns out, a noble man, a defender of the poor and oppressed. Just him alone and he went for our throats.'

'So high-spirited?' chortled one of the horsemen, advancing

on Geralt and aiming his pike at him. 'Let's have him dance a jig!'

'Drop your sword,' ordered a horseman in a plumed beret, who seemed to be the commander. 'Sword on the ground!'

'Shall I spear him, Shevlov?'

'Leave him, Sperry.'

Shevlov looked down on the Witcher from the saddle.

'You won't drop your sword, eh?' he commented. 'Are you such a hero? Such a hard man? You eat oysters in their shells? Washed down with turpentine? Bow down before no one? And only stand up for the unjustly accused? Are you so sensitive to wrongs? We'll find out. Poker, Ligenza, Floquet!'

The three armed soldiers obeyed their leader at once, clearly having experience in that regard. They dismounted, their movements well-drilled. One of them held a knife to the settler's throat, the other yanked the woman by the hair and the third grabbed the child. The child began yelling.

'Drop your sword,' said Shevlov. 'This second. Or . . . Ligenza! Slit the peasant's throat.'

Geralt dropped his sword. They immediately leaped on him, pressing him against the planks and menacing him with their blades.

'Aha!' said Shevlov, dismounting. 'Success!'

'You're in trouble, peasant champion,' he added dryly. 'You've obstructed and sabotaged a royal detachment. And I have orders to arrest and put before the courts anyone guilty of that.'

'Arrest?' The man named Ligenza scowled. 'Burden ourselves? Throw a noose round his neck and string him up! And that's that!'

'Or cut him to pieces on the spot!'

'I've seen this fellow before,' one of the riders suddenly said. 'He's a witcher.'

'A what?'

'A witcher. A wizard making his living killing monsters for money.'

'A wizard? Urgh, urgh! Kill him before he casts a spell on us.'

'Shut up, Escayrac. Speak, Trent. Where did you see him and in what circumstances?'

'It was in Maribor. In the service of the castellan there, who had

181

hired him to kill some beast. I don't recall what. But I remember him from his white hair.'

'Ha! So, if he attacked us, somebody must have hired him to.'

'Monsters are witchers' work. They just defend people from monsters.'

'Aha!' Fryga pushed back her lynx-fur calpac. 'I said so! A defender! He saw Ligenza flogging the peasant and Floquet making ready to ravish that woman . . .'

'And categorised you correctly?' Shevlov snorted. 'As monsters? So, you were lucky. I jest. Because the matter is simple, it seems to me. When serving in the army I heard something quite different about witchers. They hire themselves out for everything: to spy, to guard, even to assassinate. They called them the "Cats". Trent saw this one here in Maribor, in Temeria. Meaning he's a Temerian hireling, employed regarding the border posts. They warned me in Findetann about Temerian mercenaries and are promising a bounty for any caught. So, let's take him in fetters to Findetann, turn him in to the commandant and claim the reward. Come on, tie him up. What are you waiting for? Are you afraid? He's not offering resistance. He knows what we'd do to the little peasants if he tries anything.'

'And who's going to fucking touch him? If he's a wizard?'

'Knock on wood!' Ligenza spat on the ground.

'Lily-livered cowards!' yelled Fryga, untying the strap of her saddle bags. 'Yellow-bellies! I'll do it, since no one here has the balls!'

Geralt allowed himself to be tied up. He decided to comply. For the time being.

Two ox wagons trundled out of the forest, wagons laden with posts and elements of some kind of wooden construction.

'Someone go to the carpenters and the bailiff.' Shevlov pointed. 'Send them back. We've sunk enough posts, it'll suffice for now. We shall take a rest here, meanwhile. Search the farmyard for anything fit as fodder for the horses. And some vittals for us.'

Ligenza picked up and examined Geralt's sword, Dandelion's acquisition. Shevlov snatched it out of his hand. He hefted it, wielded it and whirled it around.

'You were lucky we came in force,' he said. 'He would have carved you up no problem: you, Fryga and Floquet. Legends circulate about these witcher swords. The best steel, oftentimes folded and forged, folded and forged again. And they're protected by special spells. Thus achieving exceptional tensile strength and sharpness. A witcher edge, I tell you, pierces armour plate and mail like a linen shift, and cuts through every other blade like noodles.'

'That cannot be,' stated Sperry. Like many of the others, his whiskers were dripping with the cream they had found in the cottage and guzzled. 'Not like noodles.'

'I can't believe it either,' added Fryga.

'Difficult to believe something like that,' threw in Poker.

'Really?' Shevlov assumed a swordsman's pose. 'Face me, one of you, and we'll find out. Come on, who's willing? Well? Why has it gone so quiet?'

'Very well.' Escayrac stepped forward and drew his sword. 'I shall face you. What do I care? We shall see whether . . . *En garde*, Shevlov.'

'*En garde*. One, two . . . three!'

The swords struck each other with a clang. The metal whined mournfully as it snapped. Fryga ducked as a broken piece of blade whistled past her temple.

'Fuck,' said Shevlov, staring disbelievingly at the blade, which had broken a few inches above the gilded cross guard.

'And not a notch on mine!' Escayrac raised his sword. 'Ha, ha, ha! Not a notch! Nor even a mark.'

Fryga giggled like a schoolgirl. Ligenza bleated like a billy goat. The rest guffawed.

'Witcher sword?' snorted Sperry. 'Cuts through like noodles? *You're* the fucking noodle.'

'It's . . .' Shevlov pursed his lips. 'It's sodding scrap. It's trash . . . And you . . .'

He tossed away the remains of the sword, glowered at Geralt and pointed an accusing finger at him.

'You're a fraudster. An imposter and a fraudster. You feign to be a witcher, and wield such trash . . . You carry junk like this instead of a decent blade? How many good people have you deceived, I wonder? How many paupers have you fleeced, swindler?

Oh, you'll confess your peccadillos in Findetann, the starosta will see to that!'

He panted, spat and stamped his foot.

'To horse! Let's get out of here!'

They rode away, laughing, singing and whistling. The settler and his family gloomily watched them go. Geralt saw their lips moving. It wasn't difficult to guess what fate and what mishaps they were wishing on Shevlov and company.

The settler couldn't have expected in his wildest dreams that his wishes would come true to the letter. And that it would happen so swiftly.

*

They arrived at the crossroads. The highway leading westwards along the ravine was rutted by wheels and hooves; the carpenters' wagons had clearly gone that way. As did the company. Geralt walked behind Fryga's horse, tied to a rope attached to the pommel of her saddle.

The horse of Shevlov – who was riding at the front – whinnied and reared up.

Something suddenly flared on the side of the ravine, lit up and became a milky, iridescent globe. Then the globe vanished and a strange group appeared in its stead. There were several figures embraced and intertwined together.

'What the devil?' cursed Poker and rode over to Shevlov, who was quietening down his horse. 'What's going on?'

The group separated. Into four figures. A slim, long-haired and slightly effeminate man. Two long-armed giants with bow legs. And a hunched dwarf with a great double-limbed steel arbalest.

'Buueh-hhhrrr-eeeehhh-bueeeeh! Bueeh-heeh!'

'Draw your weapons!' yelled Shevlov. 'Draw your weapons, stand your ground!'

First one and then the other bowstring of the great arbalest clanged. Shevlov died at once from a bolt to the head. Poker looked down at his belly, through which a bolt had just passed, before he fell from his saddle.

'Fight!' The company drew their swords as one. 'Fight!'

Geralt had no intention of standing idly by to wait for the result of the engagement. He formed his fingers in the Igni Sign and burned through the rope binding his arms. He caught Fryga by the belt and hurled her to the ground. And leaped into the saddle.

There was a blinding flash and the horses began to neigh, kick and thrash the air with their forehooves. Several horsemen fell and screamed as they were trampled. Fryga's grey mare also bolted before the Witcher could bring her under control. Fryga leaped up, jumped and seized the bridle and reins. Geralt drove her away with a punch and spurred the mare into a gallop.

Pressed to the steed's neck, he didn't see Degerlund frightening the horses and blinding their riders with magical lightning bolts. Or see Bue and Bang falling on the horsemen, roaring, one with a battleaxe, the other with a broad scimitar. He didn't see the splashes of blood, didn't hear the screams of the slaughtered.

He didn't see Escayrac die, and immediately after him Sperry, filleted like a fish by Bang. He didn't see Bue fell Floquet and his steed, and then drag him out from under the horse. But Floquet's stifled cry, the sound of a rooster being butchered, lingered long.

Until he turned from the highway and dashed into the forest.

Mahakam potato soup is prepared thus: gather chanterelles in the summer and men-on-horseback in the autumn. If it is the winter or early spring, take a sizeable handful of dried mushrooms. Put them in a pan and cover them with water, soak them overnight, salt them in the morning, toss in half an onion and boil. Drain them, but do not discard the broth; instead be vigilant in removing the sand that has surely settled at the bottom of the pan. Boil the potatoes and dice them. Take some fatty bacon, chop and fry it. Cut the onion into half slices and fry them in the bacon fat until they almost stick. Take a great cauldron, toss everything into it, not forgetting the chopped mushrooms. Pour on the mushroom broth, add water as needs be, pour on sour rye starter to taste. (How to execute the starter may be found elsewhere in another receipt.) Boil and season with salt, pepper and marjoram according to taste and liking. Add melted fatback. Stirring in cream is a matter of taste, but heed: it is against our dwarven tradition, for it is a human fashion to add cream to potato soup.

Eleonora Rhundurin-Pigott, *Perfect Mahakam Cuisine, the Precise Science of Cooking and Making Dishes from Meats, Fishes and Vegetables, also Seasoning Diverse Sauces, Baking Cakes, Making Jam, Preparing Cooked Meats, Preserves, Wines, Spirits, and Various Useful Cooking and Preserving Secrets, Essential for Every Good and Thrifty Housewife*

CHAPTER THIRTEEN

Like almost all post stations, this one was located at a junction where two roads intersected. It was a building with a shingle roof and a columned arcade with an adjoining stable and woodshed, set among white-barked birches. It was empty. There seemed to be no guests, nor travellers.

The exhausted grey mare stumbled, walking stiffly and unsteadily, her head hanging almost to the ground. Geralt led her and handed the reins over to the stable lad. He looked about forty and was bent over under the burden of his years. He stroked the mare's neck and examined his hand. He looked Geralt up and down, then spat right between his feet. Geralt shook his head and sighed. It didn't surprise him. He knew he was at fault, that he'd overdone it with the gallop, and over difficult terrain, what's more. He'd wanted to get as far away as possible from Sorel Degerlund and his minions. He was aware that it was a woeful justification; he also had a low opinion of people who drove their mounts into the ground.

The stable lad went away, leading the mare and muttering to himself. It wasn't difficult to guess what he was muttering and what he thought. Geralt sighed, pushed the door open and entered the station.

It smelled agreeable inside and the Witcher realised he hadn't eaten for more than a day.

'There's no horse,' said the postmaster, emerging from behind the counter and anticipating his question. 'And the next mail coach won't be here for two days.'

'I could use some food.' Geralt looked upwards at the ridge and rafters of the high vault. 'I'll pay.'

'We have none.'

'Oh, come, postmaster,' came a voice from the corner of the chamber. 'Does it behove you to treat a traveller so?'

In the corner, seated at a table, was a dwarf. Flaxen-haired and flaxen-bearded, he was dressed in an embroidered, patterned maroon jerkin, embellished with brass buttons on the front and sleeves. He had ruddy cheeks and a prominent nose. Geralt had occasionally seen unusually shaped, slightly pink potatoes at the market. The dwarf's nose was of an identical colour. And shape.

'You offered me potato soup.' The dwarf glared sternly at the postmaster from under very bushy eyebrows. 'You surely won't contend that your wife only prepares one portion of it. I'll wager any sum that it also suffices for this gentleman. Be seated, traveller. Will you take a beer?'

'With pleasure, thank you,' replied Geralt, sitting down and digging out a coin from the hiding place in his belt. 'But allow me to treat you, good sir. Despite the misleading impression, I am neither a tramp nor a vagrant. I am a witcher. On the job, which is why my apparel is shabby and my appearance unkempt. Which I beg you to forgive. Two beers, postmaster.'

The beers appeared on the table in no time.

'My wife will serve the potato soup shortly,' grunted the postmaster. 'And don't look askance at what just happened. I have to have vittals ready the whole time. For were some magnate, royal messengers or post to arrive . . . And were I to run out and have nothing to serve them—'

'Yes, yes . . .'

Geralt raised his mug. He knew plenty of dwarves and knew their drinking customs and proposed a toast. 'To the propitiousness of a good cause!'

'And to the confusion of whoresons!' added the dwarf, knocking his mug against Geralt's. 'It's pleasant to drink with someone who observes custom and etiquette. I am Addario Bach. Actually Addarion, but everyone calls me Addario.'

'Geralt of Rivia.'

'The Witcher Geralt of Rivia,' declared Addario Bach, wiping the froth from his whiskers. 'Your name rings a bell. You're a well-travelled fellow and it's no wonder you're familiar with customs. I, mark you, have come here on the mail coach, or the dilly, as they call it in the South. And I'm waiting for a transfer to the mail coach plying between Dorian and Tretogor in Redania. Well, that potato soup is here at last. Let's see what it's like. You ought to know that our womenfolk in Mahakam make the best potato soup, you'll never eat its like. Made from a thick starter of black bread and rye flour, with mushrooms and well-fried onions . . .'

The post station potato soup was excellent, rich with chanterelles and fried onions, and if it was inferior to the Mahakam version made by dwarven women then Geralt never found out in what respect, as Addario Bach ate briskly, in silence and without commenting.

The postmaster suddenly looked out of the window and his reaction made Geralt do likewise.

Two horses had arrived outside the station, both looking even worse than Geralt's captured mount. And there were three horsemen. To be precise, two men and a woman. The Witcher looked around the chamber vigilantly.

The door creaked. Fryga entered the station. And behind her Ligenza and Trent.

'If it's horses—' The postmaster stopped abruptly when he saw the sword in Fryga's hand.

'You guessed,' she finished his sentence. 'Horses are precisely what we need. Three. So, move yourself, bring them from the stable.'

'—you want—'

The postmaster didn't finish that time, either. Fryga leaped at him and flashed a blade before his eyes. Geralt stood up.

'Hey there!'

All three of them turned towards him.

'It's you,' drawled Fryga. 'You. Damned vagabond.'

She had a bruise on her cheek where he'd punched her.

'All because of you,' she rasped. 'Shevlov, Poker, Sperry . . . All slaughtered, the entire squad. And you, whoreson, knocked me from the saddle, stole my horse and bolted like a coward. For which I shall now repay you.'

She was short and slightly built. It didn't deceive the Witcher. He was aware, because he had experienced it, that in life – as at a post station – even very hideous things could be delivered in quite unspectacular packages.

'This is a post station!' the postmaster yelled from behind the counter. 'Under royal protection!'

'Did you hear that?' Geralt asked calmly. 'A post station. Get you gone.'

'You, O grey scallywag, are still feeble with your reckoning,' Fryga hissed. 'Do you need help counting again? There's one of you and three of us. Meaning there are more of us.'

'There are three of you.' He swept his gaze over them. 'And one of me. But there aren't more of you at all. It's something of a mathematical paradox and an exception to the rule.'

'Meaning?'

'Meaning get the fuck out of here. While you're still capable.'

He spotted a gleam in her eye and knew at once that she was one of those few who could strike in quite a different place than where they're looking. Fryga must only recently have begun perfecting that trick, for Geralt effortlessly dodged her treacherous blow. He outmanoeuvred her with a short half-twist, kicked her left leg out from under her and threw her onto the counter. She slammed against the wood with a loud thud.

Ligenza and Trent must have previously seen Fryga in action, because her failure left them simply dumbfounded. They froze open-mouthed. For long enough to allow the Witcher to seize a broom he had spied earlier in the corner. First, Trent was hit in the face with the birch twigs, then across the head with the handle. And after that Geralt put the broom in front of his legs, kicked him behind the knees and tripped him up.

Ligenza calmed down, drew his sword and leaped forward, slashing powerfully with a reverse blow. Geralt evaded it with a half-turn, spun right around, stuck out his elbow, and Ligenza – his momentum carrying him forward – jabbed his windpipe onto Geralt's elbow. He wheezed and fell to his knees. Before he fell, Geralt plucked the sword from his fingers and threw it vertically upwards. The sword plunged into a rafter and remained there.

Fryga attacked low and Geralt barely had time to dodge. He knocked her sword hand, caught her by the arm, spun her around, tripped her with the broom handle and slammed her onto the counter again.

Trent leaped for him and Geralt struck him very fast in the face with the broom: once, twice, three times. Then hit him with the handle on one temple, then on the other and then very hard in the neck. The Witcher shoved the broom handle between his legs, stepped in close, seized Trent by the wrist, twisted it, took the sword from his hand and threw it upwards. The sword sank into a rafter and remained there. Trent stepped back, tripped over a bench and fell down. Geralt decided there was no need to harm him any further.

Ligenza got to his feet, but stood motionless, with arms hanging limp, staring upwards at the swords stuck high up in the rafters, out of reach. Fryga attacked.

She whirled her blade, feinted, then made a short reverse stroke. The style was well-suited to tavern brawls, at close quarters and in poor lighting. The Witcher wasn't bothered by lighting or the lack of it, and was only too familiar with the style. Fryga's blade cut through the air and the feint wheeled her around so the Witcher ended up behind her back. She screamed as he put the broom handle under her arm and twisted her elbow. He yanked the sword from her fingers and shoved her away.

'I thought I'd keep this one for myself,' he said, examining the blade. 'As compensation for the effort I've put in. But I've changed my mind. I won't carry a bandit's weapon.'

He threw the sword upwards. The blade plunged into the rafters and shuddered. Fryga, as pale as parchment, flashed her teeth behind twisted lips. She hunched over, snatching a knife from her boot.

'That,' he said, looking her straight in the eyes, 'was a singularly foolish decision.'

Hooves thudded on the road, horses snorted, weapons clanked. The courtyard outside the station suddenly teemed with riders.

'If I were you I'd sit down on a bench in the corner.' Geralt addressed the three of them. 'And pretend I wasn't here.'

The door slammed open, spurs jangled and soldiers in fox fur hats and short black jerkins with silver braiding entered the chamber. Their leader was a man with a moustache and a scarlet sash.

'Royal forces!' he announced, resting his fist on a mace stuck into his belt. 'Sergeant Kovacs, Second Squadron of the First Company, the armed forces of graciously reigning King Foltest, the Lord of

Temeria, Pontaria and Mahakam. In pursuit of a Redanian gang!'

Fryga, Trent and Ligenza, on a bench in the corner, examined the tips of their boots.

'The border was crossed by a lawless band of Redanian marauders, hired thugs and robbers,' Kovacs went on. 'Those ne'er-do-wells are knocking over border posts, burning, pillaging, torturing and killing royal subjects. They would stand no chance in an engagement with the royal army, thus they are hiding in the forests, waiting for a chance to slip across the border. More such as them may appear in the locality. May you be warned that giving them help, information or any support will be construed as treason, and treason means the noose!

'Have any strangers been seen here at the station? Any newcomers? I mean suspicious individuals? And I say further that for identifying a marauder or helping in his capture there is a reward. Of one hundred orens. Postmaster?'

The postmaster shrugged, bowed his head, mumbled something and began wiping the counter, leaning very low over it.

The sergeant looked around and walked over to Geralt, spurs clanking.

'Who are you? Ha! I believe I've seen you before. In Maribor. I recognise you by your white hair. You are a witcher, aren't you? A tracker and despatcher of divers monsters. Am I right?'

'You are.'

'Then I have no quarrel with you; and your profession, I must say, is an honest one,' pronounced the sergeant, simultaneously eying Addario Bach appraisingly. 'Master Dwarf is also beyond suspicion, since no dwarves have been seen among the marauders. But for form's sake I ask: what are you doing at the station?'

'I came from Cidaris on a stagecoach and await a transfer. Time is dragging, so the honourable witcher and I are sitting together, conversing and converting beer into urine.'

'A transfer, you say,' repeated the sergeant. 'I understand. And you two men? Who might you be? Yes, you, I'm talking to you!'

Trent opened his mouth. Blinked. And blurted something out.

'What? Hey? Get up! Who are you, I ask?'

'Leave him, officer,' Addario Bach said freely. 'He's my servant, employed by me. He's a halfwit, an errant imbecile. It's a family

192

affliction. By great fortune his younger siblings are normal. Their mother finally understood she shouldn't drink from the puddles outside a plague house when pregnant.'

Trent opened his mouth even wider, lowered his head, grunted and groaned. Ligenza also grunted and made a movement as though to stand up. The dwarf laid a hand on his shoulder.

'Don't get up, lad. And keep quiet, keep quiet. I know the theory of evolution, I know what creature humans evolved from, you don't have to keep reminding me. Let him off, too, commandant, sir. He's also my servant.'

'Hm, yes . . .' The sergeant continued to examine them suspiciously. 'Servants, is it? If you say so . . . And she? That young woman in male attire? Hey! Get up, for I wish to look at you! Who be you? Answer when you're asked!'

'Ha, ha, commandant, sir,' the dwarf laughed. 'She? She's a harlot, I mean a wife of loose morals. I hired her in Cidaris in order to bed her. You don't miss home if you journey with a supply of fanny, any philosopher will certify to that.'

He gave Fryga a firm slap on the backside. Fryga blanched in fury and ground her teeth.

'Indeed.' The sergeant grimaced. 'How come I didn't notice at once? Why, it's obvious. A half-elf.'

'You've got half a prick,' Fryga snapped. 'Half the size of what's considered normal.'

'Quiet, quiet,' Addario Bach soothed her. 'Don't take umbrage, colonel. I simply landed an obstreperous whore.'

A soldier rushed into the chamber and submitted a report. Sergeant Kovacs stood up straight.

'The gang has been tracked down!' he declared. 'We must give chase at all speed! Forgive the disturbance. At your service!'

He exited with the soldiers. A moment later the thud of hooves reached them from the courtyard.

'Forgive me that spectacle, forgive my spontaneous words and coarse gestures,' Addario Bach said to Fryga, Trent and Ligenza, after a moment's silence. 'In truth, I know you not, I care little for you and rather don't like you, but I like scenes of hanging even less, the sight of hanged men kicking their feet depresses me deeply. Which explains my dwarven frivolity.'

'You owe your lives to his dwarven frivolity,' added Geralt. 'It would be polite to thank the dwarf. I saw you in action in the peasant homestead, and I know what kind of rogues you are. I wouldn't lift a finger in your defence. I wouldn't want or even know how to play such a scene as this noble dwarf did. And you'd already be hanging, all three of you. So be gone from here. I would advise the opposite direction to the one chosen by the sergeant and his cavalry.

'Not a chance,' he cut them off on seeing their gaze directed towards the swords stuck into the rafters. 'You won't get them back. Without them you'll be less inclined towards pillage and extortion. Begone.'

'It was tense,' sighed Addario Bach, soon after the door closed on the three of them. 'Damn it, my hands are still shaking a bit. Yours are not?'

'No.' Geralt smiled at his recollections. 'In that respect, I am . . . somewhat impaired.'

'Lucky for some.' The dwarf grinned. 'Even their impairments are nice. Another beer?'

'No thank you.' Geralt shook his head. 'Time I was going. I've found myself in a situation, so to say, where haste is rather advisable. And it would be rather unwise to stay in one place too long.'

'I rather noticed. And won't ask questions. But do you know what, Witcher? Somehow the urge to stay at this station and wait idly for the coach for two days has left me. Firstly, because the boredom would do for me. And secondly, because that maiden you defeated with a broom in that duel said goodbye to me with a strange expression. Why, in the fervour, I exaggerated a tiny bit. She probably isn't one of those you can get away with slapping on the bottom and calling a whore. She's liable to return, and I'd prefer not to be here when she does. Perhaps, then, we'll set off together?'

'Gladly.' Geralt smiled again. 'It's not so lonely on a journey with a good companion, any philosopher will certify to that. As long as the direction suits us both. I must to Novigrad. I must get there by the fifteenth of July. By the fifteenth without fail.'

He had to be in Novigrad by the fifteenth of July at the latest. He stressed that when the sorcerers were hiring him, buying two weeks of his time. *No problem.* Pinety and Tzara had looked at him superciliously. *No problem, Witcher. You'll be in Novigrad before you know it. We'll teleport you straight into the Main Street.*

'By the fifteenth, ha.' The dwarf ruffled up his beard. 'Today is the ninth. There's not much time left, for it's a long road. But there's a way for you to get there on time.'

He stood up, took a wide-brimmed, pointed hat down from a peg and put it on. He slung a bag over his shoulder.

'I'll explain the matter to you on the road. Let's be going, Geralt of Rivia. For this way suits me down to the ground.'

*

They walked briskly, perhaps too briskly. Addario Bach turned out to be a typical dwarf. Although dwarves were, when in need or for reasons of comfort, capable of using every kind of vehicle or riding, pack or harness animal, they decidedly preferred walking. They were born walkers. A dwarf was able to cover a distance of thirty miles a day, as many as a man on horseback, and, what's more, carrying luggage that a normal man couldn't even lift. A human was incapable of keeping up with an unburdened marching dwarf. And neither was the Witcher. Geralt had forgotten that, and after some time was forced to ask Addario to slow down a little.

They walked along forest trails and even at times across rough ground. Addario knew the way, he was very knowledgeable about the area. He explained that in Cidaris lived his family, which was so large that some kind of festivity was forever being held, be it a wedding, christening, funeral or wake. In keeping with dwarven customs, failure to appear at such a gathering could only be excused with a death certificate signed by a notary, and living family members could not get out of them. Thus Addario knew the way to Cidaris and back perfectly.

'Our destination,' he explained as he walked, 'is the settlement of Wiaterna, which lies in the overflow area of the Pontar. There's a port in Wiaterna where barques and boats often moor. With a bit of luck, we'll soon happen upon some specimen or other and embark. I must to Tretogor, so I shall disembark in Crane

Tussock, while you will sail further and be in Novigrad in some three or four days. Believe me, it's the quickest way.'

'I do. Slow down, Addario, please. I can barely keep up. Is your profession in some way connected to walking? Are you a hawker?'

'I'm a miner. In a copper mine.'

'Of course. Every dwarf is a miner. And works in the mine in Mahakam. Stands at the coalface with a pick and mines coal.'

'You're succumbing to stereotypes. Soon you'll be saying that every dwarf uses coarse language. And after a few stiff drinks attacks people with a battleaxe.'

'Wouldn't dream of it.'

'My mine isn't in Mahakam, but in Coppertown, near Tretogor. I don't stand up or mine, but I play the horn in the colliery brass band.'

'Interesting.'

'Actually, something else is interesting here,' laughed the dwarf. 'An amusing coincidence. One of our brass band's showpieces is called *The March of the Witchers*. It goes like this: *Tara-rara, boom, boom, umpa-umpa, rim-sim-sim, paparara-tara-rara, tara-rara, boom-boom-boom . . .*'

'How the hell did you come up with that name? Have you ever seen a witcher marching? Where? When?'

'In truth—' Addario Bach became a little disconcerted '—it's only a slightly reworked version of *The Parade of the Strongmen*. But all colliery brass bands play either *The Parade of the Strongmen*, *The Entrance of the Athletes* or *The Marches of the Old Comrades*. We wanted to be original. *Ta-ra-ra, boom-de-ay!*'

'Slow down or I'll croak!'

*

It was totally deserted in the forests. And quite the opposite in the meadows and forest clearings they often happened upon. Work was in full swing there. Hay was being mowed, raked and formed into ricks and stooks. The dwarf greeted the mowers with cheerful shouts, and they responded in kind. Or didn't.

'That reminds me of another of our band's marches.' Addario

pointed at the toiling labourers. 'Entitled *Haymaking*. We often play it, especially in the summer season. And sing along to it, too. We have a poet at the pit, he composed some clever rhymes; you can even sing it *a cappella*. It goes like this:

> *The men go forth to mow*
> *The women they follow*
> *They look up and they cower*
> *They fear a damp'ning shower*
> *We huddle to keep warm*
> *And hide from the fierce storm*
> *Our shafts we proudly vaunt*
> *And the tempest we taunt*

And from the beginning. It's fine to march to, isn't it?'

'Slow down, Addario!'

'You can't slow down! It's a marching song! With a marching rhythm and metre!'

*

There were some remains of a wall showing white on a hillock, and the ruins of a building and a familiar-looking tower. Geralt recognised the temple from the tower; he couldn't remember which deity was linked to it, but he'd heard various stories about it. Priests had lived there long ago. Rumour had it that when their rapacity, riotous debauchery and lasciviousness could no longer be tolerated, the local residents chased them away and drove them into a dense forest, where, as rumour had it, they occupied themselves converting the forest spirits. Apparently with miserable results.

'It's Old Erem,' pronounced Addario. 'We're sticking to our route and making good time. We should arrive in Sylvan Dam by evening.'

*

Upstream, the brook they were walking beside had bubbled over boulders and races, and once downstream spread out wide, forming a large pool. This was helped by a wood and earth dam that arrested the current. Some work was going on by the dam, a group of people were busily toiling there.

'We're in Sylvan Dam,' said Addario. 'The construction you can see down there is the dam itself. It's used for floating timber from the clearing. The river, as you heed, is not navigable, being too shallow. So, the water level rises, the timber is gathered and then the dam is opened. That causes a large wave facilitating the rafting. The raw material for the production of charcoal is transported this way. Charcoal—'

'—is indispensable for the smelting of iron,' Geralt finished his sentence. 'And smelting is the most important and most promising branch of industry. I know. That was clarified for me quite recently by a certain sorcerer. One familiar with charcoal and smelting.'

'No wonder he's familiar,' snorted the dwarf. 'The Sorcerers' Chapter is the major shareholder of the companies of the industrial complex at Gors Velen and it owns several foundries and metalworks outright. The sorcerers derive substantial profits from smelting. From other branches as well. Deservedly too; after all, they largely created the technology. They might, however, give up their hypocrisy and admit that magic isn't charity, isn't altruistic philanthropy, but an industry calculated to make a profit. But why am I telling you this? You know yourself. Come with me, there's a small tavern over there, let's rest. And we can doubtless get a bed there, for look, it's growing dark.'

*

The small tavern was in no way worthy of the name, but neither could one be surprised. It served woodcutters and rafters from the dam, who didn't mind where they drank as long as there was something to drink. A shack with a leaky thatched roof, an awning resting on poles, a few tables and benches made of rough planks, a stone fireplace – the local community didn't require or expect greater luxuries; what counted what was behind the partition: the barrels from which the innkeeper poured beer, and from where he occasionally served sausage, which the innkeeper's wife – if she felt like it and was in the right mood – was willing to grill over the embers for a fee.

Neither were Geralt and Addario's expectations excessive, particularly since the beer was fresh, from a newly unbunged barrel, and not many compliments were needed for the innkeeper's wife to agree to fry and serve them a skillet of blood pudding and onion. After a whole day's wandering through forests Geralt could compare the blood pudding to veal shank in vegetables, shoulder of boar, turbot in ink and the other masterpieces offered by the chef of the Natura Rerum osteria. Although to tell the truth, he did miss the osteria a little.

'Do you by any chance know the fate of that prophet?' said Addario, gesturing the innkeeper's wife over and ordering another beer.

Before they sat down to eat they had examined a moss-grown boulder standing beside a mighty oak. Carved into its surface were letters informing that in that precise place, on the day of the holiday of Birke in 1133 *post Resurrectionem*, the Prophet Lebioda gave a sermon to his acolytes, and the obelisk honouring the event was financed and erected in 1200 by Spyridon Apps, a master braidmaker from Rinde, based in the Minor Market Place, goods of excellent quality, affordable prices, please visit.

'Do you know the story of that Lebioda, whom some called a prophet?' asked Addario, scraping the rest of the blood pudding from the skillet. 'I mean the real story.'

'I don't know any stories,' replied the Witcher, running a piece of bread around the pan. 'Neither real nor invented. I was never interested.'

'Then listen. The thing occurred over a hundred years ago, I think not long after the date carved on that boulder. Today, as you well know, one almost never sees dragons, unless it's somewhere in the wild mountains, in the badlands. In those times, they occurred more often and could be vexing. They learned that pastures full of cattle were great eating places where they could stuff themselves without undue effort. Fortunately for the farmers, even a great reptile would limit itself to one or two feasts every quarter, but devoured enough to threaten the farm, particularly when it had it in for some region. One huge dragon became fixated on a certain

199

village in Kaedwen. It would fly in, eat a few sheep, two or three cows, and then catch a few carp from the fishponds for dessert. Finally, it would breathe fire, set alight a barn or hayrick and then fly off.'

The dwarf sipped his beer and belched.

'The villagers tried hard to frighten the dragon away, using various traps and trickery, but all to no avail. As luck would have it, Lebioda had just arrived in nearby Ban Ard with his acolytes. At that time, he was already celebrated, was called a prophet, and had masses of followers. The peasants asked him for help, and he, astonishingly, didn't decline. When the dragon arrived, Lebioda went to the pasture and began to exorcise it. The dragon started by singeing him, as you would a duck. And then swallowed him. Simply swallowed him. And flew off into the mountains.'

'Is that the end?'

'No. Keep listening. The acolytes wept over the prophet, despaired and then hired some hunters. Our boys, dwarven hunters, well-versed in draconian matters. They stalked the dragon for a month. Conventionally following the droppings the reptile was dumping. And the acolytes fell on their knees beside every turd and rummaged around in it, weeping bitterly, fishing out their master's remains. They finally put the whole thing together, or rather what they considered to be the whole thing, but what was actually a collection of none-too-clean human, bovine and ovine bones. Today it's all kept in the Novigrad temple in a sarcophagus. As a miraculous relic.'

'Own up, Addario. You made up that story. Or greatly embellished it.'

'Why the suspicion?'

'Because I often keep company with a certain poet. And he, when he has to choose between the real version of an event and a more attractive one, always chooses the latter, which he moreover embroiders. Regarding that, he laughs off all accusations using sophistry, saying that if something isn't truthful it doesn't mean at all that it's a lie.'

'Let me guess who the poet is. It's Dandelion, of course. And a story has its own rules.'

'"A story is a largely false account, of largely trivial events, fed to us by historians who are largely idiots",' smiled the Witcher.

'Let me also guess who the author of that quotation is.' Addario Bach grinned. 'Vysogota of Corvo, philosopher and ethicist. And also a historian. However, regarding the prophet Lebioda . . . Why, history, as it's been said before, is history. But I heard that in Novigrad the priests sometimes remove the prophet's remains from its sarcophagus and give them to the faithful to be kissed. If I were there, however, I'd refrain from kissing them.'

'I shall too,' promised Geralt. 'But as regards Novigrad, since we're on the subject—'

'Be at ease,' interrupted the dwarf. 'You won't be late. We'll rise early and go at once to Wiaterna. We'll find a good deal and you'll be in Novigrad on time.'

Let's hope, thought the Witcher. *Let's hope.*

People and animals belong to various species, while foxes live among people and animals. The quick and the dead wander along various roads, while foxes move between the quick and the dead. Deities and monsters march down various paths, while foxes walk between deities and monsters. The paths of the light and the darkness never join up or cross; vulpine ghosts lurk between them. The immortal and demons tread their own ways – vulpine ghosts are somewhere between.

Ji Yun, a scholar from the times of the Qing Dynasty

CHAPTER FOURTEEN

A storm passed in the night.

After sleeping in a hay barn, they set off at dawn on a chilly, though sunny, morning. Keeping to the waymarked path, they passed through broadleaved woodland, peat bogs and marshy meadows. After an hour of heavy marching they reached some buildings.

'Wiaterna.' Addario Bach pointed. 'This is the harbour I was telling you about.'

They arrived at the river, where a brisk wind fanned them. They stepped onto a wooden jetty. The river formed a broad water there as large as a lake and the current was scarcely perceptible, as it was flowing some way off. The branches of willows, osiers and alders on the bank hung down to the water. Waterfowl, emitting various sounds, were swimming all around: mallards, garganeys, pintails, divers and grebes. A little ship was gliding gracefully over the water, merging into the landscape without frightening the whole feathered rabble. It had a single mast, with one large sail astern and several triangular ones aft.

'Someone once rightly listed the three most beautiful sights in the world,' said Addario Bach, staring at the spectacle. 'A ship in full sail, a galloping horse and you know . . . a naked woman lying in bed.'

'Dancing.' A faint smile played around the Witcher's lips. 'A woman dancing, Addario.'

'If you say so,' the dwarf agreed. 'A naked woman dancing. And that little boat, ha, you have to admit, looks lovely on the water.'

'It's not a little boat, it's a little ship.'

'It's a cutter,' a stout, middle-aged man in an elk-skin jerkin corrected him as he approached. 'A cutter, gentlemen. Which can easily be seen from the rig. A large mainsail, a jib and two staysails on the forestays. Classic.'

The little ship – or cutter – sailed close enough to the jetty for them to admire the figurehead on the prow. The carving depicted a bald old man with an aquiline nose rather than the standard large-breasted woman, mermaid, dragon or sea serpent.

'Dammit,' Addario Bach grunted to himself. 'Does the prophet have it in for us, or what?'

'A sixty-four-footer,' went on the elderly gentleman in a proud voice. 'With a total sail area of three thousand three hundred square feet. That, gentlemen, is the *Prophet Lebioda,* a modern Koviran-type cutter, built in the Novigradian shipyard and launched almost a year ago.'

'You're familiar with that craft, as we can see.' Addario Bach cleared his throat. 'You know plenty about her.'

'I know everything about her, since I'm the owner. Do you see the ensign at the stern? There's a glove on it. It's my company's emblem. If I may: I am Kevenard van Vliet, a merchant in the glove-making trade.'

'Delighted to make your acquaintance.' The dwarf shook his right hand, eyeing up the merchant astutely. 'And we congratulate you on the little ship, for it is well-favoured and swift. It's a wonder that it's here, in Wiaterna, on the broad water, away from the main Pontarian shipping lanes. It's also a wonder that the ship's on the water and you, its owner, are on the land, in the middle of nowhere. Is anything the matter?'

'Oh, no, no, nothing the matter,' said the glove merchant, in Geralt's opinion too quickly and too emphatically. 'We're taking on provisions here, nothing more. And in the middle of nowhere, oh well, cruel necessity rather than our wishes has brought us here. For when you are hastening to rescue someone you don't pay heed to the route you take. And our rescue mission—'

'Let's not go into details, Mr van Vliet, sir,' interrupted one of a group of characters whose steps made the jetty suddenly tremble as they came closer. 'I don't think that interests the gentlemen. Nor ought it to.'

Five characters had stepped onto the jetty from the direction of the village. The one who had spoken, wearing a straw hat, was conspicuous by his well-defined jaw with several days' stubble and large protruding chin. His chin had a cleft, owing to which it looked like a miniature arse. He was accompanied by a tall bruiser, a veritable giant, although from his face and expression he was by no means a moron. The third – stocky and weather-beaten – was every inch a sailor, down to the woollen cap and earring. The other two, clearly deckhands, were lugging chests containing provisions.

'I don't think,' continued the one with the cleft chin, 'that these gentlemen, whoever they are, need know anything about us, what we're doing, or about our other private affairs. These gentlemen certainly understand that no one has the right to know our private business, in particular total strangers who we've come across by accident—'

'Perhaps not total strangers,' interjected the giant. 'Master Dwarf, I know you not, indeed, but this gentleman's white hair betrays his identity. Geralt of Rivia, I believe? The Witcher? Am I not mistaken?'

I'm becoming popular, thought Geralt, folding his hands on his chest. *Too popular. Should I dye my hair, perhaps? Or shave it off like Harlan Tzara?*

'A witcher!' Kevenard van Vliet was clearly delighted. 'A real witcher! What a stroke of luck! Noble gentlemen! Why he's a veritable godsend!'

'The famous Geralt of Rivia!' repeated the giant. 'What a stroke of luck that we've met him now, in our situation. He'll help get us out of it—'

'You talk too much, Cobbin,' interrupted the one with the chin. 'Too fast and too much.'

'What do you mean, Mr Fysh?' snorted the glove-maker. 'Can't you see what a turn-up this is? The help of someone like a witcher—'

'Mr van Vliet! Leave it to me. I have more experience in dealings with such as this one here.'

A silence fell, in which the character with the cleft chin eyed the Witcher up and down.

'Geralt of Rivia,' he finally said. 'Vanquisher of monsters and supernatural creatures. A legendary vanquisher, I would say. If I believed in the legends, that is. And where are your celebrated witcher swords? I can't seem to see them.'

'It's no wonder you can't see them,' replied Geralt. 'Because they're invisible. What, haven't you heard the legends about witcher swords? The uninitiated can't see them. They appear when I utter a spell. When the need arises. If one arises. Because I'm capable of doing a lot of damage even without them.'

'I'll take your word for it. I am Javil Fysh. I run a company in Novigrad offering various services. This is my partner, Petru Cobbin. And this is Mr Pudlorak, captain of the *Prophet Lebioda*. And the honourable Kevenard van Vliet, whom you've already met, the owner of this little ship.

'I see, Witcher, that you're standing on a jetty in the only settlement within a radius of twenty-odd miles,' Javil Fysh continued, looking around. 'In order to get out of here and find civilised roads, one must tramp through forests. It looks to me like you'd prefer to sail from this wilderness, embarking on something that floats on water. And the *Prophet* is sailing to Novigrad this very moment. And can take on passengers. Like you and your companion dwarf. Does that suit you?'

'Go on, Mr Fysh. I'm all ears.'

'Our ship, as you see, isn't any old tub, you have to pay to sail on her, and a pretty penny. Don't interrupt. Would you be prepared to take us under the protection of your invisible swords? We can pay for your valuable witcher services, meaning escorting us and protecting us during the voyage from here to the Novigradian port, as payment for the trip. What price, I wonder, do you put on your witcher services?'

Geralt looked at him.

'Including the price of getting to the bottom of this?'

'What?'

'There are tricks and catches concealed in your proposition,' Geralt said calmly. 'If I have to find them myself, I'll put a higher price on it. It'll be cheaper if you decide to be honest.'

'Your mistrust arouses suspicion,' Fysh replied coldly. 'Since swindlers forever sniff out deviousness. As it's said: a guilty conscience needs no accuser. We wish to hire you as an escort. It's rather a simple task, free of complications. What tricks could be hidden in it?'

'This whole escorting business is a tall story,' Geralt said, without lowering his gaze. 'Thought up on the spot and patently obvious.'

'Is that what you think?'

'It is. Because my lord the glove merchant let slip something about a rescue expedition, and you, Mr Fysh, are rudely silencing him. In no time, your associate will spill the beans about the situation you have to be extracted from. So, if I'm to co-operate, please leave out the fabrication. What kind of expedition is it and to whose rescue is it hastening? Why so secretive? What trouble do you need to get out of?'

'We shall explain it.' Fysh forestalled van Vliet. 'We shall explain everything, my dear witcher—'

'But on board,' croaked Captain Pudlorak, who had been silent up to then. 'There's no point dallying any longer on this jetty. We have a favourable wind. Let's sail, gentlemen.'

*

Once it had the wind in its sails, the *Prophet Lebioda* sped swiftly across the widely spread waters of the bay, holding a course for the main channel, dodging between islets. The lines rattled, the boom groaned, and the ensign with a glove flapped briskly on the flagpole.

Kevenard van Vliet kept his promise. No sooner had the cutter pushed off from the jetty in Wiaterna than he called Geralt and Addario to the bow and set about explaining.

'The expedition undertaken by us,' he began, constantly glancing at a sullen Fysh, 'is aimed at freeing a kidnapped child. Xymena de Sepulveda, the only daughter of Briana de Sepulveda. That name rings a bell with you, no doubt. Fur tanneries, soaking and stitching workshops, and furrieries. Huge annual production, immense sums of money. If you ever see a lady in a gorgeous and expensive fur, it's sure to be from her factory.'

'And it's her daughter that was abducted. For a ransom?'

'Actually no. You won't believe it, but . . . A monster seized the little girl. A she-fox. I mean a shape-changer. A vixen.'

'You're right,' said the Witcher coldly. 'I won't. She-foxes or vixens, or more precisely aguaras, only abduct elven children.'

'That's right, that's absolutely right,' snapped Fysh. 'Because although it's an unprecedented thing, the furriery in Novigrad is run by a non-human. The mother, Breainne Diarbhail ap Muigh, is a pure-blooded she-elf. The widow of Jacob de Sepulveda, whose entire estate she inherited. The family didn't manage to nullify the will, or declare the mixed marriage invalid, even though it's against custom and divine law—'

'Get to the point,' interrupted Geralt. 'Get to the point, please. You claim that this furrier, a pure-blood she-elf, charged you with recovering her kidnapped daughter?'

'You having us on?' Fysh scowled. 'Trying to catch us out? You know very well that if a she-fox kidnaps an elven child they never try to recover it. They give up on it and forget it. They accept that it was fated to happen—'

'At first, Briana de Sepulveda also pretended,' Kevenard van Vliet butted in. 'She despaired, but in the elven fashion, secretly. Outside: inscrutable, dry eyes . . . *Va'esse deireádh aep eigean, va'esse eigh faidh'ar*, she repeated, which in their tongue comes out as—'

'—something ends, something begins.'

'Indeed. But it's nothing but stupid elf talk, nothing is ending, what is there to end? And why should it? Briana has lived among humans for many years, observing our laws and customs, and is only a non-human by blood; in her heart, she's almost a human being. Elven beliefs and superstitions are powerful, I agree, and perhaps Briana is just feigning her composure to other elves, but it's clear she secretly misses her daughter. She'd give anything to get her only daughter back, she-fox or no she-fox . . . Indeed, Lord Witcher, she asked for nothing, she didn't expect help. Despite that we determined to help her, unable to look on her despair. The entire merchants' guild clubbed together and funded the expedition. I offered the *Prophet* and my own participation, as did the merchant Mr Parlaghy, whom you'll soon meet. But since we're businessmen and not thrill-seekers, we turned for help to the honourable Javil Fysh, known to us as a shrewd fellow and resourceful, unafraid of risk, adept in exacting matters, famous for his knowledge and experience . . .'

'The honourable Fysh, famous for his experience—' Geralt

glanced at him '—neglected to inform you that the rescue expedition is pointless and was doomed to failure from the start. I see
two explanations. Firstly: the honourable Fysh has no idea what
he's landing you in. Secondly, and more likely: the honourable
Fysh has received a payment, sizeable enough to lead you around
the middle of nowhere and return empty-handed.'

'You toss accusations around too eagerly!' With a gesture,
Kevenard van Vliet held back Fysh, who was spoiling to give a
furious rejoinder. 'You also too hastily predict a failure. While we,
merchants, always think positively . . .'

'You deserve credit for such thinking. But in this case it won't
help.'

'Why?'

'It's impossible to recover a child kidnapped by an aguara,' explained Geralt calmly. 'Absolutely impossible. And it's not even
that the child won't be found owing to the fact that she-foxes lead
extremely secretive lives. It's not even that the aguara won't let
you take the child away; and it's not an opponent to be trifled with
in a fight, either in vulpine or human form. The point is that a
kidnapped child ceases to be a child. Changes occur in little girls
abducted by she-foxes. They metamorphosise and became she-
foxes themselves. Aguaras don't reproduce. They maintain the
species by abducting and transforming elven children.'

'That vulpine species ought to perish.' Fysh finally had the floor.
'All those shape-changing abominations ought to perish. It's true
that she-foxes seldom get in people's way. They only kidnap elven
pups and only harm elves, which is good in itself, for the more
harm is done to non-humans, the greater the benefits for real folk.
But she-foxes are monsters, and monsters should be exterminated,
destroyed, should be wiped out as a race. You live from that, after
all, Witcher, you contribute to it. And I hope you won't bear us
a grudge either that we're contributing to the extermination of
monsters. But, it seems to me, these digressions are in vain. You
wanted explanations; you've got them. You know now what you're
being hired to do and against what . . . against what you have to
defend us.'

'No offence, but your explanations are as foggy as urine from an
infected bladder,' Geralt commented calmly. 'And the loftiness of

your expedition's goal is as dubious as a maiden's virginity after a village fête. But that's your business. It's my job to advise you that the only way to defend yourself against an aguara is to stay well away from it. Mr van Vliet?'

'Yes?'

'Return home. The expedition is senseless, so it's time to accept that and abandon it. That's as much as I can advise you as a witcher. The advice is free.'

'But you won't disembark, will you?' mumbled van Vliet, paling somewhat. 'Lord Witcher? Will you stay with us? And were . . . And were something to happen, will you protect us? Please agree . . . by the Gods, please say yes . . .'

'He'll agree, don't worry,' snorted Fysh. 'He'll sail with us. For who else will get him out of this wilderness? Don't panic, Mr van Vliet. There's nothing to fear.'

'Like hell there isn't!' yelled the glove-maker. 'That's a good one! You got us into this mess, and now you're playing the hero? I want to sail to Novigrad safe and sound. Someone must protect us, now that we're in difficulties . . . When we're in danger of—'

'We aren't in any danger. Don't fret like a woman. Go below decks like your companion Parlaghy. Drink some rum with him, then your courage will soon return.'

Kevenard van Vliet blushed, then blanched. Then met Geralt's eyes.

'Enough fudging,' he said emphatically, but calmly. 'Time to confess the truth. Master Witcher, we already have that young vixen. She's in the afterpeak. Mr Parlaghy's guarding her.'

Geralt shook his head.

'That's unbelievable. You snatched the furrier's daughter from the aguara. Little Xymena?'

Fysh spat over the side. Van Vliet scratched the back of his head.

'It wasn't what we planned,' he finally mumbled. 'A different one mistakenly fell into our hands . . . A she-fox too, but a different one . . . And kidnapped by quite another vixen. Mr Fysh bought her . . . from some soldiers who tricked the maid out of a she-fox. To begin with we thought it was Xymena, just transformed . . . But Xymena was seven years old and blonde, and this one's almost twelve and dark-haired . . .'

'We took her, even though she was the wrong one,' Fysh fore-stalled the Witcher. 'Why should elven spawn mature into an even worse monster? And in Novigrad we might be able to sell her to a menagerie; after all she's a curiosity, a savage, a half she-fox, raised in the forest by a vixen . . . An animal park will surely shower us with coin . . .'

The Witcher turned his back on him.

'Captain, steer towards the bank!'

'Not so fast,' growled Fysh. 'Hold your course, Pudlorak. You don't give the commands here, Witcher.'

'I appeal to your good sense, Mr van Vliet.' Geralt ignored him. 'The girl should be freed immediately and set down on the bank. Otherwise you're doomed. The aguara won't abandon her child. And is already certainly following you. The only way to stop her is to give up the girl.'

'Don't listen to him,' said Fysh. 'Don't let him frighten you. We're sailing on the river, on wide, deep water. What can some fox do to us?'

'And we have a witcher to protect us,' added Petru Cobbin derisively. 'Armed with invisible swords! The celebrated Geralt of Rivia won't take fright before any old she-fox!'

'I don't know, myself,' the glove-maker mumbled, his eyes sweeping from Fysh to Geralt and Pudlorak. 'Master Geralt? I'll be generous with a reward in Novigrad, I'll repay you handsomely for your exertions . . . If you'll only protect us.'

'I'll protect you by all means. In the only way possible. Captain, to the bank.'

'Don't you dare!' Fysh blanched. 'Not a step towards the after-peak, or you'll regret it! Cobbin!'

Petru Cobbin tried to seize Geralt by the collar, but was unable to because Addario Bach – up to that moment calm and taciturn – entered the fray. The dwarf kicked Cobbin vigorously behind the knee. Cobbin lurched forward into a kneeling position. Addario Bach leaped on him, gave him a tremendous punch in the kidney and then on the side of the head. The giant slumped onto the deck.

'So what if he's a big 'un?' said the dwarf, his gaze sweeping around the others. 'He just makes a louder bang when he hits the ground.'

213

Fysh's hand was hovering near his knife, but a glance from Addario Bach made him think better of it. Van Vliet stood open-mouthed. Like Captain Pudlorak and the rest of the crew.

Petru Cobbin groaned and peeled his head from the deck.

'Stay where you are,' the dwarf advised him. 'I'm neither impressed by your corpulence, nor the tattoo from Sturefors. I've done more damage to bigger fellows than you and inmates of harder prisons. So don't try getting up. Geralt, do what's necessary.

'If you're in any doubt,' he turned to the others, 'the Witcher and I are saving your lives this very moment. Captain, to the bank. And lower a boat.'

The Witcher descended the companionway, tugged open first one, then another door. And stopped dead. Behind him Addario Bach swore. Fysh also swore. Van Vliet groaned.

The eyes of the skinny girl sprawled limply on a bunk were glazed. She was half-naked, quite bare from the waist downwards, her legs spread obscenely. Her neck was twisted unnaturally. And even more obscenely.

'Mr Parlaghy . . .' van Vliet stammered out. 'What . . . What have you done?'

The bald individual sitting over the girl looked up at them. He moved his head as though he couldn't see them, as though he were searching for the origin of the glove-maker's voice.

'Mr Parlaghy!'

'She was screaming . . .' muttered the man, his double chin wobbling and his breath smelling of alcohol. 'She started screaming . . .'

'Mr Parlaghy . . .'

'I meant to quiet her . . . Only quiet her.'

'But you've killed her.' Fysh stated a fact. 'You've simply killed her!'

Van Vliet held his head in his hands.

'And what now?'

'Now,' the dwarf told him bluntly, 'we're well and truly fucked.'

*

'There's no cause for alarm!' Fysh punched the railing hard. 'We're on the river, on the deep water. The banks are far away.

Even if – which I doubt – the she-fox is following us, she can't endanger us on the water.'

'Master Witcher?' Van Vliet timidly raised his eyes. 'What say you?'

'The aguara is stalking us,' Geralt repeated patiently. 'There is no doubt about that. If anything is doubtful, it's the expertise of Mr Fysh, whom I would ask to remain silent in relation to that. Things are as follows, Mr van Vliet: had we freed the young she-fox and left her on land, the aguara might have let up on us. But what is done, is done. And now only flight can save us. The miracle that the aguara didn't attack you earlier shows indeed that fortune favours fools. But we may not tempt fate any longer. Hoist all the sails, captain. As many as you have.'

'We can also raise the lower topsail,' Pudlorak said slowly. 'The wind's in our favour—'

'And if . . .' van Vliet cut him off. 'Master Witcher? Will you defend us, sir?'

'I'll be straight, Mr van Vliet. Ideally, I'd leave you. Along with Parlaghy, the very thought of whom turns my stomach, and who's below deck, getting plastered over the corpse of the child he killed—'

'I'd also be inclined to do that,' interjected Addario Bach, looking upwards. 'For, to paraphrase the words of Mr Fysh about non-humans: the more harm happens to idiots, the greater the benefits to the judicious.'

'I'd leave Parlaghy to the mercy of the aguara. But the code forbids me. The witcher code doesn't permit me to act according to my own wishes. I cannot abandon anyone in peril of death.'

'Witcher nobility!' snorted Fysh. 'As though no one had ever heard of your villainy! But I support the idea of a swift escape. Unfurl all the canvas, Pudlorak, sail onto the shipping route and let's beat it!'

The captain issued his orders and the deckhands set about the rigging. Pudlorak himself headed for the bow, and after a moment of consideration Geralt and the dwarf joined him. Van Vliet, Fysh and Cobbin were quarrelling on the afterdeck.

'Mr Pudlorak?'

'Yes?'

'Why is the ship so named? And that pretty unusual figurehead? Was it meant to persuade the priests to finance you?'

'The cutter was launched as *Melusine*.' The captain shrugged. 'With a figurehead that suited the name and pleased the eye. Then they were both changed. Some said it was all about sponsorship. Others that the Novigradian priests were constantly accusing van Vliet of heresy and blasphemy, so he wanted to kiss their . . . Wanted to curry favour with them.'

The *Prophet Lebioda*'s prow cut through the water.

'Geralt?'

'What, Addario?'

'That she-fox . . . I mean the aguara . . . From what I've heard she can change shape. She can appear as a woman, but may also assume the form of a fox. Just like a werewolf?'

'Not exactly. Werewolves, werebears, wererats and similar creatures are therianthropes, humans able to shapeshift. The aguara is an antherion. An animal – or rather a creature – able to assume the form of a human.'

'And its powers? I've heard incredible stories . . . The aguara is said to be able to—'

'I hope we'll get to Novigrad before the aguara shows us what she's capable of,' the Witcher interrupted.

'And if—'

'It'd be better to avoid the "if".'

The wind sprang up. The sails fluttered.

'The sky's growing darker,' said Addario Bach, pointing. 'And I think I detected some distant thunder.'

The dwarf's hearing served him well. After barely a few moments it thundered again. This time they all heard it.

'A squall's approaching!' yelled Pudlorak. 'On the deep water, it'll capsize us! We must flee, hide, protect ourselves from the wind! All hands to the sails, boys!'

He shoved the steersman out of the way and took the helm himself.

'Hold on! Hold on, every man!'

The sky over starboard had turned a dark indigo. Suddenly a gale blew in, whipping the trees on the steep riverbank, tossing them around. The crowns of the larger trees swayed, the smaller

216

ones bent over. A cloud of leaves and entire branches, even large boughs, were blown away. Lightning flashed blindingly, and almost at the same moment a piercing crack of thunder reverberated. Another crash followed it almost immediately. And a third.

The next moment, presaged by a growing swooshing noise, the rain came lashing down. They could see nothing beyond the wall of water. The *Prophet Lebioda* rocked and danced on the waves, rolling and pitching sharply every few seconds. On top of that everything was creaking. It seemed to Geralt that each plank was groaning. Each plank was living its own life and moving, so it seemed, totally independently of the others. He feared that the cutter would simply disintegrate. The Witcher repeated to himself that it was impossible, that the ship had been constructed to sail even rougher waters, and that after all they were on a river, not an ocean. He repeated it to himself, spitting water and tightly clutching the rigging.

It was difficult to tell how long it lasted. Finally, though, the rocking ceased, the wind stopped raging, and the heavy downpour churning up the water eased off, becoming rain, then drizzle. At that moment, they saw that Pudlorak's manoeuvre had succeeded. The captain had managed to shelter the cutter behind a tall, forested island where the gale didn't toss them around so much. The raincloud seemed to be moving away, the squall dying down.

Fog rose from the water.

*

Water was dripping from Pudlorak's drenched cap and running down his face. In spite of that the captain didn't remove it. He probably never did.

'Blood and thunder!' he said, wiping the drops from his nose. 'Where has it taken us? Is it a distributary? Or an old river bed? The water is almost still . . .'

'But the current's still carrying us.' Fysh spat into the water and watched the spittle flow past. He'd lost his straw hat; the gale must have blown it off.

'The current is weak, but it's carrying us,' he repeated. 'We're in an inlet between some islands. Hold the course, Pudlorak. It must finally take us to the deep water.'

'I reckon the waterway is to the north,' said the captain, stooping over the compass. 'So we ought to take the starboard branch. Not the port, but the starboard . . .'

'Where do you see branches?' asked Fysh. 'There's one river. Hold the course, I say.'

'A moment ago there were two,' Pudlorak insisted. 'But maybe I had water in me eyes. Or it was that fog. Very well, let the current carry us. It's just that—'

'What now?'

'The compass. It's pointing completely . . . No, no, it's all right. I couldn't see it clearly. Water was dripping onto the glass from my cap. We're sailing.'

'So, let's sail.'

The fog was growing denser and thinner by turns, and the wind had completely died down. It had grown very warm.

'The water,' Pudlorak said. 'Can you smell it? It has a different kind of smell. Where are we?'

The fog lifted and they saw dense undergrowth on the banks, which were strewn with rotten tree trunks. Instead of the pines, firs and yews covering the islands, there were now bushy river birches and tall cypresses, bulbous at the base. The trunks of the cypresses were entwined around with climbing trumpet vines, whose garish red flowers were the only vibrant feature among the brownish green swampy flora. The water was carpeted in duckweed and was full of water weed, which the *Prophet* parted with its prow and dragged behind it like a train. The water was cloudy and indeed gave off a hideous, somehow rank odour. Large bubbles rose up from the bottom. Pudlorak was at the helm by himself again.

'There may be shallows,' he said, suddenly becoming anxious. 'Hey, there! Leadsman fore!'

They sailed on, borne by the weak current, never leaving the marshy landscape. Or rotten stench. The deckhand at the prow yelled monotonously, calling out the depth.

'Take a look at this, Master Witcher,' said Pudlorak, stooping over the compass and tapping the glass.

'At what?'

'I thought the glass was steamed up . . . But if the needle hasn't gone doolally, we're sailing eastwards. Meaning we're going back. Where we came from.'

'But that's impossible. We're being carried by the current. The river—'

He broke off.

A huge tree, its roots partly exposed, hung over the water. A woman in a long, clinging dress was standing on one of the bare boughs. She was motionless, looking at them.

'The wheel,' said the Witcher softly. 'The wheel, captain. Towards that bank. Away from the tree.'

The woman vanished. And a large fox slunk along the bough, dashed away and hid in the thicket. The animal seemed to be black and only the tip of its bushy tail white.

'She's found us.' Addario Bach had also seen her. 'The vixen has found us . . .'

'Blood and thunder—'

'Be quiet, both of you. Don't spread panic.'

They glided on. Watched by pelicans from the dead trees on the banks.

INTERLUDE

A hundred and twenty-seven years later

'That'll be Ivalo, miss, yonder, beyond the hillock,' said the merchant, pointing with his whip. 'Half a furlong, no more, you'll be there in a trice. I head eastwards towards Maribor at the crossroads, so the time has come to part. Farewell, may the gods lead you and watch over you on your way.'

'And over you, good sir,' said Nimue, hopping down from the wagon, taking her bundle and the rest of her things and then curtsying clumsily. 'My sincere thanks for the ride on your wagon. Back there in the forest . . . My sincere thanks . . .'

She swallowed at the memory of the dark forest, deep into which the highway had led her for the last two days. At the memory of the huge, ghastly trees with their twisted boughs, entwined into a canopy above the deserted road. A road where she'd suddenly found herself all alone. At the memory of the horror that had seized her. And the memory of the desire to turn tail and fly. Home. Abandoning the preposterous thought of journeying into the world alone. And banishing that preposterous thought from her memory.

'My goodness, don't thank me, it's a trifle,' laughed the merchant. 'Anyone would help a traveller. Farewell!'

'Farewell. I wish you a safe journey.'

She stood for a moment at the crossroads, looking at a stone post, polished to a smooth slipperiness by the wind and rain. *It must have stood here for ages*, she thought. *Who knows, perhaps more than a hundred years? Perhaps this post remembers the Year of the Comet? The army of the northern kings, marching to Brenna, and the battle with Nilfgaard?*

As every day, she repeated the route she'd learned by heart. Like a magical formula. Like a spell.

Vyrva, Guado, Sibell, Brugge, Casterfurt, Mortara, Ivalo, Dorian, Anchor, Gors Velen.

The town of Ivalo made itself known from a distance. By its noise and foul smell.

The forest ended at the crossroads. Further on, there was only a bare clearing, bristling with tree stumps, stretching out far away towards the horizon and the first buildings. Smoke was trailing everywhere. Rows of iron vats – retorts for making charcoal – were smoking. There was a smell of resin. The nearer the town, the louder grew the noise: a strange metallic clank, making the ground shudder perceptibly beneath her feet.

Nimue entered the town and gasped in amazement. The source of the noise and the shuddering of the ground was the most bizarre machine she had ever seen. A huge, bulbous copper cauldron with an enormous wheel, whose revolutions drove a piston shining with grease. The machine hissed, smoked, spluttered boiling water and belched steam, then at a certain moment uttered a whistle, a whistle so horrifying and dreadful that Nimue was dumbfounded. But she quickly overcame her fear, even approaching closer and curiously examining the belts which the gears of the hellish machine used to drive the saws in the mill, cutting trunks at incredible speed. She would have continued watching, but her ears began to hurt from the rumbling and grinding of the saws.

She crossed a bridge; the small river below was murky and stank repugnantly, bearing woodchips, bark and flecks of foam. The town of Ivalo, however, which she had just entered, reeked like one great latrine, a latrine, where, to make matters worse, somebody had insisted on roasting bad meat. Nimue, who'd spent the previous week among meadows and forests, began to choke. The town of Ivalo, which marked the end of another stage on her route, had seemed like a resting place to her. Now she knew she wouldn't tarry any longer than was absolutely necessary. Nor add Ivalo to her store of pleasant recollections.

As usual she sold a punnet of mushrooms and medicinal roots at the market. It didn't take long; she was now practised, knowing what there was demand for, and whom she should go to with her wares. She pretended to be half-witted, owing to which she had no problem selling, the stallholders vying with each other to outwit the dull girl. She earned little but didn't waste time. For speed mattered.

The only source of clean water in the vicinity was a well in a narrow little square, and in order to fill her canteen, Nimue had to wait her turn in a lengthy queue. Acquiring provisions for the next stage of her journey went more smoothly. Enticed by the smell, she also bought several stuffed pasties, which on closer inspection seemed suspicious. She sat down by a dairy to eat them while they were still tolerably fit to be consumed without seriously damaging her health. For it didn't look as though they would continue in that state for long.

Opposite was a tavern called the Green-something; the sign's missing lower plank had turned the name into a riddle and intellectual challenge. A moment later, Nimue became engrossed by her attempts to guess what – apart from frogs and lettuce – could be green. She was startled out of her reverie by a loud discussion being conducted on the tavern's steps by a small group of regulars.

'The *Prophet Lebioda*, I tell you,' ranted one of them. 'The legendary brig. That ghost ship that vanished without trace more than a hundred years back with all hands. And would later appear on the river when misfortune was in the air. Manned by a ghostly crew; many saw it. People said it would continue to appear as a spectre until the wreck was found. Well, and they finally found it.'

'Where?'

'In Rivermouth, on an old river bed, in the mud, in the very heart of a bog what they was drying out. It was all overgrown with weed. And moss. After they'd scraped off the weed and moss they found the inscription. The *Prophet Lebioda*.'

'And treasure? Did they find any treasure? There was meant to be treasure there, in the hold. Did they find any?'

'No one knows. The priests, they say, confiscated the wreck. Calling it a holy relic.'

'What nonsense,' hiccupped another regular. 'Believing in them childish tales. They found some old tub, and then at once: ghost ship, treasure, relics. I tell you, all that's bullshit, trashy writing, foolish rumours, old wives' tales. I say, you there! Wench! Who be you? Whose are you?'

'My own.' Nimue had a ready answer by then.

'Brush your hair aside and show us your ear! For you look like elven spawn. And we don't want elven half-breeds here!'

'Let me be, for I don't incommode you. And I'll soon be setting off.'

'Ha! And whither do you go?'

'To Dorian.' Nimue had also learned to always give as her destination only the next stage, in order never, ever, to reveal the final objective of her trek, because that only caused great merriment.

'Ho-ho! You've a long road ahead of you.'

'Hence, I am about to go. And I'll just tell you, noble gentlemen, that the *Prophet Lebioda* wasn't carrying any treasure, the legend doesn't say anything about that. The ship vanished and became a ghost because she was cursed and her skipper hadn't acted on good advice. The witcher who was there advised them to turn the ship around, not to venture into an offshoot of the river until he'd removed the curse. I read about that—'

'Still wet behind the ears and such a clever clogs?' pronounced the first regular. 'You should be sweeping floors, wench, minding pots and laundering smalls, simple as that. Says she can read – whatever next?'

'A witcher!' snorted a third. 'Tall tales, naught but tall tales!'

'If you're such a know-it-all you must have heard of our Magpie Forest,' interjected another. 'What, you haven't? Then we'll tell you: something evil lurks there. But it awakes every few years, and then woe betide anyone who wanders through the forest. And your route, if you're truly headed for Dorian, passes right through Magpie Forest.'

'And do any trees still stand there? For you've cut down everything, nothing but bare clearings remain.'

'Just look what a know-it-all she is, a mouthy stripling. What's a forest for if not to be cut down, eh? What we felled, we felled, what remains, remains. But the woodcutters fear to enter Magpie Forest, such a horror is there. You'll see for yourself if you get that far. You'll piss in your pants from fear!'

'I'd better be off then.'

Vyrva, Guado, Sibell, Brugge, Casterfurt, Mortara, Ivalo, Dorian, Anchor, Gors Velen.

I'm Nimue verch Wledyr ap Gwyn.

I'm headed for Gors Velen. To Aretuza, to the school of sorceresses on the Isle of Thanedd.

CHAPTER FIFTEEN

'You've made a pretty mess, Pudlorak!' Javil Fysh spat furiously. 'You've got us in a pretty tangle! We've been wandering around these offshoots for an hour! I've heard about these bogs, I've heard evil things about them! People and ships perish here! Where's the river? Where's the shipping channel? Why—'

'Shut your trap, by thunder!' said the captain in annoyance. 'Where's the shipping channel, where's the shipping lane? Up my arse, that's where! So clever, are you? Be my guest, now's a chance to distinguish yourself! There's another fork! Where should we sail, smart aleck? To port, as the current carries us? Or perhaps you'll order us starboard?'

Fysh snorted and turned his back on him. Pudlorak grabbed the wheel and steered the cutter into the left branch.

The leadsman gave a cry. Then a moment later Kevenard van Vliet yelled, but much louder.

'Away from the bank, Pudlorak!' screamed Petru Cobbin. 'Hard-a-starboard! Away from the bank! Away from the bank!'

'What is it?'

'Serpents! Don't you see them? Seeerpents!'

Addario Bach swore.

The left bank was teeming with snakes. The reptiles were writhing among the reeds and riverside weeds, crawling over half-submerged trunks, dangling down, hissing, from overhanging branches. Geralt recognised cottonmouths, rattlesnakes, jararacas, boomslangs, green bush vipers, puff adders, arietes, black mambas and others he didn't know.

The entire crew of the *Prophet* fled in panic from the port side, yelling at various pitches. Kevenard van Vliet ran astern and squatted down, trembling all over, behind the Witcher. Pudlorak turned the wheel and the cutter began to change course. Geralt placed his hand on Pudlorak's shoulder.

'No,' he said. 'Hold the course, as you were. Don't go near the starboard bank.'

'But the snakes . . .' Pudlorak pointed at the branch they were approaching, hung all over with hissing reptiles. 'They'll drop onto the deck—'

'There are no snakes! Hold the course. Away from the starboard bank.'

The sheets of the mainmast caught on a hanging branch. Several snakes coiled themselves around them, and several others – including two mambas – dropped onto the deck. Raising their heads and hissing, they attacked the men huddled up against the starboard side. Fysh and Cobbin fled aft and the deckhands, yelling, bolted astern. One of them jumped into the water and disappeared before he could cry out. Blood frothed on the surface.

'A lopustre!' shouted the Witcher, pointing at a wave and a dark shape moving away. 'It's real – unlike the snakes.'

'I detest reptiles . . .' sobbed Kevenard van Vliet, huddled up by the side. 'I detest snakes—'

'There aren't any snakes. And there weren't any. It's an illusion.'

The deckhands shouted and rubbed their eyes. The snakes had vanished. Both from the deck and from the bank. They hadn't even left any tracks.

'What . . .' Petru Cobbin grunted. 'What was it?'

'An illusion,' repeated Geralt. 'The aguara has caught up with us.'

'You what?'

'The vixen. She's creating illusions to confuse us. I wonder how long she's been doing it. The storm was probably genuine. But there were two offshoots, the captain's eyes didn't deceive him. The aguara cloaked one of the offshoots in an illusion. And faked the compass needle. She also created the illusion of the snakes.'

'Witcher tall tales!' Fysh snorted. 'Elven superstitions! Old wives' tales! What, some old fox has abilities like that? Hides rivers, confounds compasses? Conjures up serpents where there aren't any? Fiddlesticks! I tell you it's these waters! We were poisoned by vapours, venomous swamp gases and miasmas! That's what caused those hallucinations . . .'

'They're illusions created by the aguara.'

228

'Do you take us for fools?' yelled Cobbin. 'Illusions? What illusions? Those were real vipers! You all saw them, didn't you? Heard the hissing? I even smelled their stench!'

'That was an illusion. The snakes weren't real.'

The *Prophet*'s sheets snagged on overhanging branches again.

'That's a hallucination, is it?' asked one of the deckhands, holding out his hand. 'An illusion? That snake isn't real?'

'No! Stand still!'

The huge ariete hanging from a bough gave a blood-curdling hiss and struck like lightning, sinking its fangs into the sailor's neck: once, twice. The deckhand gave a piercing scream, fell, shaking in convulsions, banging the back of his head rhythmically against the deck. Foam appeared on his lips and blood began to ooze from his eyes. He was dead before they could get to him.

The Witcher covered the body in a canvas sheet.

'Dammit, men,' he said. 'Be heedful! Not everything here is a mirage!'

'Beware!' yelled the sailor in the bow. 'Bewaaare! There's a whirlpool ahead of us! A whirlpool!'

The old river bed branched again. The left branch, the one the current was carrying them into, was swirling and churned up in a raging whirlpool. The swirling maelstrom was surging with froth like soup in a cauldron. Logs and branches, and even an entire tree with a forked crown, were revolving in the whirlpool. The leadsman fled from the bow and the others began to yell. Pudlorak stood calmly. He turned the wheel, steering the cutter towards the calmer offshoot to the right.

'Uff!' He wiped his forehead. 'Just in time! Would have been ill if that whirlpool had sucked us in. Aye, would have given us a right old spinning . . .'

'Whirlpools!' shouted Cobbin. 'Lopustres! Alligators! Leeches! We don't need no illusions, these swamps are teeming with monstrosities, with reptiles, with every kind of venomous filth. It's too bad, too bad that we strayed here. Many ships—'

'—have vanished here.' Addario Bach finished the sentence, pointing. 'And that's probably real.'

There was a wreck lying stuck in the mud on the right bank. It was rotten and smashed, buried up to the bulwarks, covered in water weed, coiled around with vines and moss. They observed it as the *Prophet* glided past, borne by the faint current.

Pudlorak prodded Geralt with his elbow.

'Master Witcher,' he said softly. 'The compass has gone doolally again. According to the needle we've moved from an eastwards course to a southern. If it's not a vulpine trick, it's not good. No one has ever charted these swamps, but it's known they extend southwards from the shipping channel. So, we're being carried into the very heart of them.'

'But we're drifting,' observed Addario Bach. 'There's no wind, we're being borne by the current. And the current means we're joining the river, the river current of the Pontar—'

'Not necessarily,' said Geralt, shaking his head. 'I've heard about these old river courses. The direction of the flow can change. Depending on whether the tide's coming in or going out. And don't forget about the aguara. This might also be an illusion.'

The banks were still densely covered in cypresses, and large, pot-bellied tupelos, bulbous at the base, were also growing more common. Many of the trees were dead and dry. Dense festoons of bromeliads hung from the decayed trunks and branches, their leaves shining silver in the sun. Egrets lay in wait on the branches, surveying the passing *Prophet* with unmoving eyes.

The leadsman shouted.

This time everybody saw it. Once again, she was standing on a bough hanging over the water, erect and motionless. Pudlorak unhurriedly leaned on a handle, steering the cutter towards the left bank. And the vixen suddenly barked, loudly and piercingly. She barked again as the *Prophet* sailed past.

A large fox flashed across the bough and hid in the undergrowth.

*

'That was a warning,' said the Witcher, when the hubbub on deck had quietened down. 'A warning and a challenge. Or rather a demand.'

'We would free the girl,' Addario Bach added astutely. 'Of course we would. But we can't free her if she's dead.'

Kevenard van Vliet groaned and clutched his temples. Wet, dirty and terrified, he no longer resembled a merchant who could afford his own ship. More an urchin caught scrumping plums.

'What to do?' he moaned. 'What to do?'

'I know,' Javil Fysh suddenly declared. 'We'll fasten the dead wench to a barrel and toss her overboard. The vixen will stop to mourn the pup. We'll gain time.'

'Shame on you, Mr Fysh.' The glove-maker's voice suddenly hardened. 'It doesn't do to treat a corpse thus. It's not civilised.'

'And was she civilised? A she-elf, on top of that half an animal. I tell you; that barrel's a good idea . . .'

'That idea could only occur to a complete idiot,' said Addario Bach, drawing out his words. 'And it would be the death of us all. If the vixen realises we've killed the girl we're finished—'

'It wasn't us as killed the pup,' butted in Petru Cobbin, before Fysh – now scarlet with anger – could react. 'It wasn't us. Parlaghy did it. He's to blame. We're clean.'

'That's right,' confirmed Fysh, turning not towards van Vliet and the Witcher, but to Pudlorak and the deckhands. 'Parlaghy's guilty. Let the vixen take vengeance on him. We'll shove him in a boat with the corpse and they can drift away. And meanwhile, we'll . .'

Cobbin and several deckhands received the idea with an enthusiastic cry, but Pudlorak immediately dampened their enthusiasm.

'I shan't permit it,' he said.

'Nor I.' Kevenard van Vliet was pale. 'Mr Parlaghy may indeed be guilty, perhaps it's true that his deed calls for punishment. But abandon him, leave him to his death? I will not agree.'

'It's his death or ours!' yelled Fysh. 'For what are we to do? Witcher! Will you protect us when the she-fox boards the craft?'

'I shall.'

A silence fell.

The *Prophet Lebioda* drifted among the stinking water seething with bubbles, dragging behind it garlands of water weed. Egrets and pelicans watched them from the branches.

*

The leadsman in the bow warned them with a cry. And a moment later they all began to shout. To see the rotten wreck, covered in climbing plants and weed. It was the same wreck they'd passed an hour before.

'We're sailing around in circles.' The dwarf confirmed the fact. 'We're back where we started. The she-fox has caught us in a trap.'

'There's only one way out.' Geralt pointed at the left offshoot and the whirlpool seething in it. 'To sail through that.'

'Through that geyser?' yelled Fysh. 'Have you gone quite mad? It'll smash us to pieces!'

'Smash us to pieces,' confirmed Pudlorak. 'Or capsize us. Or throw us onto the bog, and we'll end up like that wreck. See those trees being tossed about in the maelstrom? That whirlpool is tremendously powerful.'

'Indeed. It is. Because it's probably an illusion. I think it's another of the aguara's illusions.'

'You think? You're a witcher and you can't tell?'

'I'd recognise a weaker illusion. And these ones are incredibly powerful. But I reckon—'

'You reckon. And if you're wrong?'

'We have no choice,' snapped Pudlorak. 'Either we go through the whirlpool or we sail around in circles—'

'—to our deaths.' Addario Bach finished his sentence. 'To our miserable deaths.'

*

Every few moments the boughs of the tree spinning around in the whirlpool stuck up out of the water like the outstretched arms of a drowned corpse. The whirlpool churned, seethed, surged and sprayed foam. The *Prophet* shivered and suddenly shot forward, sucked into the maelstrom. The tree being tossed by the whirlpool slammed against the side, splashing foam. The cutter began to rock and spin around quicker and quicker.

The entire crew were yelling at various pitches.

And suddenly everything went quiet. The water calmed down and the surface became smooth. The *Prophet Lebioda* drifted very slowly between the tupelos on the banks.

'You were right, Geralt,' said Addario Bach, clearing his throat. 'It was an illusion after all.'

Pudlorak looked long at the witcher. And said nothing. He finally took off his cap. His crown, as it turned out, was as shiny as an egg.

'I signed up for river navigation,' he finally croaked, 'because my wife asked me to. *It'll be safer on the river*, she said. *Safer than on the sea. I won't have to fret each time you set sail*, she said.'

He put his cap back on, shook his head, then tightly grabbed a handle of the wheel.

'Is that it?' Kevenard van Vliet whimpered from under the cockpit. 'Are we safe now?'

No one answered his question.

*

The water was thick with algae and duckweed. Cypresses began to dominate the riverside trees, their pneumatophores – or aerial roots, some of them almost six feet tall – sticking up densely from the bog and the shallows by the bank. Turtles basked on islands of weed. Frogs croaked.

This time they heard her before they saw her. A loud, raucous barking like a threat or a warning being intoned. She appeared on the bank in her vulpine form, on a withered, overturned tree trunk. She was barking, holding her head up high. Geralt detected strange notes in her voice and understood that apart from the threats there was an order. But it wasn't them she was giving orders to.

The water under the trunk suddenly frothed and a monster emerged. It was enormous, covered all over in a greenish-brown pattern of tear-shaped scales. It gobbled and squelched, obediently following the vixen's order, and swam, churning up the water, straight at the *Prophet*.

'Is that . . .?' Addario Bach swallowed. 'Is that an illusion too?'

'Not exactly,' said Geralt. 'It's a vodyanoy!' He yelled at Pudlorak and the deckhands. 'She's bewitched a vodyanoy and set it on us! Boathooks! All hands to the boathooks!'

The vodyanoy broke the surface alongside the ship and they saw the flat, algae-covered head, the bulging fishy eyes and the conical teeth in its great maw. The monster struck the side furiously, once, twice, making the whole ship shudder. When the crew came running up with boathooks it fled and dived, only to emerge with a splash beyond the stern a moment later, right by the rudder blade. Which it caught in its teeth and shook until it creaked.

'It'll break the rudder!' Pudlorak bellowed, trying to stab the monster with a boathook. 'It'll break the rudder! Grab the halyards and raise it! Drive the bastard away from the rudder!'

The vodyanoy chewed and jerked the rudder, oblivious to the cries and jabs of the boathooks. The blade gave way and a chunk of wood was left in the creature's teeth. It had either decided that was enough or the she-fox's spell had lost its force; suffice it to say that it dived and disappeared.

They heard the aguara barking from the bank.

'What next?' yelled Pudlorak, waving his arms. 'What will she do next? Master Witcher!'

'By the Gods . . .' sobbed Kevenard van Vliet. 'Forgive us for not believing . . . Forgive us for killing the little girl! Ye Gods, save us!'

They suddenly felt a breeze on their faces. The pennant on the *Prophet* – previously hanging pitifully – fluttered and the boom creaked.

'It's opening out!' Fysh shouted from the bow. 'Over there, over there! A broad water, there's no doubt it's the river! Sail over there, skipper! Over there!'

The river channel was indeed beginning to widen and something looking like broad water stretched beyond the green wall of reeds.

'We did it!' called Cobbin. 'Ha! We've won! We've escaped from the swamp!'

'By the mark one,' yelled the leadsman. 'By the mark o-o-one.'

'Haul her over!' roared Pudlorak, shoving the helmsman away and carrying out his own order. 'Shallooows!'

The *Prophet Lebioda*'s prow turned towards the offshoot bristling with pneumatophores.

'Where are you going?' Fysh bellowed. 'What are you doing? Sail for the broad water. Over there! Over there!'

'We can't. There's a shallow there. We'll get stuck! We'll sail to the broad water along an offshoot, it's deeper here.'

234

They heard the aguara bark again. But didn't see her.

Addario Bach tugged Geralt's sleeve.

Petru Cobbin emerged from the companionway of the after-peak, dragging Parlaghy – who could barely stay on his feet – by the collar. A sailor followed him carrying the girl, wrapped in a cloak. The other four deckhands stood steadfastly beside them, facing the Witcher. They were holding battleaxes, tridents and iron hooks.

'You can't stop us, good sir,' rasped the tallest of them. 'We want to live. The time has come to act.'

'Leave the child,' drawled Geralt. 'Let the merchant go, Cobbin.'

'No, sir.' The sailor shook his head. 'We'll toss the body and the merchant overboard; that'll stop the beast. Then we'll get away.'

'And don't you lot interfere,' wheezed another. 'We've nothing against you, but don't stand in our way. Because you'll get hurt.'

Kevenard van Vliet curled up by the side and sobbed, turning his head away. Pudlorak also looked away resignedly and pursed his lips. He clearly wouldn't react to his own crew's mutiny.

'Yes, that's right,' said Petru Cobbin, shoving Parlaghy. 'Toss the merchant and the dead vixen overboard, that's our only chance of escape. Out of the way, Witcher! Go on, boys! Into the boat with them!'

'What boat?' asked Addario Bach calmly. 'Do you mean that one, perhaps?'

Javil Fysh, hunched over the oars of a boat, was rowing, heading for the broad water, already quite far from the *Prophet*. He was rowing hard; the oar blades were splashing water and strewing water weed around.

'Fysh!' yelled Cobbin. 'You bastard! You fucking whoreson!'

Fysh turned around and raised his middle finger at them. Then took up the oars again.

But he didn't get far.

In full view of the *Prophet*'s crew the boat suddenly shot up in a jet of water and they saw the toothy jaws of a gigantic crocodile, its tail thrashing. Fysh flew overboard and began to swim – screaming all the while – towards the bank, where cypress roots bristled in the shallows. The crocodile set off in pursuit, but the palisade of

235

pneumatophores impeded its progress. Fysh swam to the bank and flopped down chest-first on a boulder lying there. But it wasn't a boulder.

An enormous lizard-like turtle opened its jaws and seized Fysh by his upper arm. He howled, struggled, kicked, flinging mud around. The crocodile broke the surface and caught him by the leg. Fysh screamed.

For a moment, it wasn't clear which of the two reptiles would catch Fysh – the turtle or the crocodile. But finally, both of them got something. An arm with a white, club-shaped bone sticking out of bloody pulp was left in the turtle's jaws. The crocodile took the rest of Fysh's body. A large red patch floated on the surface of the murky water.

Geralt took advantage of the crew's stupefaction. He snatched the dead girl from the deckhand and retreated towards the bow. Addario Bach stood beside him, armed with a boathook.

Neither Cobbin nor any of the sailors tried to oppose him. On the contrary, they all ran hastily to the stern. Hastily. Not to say in a panic. Their faces suddenly took on a deathly pallor. Kevenard van Vliet, huddled by the side, hid his head between his knees and covered it with his arms.

Geralt turned around.

Whether Pudlorak hadn't been paying attention or the rudder – damaged by the vodyanoy – wasn't working, suffice it to say that the cutter had sailed right under some hanging boughs and was caught among fallen tree trunks. The aguara took advantage of it. She leaped down onto the prow, nimbly, lightly and noiselessly. In her vulpine form. Previously he'd seen her against the sky, when she had seemed black, pitch-black. She wasn't. Her fur was dark and her brush ended in a snow-white blotch, but grey prevailed in her colouring, particularly on her head, which was more typical of a corsac fox than a silver one.

She metamorphosed, growing larger and transforming into a tall woman. With a fox's head. Pointed ears and an elongated muzzle. Rows of fangs flashed when she opened her jaws.

Geralt knelt down, placed the little girl's body gently on the deck and retreated. The aguara howled piercingly, snapped her toothy jaws and stepped towards him. Parlaghy screamed, waving his arms in panic, tore himself away from Cobbin's grasp and jumped overboard. He sank at once.

Van Vliet was weeping. Cobbin and the deckhands, still pale, gathered around Pudlorak. Pudlorak removed his cap.

The medallion around the Witcher's neck twitched powerfully, vibrated and made its presence felt. The aguara kneeled over the girl, making strange noises, neither growling nor hissing. She suddenly raised her head and bared her fangs. She snarled softly and a fire flared up in her eyes. Geralt didn't move.

'We are to blame,' he said. 'Something truly ill has happened. But may no worse things occur. I cannot allow you to harm these men. I shall not allow it.'

The vixen stood up, lifting the little girl. She swept her gaze over them all. And finally looked at Geralt.

'You stood in my way,' she barked, clearly, slowly enunciating each word. 'In their defence.'

He didn't answer.

'I am taking my daughter,' she finished. 'That is more important than your lives. But it was you who stood in their defence, O White-Haired One. Thus, I shall come looking for you. One day. When you have forgotten. And will be least expecting it.'

She hopped nimbly onto the bulwark and then onto a fallen trunk. And disappeared into the undergrowth.

In the silence that fell only van Vliet's sobbing could be heard.

The wind dropped and it became muggy. The *Prophet Lebioda*, pushed by the current, freed itself from the boughs and drifted down the middle of the offshoot. Pudlorak wiped his eyes and forehead with his cap.

The leadsman cried. Cobbin cried. And then the others added their voices.

The thatched roofs of cottages could suddenly be seen beyond the thicket of reeds and wild-rice. They saw nets drying on poles. A yellow strip of sandy beach. A jetty. And further away, beyond the trees on the headland, the wide river beneath a blue sky.

'The river! The river! At last!'

They all shouted. The deckhands, Petru Cobbin and van Vliet. Only Geralt and Addario Bach didn't join in the yelling.

Pudlorak, pushing on the wheel, also said nothing.

'What are you doing?' yelled Cobbin. 'Where are you going? Head for the river! Over there! For the river!'

'Not a chance,' said the captain, and there was despair and resignation in his voice. 'We're becalmed, the ship barely responds to the wheel and the current grows stronger. We're drifting, it's pushing us, carrying us into the offshoot again. Back into the swamp.'

'No!' Cobbin swore. And leaped overboard. And swam towards the beach.

All the sailors followed his example. Geralt was unable to stop any of them. Addario Bach roughly shoved down van Vliet, who was preparing to jump.

'Blue sky,' he said. 'A golden, sandy beach. The river. It's too beautiful to be true. Meaning it isn't.'

And suddenly the image shimmered. Suddenly, where a moment earlier there had been fishing cottages, a golden beach and the river beyond the headland, the Witcher for a brief moment saw a spider's web of tillandsia trailing right down to the water from the boughs of decaying trees. Swampy banks, cypresses bristling with pneumatophores. Bubbles rising up from the murky depths. A sea of water plants. An endless labyrinth of branches.

For a second, he saw what the aguara's final illusion had been hiding.

The men in the water began to suddenly scream and thrash around. And disappear below the surface, one by one.

Petru Cobbin came up for air, choking and screaming, covered entirely in writhing, striped leeches, as fat as eels. Then he sank below the water and didn't come up again.

'Geralt!'

Addario Bach used the boathook to pull the small boat, which had survived the encounter with the crocodile and had now drifted to the side of the ship. The dwarf jumped in and Geralt passed him the still stupefied van Vliet.

'Captain.'

Pudlorak waved his cap at them.

'No, Master Witcher! I shall not abandon my ship. I'll guide her into port, whatever happens! And if not, I'll go down to the bottom with her! Farewell!'

The *Prophet Lebioda* drifted calmly and majestically, gliding into an offshoot and vanishing from sight.

Addario Bach spat on his hands, hunched forward and pulled on the oars. The boat sped over the water.

'Where to?'

'To the broad water, beyond the shallows. The river's there. I'm certain. We'll join the shipping channel and come across a ship. And if not, we'll row this boat all the way to Novigrad.'

'Pudlorak . . . ?'

'He'll cope. If it's his destiny.'

Kevenard van Vliet wept. Addario rowed.

The sky had grown dark. They heard the distant rumble of thunder.

'A storm's coming,' said the dwarf. 'We'll get bloody soaked.'

Geralt snorted. And then began to laugh. Heartily and sincerely. And infectiously. Because a moment later they were both laughing.

Addario rowed with powerful, even strokes. The boat skipped over the water like an arrow.

'You row as though you've been doing it all your life,' said Geralt, wiping his eyes, wet with tears. 'I thought dwarves didn't know how to sail or swim . . .'

'You're succumbing to stereotypes.'

INTERLUDE

Four days later

The auction house of the brothers Borsody was located in a small
square off the Main Street, which was indeed Novigrad's main road,
and connected the town square with the temple of Eternal Fire. At
the beginning of the brothers' career, when they traded horses and
sheep, they had only been able to afford a shack beyond the town
walls. Forty-two years after founding their auction house they now
occupied an impressive, three-storey building in the most elegant
quarter of the city. It had remained in the family's possession, but
the objects at auction were now exclusively precious stones, chiefly
diamonds, and works of art, antiques and collectors' items. The
auctions took place once a quarter, always on a Friday.

That day the auction room was full to bursting. *There are a good
hundred people*, thought Antea Derris.

The buzz and murmur quietened down. The auctioneer, Abner
de Navarette, took his place behind the podium.

As usual, de Navarette looked splendid in a black velvet jerkin
and waistcoat with golden brocade. Princes could have envied him
his noble looks and physiognomy, and aristocrats his bearing and
manners. It was an open secret that Abner de Navarette really
was an aristocrat, banished from his family and disinherited for
drunkenness, profligacy and debauchery. Had it not been for the
Borsody family, Abner de Navarette would have lived by begging.
But the Borsodys needed an auctioneer with aristocratic looks.
And none of the other candidates could equal Abner de Navarette
in that regard.

'Good evening, ladies and gentlemen,' he said in a voice as vel-
vety as his jacket. 'Welcome to the Borsodys' Auction House for
the quarterly auction of art treasures and antiques. The collection
under the hammer today, which you became acquainted with in

our gallery, is unique and comes entirely from private owners.

'The vast majority of you, I note, are regular guests and clients, familiar with the rules of our House and the regulations that apply during auctions. Everybody here was given on entry a brochure containing the regulations. I thus presume that you are all informed regarding the rules and aware of the consequences of breaking them. Let us then begin without delay.

'Lot number one: a nephrite group figure, depicting a nymph . . . hmm . . . with three fauns . . . It was made, according to our experts, by gnomes, dated as being a hundred years old. Starting price: two hundred crowns. I see two hundred and fifty. Going once. Going twice. Going three times. Sold to the gentleman with number thirty-six.'

Two clerks perched at neighbouring desks diligently wrote down the results of the sales.

'Lot number two: *Aen N'og Mab Taedh'morc*, a collection of elven tales and poems. Richly illustrated. Mint condition. Starting price: five hundred crowns. Five hundred and fifty, to Merchant Hofmeier. Councillor Drofuss, six hundred. Mr Hofmeier, six hundred and fifty. No more bids? Sold for six hundred and fifty crowns to Mr Hofmeier of Hirundum.

'Lot number three: an ivory device, of a . . . hmm . . . curved and elongated shape . . . hmm . . . probably used for massage. Foreign provenance, age unknown. Starting price: a hundred crowns. To my left, a hundred and fifty. Two hundred, the lady in the mask with number forty-three. Two hundred and fifty, the lady in the veil with number eight. Do I hear three hundred? Three hundred, to the wife of apothecary Vorsterkranz. Three hundred and fifty! Going for the last time. Sold for three hundred and fifty crowns to the lady with number forty-three.

'Lot number four: *Antidotarius magnus*, a unique medical treatise, published by Castell Graupian University at the beginning of the academy's existence. Starting price: eight hundred crowns. I see eight hundred and fifty. Doctor Ohnesorg, Nine hundred. One thousand, the Honourable Marti Sodergren. Any more bids? Sold for one thousand crowns to the Honourable Sodergren.

'Lot number five: *Liber de naturis bestiarum*, a rare edition, bound in beechwood boards, ornately illustrated . . .

'Lot number six: *Girl with a Kitten*, portrait *en trois quarts*, oil on canvas, the Cintran school. Starting price . . .

'Lot number seven: a bell with a handle, brass, dwarven work, the age of the item is difficult to ascertain, but it is without doubt antique. There is an engraving on the rim in dwarven runes, reading: "Why are you ringing it, you twat?" Starting price . . .

'Lot number eight: oils and tempera on canvas, artist unknown. A masterpiece. Please observe the rare use of colour, the play of pigments and the dynamics of the light. The semi-dark mood and the splendid colours of a majestically rendered sylvan landscape. And please note the main figure in the work's central position: a stag in its rutting ground, in atmospheric chiaroscuro. Starting price . . .

'Lot number nine: *Ymago mundi*, also known as *Mundus novus*. An extremely rare book, only one copy in the possession of the University of Oxenfurt and a few in private hands. Bound in cordovan. Excellent condition. Starting price: one thousand five hundred crowns. One thousand six hundred, the Honourable Vimme Vivaldi. One thousand six hundred and fifty, the Reverend Prochaska. One thousand seven hundred, the lady at the back of the room. One thousand eight hundred, Master Vivaldi. One thousand eight hundred and fifty, the Reverend Prochaska. One thousand nine hundred, Mr Vivaldi. Bravo, Reverend Prochaska, two thousand crowns. Two thousand one hundred, Mr Vivaldi. Do I hear two thousand two hundred?'

'That book is godless, it contains a heretical message! It ought to be burned! I want to buy it to burn it! Two thousand two hundred crowns!'

'Two thousand five hundred!' snorted Vimme Vivaldi, stroking a well-groomed white beard. 'Can you top that, you devout arsonist?'

'It's a scandal! Mammon is triumphing over probity! Pagan dwarves are treated better than people! I shall complain to the authorities!'

'Sold for two thousand five hundred crowns to Mr Vivaldi,' Abner de Navarette announced calmly. 'However, I remind the Reverend Prochaska about the rules and regulations of the Borsody Auction House.'

'I'm leaving.'

'Farewell. Please forgive the disturbance. It can happen that the uniqueness and wealth of the Borsody Auction House's portfolio calls forth strong emotions. Let us continue. Lot number ten: an absolute curio, an exceptional find, two witcher swords. The House has decided not to offer them separately, but as a set, in honour of the witcher whom they served years ago. The first sword, made of steel from a meteorite. The blade was forged and sharpened in Mahakam, there are authentic dwarven punched patterns confirmed by our experts.

'The other sword is silver. There are runic signs and glyphs, confirming its originality, on the cross guard and along the entire length of the blade. Starting price: one thousand crowns for the set. The gentleman with number seventeen, one thousand and fifty. Any more bids? Do I hear one thousand one hundred? For such rare items?'

'Shit, not much money,' muttered Nikefor Muus, court clerk, who was sitting in the back row, by turns nervously clenching his ink-stained fingers into a fist and pulling his fingers through his thinning hair. 'I knew it wasn't worth bothering—'

Antea Derris shut him up with a hiss.

'Count Horvath, one thousand one hundred. The gentleman with number seventeen, one thousand two hundred. The Honourable Nino Cianfanelli, one thousand five hundred. The gentleman in the mask, one thousand six hundred. The gentleman with number seventeen, one thousand seven hundred. Count Horvath, one thousand eight hundred. The gentleman in the mask, two thousand. The Honourable Master Cianfanelli, two thousand one hundred. The gentleman in the mask, two thousand two hundred. Any more bids? The Honourable Master Cianfanelli, two thousand five hundred . . . The gentleman with number seventeen . . .'

The gentleman with number seventeen was suddenly seized under the armpits by two burly thugs who had entered the room unnoticed.

'Jerosa Fuerte, known as Needle,' drawled a third thug, tapping the arrested man in the chest with a club. 'A hired killer, with a warrant issued for his apprehension. You are under arrest. Take him away.'

'Three thousand!' yelled Jerosa Fuerte, known as Needle, waving the sign with the number seventeen that he was still holding. 'Three . . . thousand . . .'

'I'm sorry,' said Abner de Navarette coldly. 'It's the rules. A bidder's offer is cancelled on the event of his arrest. The current bid is two thousand five hundred, offered by the Honourable Master Cianfanelli. Do I hear a higher bid? Count Horvath, two thousand six hundred. The gentleman in the mask, two thousand seven hundred. The Honourable Master Cianfanelli, three thousand. Going once, going twice . . .'

'Four thousand.'

'Oh. The Honourable Molnar Giancardi. Bravo. Four thousand crowns. Do I hear four thousand five hundred?'

'I wanted them for my son,' snapped Nino Cianfanelli. 'And you have only daughters, Molnar. What do you want with those swords? Ah well, have it your own way. I yield.'

'Sold,' declared de Navarette, 'to the Honourable Master Molnar Giancardi for four thousand crowns. Let us go on, noble ladies and gentlemen. Lot number eleven: a cloak of monkey fur . . .'

Nikefor Muus, joyful and grinning like a weasel in a chicken coop, slapped Antea Derris on the back. Hard. Only the last remnants of her will prevented Antea from punching him in the mouth.

'We're leaving,' she hissed.

'And the money?'

'After the auction is over and the formalities have been completed. That will take some time.'

Ignoring the grumbling of Nikefor Muus, Antea walked towards the door. She was aware of somebody observing her and glanced surreptitiously. A woman. With black hair. Attired in black and white. With an obsidian star hanging in her cleavage.

She felt a shiver.

*

Antea had been right. The formalities did take some time. They could only go to the bank two days later. It was a branch of one of the dwarven banks, smelling – like all the others – of money, wax and mahogany panelling.

'The sum to be paid is three thousand three hundred and sixty-six crowns,' declared the clerk. 'After subtracting the bank's charges of one per cent.'

'The Borsodys: fifteen, the bank: one,' growled Nikefor Muus. 'They'd take a cut from everything! Daylight robbery! Hand over the cash!'

'One moment.' Antea stopped him. 'First, let's sort out our affairs, yours and mine. I'm also due a commission. Of four hundred crowns.'

'Hold on, hold on!' yelled Muus, attracting the gaze of other clerks and customers. 'What four hundred? I've barely got three thousand and a few pennies from the Borsodys . . .'

'According to the contract I'm owed ten per cent of the sale price. The costs are your affair. And they apply only to you.'

'What are you—?'

Antea Derris looked at him. That was enough. There wasn't much resemblance between Antea and her father. But Antea could glare just like he did. Just like Pyral Pratt. Muus cringed beneath her gaze.

'Please make out a cheque for four hundred crowns from the sum to be paid,' she instructed the clerk. 'I know the bank takes a commission, I accept that.'

'And my dough in cash!' The court scribe pointed to the large leather satchel he was lugging. 'I'll take it home and hide it away safely! No thieving banks are going to fleece me for a commission!'

'It's a considerable sum,' said the clerk, standing up. 'Please wait here.'

As he left the counter the clerk opened the door leading to the rear for a moment, but Antea could have sworn that for a second she saw a black-haired woman dressed in black and white.

She felt a shiver.

*

'Thank you, Molnar,' said Yennefer. 'I won't forget this favour.'

'What are you thanking me for?' smiled Molnar Giancardi. 'What have I done, what service have I rendered? That I bought a certain lot at auction? Paying for it with money from your private account? And perhaps that I turned away when you cast that spell a moment ago? I turned away, because I was watching that agent from the window as she walked away, gracefully swaying this and that. She's a dame to my taste, I don't deny it, although I'm not fond of human females. Will your spell . . . cause her problems too—?'

'No,' interrupted the sorceress. 'Nothing will happen to her. She took a cheque, not gold.'

'Indeed. You will take away the Witcher's swords at once, I presume. After all, to him they mean—'

'—everything.' Yennefer completed his sentence. 'He's bound to them by destiny. I know, I know, indeed. He told me. And I've begun to believe it. No, Molnar, I won't take the swords today. They can remain in the safe deposit. I'll soon send an authorised person to collect them. I leave Novigrad this very day.'

'As do I. I'm riding to Tretogor, I have to inspect the branch there. Then I'm going home to Gors Velen.'

'Well, thank you once again. Farewell, O dwarf.'

'Farewell, O sorceress.'

INTERLUDE

Precisely one hundred hours after the gold was taken from the Giancardis' bank in Novigrad

'You're banned from entry,' said the doorman Tarp. 'And well aware of that. Move away from the steps.'

'Ever seen this, peasant?' Nikefor Muus shook and jingled a fat pouch. 'Ever seen so much gold at one time? Out of my way, a nobleman is coming through! A wealthy lord! Stand aside, churl!'

'Let him in, Tarp.' Febus Ravenga emerged from inside the osteria. 'I don't want any disturbance here; the customers are growing anxious. And you, beware. You've cheated me once, there won't be a second time. You'd better have the means to pay this time, Muus.'

'*Mr* Muus!' The scribe shoved Tarp aside. '*Mr!* Beware how you address me, innkeeper!'

'Wine,' he cried, lounging back in a chair. 'The dearest you have!'

'Our dearest costs sixty crowns . . .' the maître d'hôtel stated gravely.

'I can afford it! Give me a whole jug and pronto!'

'Be quiet,' Ravenga admonished him. 'Be quiet, Muus.'

'Don't silence me, mountebank! Trickster! Upstart! Who are you to silence me? A gilded sign, but with muck still on your boots. And shit will always be shit! Take a look here! Ever seen so much gold at one time? Well?'

Nikefor Muus reached into the pouch, pulled out a handful of gold coins and tossed them contemptuously on the table.

The coins landed with a splash, melting into a brown gunk. A ghastly stench of excrement spread around.

The customers of the Natura Rerum osteria leaped to their feet and dashed for the exit, choking and covering their noses with napkins. The maître d'hôtel bent over and retched. There was a scream and a curse. Febus Ravenga didn't even twitch. He stood like a statue, arms crossed on his chest.

Muus, dumbfounded, shook his head, goggled and rubbed his eyes, staring at the stinking pile of shit on the tablecloth. He finally roused himself and reached into the pouch. And pulled out a handful of soft gunk.

'You're right, Muus,' said Febus Ravenga in an icy voice. 'Shit will always be shit. Into the courtyard with him.'

The court scribe didn't even put up any resistance as he was hauled away, too bewildered by what had happened. Tarp dragged him to the outhouse. At a sign from Ravenga, two servants removed the wooden cover of the latrine. Muus became animated at the sight and began to yell, struggle and kick. It didn't help much. Tarp hauled him to the earth closet and threw him down the opening. The young man tumbled into the sloppy excrement. But he didn't go under. He spread out his arms and legs and held his head up, keeping himself on the surface of the muck with his arms on bunches of straw, rags, sticks and crumpled pages from various learned and pious books.

Febus Ravenga took down from the wall of the granary a wooden pitchfork made from a single forked branch.

'Shit was, is and will remain shit,' he said. 'And always ends up where shit is.'

He pressed down on the pitchfork and submerged Muus. Completely. Muus broke the surface, roaring, coughing and spitting. Ravenga let him cough a little and get his breath back and then submerged him again. This time much deeper.

After repeating the operation several times, he threw down the pitchfork.

'Leave him,' he ordered. 'Let him crawl out by himself.'

'That won't be easy,' adjudged Tarp. 'And it'll take some time.'

'Let it. There's no rush.'

A mon retour (hé! je m'en désespere!)
Tu m'as reçu d'un baiser tout glacé.

Pierre de Ronsard

CHAPTER SIXTEEN

Just at that moment, the Novigradian schooner *Pandora Parvi*, a beautiful ship indeed, was sailing to its mooring place under full sail. *Beautiful and swift*, thought Geralt, descending the gangway onto the busy wharf. He had seen the schooner in Novigrad, asked around and knew it had set sail from there two whole days after the galley *Stinta*, on which he had sailed. In spite of that, he had essentially reached Kerack at the same time. *Perhaps I ought to have waited and boarded the schooner*, he thought. *Two days more in Novigrad. Who knows, perhaps I would have acquired some more information?*

Vain digressions, he decided. Perhaps, who knows, maybe. What has happened has happened, nothing can change it now. And there's no sense going on about it.

With a glance, he bade farewell to the schooner, the lighthouse, the sea and the horizon, darkening with storm clouds. Then he set off for the town at a brisk pace.

*

Just at that moment, two porters were coming out carrying a sedan chair, a dainty construction with delicate lilac curtains. It had to be Tuesday, Wednesday or Thursday. On those days Lytta Neyd saw patients: usually wealthy, upper-class ladies, who arrived in sedan chairs like that.

The doorman let him in without a word. Just as well. Geralt wasn't in the best of moods and would certainly have retaliated with a word. Or even two or three.

The patio was deserted and the water in the fountain burbled softly. There was a carafe and some cups on a small malachite table. Without further ado, Geralt poured himself a cup.

When he raised his head, he saw Mozaïk. In a white coat

and apron. Pale. With her hair slicked down.

'It's you,' she said. 'You're back.'

'It certainly is,' he confirmed dryly. 'I most certainly am. And this wine is most certainly a little sour.'

'*Such* a pleasure seeing you again.'

'Coral? Is she here? And if so, where?'

'I saw her between the thighs of a patient a moment ago,' she shrugged. 'She's most certainly still there.'

'You indeed have no choice, Mozaïk,' he responded calmly, looking her in the eyes. 'You'll have to become a sorceress. In sooth, you have a great predisposition for it and the makings of one. Your caustic wit wouldn't be appreciated in a weaving manufactory. Nor yet in a bawdy house.'

'I'm learning and growing.' She withstood his gaze. 'I don't cry myself to sleep any longer. I've done all my crying. I'm over that stage.'

'No, no you're not, you're deluding yourself. There's still a lot ahead of you. And sarcasm won't protect you from it. Especially as it's forced, and a pale imitation. But enough of that, it's not my job to give you lessons in life. I asked where Coral was.'

'Here. Greetings.'

The sorceress emerged from behind a curtain like a ghost. Like Mozaïk, she was wearing a white doctor's coat, and her red hair was pinned up and hidden by a linen cap which in ordinary circumstances he would have thought ridiculous. But the circumstances weren't ordinary and laughter would have been out of place. He needed a few seconds to understand that.

She walked over and kissed him on the cheek without a word. Her lips were cold. And she had dark circles under her eyes.

She smelled of medicine. And the fluid she used as disinfectant. It was a nasty, repulsive, morbid scent. A scent full of fear.

'I'll see you tomorrow,' she forestalled him. 'Tomorrow I'll tell you everything.'

'Tomorrow.'

She looked at him and it was a faraway look, from beyond the chasm of time and events between them. He needed a few seconds to understand how deep that chasm was and how remote were the events separating them.

'Maybe the day after tomorrow would be better. Go to town. Meet that poet, he's been worried about you. But now go, please. I have to see a patient.'

After she had gone, he glanced at Mozaïk. Probably meaningfully enough for her not to delay with an explanation.

'We had a birth this morning,' she said, and her voice was a little different. 'A difficult one. She decided to use forceps. And everything that could have gone badly did.'

'I understand.'

'I doubt it.'

'Goodbye, Mozaïk.'

'You were away for a long time.' She raised her head. 'Much longer than she had expected. At Rissberg they didn't know anything, or at least pretended not to. Something happened, didn't it?'

'Yes, it did.'

'I understand.'

'I doubt it.'

*

Dandelion impressed with his intelligence. By stating something so obvious that Geralt was still unable to completely adjust himself to it. Or completely accept it.

'It's the end, isn't it? Gone with the wind? Of course, she and the sorcerers needed you, you've done the job, now you can go. And know what? I'm glad it's happening now. You had to finish that bizarre affair some time, and the longer it went on the more dangerous the consequences were potentially becoming. If you want to know my opinion, you should also be glad it's over and that it went so smoothly. You should then dress your countenance in a joyful smile, not a saturnine and gloomy grimace which, believe me, doesn't suit you at all. With it, you look quite simply like a man with a serious hangover, who to cap it all has got food poisoning and doesn't remember when he broke a tooth and on what, or how he got the semen stains on his britches.

'Or perhaps your melancholy results from something else?' continued the bard, completely undaunted by the Witcher's lack of reaction. 'If only from the fact that you were thrown out on your ear when you were planning a finale in your own, inimitable style? The one with the flight at dawn and flowers on the bedside table? Ha, ha, being in love is like being at war, my friend, and your beloved behaved like an expert strategist. She acted pre-emptively, with a preventative strike. She must have read Marshal Pelligram's *The History of Warfare*. Pelligram cites many examples of victories won using a similar stratagem.'

Geralt still didn't react. It was apparent that Dandelion didn't expect a reaction. He finished his beer and gestured to the innkeeper's wife to bring another.

'Taking the above into consideration,' he continued, twisting the pegs of his lute, 'I'm generally in favour of sex on the first date. In the future, I recommend it to you in every respect. It eliminates the necessity of any further rendezvous with the same person, which can be wearisome and time-consuming. While we're on the subject, that lady lawyer you recommended turned out indeed to be worth the bother. You wouldn't believe—'

'I would,' the Witcher spat, interrupting him quite bluntly. 'I can believe it without hearing an account, so you can give it a miss.'

'Indeed,' the bard noted. 'Dejected, distressed and consumed by care, owing to which you're tetchy and brusque. It's not just the woman, it seems to me. There's something else. I know it, dammit. And see it. Did you fail in Novigrad? Didn't you get your swords back?'

Geralt sighed, although he had promised himself he wouldn't.

'No, I didn't. I was too late. There were complications, and various things took place. We were caught by a storm, then our boat began to ship water . . . And then a certain glove-maker was taken seriously ill . . . Ah, I won't bore you with the details. In brief, I didn't make it in time. When I reached Novigrad the auction was over. They gave me short shrift at the Borsodys. The auctions are shrouded in commercial confidentiality, protecting both the sellers and the buyers. The company doesn't issue any information to outsiders, blah, blah, blah, farewell, sir. I didn't find anything out. I don't know whether the swords were sold, and if so, who purchased them. I don't even know if the thief put the swords up for auction at all. For he might have ignored Pratt's advice; another opportunity might have occurred. I don't know anything.'

'Too bad.' Dandelion shook his head. 'It's a streak of unfortunate incidents. Cousin Ferrant's investigation is at a standstill, it seems to me. Cousin Ferrant, while we're on the subject, asks about you endlessly. Where you are, whether I have any tidings from you, when you're returning, whether you'll make it to the royal nuptials in time, whether you've forgotten your promise to Prince Egmund. Naturally, I haven't said a word about your endeavours or the auction. But the holiday of Lughnasadh, I remind you, is getting closer. Only ten days remain.'

'I know. But perhaps something will happen in the meantime. Something lucky, let's say? After the streak of unfortunate incidents, we could do with a change.'

'I don't deny it. But if—'

'I'll think it over and make a decision.' Geralt didn't let the bard finish. 'Nothing in principle binds me to appear at the royal nuptials as his bodyguard: Egmund and the instigator didn't recover my swords, and that was the condition. But I absolutely don't rule out fulfilling the ducal wish. Material considerations – if nothing else – argue for it. The prince boasted he wouldn't skimp on a penny. And everything suggests that I'll be needing new swords, bespoke ones. And that will cost a great deal. What can I say? Let's go and eat. And drink.'

'To the Natura in Ravenga?'

'Not today. Today I feel like simple, natural, uncomplicated and honest things. If you know what I mean.'

'Of course, I do,' said Dandelion, standing up. 'Let's go down to the sea, to Palmyra. I know a place there. They serve herrings, vodka and soup made from a fish called the bighead carp. Don't laugh! That really is its name!'

'They can call themselves whatever they want. Let's go.'

*

The bridge over the Adalatte was blocked, for at that very moment a column of laden wagons and a troop of horsemen pulling riderless horses were passing over it. Geralt and Dandelion had to wait and step out of the way.

A rider on a bay mare brought up the rear of the cavalcade. The mare tossed her head and greeted Geralt with a long-drawn-out neigh.

'Roach!'

'Greetings, Witcher,' said the horseman, removing his hood to reveal his face. 'I was just coming to visit you. Although I hadn't expected we'd bump into each other so soon.'

'Greetings, Pinety.'

Pinety dismounted. Geralt noticed he was armed. It was quite strange, since mages almost never bore arms. A sword in a richly decorated scabbard was hanging from the sorcerer's brass-studded belt. There was also a dagger, solid and broad.

He took Roach's reins from the sorcerer and stroked the mare's nostrils and mane. Pinety took off his gloves and stuck them into his belt.

'Please forgive me, Master Dandelion,' he said, 'but I'd like to be alone with Geralt. What I must say to him is meant for his ears only.'

'Geralt has no secrets before me,' Dandelion said, puffing himself up.

'I know. I learned many details of his private life from your ballads.'

'But—'

'Dandelion,' the Witcher interrupted. 'Take a walk.'

'Thank you,' he said when they were alone. 'Thank you for bringing me my horse, Pinety.'

'I observed that you were attached to her,' replied the sorcerer. 'So, when I found her in Pinetops—'

'You were in Pinetops?'

'We were. Constable Torquil summoned us.'

'Did you see—?'

'We did.' Pinety cut him off curtly. 'We saw everything. I don't understand, Witcher. I don't understand. Why didn't you hack him to death when you could? On the spot? You didn't act too prudently, if I may say so.'

I know, thought Geralt to himself. *I know, how well I know. I turned out to be too stupid to take advantage of the chance fate had given me. For what harm would there have been in that, one more corpse in the statistics? What does that mean to a hired killer? So what*

258

*if it sickened me to be your tool? I'm always somebody's tool, after all.
I ought to have gritted my teeth and done what had to be done.*

'This is sure to astonish you,' said Pinety, looking him in the
eyes, 'but we immediately came to help, Harlan and I. We guessed
you were in need of assistance. We caught Degerlund the following day when he was tearing apart some random gang.'

*You caught him, the Witcher thought to himself. And broke his
neck without thinking twice? Since you're cleverer than me, you didn't
repeat my mistake? Like hell you didn't. If it had been like that you
wouldn't be wearing a face like that now, Guincamp.*

'We aren't murderers,' stammered the sorcerer, blushing. 'We
hauled him off to Rissberg. And caused a mild commotion . . .
Everybody was against us. Ortolan, astonishingly, behaved
cautiously, and we'd actually expected the worst from him. But
Biruta Icarti, Pockmarked Axel, Sandoval, even Zangenis, who
had previously been on our side . . . We had to listen to a lengthy
lecture about the solidarity of the fellowship, about fraternity,
about loyalty. We learned that only utter good-for-nothings send
hired killers after confraters, that you have to fall very low to hire a
witcher to go after a comrade. For low reasons. Out of envy for our
comrade's talent and prestige; jealousy over his scientific achieve-
ments and successes.'

*Citing the incidents in the Hills and the forty-four corpses achieved
nothing, the Witcher thought to himself. Unless you count shrugs
of the shoulders. And probably a lengthy lecture about science and the
need to make sacrifices. About the end justifying the means.*

'Degerlund,' Pinety continued, 'was hauled before the commission and dealt a severe reprimand. For practicing goetia, for the
people killed by the demon. He was haughty, clearly counting on
an intervention by Ortolan. But Ortolan had somehow forgotten
about him, having devoted himself utterly to a fresh new passion:
developing a formula for an extremely effective and universal
manure, meant to revolutionise agriculture. Left to fend for himself, Degerlund struck a different tone. Tearful and pathetic. He
played the victim. A victim in equal measure of his own ambition
and magical talent, owing to which he evoked a demon so powerful
it was uncontrollable. He swore to abandon the practice of goetia,
that he would never touch it again. That he would utterly devote

himself to research into perfecting the human species, into trans-humanism, speciation, introgression and genetic modification.'

And they lent credence to him, the Witcher thought to himself.

'They lent credence to him. Ortolan, who suddenly appeared before the commission stinking of manure, influenced them. He denominated Degerlund a "dear youth" who had admittedly committed grievous miscalculations, but who is infallible? He didn't doubt that the youth would calibrate himself and that he would vouch for it. He asked for the commission to temper its ire, to show compassion and not excoriate the youth. He finally promulgated Degerlund his heir and successor, fully transferring his private laboratory in the Citadel to him. He himself, he declared, didn't need a laboratory, for he had resolved to toil and take exercise under the open sky, on vegetable patches and flower beds. This plan appealed to Biruta, Pockmarked Axel and the rest. The Citadel, bearing in mind its inaccessibility, could successfully be considered a place of correction. Degerlund had ensnared himself. He found himself under house arrest.'

And the affair was swept under the carpet, the Witcher thought to himself.

'I suspect that consideration for you and your reputation had an influence on it,' said Pinety, looking at him keenly.

Geralt raised his eyebrows.

'Your witcher code,' continued the sorcerer, 'reportedly forbids the killing of people. But it is said about you that you don't treat the code with due reverence. That this and that has occurred, that several people have departed this life thanks to you. Biruta and the others got cold feet, fearing that you'd return to Rissberg and finish the job, and that they were in line for a beating too. But the Citadel is a fully secure refuge, a former gnomish mountain fortress converted into a laboratory and currently under magical protection. No one can get into the Citadel, there is no possibility. Degerlund is thus not only isolated but also safe.'

Rissberg is also safe, the Witcher thought to himself. *Safe from scandals and embarrassment. With Degerlund in isolation there's no scandal. No one will ever know that the crafty bastard and careerist tricked and led up the garden path the sorcerers of Rissberg, who believe themselves and declare themselves to be the elite of the magical fraternity. Or know that a degenerate psychopath took advantage of the naivety and stupidity of that elite and managed without any hindrance to kill almost four dozen people.*

'Degerlund will be under supervision and observation in the Citadel,' the sorcerer said, looking him in the eye the whole time. 'He won't call forth any demon.'

There never was a demon. And you, Pinety, know that only too well.

'The Citadel,' said the sorcerer, looking away and observing the ships at anchor, 'is built into the rock of the Mount Cremora massif, at the foot of which lies Rissberg. An attempt to storm it would be tantamount to suicide. Not only owing to the magical protection. Do you remember what you told us back then? About that possessed person whom you once killed? In case of absolute necessity, protecting one good at the cost of another, precluding the lawlessness of a forbidden deed in the process. Well, you must understand that the circumstances are now quite different. In isolation, Degerlund doesn't represent a genuine or direct threat. Were you to lay a finger on him, you would be committing a forbidden and lawless deed. Were you to try to kill him, you would go to court accused of attempted murder. Some of our people, I happen to know, hope you will nonetheless try. And end up on the scaffold. So, I advise you: let it go. Forget about Degerlund. Leave it to run its course.

'You say nothing.' Pinety stated a fact. 'You're keeping your comments to yourself.'

'Because there's nothing to say. I'm only curious about one thing. You and Tzara. Will you remain at Rissberg?'

Pinety laughed. Dryly and hollowly.

'Both Harlan and I were asked to tender our resignation, at our own request, by virtue of our state of health. We left Rissberg and we'll never return there. Harlan is going to Poviss to serve King Rhyd. And I'm inclined to continue travelling. In the Empire of Nilfgaard, I hear, they treat mages functionally and without undue respect. But they pay them well. And while we're on the subject of Nilfgaard . . . I almost forgot. I have a farewell gift for you, Witcher.'

He undid his baldric, wrapped it around the scabbard and

handed the sword to Geralt.

'It's for you,' he said before the Witcher could speak. 'I received it on my sixteenth birthday. From my father, who couldn't get over the fact that I'd decided to study magic. He hoped the gift would influence me and that as the owner of such a weapon I would feel obliged to continue the family tradition and choose a military career. Why, I disappointed my father. In everything. I didn't like hunting, I preferred angling. I didn't marry the only daughter of his closest friend. I didn't become a military man, and the sword gathered dust in a cupboard. I have no need of it. It will serve you better.'

'But . . . Pinety . . .'

'Take it, don't make a fuss. I know your swords went missing and you're in need.'

Geralt grasped the lizard-skin hilt and drew the blade halfway out of the scabbard. One inch above the cross guard, he saw a punch in the shape of the sun in its glory with sixteen rays, alternating straight and wavy, symbolising heraldically the light and heat of the sun. A beautifully executed inscription in stylised lettering – a famous trademark – began two inches beyond the sun.

'A blade from Viroleda.' The Witcher stated a fact. 'This time authentic.'

'I beg your pardon?'

'Nothing, nothing. I'm admiring it. And I still don't know if I can accept it . . .'

'You can. In principle, you already have received it, since you're holding it. Hell's bells, don't make a fuss, I said. I'm giving you the sword because I like you. So that you'll realise not every sorcerer has it in for you. Anyway, fishing rods are more use to me. The rivers are beautiful and crystal clear in Nilfgaard, there's plenty of trout and salmon in them.'

'Thank you. Pinety?'

'Yes?'

'Are you giving me the sword purely because of liking me?'

'Why, because I like you, indeed.' The sorcerer lowered his voice. 'But perhaps not only. What does it bother me what happens here and what purposes that sword will serve? I'm leaving these parts, never to return. You see that splendid galleon lying at anchor? It's *Euryale*, its home port is Baccalá. I sail the day after tomorrow.'

'You arrived a little early.'

'Yes . . .' said the mage, stammering slightly. 'I wanted to say goodbye . . . to someone.'

'Good luck. Thanks for the sword. And for the horse, thanks again. Farewell, Pinety.'

'Farewell.' The sorcerer shook Geralt's extended hand without thinking. 'Farewell, Witcher.'

*

He found Dandelion – where else? – in the portside tavern, slurping fish soup from a bowl.

'I'm leaving,' he announced briefly. 'Right away.'

'Right away?' Dandelion froze with the spoon halfway to his mouth. 'Right now? I thought—'

'It doesn't matter what you thought. I ride immediately. Reassure your cousin, the instigator. I'll be back for the royal nuptials.'

'What's that?'

'What does it look like?'

'A sword, naturally. Where did you get it? From the sorcerer, was it? And the one I gave you? Where's that?'

'It got lost. Return to the upper town, Dandelion.'

'What about Coral?'

'What *about* Coral?'

'What do I say if she asks . . .'

'She won't. She won't have time. She'll be saying farewell to somebody.'

INTERLUDE

CONFIDENTIAL
Illustrissimus et Reverendissimus
Magnus Magister Narses de la Roche
The Head of the Chapter of the Gift and the Art
Novigrad
Datum ex Castello Rissberg,
die 15 mens. Jul. anno 1245 post Resurrectionem

Re:
Master of the Arts
Sorel Albert Amador Degerlund

Honoratissime Grandmaster,

Rumours about the incidents which occurred on the western bor-
ders of Temeria, in the summer of *anno currente*, have doubtless
reached the ears of the Chapter. The result of the said incidents,
presumably, is that around forty – it is impossible to state precisely
– persons, mainly unschooled forestry labourers, lost their lives.
These incidents are associated – regrettably – with the person of
Master Sorel Albert Amador Degerlund, a member of the research
team at the Rissberg Complex.

The research team of the Rissberg Complex is united in sympathy with the families of the victims of the incidents, although
the victims – who stand very low in the social hierarchy, abusing
alcohol and leading immoral lives – were probably not in legalised
unions.

We wish to remind the Chapter that Master Degerlund, a pupil
and acolyte of Grandmaster Ortolan, is an outstanding scientist,
a specialist in the field of genetics, boasting immense, simply in-
calculable accomplishments in transhumanism, introgression and

265

speciation. The research that Master Degerlund is conducting may turn out to be pivotal for the development and evolution of the human race. As is known, the human race is no match for the non-human races in terms of many physical, psychological and psychomagical traits. Master Degerlund's experiments, based on the hybridisation and combination of the gene pool, are intended – in the beginning – to equalise the human race with non-human races, while in the long term – by the application of speciation – to permit humans to dominate non-humans and subdue them utterly. It is probably unnecessary to explain what cardinal significance this matter has. It would be inadvisable for some trifling incidents to impede or stop the above-mentioned scientific studies.

As far as Master Degerlund himself is concerned, the research team of the Rissberg Complex takes full responsibility for his medical care. Master Degerlund was previously diagnosed with narcissistic tendencies, absence of empathy and slight emotional disturbances. During the time preceding the perpetration of the acts he is accused of, the condition intensified until symptoms of bipolar disorder occurred. It may be stated that at the time the acts he is accused of were committed Master Degerlund was not in control of his emotional reactions and his ability to differentiate between good and evil was impaired. It may be assumed that Degerlund was *non compos mentis, eo ipso* was temporarily insane, hence he cannot take criminal responsibility for the acts ascribed to him, since *impune est admittendum quod per furorem alicuius accidit.*

Master Degerlund has been placed *ad interim* in a secret locality where he is being treated and is continuing his research.

Since we consider the matter closed, we wish to draw the Chapter's attention to Constable Torquil, who is conducting the investigation into the matter of the Temerian incidents. Constable Torquil, a subordinate of the bailiff in Gors Velen, otherwise known as a diligent functionary and staunch defender of law, is exhibiting excessive zeal as regards the incidents in the above-mentioned settlements and is following – from our point of view – a decidedly inappropriate trail. His superiors ought to be persuaded to temper his enthusiasm. And were that not to be effective it would be worth investigating the personal files of the constable, his wife, parents, grandparents, children and other members of his family, paying special attention to his private life, past, criminal record, material affairs and sexual preferences. We suggest contacting the law firm of Codringher and Fenn, whose services, if I may remind the Chapter, were taken advantage of three years ago with the aim of discrediting and ridiculing the witnesses in the case known as the 'corn affair'.

Item, we would like to draw the Chapter's attention to the fact that unfortunately the witcher called Geralt of Rivia has become embroiled in the matter in question. He had direct access to the incidents in the settlements, and we also have reason to suppose that he connects those events with Master Degerlund. The said witcher ought also to be silenced, should he begin to delve too deeply into the matter. We would like to point out that the asocial attitude, nihilism, emotional instability and chaotic personality of the aforementioned witcher may mean that a stark warning may prove to be *non sufficit* and extreme measures will turn out to be necessary. The witcher is under permanent surveillance and we are prepared to apply such measures if, naturally, the Chapter approves and orders it.

In hopes that the above explanation will turn out to be sufficient for the Chapter to close the matter, *bene valere optamus* and we remain yours sincerely

on behalf of the Rissberg Complex research team
semper fidelis vestrarum bona amica

Biruta Anna Marquette Icarti *manu propria*

CHAPTER SEVENTEEN

'Just in time,' said Frans Torquil morosely. 'You made it on time, Witcher, right on time. The spectacle's about to begin.'

He lay on his back on a bed, as pale as a whitewashed wall, his hair wet with sweat and plastered to his forehead. He was wearing nothing but a coarse linen shirt that at once reminded Geralt of a winding sheet. His left thigh was swathed down to the knee in a blood-soaked bandage.

A table had been put in the centre of the room and covered in a sheet. A squat individual in a black jerkin was setting out tools on the table, one after the other, in turn. Knives. Forceps. Chisels. Saws.

'I regret but one thing,' said Torquil, grinding his teeth. 'That I didn't catch the whoresons. It was the gods' will, it wasn't written for me . . . And now it won't come to pass.'

'What happened?'

'The sodding same as in Yew Trees, Rogovizna and Pinetops. Except it wasn't like the others, but at the very edge of the forest. And not in a clearing, but on the highway. They'd surprised some travellers. They killed three and abducted two bairns. As luck would have it, I was nearby with my men. We gave chase at once, soon had them in sight. Two great bruisers as big as oxen and one misshapen hunchback. And that hunchback shot me with a crossbow.'

The constable gritted his teeth and waved a hand at his bandaged thigh.

'I ordered my men to leave me and follow them. They disobeyed, the curs. And as a result, they made off. And me? So what if they saved me? When they're cutting my leg off now? I'd rather have fucking pegged it there, but seen them 'uns kicking their legs on the scaffold before my eyes clouded over. The wretches didn't obey my orders. Now they're sitting there, hangdog.'

To a man, the constable's subordinates were indeed sitting shamefacedly on a bench by the wall. They were accompanied by a wrinkled old woman with a garland on her head that didn't match her grey hair at all, who looked completely out of place.

'We can begin,' said the man in the black jerkin. 'Put the patient on the table and strap him down tightly. All outsiders to leave the chamber.'

'They can stay,' growled Torquil. 'I want to know they're watching. I'll be too ashamed to scream.'

'One moment,' Geralt said, straightening up. 'Who decided that amputation is inevitable?'

'I did,' said the man in black, also drawing himself up to his full height, but having to lift his head up high to look Geralt in the face. 'I'm Messer Luppi, physician to the bailiff in Gors Velen, specially sent for. An examination has confirmed that the wound is infected. The leg has to go, there's no hope for it.'

'How much do you charge for this procedure?'

'Twenty crowns.'

'Here's thirty,' said Geralt, digging three ten-crown coins from a pouch. 'Take your instruments, pack up and return to the bailiff. Should he ask, say the patient is improving.'

'But . . . I must protest . . .'

'Get packed and return. Which of those words don't you understand? And you, nana, to me. Unwind the bandage.'

'He forbade me from touching the patient,' she said, nodding at the court physician. 'Says I'm a quack and a witch. Threatened to inform on me.'

'Ignore him. Indeed, he's just leaving.'

The old woman, whom Geralt at once recognised as a herbalist, did as she was told. She unwound the bandage with great care, but it was enough to make Torquil shake his head, hiss and groan.

'Geralt . . .' he groaned. 'What are you playing at? The physician said there's no hope . . . Better to lose a leg than my life.'

'Bullshit. It's not better at all. And now shut up.'

The wound looked hideous. But Geralt had seen worse.

He took a box from the pouch containing elixirs. Messer Luppi, now packed, looked on, shaking his head.

'Those decocts are fit for nothing,' he pronounced. 'Those

quack tricks and that bogus magic is fit for nothing. It's nothing but charlatanism. As a physician, I must protest—'

Geralt turned around and stared. The physician exited. In a hurry. Tripping over the doorstop.

'Four men to me,' said the Witcher, uncorking a vial. 'Hold him fast. Clench your teeth, Frans.'

The elixir foamed copiously as it was poured over the wound. The constable groaned heart-rendingly. Geralt waited a while and then poured on another elixir. That one also foamed, and hissed and smoked as well. Torquil screamed, tossed his head around, tensed up, rolled his eyes and fainted.

The old woman took a canteen from her bundle, scooped out a handful of green ointment, smeared it thickly on a piece of folded linen and applied it to the wound.

'Knitbone,' guessed Geralt. 'A poultice of knitbone, arnica and marigold. Good, nana, very good. Goatweed and oak bark would also come in use—'

''ark at 'im,' interrupted the old woman, without raising her head from the constable's leg. 'Trying to teach me herbalism. I was healing people with herbs when you were still puking your porridge over your wet nurse, laddie. And you, lummoxes, away with you, for you're blocking out the light. And you stink dreadfully. You ought to change your footwraps. From time to time. Out with you, hear me?'

'His leg will have to be immobilised. Set in long splints—'

'Don't instruct me, I said. And get you gone as well. Why are you still here? What are you waiting for? For thanks that you nobly gave up your magical witcher medicaments? For a promise that he won't forget it till his dying day?'

'I want to ask him something.'

'Promise me, Geralt, that you'll catch them,' said Frans Torquil, suddenly quite lucid. 'That you won't let them off—'

'I'll give him a sleeping draught and something for the fever, because he's raving. And you, witcher, get out. Wait in the yard.'

He didn't have to wait long. The old woman came out, hitched up her dress and straightened her crooked garland. She sat beside him on the step. And rubbed one foot against the other. She had extremely small feet.

'He's sleeping,' she announced. 'And will probably live, if nothing evil sets in, touch wood. The bone will knit. You saved his pin with them witcher charms. He'll always be lame and he'll never mount a horse again, I dare say, but two legs are better than one, hee, hee.'

She reached into her bosom, beneath her embroidered sheepskin vest, making the air smell even more strongly of herbs. She drew out a wooden casket and opened it. After a moment's hesitation, she proffered it to Geralt.

'Want a snort?'

'No thank you. I don't use fisstech.'

'But I . . .' said the herbalist, sniffing up the drug, first into one, then the other nostril. 'But I do, from time to time. Sharpens up the mind like no one's bloody business. Increases longevity. And improves the looks. Just look at me.'

He did.

'Thanking you for the witcher medicaments for Frans,' she said, wiping a watering eye and sniffing. 'I won't forget it. I know you jealously guard those decocts of yours. And you gave them to me, without a second thought. Even though you may run short when you're next in need. Aren't you afraid?'

'I am.'

She turned her head to show her profile. She must indeed have been a beautiful woman once, a long time ago.

'And now.' She turned to face him. 'Speak. You meant to ask Frans something?'

'Never mind. He's sleeping and it's time I was off.'

'Speak.'

'Mount Cremora.'

'You should have said. What do you want to know about that mountain?'

*

The cottage stood quite far outside the village, hard by the wall of the forest which began just beyond a fence surrounding an orchard full of small trees laden with apples. The rest had all the hallmarks of a typical homestead: a barn, a shed, a hen house, several beehives, a vegetable patch and a muck heap. A thin trail of white, pleasant-smelling smoke was wafting from the chimney.

The guinea fowl scurrying around by the wattle fencing noticed him first, raising the alarm with a hellish screeching. Some children playing in the farmyard dashed towards the cottage. A woman appeared in the doorway. Tall, fair-haired and wearing an apron over a coarse linen frock. He rode closer and dismounted.

'Greetings,' he said. 'Is the man of the house at home?'

The children – all of them little girls – clung to their mother's skirts and apron. The woman looked at the Witcher and any search for friendliness in those eyes would have been in vain. No wonder. She caught a good sight of the sword hilt over his shoulder. Of the medallion on his neck. And of the silver studs on his gloves which the Witcher was by no means hiding. Rather, he was flaunting them.

'The man of the house,' he repeated. 'I mean Otto Dussart. I want to talk to him about something.'

'What?'

'It's private. Is he at home?'

She stared at him in silence, slightly tilting her head. She had rustic looks and he guessed she might be aged anything between twenty-five and forty-five. A more precise assessment – as with the majority of village women – was impossible.

'Is he at home?'

'No.'

'Then I'll wait until he returns,' he said, tossing the mare's reins over a pole.

'You might have to wait a while.'

'I'll hold out somehow. Although in truth I'd prefer to wait inside than by the fence.'

The woman eyed him up and down for a moment. Him and his medallion.

'Accept our invitation, guest,' she said finally. 'Step inside.'

'Gladly,' he answered, using the customary formula. 'I won't transgress the rules of hospitality.'

'You won't,' she repeated in a slow, drawling voice. 'Yet you wear a sword.'

'Such is my profession.'

273

'Swords injure. And kill.'

'So does life. Does the invitation still apply?'

'Please enter.'

One entered – typically for such homesteads – through a gloomy, cluttered passage. The main chamber turned out to be quite spacious, light and clean, with only the walls near the range and chimney bearing sooty streaks. Otherwise, the walls were painted freshly white and decorated with gaily embroidered wall hangings. Various household utensils, bunches of herbs, plaits of garlic and strings of capsicums enlivened the walls. A woven curtain separated the chamber from the larder. It smelt of cooking. Cabbage, to be precise.

'Please be seated.'

The housewife remained standing, crumpling her apron in her hands. The children crouched by the stove on a low bench.

The medallion on Geralt's neck was vibrating. Powerfully and constantly. It fluttered under his shirt like a captured bird.

'You ought to have left the sword in the passage,' the woman said, walking over to the range, 'It's indecent to sit down to table with a weapon. Only brigands do so. Be you a brigand—?'

'You know who I am,' he cut her off. 'And the sword stays where it is. To act as a reminder.'

'Of what?'

'That hasty actions have perilous consequences.'

'There's no weapons here, so—'

'Yes, yes,' he interrupted bluntly. 'Let's not kid ourselves, missus. A peasant's cottage and farmyard is an arsenal; many have died from hoes, not to mention flails and pitchforks. I heard that someone was killed with the plunger from a butter churn. You can do harm with anything if you want to. Or have to. And while we're on the subject, leave that pot of boiling water alone. And move away from the stove.'

'I meant nothing,' the woman said quickly, evidently lying. 'And it's not boiling water, it's borscht. I meant to offer you some—'

'No, thank you. I'm not hungry. So don't touch the pot and move away from the stove. Sit down by the children. And we'll wait nicely for the man of the house.'

They sat in a silence broken only by the buzzing of flies. The medallion twitched.

'A pan of cabbage in the oven is almost ready,' said the woman, interrupting the awkward silence. 'I must take it out and stir it, or it'll burn.'

'Her.' Geralt pointed to the smallest of the girls. 'She can do it.'

The girl stood up slowly, glaring at him from under a flaxen fringe. She took hold of a long-handled fork and bent over towards the stove door. And suddenly launched herself at Geralt like a she-cat. She aimed to pin him by his neck to the wall with the fork, but he dodged, jerked the fork handle, and knocked her over. She began to metamorphosise before even hitting the floor.

The woman and the other two girls had already managed to transform. Three wolves – a grey she-wolf and two cubs – bounded towards the Witcher, with bloodshot eyes and bared fangs. They bounded apart, quite like wolves, attacking from all sides. He dodged, shoved the bench at the she-wolf, fending the cubs away with blows of his fists in his silver-studded gloves. They howled and flattened themselves against the floor, baring their fangs. The she-wolf howled savagely and leaped again.

'No! Edwina! No!'

She fell on him, pressing him to the wall. But now in human form. The wolf-girls immediately fled and hunkered down by the stove. The woman remained, crouching before him, staring with embarrassed eyes. He didn't know if she was ashamed because of attacking him, or because the attack had failed.

'Edwina! What is the meaning of this?' bellowed a bearded man of impressive height, arms akimbo. 'What are you doing?'

'It's a witcher!' the woman snorted, still on her knees. 'A brigand with a sword! He came for you! The murderer! He reeks of blood!'

'Silence, woman. I know him. Forgive her, Master Geralt. Everything in order? Forgive her. She didn't know . . . She thought that since you're a witcher—'

He broke off and looked nervously. The woman and the little girls were gathered by the stove. Geralt could have sworn he heard a soft growling.

'It's all right,' he said. 'I bear no ill will. But you showed up just in time. Not a moment too soon.'

'I know,' said the bearded man, shuddering perceptibly. 'Sit you down, sir, sit down at table . . . Edwina! Bring beer!'

'No. Outside, Dussart. For a word.'

In the middle of the farmyard sat a grey cat that fled in a trice at the sight of the Witcher and hid in the nettles.

'I don't wish to upset your wife or frighten your children,' Geralt announced. 'And what's more, I have a matter I'd prefer to talk about in private. It concerns a certain favour.'

'Whatever you want, sir,' said the bearded man. 'Just say it. I'll fulfil your every wish, if it's in my power. I am indebted to you, greatly indebted. Thanks to you I walk alive through this world. Because you spared me then. I owe you—'

'Not me. Yourself. Because even in lupine form you remained a man and never harmed anybody.'

'I never harmed anybody, 'tis true. And how did I benefit? My neighbours, having become suspicious, brought a witcher down on me at once. Though paupers, they scrimped and saved in order to hire you.'

'I thought about giving them back their money,' admitted Geralt. 'But it might have aroused suspicion. I gave them my witcher word that I'd removed the werewolf spell from you and had completely healed you of lycanthropy, that you are now as normal as the next man. Such a feat has to cost. If people pay for something they believe in it: whatever is paid for becomes real and legal. The more expensive, the better.'

'Recalling that day sends shivers down my spine,' said Dussart, paling under his tan. 'I almost died of fear when I saw you with that silver blade. I thought my last hour had come. There's no end of stories. About witcher-murderers relishing blood and torture. You, it turned out, are a decent fellow. And a good one.'

'Let's not exaggerate. But you followed my advice and moved out of Guaamez.'

'I had to,' Dussart said gloomily. 'The people of Guaamez believed in theory that I was free of the spell, but you were right, a former werewolf doesn't have it easy either. It was as you said: what you used to be means more to people than what you are. I was compelled to move out, and roam through strange surroundings where no one knew me. I wandered and wandered . . . Until I finally ended up here. And met Edwina.'

'It rarely happens for two therianthropes to form a couple,' said Geralt, shaking his head. 'It's even more seldom for children to be born to such couples. You're a lucky man, Dussart.'

'If only you knew,' grinned the werewolf. 'My children are as pretty as a picture, they're growing up into beautiful maidens. And Edwina and I were made for each other. I wish to be with her to the end of my days.'

'She knew me as a witcher at once. And was prepared to defend herself. She meant to throw boiling borscht over me, would you believe? She must also have heard her fill of werewolf tales about bloodthirsty witchers relishing torture.'

'Forgive her, Master Geralt. And we shall soon savour that borscht. Edwina makes delicious borscht.'

'It might be better if I don't impose,' said the Witcher, shaking his head. 'I don't want to scare the children, much less worry your wife. To her I'm still a brigand with a sword, it'd be hard to expect her to take to me at once. She said I reek of blood. Metaphorically, I understand.'

'Not really. No offence, Master Witcher, but you stink to high heaven of it.'

'I haven't had any contact with blood for—'

'—for about two weeks, I'd say.' The werewolf finished his sentence. 'It's clotted blood, dead blood, you touched someone who was bleeding. There's also earlier blood, over a month old. Cold blood. Reptile blood. You've also bled. Living blood, from a wound.'

'I'm full of admiration.'

'Us werewolves,' said Dussart, standing up proudly, 'have a slightly more sensitive sense of smell than you humans.'

'I know,' smiled Geralt. 'I know that the werewolf sense of smell is a veritable wonder of nature. Which is why I've come to ask you for a favour.'

*

'Shrews,' said Dussart, sniffing. 'Shrews. And voles. Lots of voles. Dung. Lots of dung. Mainly marten. And weasel. Nothing else.'

The Witcher sighed and then spat. He didn't conceal his disappointment. It was the fourth cave where Dussart hadn't smelt anything apart from rodents and the predators that hunted them. And an abundance of both the former and latter's dung.

They moved on to the next opening gaping in the rock wall. Pebbles shifted under their feet and rolled down the scree. It was steep, they proceeded with difficulty and Geralt was beginning to feel weary. Dussart either turned into a wolf or remained in human form depending on the terrain.

'A she-bear,' he said, looking into the next cave and sniffing. 'With young. She was there but she's not any more. There are marmots. Shrews. Bats. Lots of bats. Stoat. Marten. Wolverine. Lots of dung.'

The next cavern.

'A female polecat. She's on heat. There's also a wolverine . . . No, two. A pair of wolverines.

'An underground spring, the water's slightly sulphurous. Gremlins, a whole flock, probably ten of them. Some sort of amphibians, probably salamanders . . . Bats . . .'

An immense eagle flew down from a rocky ledge located somewhere overhead and circled above, crying out repeatedly. The werewolf raised his head and glanced at the mountain peaks. And the dark clouds gliding out from behind them.

'There's a storm coming. What a summer, when there's almost not a day without a storm . . . What shall we do, Master Geralt? Another hole?'

'Another hole.'

In order to reach the next one, they had to pass under a waterfall cascading down from a cliff; not very large, but sufficient to wet them through. The moss-covered rocks were as slippery as soap. Dussart metamorphosed into a wolf to continue. Geralt, after slipping dangerously several times, forced himself onward, cursed and overcame a difficult section on all fours. *Lucky Dandelion's not here*, he thought, *he'd have turned it into a ballad*. The lycanthrope in front in wolfish form with a witcher behind him on all fours. People would have had a ball.

'A large hole, Master Witcher,' said Dussart, sniffing. 'Broad and deep. There are mountain trolls there. Five or six hefty trolls. And bats. Loads of bat dung.'

'We'll go on. To the next one.'

'Trolls . . . The same trolls as before. The caves are connected.'

'A bear. A cub. It was there, but it's gone. Not long since.'

'Marmots. Bats. Vampyrodes.'

The werewolf leaped back from the next cave as though he'd been stung.

'A gorgon,' he whispered. 'There's a huge gorgon deep in the cave. It's sleeping. There's nothing else apart from it.'

'I'm not surprised,' the Witcher muttered. 'Let's go away. Silently. Because it's liable to awaken . . .'

They walked away, looking back anxiously. They approached the next cave, fortunately located away from the gorgon's lair, slowly, aware that it wouldn't do any harm to be cautious. It didn't do any harm, but turned out to be unnecessary. The next few caves didn't hide anything in their depths other than bats, marmots, mice, voles and shrews. And thick layers of dung.

Geralt was weary and resigned. Dussart clearly was too. But he kept his chin up, you had to grant him that, and didn't betray any discouragement by word or gesture. But the Witcher didn't have any illusions. The werewolf had his doubts about the operation's chances of success. In keeping with what Geralt had once heard and what the old herbalist had confirmed, the steep, eastern cliff of Mount Cremora was riddled with holes, penetrated by countless caves. And indeed, they found countless caves. But Dussart clearly didn't believe it was possible to sniff out and find the right one, which was an underground passage leading inside the rocky complex of the Citadel.

To make matters worse there was a flash of lightning. And a clap of thunder. It began to rain. Geralt had a good mind to spit, swear coarsely and declare the enterprise over. But he overcame the feeling.

'Let's go on, Dussart. Next hole.'

'As you wish, Master Geralt.'

And suddenly, quite like in a cheap novel, a turning point in the action occurred by the next opening gaping in the rock.

'Bats,' announced the werewolf, sniffing. 'Bats and a . . . cat.'

279

'A lynx? A wild cat?'

'A cat,' said Dussart, standing up. 'An ordinary domestic cat.'

*

Otto Dussart looked at the small bottles of elixirs with curiosity and watched the Witcher drinking them. He observed the changes taking place in Geralt's appearance, and his eyes widened in wonder and fear.

'Don't make me enter that cave with you,' he said. 'No offence, but I'm not going. The fear of what might be there makes my hair stand on end.'

'It never occurred to me to ask you to. Go home, Dussart, to your wife and children. You've done me a favour, you've done what I asked of you, so I can't demand any more.'

'I'll wait,' protested the werewolf. 'I'll wait until you emerge.'

'I don't know when I'll be coming out,' said Geralt, adjusting the sword on his back. 'Or if I'll come out at all.'

'Don't say that. I'll wait . . . I'll wait until dusk.'

*

The cave bottom was carpeted in a dense coat of bat guano. The bats themselves – pot-bellied flittermice – were hanging in whole clusters on the cave ceiling, wriggling and squeaking drowsily. At first, the ceiling was high above Geralt's head and he could walk along the level bottom tolerably quickly and comfortably. The comfort soon ended, however – first he had to stoop, then stoop lower and lower, and finally nothing remained but to move along on his hands and knees. And ultimately crawl.

There was a moment when he stopped, determined to turn back, when the cramped conditions represented a grave risk of getting stuck. But he could hear the whoosh of water and feel on his face a current of cold air. Aware of the risk, he forced his way through a crack and sighed in relief as it began to open out. All of a sudden, the corridor turned into a chute down which he slid straight into the channel of an underground stream, gushing out from under a rock and disappearing under another. Somewhere above was a weak light, emanating from the same place as cold gusts of air.

The pool the stream vanished into appeared to be totally under water, and the Witcher wasn't keen on the idea of swimming through, although he suspected it was a sump. He chose a route upstream, against the fast-flowing current, along a ramp leading upwards. Before emerging from the ramp into a great chamber, he was completely drenched and covered in silt from the lime deposits.

The chamber was huge, covered all over with majestic dripstones, draperies, stalagmites, stalactites and stalagnates. The stream flowed along the bottom in a deeply hollowed out meander. There was also a gentle glow of light and a weak draught. There was a faint odour. The Witcher's sense of smell couldn't compete with the werewolf's, but he also smelled what the werewolf had earlier – the faint odour of cat urine.

He stopped for a moment and looked around. The draught pointed to the exit, an opening like a palace portal flanked by pillars of mighty stalagmites. Right alongside he saw a hollow full of fine sand. That hollow was what smelt of cat. He saw numerous feline pawprints in the sand.

He slung his sword – which he'd had to remove in the cramped space of the fissure – across his back. And passed between the stalagmites.

The corridor leading gently upwards had a high ceiling and was dry. There were large rocks on the bottom but it was possible to walk. He set off. Until his way was blocked by a door. Robust and typical of a castle.

Until that moment, he hadn't been at all certain if he was following the right track, had no certainty that he had entered the right cave. The door seemed to confirm his choice.

There was a small opening in the door just above the threshold which had quite recently been carved out. A passage for the cat. He pushed the door – it didn't budge. But the Witcher's amulet quivered slightly. The door was magical, protected by a spell. The weak vibration of the medallion suggested, however, that it wasn't a powerful spell. He brought his face close to the door.

'Friend.'

The door opened noiselessly on oiled hinges. As he had

accurately guessed, it had been equipped with standard weak magical protection and a basic password, as no one – fortunately for him – had felt like installing anything more sophisticated. It was intended to separate the castle from the cave complex and deter any creatures incapable of using even simple magic.

The natural cave ceased beyond the door – which he wedged open with a stone. A corridor carved out of the rock with pickaxes extended before him.

In spite of all the evidence, he still wasn't certain. Until the moment he saw light in front of him. The flickering light of a brand or a cresset. And a moment later heard some very familiar laughter. Cackling.

'Buueh-hhhrrr-eeeehhh-bueeeeh!'

The light and cackling, it turned out, were coming from a large room, illuminated by a torch stuck into an iron basket. Trunks, boxes and barrels were piled up against the walls. Bue and Bang were sitting at one of the crates using barrels as seats. They were playing dice. Bang was cackling, clearly having thrown a higher number.

There was a demijohn of moonshine on the crate. And beside it some kind of snack.

A roast human leg.

The Witcher drew his sword.

'Hello, boys.'

Bue and Bang stared at him open-mouthed for some time. Then they roared and leaped to their feet, knocking over the barrels and snatching up their weapons. Bue a scythe, and Bang a broad scimitar. And charged the Witcher.

They took him by surprise, although he hadn't expected it to be an easy fight. But he hadn't expected the misshapen giants to move so fast.

Bue swung his scythe low and had it not been for a jump Geralt would have lost both legs. He barely dodged Bang's blow, the scimitar striking sparks from the rock wall.

The Witcher was able to cope with fast opponents. And large ones too. Fast or slow, large or small, they all had places sensitive to pain.

And they had no idea how fast a witcher could be after drinking his elixirs.

Bue howled, lacerated on the elbow, and Bang, cut on the knee, howled even louder. The Witcher deceived Bue with a swift spin, jumped over the scythe blade and cut him in the ear with the very tip of his blade. Bue roared, shaking his head, swung the scythe and attacked. Geralt arranged his fingers and struck him with the Aard Sign. Assaulted by the spell, Bue flopped onto his backside on the floor and his teeth rang audibly.

Bang took a great swing with the scimitar. Geralt nimbly ducked under the blade, slashing the giant's other knee in passing, spun around and leaped at Bue, who was struggling to stand up, cutting him across the eyes. Bue managed to pull his head back, however, and was caught on the brow ridge; blood instantly blinded the ogrotroll. Bue yelled and leaped up, attacking Geralt blindly. Geralt dodged away, Bue lurched towards Bang and collided with him. Bang shoved him away and charged the Witcher, roaring furiously, to aim a fierce backhand blow at him. Geralt avoided the blade with a fast feint and a half-turn and cut the ogrotroll twice, on both elbows. Bang howled, but didn't release the scimitar, and took another swing, slashing broadly and chaotically. Geralt dodged, spinning beyond the blade's range. His manoeuvre carried him behind Bang's back and he had to take advantage of a chance like that. He turned his sword around and cut from below, vertically, right between Bang's buttocks. The ogrotroll seized himself by the backside, howled, squealed, hobbled, bent his knees and pissed himself.

Bue, blinded, swung his scythe. And struck. But not the Witcher, who had spun away in a pirouette. He struck his comrade, who was still holding himself by the buttocks. And hacked his head from his shoulders. Air escaped from the severed windpipe with a loud hiss, blood burst from the artery like lava erupting from a volcano, high, right up to the ceiling.

Bang stood, gushing blood, like a headless statue in a fountain, held up by his huge, flat feet. But he finally tipped over and fell like a log.

Bue wiped the blood from his eyes. He roared like a buffalo when it finally dawned on him what had happened. He stamped his feet and swung his scythe. He whirled around on the spot, look-ing for the Witcher. He didn't find him. Because the Witcher was behind him. On being cut in the armpit he dropped the scythe, attacking Geralt with his bare hands, but the blood had blinded him again and he careered into the wall. Geralt was upon him and slashed.

Bue obviously didn't know an artery had been severed. And that he ought to have died long ago. He roared and spun around on the spot, waving his arms about. Until his knees crumpled beneath him and he dropped down in a pool of blood. Now kneeling, he roared and carried on swinging, but quieter and quieter and more drowsily. In order to end it, Geralt went in close and thrust his sword under Bue's sternum. That was a mistake.

The ogrotroll groaned and grabbed the blade, cross guard and the Witcher's hand. His eyes were already misting over, but he didn't relax his grip. Geralt put a boot against his chest, braced himself and tugged. Bue didn't let go even though blood was spurting from his hand.

'You stupid whoreson,' drawled Pastor, entering the cavern and aiming at the Witcher with his double-limbed lathe arbalest. 'You've come here to die. You're done for, devil's spawn. Hold him, Bue!'

Geralt tugged. Bue groaned, but didn't let go. The hunchback grinned and released the trigger. Geralt crouched to evade the heavy bolt and felt the fletching brush against his side before it slammed into the wall. Bue released the sword and – lying on his stomach – caught the Witcher by the legs and held him fast. Pastor croaked in triumph and raised the crossbow.

But didn't manage to fire.

An enormous wolf hurtled into the cavern like a grey missile. It struck Pastor in the legs from behind in the wolfish style, tearing his cruciate ligaments and popliteal artery. The hunchback yelled and fell over. The bowstring of the released arbalest clanged and Bue rasped. The bolt had struck him right in the ear and entered up to the fletching. And the bolt protruded from his other ear.

Pastor howled. The wolf opened its terrible jaws and seized him by the head. The howling turned into wheezing.

Geralt pushed away the finally dead ogrotroll from his legs.

Dussart, now in human form, stood up over Pastor's corpse and wiped his lips and chin.

'After forty-two years of being a werewolf,' he said, meeting the Witcher's gaze, 'it was about time I finally bit someone to death.'

*

'I had to come,' Dussart said, explaining his actions. 'I knew, Master Geralt, that I had to warn you.'

'About them?' Geralt wiped his blade and pointed to the lifeless bodies.

'Not only.'

The Witcher entered the room the werewolf was pointing at. And stepped back involuntarily.

The stone floor was black with congealed blood. A black-rimmed hole gaped in the centre of the room. A pile of bodies was heaped up beside it. Naked and mutilated, cut up, quartered, occasionally with the skin flayed off them. It was difficult to estimate how many there were.

The sound of bones being crunched and cracked rose up very audibly from deep in the hole.

'I wasn't able to smell it before,' mumbled Dussart, in a voice full of disgust. 'I only smelled it when you opened the door down there at the bottom. Let's flee from here, master. Far from this charnel house.'

'I still have something to sort out here. But you go. I thank you very much for coming to help.'

'Don't thank me. I owed you a debt. I'm glad I was able to pay it back.'

*

A spiral staircase led upwards, winding up a cylindrical shaft carved into the rock. It was difficult to estimate precisely, but Geralt roughly calculated that had it been a staircase in a typical tower, he would have climbed to the first – or possibly the second – storey. He had counted sixty-two steps when a door finally barred his way.

Like the one down in the cave, that door also had a passage carved in it for a cat. Unlike the heavy doors in the cave it wasn't magical and yielded easily after the handle had been pushed down.

The room he entered had no windows and was dimly lit. Beneath the ceiling hung several magical globes, but only one was active. The room stank acridly of chemicals and every possible kind of monstrosity. A quick glance revealed what it contained. Specimen jars, demijohns and flagons on shelves, retorts, glass spheres and tubes, steel instruments and tools – unmistakably a laboratory, in other words.

Large specimen jars were standing in a row on a bookshelf by the entrance. The nearest one was full of human eyeballs, floating in a yellow liquid like mirabelle plums in compote. In another jar, there was a tiny homunculus, no larger than two fists held together. In a third . . .

A human head was floating in the third jar. Geralt might not have recognised the features, which were distorted by cuts, swelling and discolouration, barely visible through the cloudy liquid and thick glass. But the head was quite bald. Only one sorcerer shaved his head.

Harlan Tzara – it transpired – had never made it to Poviss.

Things were suspended in other jars: various blue and pale horrors. But there were no more heads.

There was a table in the middle of the room. A steel, purpose-built table with a gutter.

A naked corpse was lying on the table. A diminutive one. The remains of a child. A fair-haired little girl.

The remains had been slit open with a cut in the shape of a letter 'Y'. The internal organs, removed, had been arranged on both sides of the body, evenly, neatly and orderly. It looked just like an engraving from an anatomical atlas. All that was missing were plate numbers: fig. 1, fig. 2 and so on.

He caught sight of movement out of the corner of his eye. A large black cat flashed by close to the wall, glanced at him, hissed and fled through the open door. Geralt set off after him.

'Mester . . .'

He stopped. And turned around.

In the corner stood a low cage, resembling a chicken coop. He saw thin fingers clenching the iron bars. And then two eyes.

'Mester . . . Help me . . .'

It was a little boy, no more than ten years old. Cowering and trembling.

'Help me . . .'

'Sssh, be quiet. You're in no danger now, but hold on a little longer. I'll be back soon to get you.'

'Mester! Don't go!'

'Be quiet, I said.'

First there was a library with dust that made his nose tingle. Then something like a drawing room. And then a bedchamber. A huge bed with a black canopy on ebony columns.

He heard a rustle. And turned around.

Sorel Degerlund was standing in the doorway. Coiffured, in a mantle embroidered with gold stars. A smallish, quite grey creature armed with a Zerrikanian sabre was standing beside him.

'I have a specimen jar full of formalin prepared,' said the sorcerer. 'For your head, you abomination. Kill him, Beta!'

The creature, an incredibly fast grey apparition, an agile and noiseless grey rat, had already attacked with a whistle and a flash of the sabre before Degerlund had finished his sentence and while he was still delighting in his own voice. Geralt avoided two blows, delivered diagonally in classic style. The first time he felt the movement of air pushed by a blade by his ear, and the second a brush on his sleeve. He parried the third blow, and for a moment they crossed swords. He saw the face of the grey creature, its large yellow eyes with vertical pupils, narrow slits instead of a nose and pointed ears. The creature had no mouth at all.

They parted. The creature turned around nimbly, attacked at once, with an ethereal, dancing step, once again diagonally. Once again predictably. It was inhumanly energetic, incredibly agile, hellishly swift. But stupid.

It had no idea how fast a witcher could be after drinking his elixirs.

Geralt allowed it only one blow, which he outmanoeuvred. Then he attacked with a trained sequence of movements he had practised a hundred times. He encircled the grey creature with a fast half-turn, executed a deceptive feint and slashed it across the collarbone. The blood hadn't even had time to spurt when he slashed it under the arm. And jumped aside, ready for more. But no more was needed.

It turned out that the creature did have a mouth. It opened in the grey face like a wound, splitting widely from ear to ear, although no more than half an inch. But the creature didn't utter a word or a sound. It fell onto its knees and then its side. For a moment it twitched, moving its limbs like a dog dreaming. And died. In silence.

It was then that Degerlund committed an error. Rather than fleeing, he raised both hands and began to bark out a spell, in a furious voice full of rage and hatred. Flames whirled around his hands, forming a fiery globe. It looked a little like candyfloss being made. It even smelled similar.

Degerlund didn't manage to create a complete globe. He had no idea how fast a witcher could be after drinking his elixirs.

Geralt was upon him and cut across the globe and the sorcerer's hands. There was a roar like a furnace being ignited, and sparks flew. Degerlund yelled, releasing the flaming globe from his blood-ied hands. The globe went out, filling the chamber with the smell of burning caramel.

Geralt dropped his sword. He slapped Degerlund hard in the face with his open palm. The sorcerer screamed, cowered and turned his back on him. The Witcher seized him, caught him by a buckle and clasped his neck in his forearm. Degerlund yelled and began to kick out.

'You cannot!' he wailed. 'You cannot kill me! It is forbidden . . . I am . . . I am a human being!'

Geralt tightened his forearm around his neck. Not too tightly at first.

'It wasn't me!' wailed the sorcerer. 'It was Ortolan! Ortolan forced me! He forced me! And Biruta Icarti knew about everything! She did! Biruta! That medallion was her idea! She made me do it!'

The Witcher tightened his grip.

'Heeeeelp! Somebody heeelp meeee!'

Geralt tightened his grip.

'Somebody . . . Heeelp . . . Noooo . . .'

Degerlund wheezed, saliva dripping copiously from his mouth. Geralt turned his head away. And tightened his grip.

Degerlund lost consciousness and went limp. Tighter. The hyoid bone cracked. Tighter. His larynx gave way. Tighter. Even tighter.

The cervical vertebrae cracked and dislocated.

Geralt held Degerlund up a moment longer. Then he jerked the sorcerer's head hard sideways, to be quite certain. Then he let him go. The sorcerer slid down onto the floor, softly, like a silk cloth.

The Witcher wiped the saliva from his sleeve on a curtain. The large black cat appeared from nowhere. It rubbed itself against Degerlund's body. Licked his motionless hand. Meowed and cried mournfully. It lay down beside the corpse, cuddling up against its side. And looked at the Witcher with its wide-open golden eyes.

'I had to,' said the Witcher. 'It was necessary. If anyone, you ought to understand.'

The cat narrowed its eyes. To indicate it did.

For God's sake let us sit upon the ground
And tell sad stories of the death of kings;
How some have been depos'd, some slain in war,
Some haunted by the ghosts they have depos'd;
Some poison'd by their wives, some sleeping kill'd;
All murder'd.

William Shakespeare,
Richard II

CHAPTER EIGHTEEN

The weather on the day of the royal wedding had been wonderful from early morning, the blue sky over Kerack not sullied by even a single cloud. It had been very warm since the morning, but the hot weather was tempered by a sea breeze.

There had been a commotion in the upper town from the early morning. The streets and squares had been thoroughly swept, the house fronts decorated with ribbons and garlands, and pennants put on flagpoles. Since the morning, a line of suppliers had streamed along the road leading to the royal palace. Laden wagons and carts passed empty ones on their way back, and porters, craftsmen, merchants, messengers and couriers ran up the hill. Some time after, the road had teemed with sedan chairs carrying wedding guests to the palace. *My nuptials are no laughing matter*, King Belohun was heard to have said, *my nuptials will become lodged in people's memory and talked about through the whole wide world.* On the order of the king, the celebrations were thus meant to begin in the morning and last long into the night. The guests would be facing quite unprecedented attractions throughout the whole day. Kerack was a tiny kingdom and actually fairly insignificant, hence Geralt doubted whether the world was particularly bothered about Belohun's nuptials, even though he had decided to hold balls the entire week and God knows what attractions he had come up with, and there was no chance the people living more than a hundred miles away could have heard of the event. But to Belohun – as was universally known – the city of Kerack was the centre of the world and the world was the small region surrounding Kerack.

Geralt and Dandelion were both dressed as elegantly as they could manage, and the Witcher had even purchased for the celebrations a brand new calfskin jacket, for which he had paid well over the odds. As for Dandelion, he had announced from the beginning that he would scorn the royal nuptials and take no part in them. For he had been added to the guest list as a relative of the royal instigator and not as the world-famous poet and bard. And he had not been invited to perform. Dandelion regarded that as a slight and took umbrage. As was customary with him his resentment didn't last long, no more than half a day.

Flagpoles were erected along the entire road winding up the hillside to the palace and on them hung yellow pennants with the coat of arms of Kerack, a blue dolphin *naiant* with red fins and tail, languidly fluttering in the breeze.

Dandelion's kinsman, Ferrant de Lettenhove, assisted by several royal guardsmen wearing livery with the heraldic dolphin – in other words blue and red – was waiting for them outside the entrance to the palace complex. The instigator greeted Dandelion and called over a page who was charged with assisting the poet and escorting him to the place of the party.

'And I would ask you, M'lord Geralt, to come with me.'

They walked through the grounds along a side avenue, passing an area obviously used for utilities, from where they could hear the clank of pots and kitchen utensils, as well as the vile insults the chefs were dishing out to the kitchen porters. On top of that, however, was the pleasant and appetising smell of food. Geralt knew the menu and knew what the guests would be served during the wedding party. A few days before, he and Dandelion had visited the Natura Rerum osteria. Febus Ravenga – not concealing his pride – had boasted that he and several other restaurateurs were organising the feast and composing a list of dishes, for the preparation of which only the most distinguished of local chefs would be hired. *Sautéed oysters, sea urchins, prawns and crabs will be served for breakfast*, he had said. *For a mid-morning snack there will be meat jellies and various pasties, smoked and marinated salmon, duck in aspic, sheep and goats cheese. For luncheon there will be ad libitum meat or fish broth, on top of that meat or fish patties, tripe with liver meatballs, grilled monkfish glazed with honey and sea perch with saffron and cloves.*

Afterwards, Ravenga intoned, modulating his breathing like a trained orator, *will be served cuts of roast meat in white sauce with capers, eggs and mustard, swans' knees in honey, capons draped in fatback, partridges and quince conserve, roast pigeon and mutton liver pie with barley groats. Salads and diverse vegetables. Then caramels, nougats, stuffed cakes, roast chestnuts, preserves and marmalades. Wine from Toussaint, naturally, will be served continuously and without pause.*

Ravenga described it so vividly it was mouth-watering. Geralt doubted, however, that he would manage to taste anything from the extensive menu. He was by no means a guest at the nuptials. He was in a worse situation than the pages, who could always pluck some morsels from the dishes or at least stick a finger in the creams, sauces or forcemeats as they hurried by.

The main location of the celebrations was the palace grounds, once the temple orchard, with modifications and extensions by the kings of Kerack, mainly in the form of colonnades, bowers and temples of contemplation. Today, many colourful pavilions had been additionally erected among the trees and buildings, and sheets of canvas stretched over poles offered shelter from the heat of the day. A small crowd of guests had already gathered. There weren't meant to be too many; some two hundred in total. It was rumoured that the king himself had drawn up the list and only a select circle – *la crème de la crème* itself – would be receiving invitations. For Belohun, it turned out, his close and distant relatives constituted the larger part of the elite. Aside from them, the local high society, key administrative officials, and the wealthiest local and foreign businessmen and diplomats – meaning spies from neighbouring countries posing as commercial attachés – had also been invited. The list was completed by quite a large group of sycophants, grovellers and pre-eminent arse-kissers.

Prince Egmund was waiting outside one of the side entrances to the palace, dressed in a short black jacket with rich silver and gold embroidery. He was accompanied by a few young men. They all had long, curled hair and were wearing padded doublets and tight hose with terribly fashionable and excessively large codpieces. Geralt didn't like the look of them. Not just because of the mocking glances they were shooting at his apparel. They reminded him too much of Sorel Degerlund.

At the sight of the instigator and the Witcher, the prince immediately dismissed his entourage. Only one individual remained. He had short hair and wore normal trousers. In spite of that, Geralt didn't like the look of him either. He had strange eyes. And an unprepossessing look.

Geralt bowed before the prince. The prince didn't return the bow, naturally.

'Hand over your sword,' he said to Geralt right after his greeting. 'You may not parade around with a weapon. Don't fret, although you won't see your sword it will be close at hand the whole time. I've issued orders. Should anything occur, the sword will immediately be returned to you. Captain Ropp here will take charge of that.'

'And what's the likelihood of anything happening?'

'Were there no chance or little chance, would I be bothering you?' Egmund examined the scabbard and blade. 'Oh! A sword from Viroleda! Not a sword, but a work of art. I know, for I once had a similar one. My half-brother, Viraxas, stole it from me. When my father banished him, he appropriated a great deal of things that didn't belong to him before leaving. No doubt as souvenirs.'

Ferrant de Lettenhove cleared his throat. Geralt recalled Dandelion's words. It was forbidden to utter the name of the banished first-born son at court. But Egmund was clearly ignoring the prohibitions.

'A work of art,' repeated the prince, still examining the sword. 'Without asking how you came by it, I congratulate you on the acquisition. For I can't believe the stolen ones were any better than this.'

'That's a matter of taste and preference. I'd prefer to recover the stolen ones. Your Royal Highness and my Lord Instigator vouched that you would find the thief. It was, I take the liberty of recalling, the condition on which I undertook the task of protecting the king. The condition has clearly not been met.'

'It clearly hasn't,' Egmund admitted coldly, handing the sword to Captain Ropp, the man with the malevolent gaze. 'I thus feel obliged to compensate you for it. Instead of the three hundred crowns I had planned to pay you for your services, you will receive five hundred. I also add that the investigation regarding your swords is ongoing and you may yet recover them. Ferrant allegedly has a suspect. Haven't you?'

'The investigation explicitly indicated the person of Nikefor

Muus, a municipal and judicial clerk,' Ferrant de Lettenhove announced dryly. 'He has fled, but his recapture is imminent.'

'I trust so.' The prince snorted. 'It can't be such a feat to catch an ink-stained petty clerk. Who, in addition, must have acquired piles from sitting at a desk, which hinder escape, both on foot and horseback. How did he manage to escape at all?'

'We are dealing with a very volatile person.' The instigator cleared his throat. 'And probably a madman. Before he vanished, he caused a revolting scene in Ravenga's restaurant, concerning, forgive me, human faeces . . . The restaurant had to be closed for some time, because . . . I shall spare you the gory details. The stolen swords were not discovered during a search carried out at Muus's lodgings, but instead . . . Forgive me . . . A leather satchel, filled to the brim with—'

'Enough, enough, I can guess what.' Egmund grimaced. 'Yes, that indeed says a great deal about the individual's psychological state. Your swords, Witcher, have probably been lost, then. Even if Ferrant captures him he won't learn anything from a madman. It's not even worth torturing men like him, they only talk gibberish on the rack. And now forgive me, duty calls.'

Ferrant de Lettenhove escorted Geralt towards the main entrance to the palace grounds. Shortly after, they found themselves in a stone-slabbed courtyard where seneschals were greeting the guests as they arrived, and guardsmen and pages were escorting them further into the grounds.

'What may I expect?'

'I beg your pardon?'

'What may I expect today? What part of that didn't you understand?'

'Prince Xander has boasted in front of witnesses that he will be crowned king tomorrow,' said the instigator in a low voice. 'But it isn't the first time he's said that and he's always been in his cups when he has.'

'Is he capable of carrying out a coup?'

'Not especially. But he has a camarilla, confidants and favourites. They are more capable.'

'How much proof is there in the rumour that Belohun will today announce as his successor the son his betrothed is carrying?'

'Quite some.'

'And Egmund, who's losing his chances for the throne, lo and behold, is hiring a witcher to guard and protect his father. What commendable filial love.'

'Don't digress. You took on the task. Now execute it.'

'I did and I shall. Although it's extremely vague. I don't know who, if anything happens, will be pitted against me. But I probably ought to know who will support me if anything happens.'

'If such a need arises, the sword, as the prince promised, will be given to you by Captain Ropp. He will also back you up. I shall help, as far as I'm able. Because I wish you well.'

'Since when?'

'I beg your pardon?'

'We've never spoken face to face. Dandelion has always been with us and I didn't want to bring up the subject with him there. The detailed documentation about my alleged frauds. How did Egmund come by it? Who forged it? Not him, of course. You did, Ferrant.'

'I had nothing to do with it. I assure you—'

'You're a rotten liar for a guardian of the law. It's a mystery how you landed your position.'

Ferrant de Lettenhove pursed his lips.

'I had to,' he said. 'I was carrying out orders.'

The Witcher looked long and hard at him.

'You wouldn't believe how many times I've heard similar words,' he finally said. 'But it's comforting to think it was usually from the mouths of men who were about to hang.'

*

Lytta Neyd was among the guests. He spotted her easily. Because she looked eye-catching.

The bodice of her vivid green *crêpe de chine* gown with its plunging neckline was decorated with embroidery in the form of a stylised butterfly sparkling with tiny sequins. It was edged with frills. Frilly dresses on women older than ten usually evoked ironic sympathy in the Witcher, while on Lytta's dress they harmonised with the rest of it with more than attractive results.

The sorceress's neck was adorned with a necklace of polished emeralds. None smaller than an almond. And one considerably larger.

Her red hair was like a forest fire.

Mozaïk was standing at Lytta's side. In a black and astonishingly bold dress of silk and chiffon, quite transparent on the shoulders and sleeves. The girl's neck and cleavage were veiled in something like a fancifully draped chiffon ruff which, in combination with the long black sleeves, gave her figure an aura of flamboyance and mystery.

They were both wearing four-inch heels. Lytta's were made of iguana skin and Mozaïk's of patent leather.

Geralt hesitated to approach for a moment. But only a moment.

'Greetings,' Lytta she said guardedly. 'What a pleasant surprise, it's lovely to see you. Mozaïk, you won, the white slippers are yours.'

'A wager,' he guessed. 'What did it concern?'

'You. I thought we wouldn't see you again and wagered that you wouldn't show up. Mozaïk took the bet, because she thought differently.'

Lytta gave him a deep, jade-green glance, clearly waiting for a response. For a word. For anything. Geralt remained silent.

'Greetings, fair ladies!' said Dandelion, springing up from nowhere, a veritable *deus ex machina*. 'My respects, I bow before your beauty. Madame Neyd, Miss Mozaïk. Forgive the absence of flowers.'

'We forgive you. What of the arts?'

'All that you'd expect: everything and nothing,' said Dandelion, snatching two goblets of wine from a passing page and handing them to the women. 'The party's somewhat dull, isn't it? But the wine's good. Est Est, forty a pint. The red's not bad, either, I've tried it. Just don't drink the hippocras, they don't know how to spice it. And there's no end of guests, have you seen? As usual in high society, the race is back-to-front, it's *à rebours*; whoever arrives last wins and claims the laurels. And will have a splendid entrance. I think we're observing the finish right now. The owner of a chain of lumber mills and wife are crossing the finishing line, losing out in the process to the harbourmaster and wife who are just behind. Who in turn are losing out to a dandy I don't know . . .'

'That's the head of the Koviran commercial mission. And wife,' explained Coral. 'I wonder whose.'

'Pyral Pratt, that old villain, will make it into the leading pack. With a pretty good-looking partner . . . Bloody hell!'

'What's the matter?'

'The woman beside Pratt . . .' Dandelion choked. 'Is . . . is Etna Asider . . . The little widow who sold me the sword . . .'

'Is that how she introduced herself?' snorted Lytta. 'Etna Asider? A cheap anagram. She's Antea Derris. Pratt's eldest daughter. And no little widow, for she's never married. Rumour has it she isn't fond of men.'

'Pratt's daughter? Impossible! I've visited him—'

'But you didn't meet her there,' the sorceress cut him off. 'Nothing strange. Antea doesn't get on very well with her family, she doesn't even use her surname, but an alias made up of two given names. She only contacts her father regarding her business affairs, which as a matter of fact are booming. But I'm surprised to see them here together.'

'They must have their reasons,' the Witcher observed astutely.

'I dread to think what. Officially, Antea is a commercial agent, but her favourite sports are swindles, fraud and rackets. Poet, I have a favour to ask. You're worldly-wise, but Mozaïk isn't. Lead her among the guests and introduce her to anyone worth knowing. And point out any who aren't.'

Assuring Coral that her wish was his command, Dandelion proffered Mozaïk his arm. They were left alone.

'Come,' Lytta interrupted the lengthening silence. 'Let's take a walk. Up that little hill over there.'

A view of the city, Palmyra, the harbour and the sea, spread out from high up on the hill, from the temple of contemplation. Lytta shielded her eyes with a hand.

'What's that sailing into harbour? And dropping anchor? A three-masted frigate of curious construction. Under black sails, ha, it's quite remarkable—'

'Forget the frigates. Dandelion and Mozaïk having been sent away, we're alone and out of the way.'

'And you're wondering why.' She turned around. 'Waiting for me to tell you something. You're waiting for the questions I shall ask you. But perhaps I only want to tell you the latest gossip? From the wizarding community? Oh, no, never fear, it's not about Yennefer. It's about Rissberg, a place you know well, after all. Plenty of changes have taken place there . . . But I fail to see the glint of curiosity in your eyes. Shall I go on?'

'By all means, do.'

'It began when Ortolan died.'

'Ortolan's dead?'

'He passed away almost a week ago. According to the official version he was lethally poisoned by the fertiliser he was working on. But rumour has it that it was a stroke caused by the news of the sudden death of one of his favourites, who died as a result of an unsuccessful and highly suspicious experiment. I'm talking about a certain Degerlund. Does that name ring a bell? Did you meet him when you were at the castle?'

'I may have. I met many sorcerers. They weren't all memorable.'

'Ortolan apparently blamed the entire council at Rissberg for his favourite's death, became enraged and suffered a stroke. He was really very old and had suffered from high blood pressure. His addiction to fisstech was an open secret, and fisstech and high blood pressure are a potent mixture. But there must have been something fishy, because significant staffing changes have taken place at Rissberg. Even before Ortolan's death there had been conflicts. Algernon Guincamp, more commonly known as Pinety, was forced to resign, among others. You remember him, I'm certain. Because if anyone was memorable there, he was.'

'Indeed.'

'Ortolan's death—' Coral glared at him keenly '—provoked a swift response from the Chapter, who had much earlier been aware of some worrying tidings concerning the antics of the deceased and his favourite. Interestingly – and increasingly typically in our times – a tiny pebble triggered the landslide. An insignificant commoner, an over-zealous shire-reeve or constable. He forced his superior – the bailiff from Gors Velen – to take action. The bailiff took the accusations higher up and thus, rung by rung, the affair reached the royal council and thence the Chapter. To keep things brief: people were accused of negligence. Biruta Icarti had to leave the board. She went back to lecture at Aretuza. Pockmarked Axel and Sandoval left. Zangenis kept his job, gaining the Chapter's pardon by informing on the others and shifting all the blame onto them. What do you say to that? Do you have anything to say?'

'What can I say? It's your business. And your scandals.'

'Scandals that erupted at Rissberg soon after your visit.'

'You overrate me, Coral. And my influence.'

'I never overrate anything. And seldom underrate.'

'Mozaïk and Dandelion will be back any moment,' he said, looking her in the eyes. 'And after all, you didn't bring me here without a reason. Will you tell me what this is about?'

She withstood his gaze.

'You know very well what this is about,' she replied. 'So don't offend my intelligence by lowering your own. You haven't come to see me in over a month. No, don't think I desire mawkish melodrama or pathetic sentimental gestures. I don't expect anything more from the relationship that's finishing than a pleasant memory.'

'It seems to me you used the word "relationship"? Its semantic capacity is indeed astounding.'

'Nothing but a pleasant memory,' she said, ignoring his comment and holding his gaze. 'I don't know what it's like for you, but as far as I'm concerned, I'll be frank, things aren't that good. It would, I think, be worth making some serious efforts to that end. I don't think much would be necessary. Why, something small but nice, a nice final note, something to leave a pleasant memory. Could you manage something like that? Would you like to visit me?'

He didn't manage to answer. The bell in the belfry began to toll deafeningly, striking ten times. Then trumpets sounded a loud, brassy and slightly cacophonous fanfare. The crowd of guests was parted by blue and red guardsmen forming a double file. The marshal of the court appeared beneath the portico in the entrance to the palace wearing a gold chain around his neck and holding a staff as a big as a fence post. Behind him strode heralds and behind the heralds, seneschals. And behind the seneschals, wearing a sable calpac and holding a sceptre, marched Belohun, King of Kerack, in bony and wiry person. At his side walked a willowy young blonde in a veil, who could only have been the royal betrothed, and in the very near future his wife and queen. The blonde was wearing a snow-white dress and was bedecked in diamonds, perhaps rather too lavishly, in a rather nouveau-riche and rather tasteless style. Like the king, she bore on her shoulders an ermine cloak which was held by pages.

The royal family followed on behind the royal couple, at least a dozen paces behind the pages holding the train, which spoke volumes about their status. Egmund was there, naturally, and beside him a man as fair-skinned as an albino, who could only have been his brother Xander. Beyond the brothers walked the rest of the relatives: several men, several women, and a few teen-aged boys and girls, evidently the king's legitimate and illegitimate offspring.

Amid the bowing male and low-curtsying female guests, the royal procession reached its destination, which was a raised platform somewhat resembling a scaffold. Two thrones had been placed on the platform, which was roofed over by a canopy and covered at the sides by tapestries. The king and the bride sat down on the thrones. The rest of the family had to stand.

The trumpets assaulted the ears a second time with their brassy braying. The marshal of the court – brandishing his arms like a conductor in front of an orchestra – encouraged the guests to shout, cheer and toast the duo. The guests and courtiers tried to outdo each other by showering the soon-to-be-wed couple from all sides with wishes for eternal good health, happiness, success, long, longer and even longer lives. King Belohun maintained his haughty and huffy expression, and only demonstrated his pleasure with the good wishes, compliments and praises being sung to him and his bride-to-be by subtle twitches of his sceptre.

The marshal of the court silenced the guests and gave a long speech, smoothly shifting from grandiloquence to bombast and back again. Geralt devoted all his attention to watching the crowd, hence he only listened with half an ear. King Belohun – the marshal of the court proclaimed to all and sundry – was genuinely glad that so many people had come, was overjoyed to welcome everybody on such an auspicious occasion and wished them precisely the same as they wished him. The wedding ceremony would be taking place in the afternoon, and until then the guests were invited to eat, drink and be merry and avail themselves of the numerous attractions planned for the event.

The braying of the trumpets proclaimed the end of the official part. The royal procession began to leave the gardens. Among the guests, Geralt had managed to observe several small groups behaving quite suspiciously. One group in particular bothered him, because they hadn't bowed to the procession as low as the others and were attempting to shove their way towards the palace gate. He drifted towards the double file of soldiers in blue and red. Lytta walked beside him.

Belohun strode with his eyes fixed straight ahead. The bride-to-be was looking around, occasionally nodding at the guests greeting her. A gust of wind raised her veil for a moment. Geralt saw her large blue eyes. He saw those eyes suddenly find Lytta Neyd amid the throng. And saw the eyes light up with hatred. Pure, unadulterated, distilled hatred.

It lasted a second and then the trumpets resounded, the procession passed and the guardsmen marched on. The suspiciously behaving little group had, as it turned out, only been aiming at the table laden with wine and *hors d'oeuvres*, which they besieged and stripped ahead of the other guests. Performances began on makeshift stages dotted here and there: musicians played fiddles, lyres, pipes and recorders, and choirs sang. Jugglers took turns with tumblers, strongmen made way for acrobats, and tightrope walkers were replaced by scantily clad dancers with tambourines. People became merrier and merrier. The ladies' cheeks began to glow, the gentlemen's foreheads to glisten with sweat, and the speech of both the former and the latter became very loud. And somewhat incoherent.

Lytta pulled him beyond a pavilion. They surprised a couple that had concealed themselves there for explicitly sexual purposes. The sorceress wasn't bothered and paid almost no attention to them.

'I don't know what's afoot,' she said. 'And I don't know why you're here, though I can guess. But keep your eyes open and anything you do, do with prudence. The royal betrothed is none other than Ildiko Breckl.

'I won't ask you if you know her. I saw that look.'

'Ildiko Breckl,' Coral repeated. 'That's her name. She was turfed out of Aretuza in the third year. For petty theft. She's done well for herself, as you can see. She didn't become a sorceress, but she'll be a queen in a few hours. The cherry on the tart, dammit? She's only meant to be seventeen. The old fool. Ildiko is a good twenty-five.'

'And appears not to like you.'

'The feeling's mutual. She's a born schemer, trouble always follows her around. But that's not all. The frigate that sailed into the harbour under black sails? I know what she is, I've heard about her. She's *Acherontia*. And is extremely infamous. Wherever she appears something happens.'

'What, for example?'

'She has a crew of mercenaries who can allegedly be hired to do anything. And what do you hire mercenaries for? Bricklaying?'

'I have to go. Forgive me, Coral.'

'Whatever occurs,' she said slowly, looking him in the eyes, 'whatever happens, I can't be embroiled in it.'

'Never fear. I don't mean to ask for your help.'

'You misunderstood me.'

'No doubt. Forgive me, Coral.'

*

Just beyond the ivy-grown colonnade he bumped into Mozaïk coming the other way. Astonishingly calm and cool among the heat, hubbub and commotion.

'Where's Dandelion? Did he leave you?'

'He did,' she sighed. 'But excused himself politely and also asked me to apologise to you. He was invited to perform in private. In the palace chambers, for the queen and her ladies-in-waiting. He couldn't refuse.'

'Who asked him?'

'A man with a soldierly look. And a strange expression in his eyes.'

'I have to go. Forgive me, Mozaïk.'

A small crowd had gathered beyond the pavilion, which was decorated with colourful ribbons. Food was being served: pasties, salmon and duck in aspic. Geralt cleared a path for himself, looking out for Captain Ropp or Ferrant de Lettenhove. Instead he ran straight into Febus Ravenga. The restaurateur resembled an aristocrat. He was dressed in a brocade doublet, while his head was adorned with a hat bearing a plume of ostrich feathers. He was accompanied by Pyral Pratt's daughter, chic and elegant in a black male outfit.

'Oh, Geralt,' said Ravenga, looking pleased. 'Antea, let me introduce you: Geralt of Rivia, the famous witcher. Geralt, this is Madam Antea Derris, commercial agent. Have a glass of wine with us . . .'

'Forgive me but I'm in a hurry,' he apologised. 'I'm aware of Madam Antea, although I haven't met her personally. In your shoes, I wouldn't buy anything from her, Febus.'

The portico over the palace entrance had been decorated by some scholarly linguist with a banner reading CRESCITE ET MULTIPLICAMINI. And Geralt was stopped by crossed halberd shafts.

'No entry.'

'I have to see the royal instigator urgently.'

'No entry.' The commander of the guard emerged from behind the halberdiers. He was holding a half-pike in his left hand. He aimed the dirty index finger of his right hand straight at Geralt's nose. 'No entry, do you understand, sire?'

'If you don't take that finger away from my face, I'll break it in several places. Ah, precisely, that's much better. And now take me to the instigator.'

'Whenever you happen upon guards there's always a row,' said Ferrant de Lettenhove from behind the Witcher. He must have followed Geralt. 'It's a grave character flaw. And may have disagreeable consequences.'

'I don't like it when anybody bars my way.'

'But that's what guards and sentries are for, after all. They wouldn't be necessary if there was free entry everywhere. Let him through.'

'We have orders from the king himself.' The commander of the guard frowned. 'We're to admit no one without being searched!'

'Then search him.'

The search was thorough and the guardsmen took it seriously.

They searched him thoroughly, not limiting themselves to a cursory pat. They didn't find anything, Geralt hadn't taken the dagger he usually carried stuck down his boot to the wedding.

'Happy?' asked the instigator, looking down at the commander. 'Now step aside and let us through.'

'May Your Excellency forgive me,' the commander drawled. 'The king's order was unequivocal. It applied to everyone.'

'Whatever next? Don't forget yourself, lad! Do you know who stands before you?'

'Everyone is to be searched,' said the commander, nodding towards the guardsmen. 'The order was clear. Please don't make problems, Your Excellency. For us . . . or for yourself.'

'What's happening today?'

'Regarding that, please see my superiors. They ordered me to search everybody.'

The instigator swore under his breath and yielded to the search. He didn't even have a penknife.

'I'd like to know what this is all about,' he said when they were finally walking along the corridor. 'I'm seriously perturbed. Seriously perturbed, Witcher.'

'Did you see Dandelion? He was apparently summoned to the palace to sing.'

'I know nothing of that.'

'But did you know that the *Acherontia* has sailed into harbour? Does that name mean anything to you?'

'A great deal. And my anxiety grows. By the minute. Let's make haste!'

Guardsmen armed with partisans were moving around the vestibule – once the temple cloisters – and blue and red uniforms also flitted through the cloisters. The clatter of boots and raised voices reached them from the corridor.

'I say!' said the instigator, beckoning at a passing soldier. 'Sergeant! What's going on here?'

'Forgive me, Your Excellency . . . I'm hurrying with orders . . .'

'Stand still, I say! What's going on? I demand an explanation! Is something the matter? Where is Prince Egmund?'

'Mr Ferrant de Lettenhove.'

King Belohun himself stood in a doorway, beneath standards

bearing the blue dolphin, accompanied by four sturdy toughs in leather jerkins. He had disposed of his royal trappings, so he didn't look like a king. He looked like a peasant whose cow had just calved and given birth to a gorgeous specimen.

'Mr Ferrant de Lettenhove.' Joy at the calf could also be heard in the king's voice. 'The royal instigator. I mean, *my* instigator. Or perhaps not mine. Perhaps my son's. You appear, although I haven't summoned you. In principle, being here at this moment was your professional duty, but I didn't summon you. *Let Ferrant,* I thought to myself, *let Ferrant eat, drink, pick up a bit of skirt and shag her in the bower. I won't summon him, I don't want him here.* Do you know why I didn't want you? Because I wasn't certain who you serve. Whom do you serve, Ferrant?'

'I serve Your Majesty,' replied the instigator, bowing low. 'And I'm utterly devoted to Your Majesty.'

'Did you all hear that?' asked the king, looking around theatrically. 'Ferrant is devoted to me! Very well, Ferrant, very well. I expected an answer like that, O royal instigator. You may remain, you'll come in useful. I shall at once charge you with a task befitting an instigator . . . I say! And this one? Who is it? Just a minute! Could it be that witcher who engages in swindles? Whom the sorceress fingered?'

'He turned out to be innocent, the sorceress was misled. He had been informed upon—'

'The innocent are not informed upon.'

'It was a decision of the court. The case was closed owing to lack of evidence.'

'But there was a case, meaning there was a stink. Decisions of the court and its verdicts derive from the imaginations and caprices of court officers, while the stink issues from the very nub of the case. That's all I wish to say, I won't waste time on lectures about jurisprudence. On the day of my marriage I can show magnanimity, not order him locked up, but get that witcher out of my sight at once. And may he never darken my door again!'

'Your Majesty . . . I am perturbed . . . *Acherontia* has allegedly sailed into port. In this situation safety considerations dictate the need for protection . . . The Witcher could . . .'

'Could what? Shield me with his own bosom? Paralyse the

assassins with a witcher spell? For did Egmund, my loving son, charge him with such a task? To protect his father and ensure his safety? Step this way, Ferrant. Why, and you bloody come too, Witcher. I'll show you something. You'll see how one takes care of one's own safety and guarantees oneself protection. Have a good look. Listen. Perhaps you'll learn something. And find something out. About yourselves. Come on, follow me!'

They set off, urged by the king and surrounded by the bruisers in leather jerkins. They entered a large room where a throne stood on a dais beneath a plafond decorated with waves and sea monsters. Belohun seated himself on the throne. Opposite, beneath a fresco portraying a stylised map of the world, the king's sons sat on a bench, guarded by other bruisers. The princes of Kerack. The coal-black-haired Egmund and the albino-blonde Xander.

Belohun sat back comfortably on his throne. He looked down on his sons with the air of a victorious commander before whom kneel his enemies, crushed in battle, begging for mercy. However, the victors on the paintings Geralt had seen usually wore expressions of gravity, dignity, nobility and magnamity for the vanquished. One would have searched in vain for that on Belohun's face. It was painted with nothing but scathing derision.

'My court jester fell ill yesterday,' spoke the king. 'He came down with the shits. *What bad luck,* I thought, *there'll be no jokes, no japes, no fun and games.* I was wrong. It's funny. So funny, it's side-splitting. For you, you two, my sons, are hilarious. Pathetic, but hilarious. In the coming years, I guarantee, lying in bed with my little wife, after amorous capers and frolics, whenever we recall you and this day, we shall laugh until we weep. For there's nothing funnier than a fool.'

Xander, it was readily apparent, was afraid. His eyes were sweeping over the chamber and he was sweating profusely. Egmund, on the contrary, didn't evince any fear. He looked his father straight in the eyes and returned the derision as his father spoke on.

'Folk wisdom declares: hope for the best, expect the worst. So, I was prepared for the worst. For could there be anything worse than betrayal by one's own sons? I placed agents among your most trusted comrades. Your accomplices betrayed you immediately, as soon as I put the screws on them. Your factotums and favourites are right now fleeing the city.

'Yes, my sons. You thought me deaf and blind? Old, senile and decrepit? You thought I couldn't see that you both craved the throne and crown? That you desired them like a swine desires truffles? A swine that sniffs out a truffle loses its head. From desire, lust, urges and untamed appetite. The swine goes insane, squeals, burrows, paying no heed, as long as it can get hold of the truffles. You need to whack it severely with a stick to drive it away. And you, my sons, turned out to be just such swine. You sniffed out a mushroom and went berserk with lust and cravings. But you'll receive shit – and no truffles. Though you *will* taste a thrashing. You acted against me, my sons, you violated my authority and person. The health of people who act against me usually deteriorates violently. It's a fact confirmed by medical science.

'The frigate *Acherontia* has dropped anchor in the harbour. It sailed here on my orders, it was I who commissioned the captain. The court will convene tomorrow morning and the verdict will be reached before noon. And at noon the two of you will be aboard the ship. They'll only allow you to disembark once the frigate passes the lighthouse at Peixe de Mar. Which means in practical terms that your new place of abode will be Nazair. Ebbing. Maecht. Or Nilfgaard. Or the very end of the world and the gates of hell, if it's your will to travel there. For you shall never return to these parts. Ever. If you want your heads to remain on your shoulders.'

'You mean to banish us?' howled Xander. 'As you banished Viraxas? Will you also forbid our names from being mentioned at court?'

'I banished Viraxas in wrath and without a judgement. Which doesn't mean I wouldn't have him beheaded should he dare to return. The tribunal will sentence you to exile. Legally and bindingly.'

'Are you so sure of that? We shall see! We shall see what the court has to say about such lawlessness!'

'The court knows what verdict I expect and that's the one it will pronounce. Unanimously.'

'Like hell it'll be unanimous! The courts are independent in this country.'

'The courts may be. But the judges aren't. You're a fool, Xander. Your mother was as thick as two short planks and you take after her. You certainly didn't concoct the murder plot yourself, one of your favourites planned it all. But actually, I'm glad you did, I'll gleefully rid myself of you. It's different with Egmund, yes, Egmund is cunning. The Witcher, hired by the caring son to protect his father, ah, how shrewdly you kept that a secret, so that everybody found out. And then the contact poison. A wily thing, poison like that, my food and drink is tasted, but who would have thought of the handle of the poker from the fireplace in the royal bedchamber? The poker I use and don't let anybody touch? Cunning, my son, cunning. Pity that your poisoner betrayed you, but that's the way it is, traitors betray traitors. Why do you say nothing, Egmund? Do you have nothing to say?'

Egmund's eyes were cold and still showed no traces of fear. *He isn't at all daunted by the prospect of banishment,* thought Geralt. *He isn't thinking about banishment or going into exile, isn't thinking about Acherontia, isn't thinking about Peixe de Mar. So what is he thinking about?*

'Nothing to say, son?' repeated the King.

'Only one thing,' Egmund said through pursed lips. 'From the folk wisdom you're so fond of. "There's no fool like an old fool". Remember my words, father dear. When the time comes.'

'Take them away, lock them up and guard them,' ordered Belohun. 'That's your job, Ferrant, the job of the instigator. And now call the tailor in here, the marshal of the court and the notary, everyone else – out. And you, Witcher . . . You've learned something today, haven't you? Have you learned something about yourself? Namely, that you're a naive chump? If you've understood that then there'll be some benefit from your visit today. A visit which has just finished. Hi, over there, two men to me. Escort this witcher to the gate and eject him from it. Making sure first that he hasn't swiped any of the silverware!'

*

Captain Ropp barred their way in the corridor outside the throne room. Accompanied by two individuals with similar eyes,

309

movements and bearing. Geralt would have wagered that all three of them had once served in the same unit. He suddenly understood. He suddenly realised he knew what was about to happen, how things would develop. Thus, it came as no surprise to him when Ropp announced he was taking control of the escort and ordered the guardsmen away. The Witcher knew the captain would order him to follow. As he had expected, the other two men were close behind.

He had a foreboding about who he would find in the chamber they were about to enter.

Dandelion was as white as a sheet and clearly terrified. But probably unharmed. He was sitting on a chair with a high backrest. Behind the chair stood a skinny character with hair combed and plaited into a queue. The character was holding a misericorde with a long, narrow, four-sided blade. The blade was pressed against the poet's neck, below his jaw, slanting upwards.

'No funny business,' warned Ropp. 'No funny business, witcher. One false move, even one twitch, and Mr Samsa will stick the minstrel like a hog. He won't hesitate.'

Geralt knew that Mr Samsa wouldn't hesitate. Because Mr Samsa's eyes were even nastier than Ropp's. They were eyes with a very specific expression. People with eyes like that could occasionally be come across in morgues and anatomy laboratories. They weren't employed there by any means to support themselves, but to have the opportunity to indulge their dark predilections.

Geralt now understood why Prince Egmund had been so calm. Why he had been looking ahead fearlessly. And into his father's eyes.

'We ask you to be obedient,' said Ropp. 'If you're obedient, you'll both get out alive.

'Do what we ask and we'll release you and the poetaster,' the captain continued to lie. 'If you're obstructive we'll kill you both.'

'You're making a mistake, Ropp.'

'Mr Samsa will remain here with the minstrel,' said Ropp, unconcerned by the warning. 'We – I mean you and I – will go to the royal chambers. There'll be a guard. I have your sword, as you see. I'll give it back to you and you'll deal with the sentries. And the reinforcements that the guards will summon before you kill them

310

all. On hearing the din, the chamber man will spirit the king away through a secret exit, and Messrs Richter and Tverdoruk will be waiting there. They will change the succession of the throne and the history of the local monarchy.'

'You're making a mistake, Ropp.'

'Now,' said the captain, moving in very close. 'Now you will confirm that you've understood the task and will execute it. Should you not, before I count to ten under my breath, Mr Samsa will rupture the minstrel's right eardrum and I shall carry on counting. If the desired result does not ensue, Mr Samsa stabs the other ear. And will then gouge out the poet's eye. And so on, to the bitter end, which is a jab to the brain. I'm starting to count, Witcher.'

'Don't listen to him, Geralt!' Dandelion somehow managed to make a sound from his constricted throat. 'They won't dare to touch me! I'm famous!'

'He doesn't seem to be taking us seriously. Mr Samsa, the right ear.'

'Stop! No!'

'That's better,' nodded Ropp. 'Much better, Witcher. Confirm that you've understood the task. And that you'll execute it.'

'First, move that dagger away from the poet's ear.'

'Ha,' snorted Mr Samsa, lifting the misericorde high over his head. 'Is that better?'

'Better.'

Geralt's left hand caught Ropp by the wrist and his right seized the hilt of his sword. He pulled the captain towards him with a powerful tug and headbutted him in the face with all his strength. There was a crunching sound. The Witcher jerked the sword from the scabbard before Ropp fell and with one fluid movement coming out of a short spin hacked off Samsa's raised hand. Samsa yelled and dropped to his knees. Richter and Tverdoruk, daggers drawn, fell on the Witcher, who spun among them. In passing, he slit open Richter's neck and blood spurted right up to the chandelier on the ceiling. Tverdoruk attacked, leaping in knifeman's feints, but he tripped on Ropp's inert body, losing his balance for a moment. Geralt didn't let him recover. With a rapid lunge, he slashed him from below in the groin and a second time from above in the carotid artery. Tverdoruk fell over and curled up in a ball.

Mr Samsa took him by surprise. Although lacking his right hand, although gushing blood from the stump, he found the misericorde on the floor with his left hand. And aimed it at Dandelion. The poet screamed, yet demonstrated presence of mind. He fell from his chair and put it between himself and the assailant. Geralt didn't let Mr Samsa do anything else. Blood once again splashed the ceiling, the chandelier and the candle-ends stuck into it.

Dandelion got up from his knees, rested his forehead against the wall, then vomited extremely copiously and splattering the floor.

Ferrant de Lettenhove rushed into the chamber with several guardsmen.

'What's going on? What happened? Julian! Are you in one piece? Julian!'

Dandelion raised a hand, signalling that he would answer in a moment, because he didn't have time right then. And vomited again.

The instigator ordered the guardsmen to leave and closed the door behind them. He looked at the bodies, cautiously, so as not to tread in the spilt blood and making certain that the blood dripping from the chandelier didn't stain his doublet.

'Samsa, Tverdoruk, Richter,' he said, listing them. 'And Master Captain Ropp. Prince Egmund's confidants.'

'They carried out their orders,' said the Witcher, shrugging, looking down at his sword. 'Like you, they obeyed their orders. And you didn't know anything about it. Confirm that, Ferrant.'

'I didn't know anything about it,' the instigator confirmed hastily and stepped back, leaning against the wall. 'I swear! You can't possibly suspect . . . You don't think . . .'

'If I did you'd be dead. I believe you. You wouldn't have risked Dandelion's life, after all.'

'The king must be informed. I'm afraid that for Prince Egmund it may mean amendments and appendices to the indictment. Ropp is alive, I think. He'll testify . . .'

'I doubt he'll be in a fit state.'

The instigator examined the captain, who was lying, stretched out in a pool of urine, salivating copiously and trembling incessantly.

'What's wrong with him?'

'Shards of nasal bones in the brain. And probably several splinters in his eyeballs.'

'You struck him too hard.'

'That was my intention,' said Geralt, wiping the sword blade with a napkin taken from the table. 'Dandelion, how are you? Everything in order? Can you stand?'

'I'm good, I'm good,' gibbered Dandelion. 'I'm feeling better. Much better . . .'

'You don't look like someone who's feeling better.'

'Dammit, I've barely escaped with my life!' said the poet, getting to his feet and holding on to a bureau. 'For fuck's sake, I've never been so afraid . . . I felt like the insides were falling out of my arse. And that everything would drop out of me, teeth included. But when I saw you I knew you'd save me. I mean, I didn't, but I was counting strongly on it . . . How much sodding blood there is . . . How it stinks in here! I think I'm going to puke again . . .'

'We're going to the king,' said Ferrant de Lettenhove. 'Give me your sword, Witcher . . . And clean it a little. You stay here, Julian—'

'Fuck that. I'm not staying here for a moment. I prefer sticking close to Geralt.'

*

The entrance to the royal antechambers was being guarded by sentries who, however, recognised the instigator and let him through. But getting into the actual chambers was not so straightforward. A herald, two seneschals and their entourage, consisting of four bruisers, turned out to be an insurmountable obstacle.

'The king is being fitted for his wedding outfit,' the herald pronounced. 'He made it clear he is not to be disturbed.'

'We have an important matter requiring urgent attention!'

'The king made it categorically clear he is not to be disturbed. While Master Witcher had, as I recall, orders to leave the palace. What, then, is he still doing here?'

'I'll explain that to the king. Admit us!'

Ferrant pushed the herald away and shoved the seneschal. Geralt followed him. But they were still only able to reach the chamber's threshold, stuck behind several courtiers gathered there. Their further progress was thwarted by bruisers in leather jerkins who pushed them against the wall on the order of the herald. They were pretty rough, but Geralt followed the instigator's example and gave up any resistance.

The king was standing on a low stool. A tailor with pins in his mouth was adjusting the royal breeches. Beside the king stood the marshal of the court and somebody dressed in black, probably the notary.

'Right after the wedding ceremony,' said Belohun, 'I shall announce that my successor will be the son who my little wedded wife will bear me today. That measure ought to assure me her favour and submission, hee, hee. It will also give me a little time and peace. About twenty years will pass before the pup reaches an age when he'll start scheming.

'But if I so wish I shall call it all off and designate somebody quite different as my successor.' The king grimaced and winked at the marshal of the court. 'After all, it is a morganatic marriage and issue from such unions don't inherit titles, do they? And who's capable of predicting how long I'll stand her? For are there no other prettier and younger wenches in the world? It'll be necessary to draw up the appropriate documents, a prenuptial agreement or something. Hope for the best, expect the worst, hee, hee, hee.'

The chamber man handed the king a tray piled up with jewels.

'Take it away.' Belohun grimaced. 'I won't be bedecking myself with trinkets like some fop or arriviste. I'll only put this on. It's a gift from my betrothed. Small, but tasteful. A medallion with the crest of my country, it behoves me to wear such a coat of arms. They are her words: the country's crest on my chest, the country's good in my heart.'

Some time passed before Geralt, standing pressed against the wall, put two and two together.

The cat, patting the medallion with its paw. The golden medallion on a chain. The blue enamel, the dolphin. *D'or, dauphin naiant d'azur, lorré, peantré, oreillé, barbé et crêté de gueules.*

It was too late to react. He didn't even manage to cry out or give a warning. He saw the golden chain suddenly contract and tighten around the king's neck like a garrotte. Belohun flushed and opened his mouth, but was incapable of taking a breath or screaming. He grabbed his neck with both hands, struggling to tear the medallion off or at least jam his fingers under the chain. He couldn't, as the chain had cut deeply into his flesh. The king fell from the stool, and danced, bumping into the tailor. The tailor staggered and choked; he'd probably swallowed his pins. He fell against the notary and they both went over. Meanwhile, Belohun turned blue, eyes goggling, tumbled onto the floor, kicked out with his legs a few times and tensed up. And stopped moving.

'Help! The king has collapsed!'

'The physician!' called the marshal of the court. 'Summon the physician!'

'Ye Gods! What has happened? What's happened to the king?'

'The physician! Quickly!'

Ferrant de Lettenhove put his hands to his brow. His face wore a strange expression. The expression of a man who was slowly beginning to understand.

The king was laid down on a chaise longue. The physician took a long time examining him. Although close by, Geralt wasn't allowed through, couldn't watch. In spite of that, he knew that the chain had already loosened before the physician came running.

'Apoplexy,' the physician pronounced, straightening up. 'Brought on by airlessness. Bad vapours entered the body and poisoned the humours. The unceasing storms raising the heat of the blood are to blame. Science is powerless, I can do nothing. Our good and gracious king is dead. He has departed this life.'

The marshal of the court gave a cry, burying his face in his hands. The herald seized his beret in both hands. A courtier sobbed. Others knelt down.

The corridor and vestibule abruptly resounded with the echo of heavy steps. In the doorway appeared a giant, a fellow measuring a good seven feet tall. In the uniform of a guardsman, but a senior one. The giant was accompanied by men in headscarves and earrings.

'Gentlemen, you are to proceed to the throne room. At once,' said the giant amid the silence.

'What throne room?' retorted the marshal of the court, irritably.

315

'And why? Do you realise, Lord de Santis, what has just happened? What misfortune has occurred? You don't understand—'

'To the throne room. By order of the king.'

'The king is dead!'

'Long live the king. To the throne room, please. Everybody. At once.'

About a dozen men were gathered in the throne room, beneath the maritime plafond with the tritons, mermaids and hippocampi. Some were wearing colourful scarves, some sailor's caps with ribbons. They were all weather-beaten and had earrings.

Mercenaries. It wasn't difficult to guess. The crew of the frigate *Acherontia*.

A dark-haired, dark-eyed man with a prominent nose was sitting on the throne on a dais. He was also weather-beaten. But he didn't have an earring.

Beside him sat Ildiko Breckl on an extra chair, still in her snow-white gown and still bedecked in diamonds. The – until recently – royal fiancée and betrothed was staring at the dark-haired man with an expression of adoration. For some time, Geralt had been wondering how events would proceed and guessing at their causes, had been connecting facts and putting two and two together. Now, though, at that moment someone with even very limited intellect would have seen and understood that Ildiko Breckl and the dark-haired man knew each other. And very well, at that. And had for quite some time.

'Prince Viraxas, Prince of Kerack, a moment ago still the heir to the throne and crown, now the King of Kerack, the rightful ruler of the country,' announced the giant, de Santis, in a booming baritone.

The marshal of the court was the first to bow and then go down on one knee. After him, the herald paid homage. The seneschals, bowing low, followed suit. The last person to bow was Ferrant de Lettenhove.

'Your Royal Highness.'

'"Your Highness" will do for the moment,' corrected Viraxas. 'I shall be entitled to style myself in full after the coronation. Which, indeed, we shall not delay. The sooner, the better. Am I right, marshal?'

It was very quiet. The stomach of one of the courtiers could be heard rumbling.

'My late lamented father is dead,' said Viraxas. 'He has joined his revered forebears. Both of my younger brothers, unsurprisingly, have been accused of treason. The trial will be conducted in keeping with the dead king's will, both brothers will turn out to be guilty and will leave Kerack forever on the strength of the court's verdict. Aboard the frigate *Acherontia*, hired by me . . . and my powerful friends and patrons. The dead king, I happen to know, didn't leave a valid will and testament or any official directives regarding the succession. I would have respected the king's will had there been any such directives. But there are none. By right of inheritance, the crown thus belongs to me. Does anyone of the people gathered here wish to oppose that?'

No one among the people gathered there did. Everybody present was sufficiently endowed with good sense and the instinct of self-preservation.

'So please begin the preparations for the coronation. May the people within whose jurisdiction it falls busy themselves with it. The coronation will be combined with my nuptials. For I have decided to revive the ancient custom of the kings of Kerack, a law enacted centuries ago. Which declares that if the groom dies before his wedding, the fiancée will wed his closest unmarried relative.'

Ildiko Breckl – as was clear from her radiant expression – was prepared to submit to the ancient custom that very minute. Others of those present remained quiet, undoubtedly trying to recall who had enacted the law, when and on what occasion. And how that custom could have been enacted centuries ago, since the kingdom of Kerack had existed for less than a hundred years. But the brows of the courtiers wrinkled with mental effort then quickly became smooth. Unanimously, they came to the correct conclusion. That although the coronation hadn't taken place yet, and although he was only His Highness, Viraxas was already essentially king, and the king is always right.

'Get out of here, Witcher,' whispered Ferrant de Lettenhove, pushing Geralt's sword into his hand. 'Take Julian away. Vanish, both of you. You haven't seen anything, haven't heard anything. Let no one link you with all this.'

'I realise—' Viraxas swept his gaze over the assembled company '—and understand that for some of you gathered here the situation may seem astonishing. That for some of you the changes are occurring too unexpectedly and without warning, and events are moving too fast. Nor can I rule out that for some of the assembled company things are not happening as they intended and the state of affairs is not to their liking. Colonel de Santis immediately threw in his lot on the right side and swore loyalty to me. I expect the same from everybody gathered here.

'Let us begin with the faithful servants of my late lamented father.' He indicated them with a nod. 'As well as the executors of the orders of my brother, who made an attempt on my father's life. We shall start with the royal instigator, Lord Ferrant de Lettenhove.'

The instigator bowed.

'You will submit to an investigation,' warned Viraxas. 'Which will reveal what role you played in the princes' plot. The plot was a fiasco, which thus qualifies the plotters as inept. I may forgive errors but not ineptitude. Not when it concerns the instigator, the guardian of law. But that will be later, for we shall begin with essential matters. Come closer, Ferrant. We wish you to demonstrate and prove whom you serve. We desire you to pay due homage to us. To kneel at the foot of the throne. And kiss our royal hand.'

The instigator moved obediently towards the dais.

'Get out of here,' Ferrant managed to whisper again. 'Vanish as quickly as you can, Witcher.'

*

The party in the grounds was in full swing.

Lytta Neyd immediately noticed blood on Geralt's shirtsleeve. Mozaïk also noticed and – unlike Lytta – went pale.

Dandelion grabbed two goblets from the tray of a passing page and downed one after the other in single draughts. He grabbed two more and offered them to the ladies. They declined. Dandelion drank one and gave the other reluctantly to Geralt. Coral stared at the Witcher with narrowed eyes, clearly tense.

'What's happening?'

'You'll soon find out.'

The bell in the belfry began to toll. It tolled so ominously, so gloomily and so mournfully, that the guests fell silent.

The marshal of the court and the herald stepped onto the scaffold-like platform.

'Fraught with regret and distress,' the marshal said into the silence, 'I must inform you, honourable guests, that King Belohun the First, our beloved, good and gracious ruler, has suddenly passed away. Struck down by the stern hand of fate, he has departed this life. But the kings of Kerack do not die! The king is dead, long live the king! Long live His Royal Highness, King Viraxas! The firstborn son of the deceased king, the rightful heir to the throne and the crown! King Viraxas the First! Let us proclaim it three times: Long live the king! Long live the king! Long live the king!'

A choir of sycophants, toadies and arse-kissers took up the cry. The marshal of the court quietened them with a gesture.

'King Viraxas is plunged in mourning, as is the entire court. The banquet has been abandoned and the guests are asked to leave the palace and grounds. The king plans his own nuptials soon and then the banquet will be repeated. So as not to waste the vittals, the king has ordered for them to be taken to the city and placed in the town square. The vittals will also be shared with the folk of Palmyra. A time of happiness and prosperity is coming to Kerack!'

'My, my,' announced Coral, straightening her hair. 'There is much truth in the claim that the death of the bridegroom is capable of seriously disrupting a wedding celebration. Belohun was not without his flaws, but there have been worse kings. May he rest in peace and may the earth rest lightly on him. Let's go from here. In any case, it's begun to be boring. And since it's a beautiful day, let's take a walk along the terraces and gaze at the sea. Poet, be so kind as to proffer your arm to my pupil. I'll walk with Geralt. For he has something to tell me, methinks.'

It was still early afternoon. It was hard to believe that so much had happened in such a short time.

CHAPTER NINETEEN

'Hey! Look!' Dandelion said suddenly. 'A rat!'

Geralt didn't react. He knew the poet and knew he tended to be afraid of any old thing or become enraptured by any old thing and sought out sensation where there was nothing worthy of the name.

'A rat!' said Dandelion, not giving up. 'Oh, another! A third! A fourth! Bloody hell! Geralt, look.'

Geralt sighed and looked.

The foot of the cliff beneath the terrace was teeming with rats. The ground between Palmyra and the hill was alive, moving, undulating and squeaking. Hundreds – perhaps thousands – of rodents were fleeing from the harbour area and river mouth and scurrying uphill, along the palisade, onto the hill and into the trees. Other passers-by also noticed the phenomenon, and cries of amazement and fright rang out on all sides.

'The rats are fleeing Palmyra and the harbour because they're frightened!' pronounced Dandelion. 'I know what's happened. A ship full of rat-catchers has probably tied up to the quay.'

No one felt like commenting. Geralt wiped the sweat from his eyelids. The heat was oppressive, and the hot air made breathing difficult. He looked up at the sky, which was clear, quite cloudless.

'There's a storm coming,' Lytta said, articulating what he had thought himself. 'A tremendous storm. The rats can sense it. And I can too. I can feel it in the air.'

I can too, thought the Witcher.

'A storm,' Coral repeated. 'There's a storm coming from the sea.'

'What do you mean a storm?' Dandelion fanned himself with his bonnet. 'Not at all! The weather's as pretty as a picture, the sky's pristine, without the faintest zephyr. Pity, we could do with a breath of wind in this heat. A sea breeze . . .'

The wind began to blow before he finished his sentence. A faint breeze bore the smell of the sea. It was refreshing, and gave pleasant relief. And quickly intensified. Pennants on masts – not long before hanging limply and pitifully – moved and fluttered.

The sky over the horizon grew dark. The wind increased. The faint soughing became a swoosh, the swoosh a whistle.

The pennants on the masts fluttered and flapped violently. Weathervanes on roofs and towers creaked, tin chimney pots grated and clanged. Shutters banged. Clouds of dust swirled up.

Dandelion seized his bonnet in both hands at the last moment, preventing it from being blown away.

Mozaïk caught her dress, a sudden gust lifting up the chiffon almost to her hips. Before she could bring the billowing material under control, Geralt had an enjoyable view of her legs. She saw him looking. And held his gaze.

'A storm . . .' Coral had to turn away in order to speak. The wind was blowing so hard it drowned out her words. 'A storm! There's a storm coming!'

'Ye gods!' cried Dandelion, who didn't believe in any. 'Ye gods! What's happening? Is it the end of the world?'

The sky darkened quickly. And the horizon went from deep blue to black.

The wind grew stronger, whistling hellishly.

The sea was rough in the anchorage beyond the headland, the waves were crashing against the breakwater, white foam was splashing. The crashing of the waves intensified. It became as dark as night.

There was a commotion among the ships lying at anchor. Several – including the post clipper *Echo* and the Novigradian schooner *Pandora Parvi* – hurriedly hoisted their sails, ready to make for open sea. The rest of the ships dropped theirs and remained at anchor. Geralt remembered some of them, he had observed them from the terrace of Coral's villa. *Alke*, a cog from Cidaris. *Fuchsia*, he couldn't recall where it was from. And galleons: *Pride of Cintra* under a flag with a blue cross. The three-master *Vertigo* from Lan Exeter. The Redanian *Albatross*: a hundred and twenty feet from prow to stern. And several others. Including the frigate *Acherontia* under black sails.

The wind wasn't whistling now. It was howling. Geralt saw the first thatched roof from the Palmyra district fly up and disintegrate in mid-air. A second followed soon after. A third. And a fourth. And the wind was growing ever stronger. The flapping of pennants became a constant clatter, shutters banged, tiles and gutters hailed down, chimneys tumbled, flowerpots smashed on the cobbles. The bell in the belfry, set in motion by the gale, began to toll with an intermittent, anxious, ominous sound.

And the gale blew, blew more and more strongly. And drove bigger and bigger waves towards the shore. The crashing of the waves intensified, becoming louder and louder. It soon stopped being just a crash. It was a monotonous and dull booming, like the thudding of some infernal machine. The waves grew, rollers topped by white foam crashed onto the shore. The ground was trembling beneath people's feet. The gale howled.

Echo and *Pandora Parvi* were unable to flee. They returned to the harbour and dropped anchor.

The awestruck and terrified cries of the people gathered on terraces sounded louder and louder. Outstretched arms pointed at the sea.

The sea was one great wave. A colossal wall of water. Apparently rising to the height of the galleons' masts.

Coral grabbed the Witcher by the arm. She said something, or rather tried to speak, but the gale gagged her effectively.

'—way! Geralt! We have to get away from here!'

The wave descended on the harbour. People were screaming. The pier splintered and disintegrated under the weight of the mass of water, posts and planks went flying. The dock collapsed, cranes broke and fell over. A boat and launches moored by the wharf flew into the air like children's toys, like boats made of bark launched in the gutter by street urchins. The cottages and shacks near the beach were simply washed away without leaving a trace. The wave burst into the river mouth, immediately turning it into some diabolical whirlpool. Crowds of people were fleeing from Palmyra, now under water, most of them running towards the upper city and the guardhouse. They survived. Others chose the riverbank as their escape route. Geralt saw them engulfed by the water.

'Another wave!' yelled Dandelion. 'Another wave!'

It was true, there was another. And then a third. A fourth. A fifth. And a sixth. Walls of water rolled into the harbour and the port.

The waves struck the ships at anchor with immense force, and they thrashed about frantically. Geralt saw men falling from the decks.

Ships with their prows turned to windward fought bravely. For some time. They lost their masts, one after the next. Then the waves began to wash over them. They were engulfed by the foam and then re-emerged, were engulfed and re-emerged.

The first not to reappear was the post clipper *Echo*. It quite simply vanished. A moment later the same fate befell *Fuchsia*; the galley simply disintegrated. The taut anchor chain tore out the hull of *Alke* and the cog disappeared into the abyss in a flash. The prow and fo'c'sle of *Albatross* broke off under the pressure and the remains of the ship sank to the bottom like a stone. *Vertigo*'s anchor was wrenched off, the galleon danced on the crest of a wave, was spun around and shattered against the breakwater.

Acherontia, *Pride of Cintra*, *Pandora Parvi* and two galleons Geralt didn't recognise raised their anchors and the waves bore them to the shore. This strategy was only seemingly an act of suicidal desperation. The captains had to choose between certain destruction in the bay and the risky manoeuvre of sailing into the river mouth.

The unknown galleons had no chance. Neither of them managed to align itself correctly. Both were smashed against the wharf.

Pride of Cintra and *Acherontia* lost their manoeuvrability too. They lurched into each other and became entangled, the waves tossing them onto the wharf and rending them to shreds. The water carried away the wreckage.

Pandora Parvi danced and leaped on the waves like a dolphin. But she held her course, borne straight into the mouth of the Adalatte which was roiling like a cauldron. Geralt heard the cries of people cheering the captain on.

Coral yelled, pointing.

A seventh wave was coming.

Geralt had estimated the previous ones – which were level with the ships' masts – at about five or six fathoms or thirty to forty feet. The wave which was approaching now, obliterating the sky, was twice as high.

The people fleeing Palmyra, crowded by the guardhouse, began to scream. The gale knocked them down, hurled them to the ground and pinned them to the stockade.

The wave crashed down on Palmyra. And simply pulverised it, washed it off the face of the earth. The water reached the palisade in an instant, engulfing the people crowded there. The mass of timber being carried by the sea dropped onto the palisade, breaking the piles. The guardhouse collapsed and floated away.

The relentless watery battering ram struck the precipice. The hill shook so hard that Dandelion and Mozaïk fell down and Geralt only kept his balance with great difficulty.

'We must fly!' screamed Coral, hanging on to the balustrade. 'Geralt! Let's get out of here! More waves are coming!'

A wave crashed over them, swamping them. The people on the terrace who hadn't fled earlier did now. They fled screaming, higher, ever higher, up the hill, towards the royal palace. A few stayed. Geralt recognised Ravenga and Antea Derris among them.

People screamed and pointed. To their left the waves were washing away the cliff beneath the villa district. The first villa crumpled like a house of cards and slid down the slope, straight into the maelstrom. Then a second, a third and a fourth.

'The city is disintegrating!' wailed Dandelion. 'It's falling apart!'

Lytta Neyd raised her arms. Chanted a spell. And vanished.

Mozaïk clutched Geralt's arm. Dandelion yelled.

The water was right beneath them, below the terrace. And there were people in the water. Others were lowering poles and boathooks to them, ropes were being thrown and they were being pulled out. Not far from them, a powerfully built man dived into the whirlpool and swam to rescue a drowning woman.

Mozaïk screamed.

She saw a fragment from the roof of a cottage floating past. With some children clinging to it. Three children. Geralt unslung his sword from his back.

'Hold it, Dandelion!'

Geralt threw off his jacket. And dived into the water.

It wasn't normal swimming and his normal swimming skills were fit for nothing. The waves tossed him upwards, downwards and sideways, pummelled him with the beams, planks and furniture spinning in the whirlpool. The mass of timber bearing down on him threatened to crush him to a pulp. When he finally swam over and caught hold of the roof he was already severely battered. The roof bucked and whirled in the waves like a spinning top. The children were bawling at various pitches.

Three, he thought. *No way will I manage to carry all three of them.* He felt a shoulder alongside his.

'Two!' Antea Derris spat water and seized one of the children. 'Take two!'

It wasn't so simple. He peeled a little boy off and pinned him under one arm. A little girl was clinging to the rafters in such desperation that it took Geralt a long time to pry open her fingers. The waves, swamping and covering them, helped. The half-drowned little girl released the roof timbers and Geralt shoved her beneath his other arm. And then all three of them began to go under. The children gurgled and struggled. Geralt fought.

He had no idea how, but he swam up to the surface. A wave tossed him against the wall of the terrace, knocking the wind out of him. He didn't release the children. The people above shouted, tried to help, reaching down with anything they could seize hold of. But to no avail. The whirlpool snatched them and carried them away. The Witcher slammed into somebody. It was Antea Derris with the little girl in her arms. She was putting up a fight, but he saw she was exhausted. She was struggling to hold her head and that of the child above water.

A splash alongside and faltering breathing. It was Mozaïk. She tore one of the children from Geralt's arms and swam off. Geralt saw her being struck by a beam carried by the waves. She screamed but kept hold of the child.

The waves flung them against the wall of the terrace again. This time the people above were prepared, they'd even brought a ladder and were hanging from it with outstretched arms. They lifted up the children. The Witcher saw Dandelion grab Mozaïk and drag her onto the terrace.

Antea Derris looked at him. She had beautiful eyes. She smiled.

They were struck by the mass of timber – heavy stakes from the palisade – being carried on the wave.

One of them jabbed Antea Derris and crushed her against the terrace. She coughed up blood. A lot of blood. Then her head lolled on her chest and she vanished beneath the waves.

Geralt was hit by two stakes, one in the shoulder, the other in the hip. The impact paralysed him, totally numbing him in an instant. He choked on water and began to sink.

Someone seized him in a painful, iron grip and snatched him upwards, towards the surface and the light. He groped around and felt a powerful bicep as hard as rock. The strongman was pumping with his legs, forging through the water like a triton, shoving away the wood floating around and the drowned corpses spinning in the turmoil. Geralt came up right by the terrace. Shouts and cheers from above. Arms reaching out.

A moment later the Witcher was lying in a pool of water, coughing, spluttering and retching onto the terrace. Dandelion knelt beside him, as white as a sheet. Mozaïk was on his other side. Also pale-faced. But with trembling hands. Geralt sat up with difficulty.

'Antea?'

Dandelion shook his head and looked away. Mozaïk lowered her head onto her lap. He saw the sobbing shaking her shoulders.

His rescuer was sitting beside him. The strongman. Or to be more precise, strongwoman. The untidy bristles on the shaven head. The belly like pork shoulder covered in netting. The shoulders like a wrestler's. The calves like a discus thrower's.

'I owe you my life.'

'Don't be soft . . .' said the commandant of the guardhouse, waving a dismissive arm. 'Think nothing of it. And anyway, you're an arse, and me and the girls are pissed off with you about that rumpus. So you'd better steer clear of us, or you'll get a good hiding. Is that clear?'

'Indeed.'

'But I have to admit,' said the commandant, hawking noisily and shaking water from an ear. 'You're a courageous arse. A courageous arse, Geralt of Rivia.'

'What about you?' What's your name?'

'Violetta,' said the commandant and suddenly turned gloomy. 'What about her? That one . . .'

'Antea Derris.'

'Antea Derris,' she repeated, grimacing. 'Pity.'

'Pity.'

More people came to the terrace, it became crowded. The danger had passed, the sky had brightened up, the gale had stopped blowing, the pennants were hanging limp. The sea was calm, the water had receded. Leaving devastation and disarray. And corpses which the crabs were already scuttling over.

Geralt stood up with difficulty. Every movement and every breath returned as a throbbing pain in his side. His knee was aching intensely. Both his shirtsleeves had been torn off, he couldn't recall exactly when he had lost them. The skin on his left elbow, right shoulder and probably his shoulder blade had been rubbed raw. He was bleeding from numerous shallow cuts. All in all, nothing serious, nothing he needed to worry about.

The sun had broken through the clouds, the sunlight glistened on the calming sea. The roof of the lighthouse at the end of the headland was sparkling. It was built of white and red brick, a relic of elven times. A relic that had endured many storms like that. And would endure many more, it would seem.

The schooner *Pandora Parvi*, having overcome the river mouth, which was now calm although still densely encumbered with flotsam, sailed out to anchor under full canvas as though taking part in a regatta. The crowd cheered.

Geralt helped Mozaïk stand up. Not many of her clothes remained on her, either. Dandelion gave her his cloak to cover herself up. And cleared his throat meaningfully.

Lytta Neyd was standing in front of them. With her medical bag on her shoulder.

'I came back,' she said, looking at the Witcher.

'No, you didn't,' he retorted. 'You left.'

She looked at him. With cold, strange eyes. And soon after fixed her gaze on something very distant, located very far over the Witcher's right shoulder.

'So, you want to play it like that,' she stated coolly. 'And leave a memory like that. Well, it's your will, your choice. Although you might have chosen a little less lofty style. Farewell then. I'm going to offer help to the wounded and the needy. You clearly don't need my help. Or me. Mozaïk!'

Mozaïk shook her head. And linked her arm through Geralt's. Coral snorted.

'It's like that, is it? That's what you want? Like that? Well, it's your will. Your choice. Farewell.'

She turned and walked away.

*

Febus Ravenga appeared in the crowd that had begun to gather on the terrace. He must have taken part in the rescue, because his wet clothes were hanging on him in shreds. An attentive factotum approached and handed him his hat. Or rather what remained of it.

'What now?' called a voice in the crowd. 'What now, councillor?'

'What now? What shall we do?'

Ravenga looked at them. For a long time. Then straightened up, wrung out his hat and put it on.

'Bury the dead,' he said. 'Take care of the living. And start rebuilding.'

*

The bell in the belfry tolled. As though it wanted to assert that it had survived. That although much had changed, certain things were unchanging.

'Let's go,' said Geralt, pulling wet seaweed from his collar. 'Dandelion? Where's my sword?'

Dandelion choked, pointing at an empty place at the foot of a wall.

'A moment ago . . . They were here a moment ago! Your sword and your jacket. They've been stolen! The fucking bastards! They've been stolen! Hey, you there! There was a sword here! Give it back! Come on! Oh, you whoresons! Damn you!'

The Witcher suddenly felt weak. Mozaïk held him up. *I must*

329

be in poor shape, he thought. *I must be in poor shape if a girl has to hold me up.*

'I've had enough of this town,' he said. 'Enough of everything this town is. And represents. Let's get out of here. As soon as possible. And as far away as possible.'

INTERLUDE

Twelve days later.

The fountain splashed very softly, the basin smelled of wet stone. There was a scent of flowers and of the ivy growing up the walls of the patio. And it smelled of the apples in a dish on the marble table top. There were beads of condensation on two goblets of chilled wine.

Two women were seated at the table. Two sorceresses. If, as luck would have it, someone with artistic sensibilities had been in the vicinity, full of painterly imagination and capable of lyrical allegories, that person wouldn't have had any problem portraying the two of them. The flame-haired Lytta Neyd in a vermillion and green gown was like a sunset in September. Yennefer of Vengerberg, black-haired, dressed in a composition of black and white, evoked a December morning.

'Most of the neighbouring villas are lying in rubble at the foot of the cliff,' Yennefer said, breaking the silence. 'But yours is untouched. Not even a single roof tile was lost. You're a lucky woman, Coral. I advise you to consider buying a ticket in the lottery.'

'The priests wouldn't call that luck.' Lytta Neyd smiled. 'They'd say it was protection by the divinities and heavenly forces. The divinities safeguard the just and protect the virtuous. They reward goodness and righteousness.'

'Indeed. Reward. If they want to and happen to be nearby. Your good health, my friend.'

'And yours, my friend. Mozaïk! Fill up Madam Yennefer's goblet. It's empty.

'Regarding the villa, though.' Lytta followed Mozaïk with her eyes. 'It's for sale. I'm selling it, because . . . Because I have to move out. The weather in Kerack has stopped suiting me.'

Yennefer raised an eyebrow. Lytta didn't keep her waiting.

'King Viraxas has begun his reign with truly royal edicts,' she said in a barely audible sneer. '*Primo*, his coronation day has been declared a state holiday in the Kingdom of Kerack. *Secundo*, an amnesty is being proclaimed . . . for criminals. Political prisoners remain in prison without the right to be visited or conducting correspondence. *Tertio*, customs and port fees are being increased by a hundred per cent. *Quarto*, all non-humans and residents that harm the state's economy and take jobs away from pure-blooded people are to leave Kerack within two weeks. *Quinto*, in Kerack it is forbidden to work any magic without the king's permission and mages are not allowed to possess land or property. Sorcerers living in Kerack must dispose of their property and obtain a licence. Or leave the kingdom.'

'A marvellous demonstration of gratitude.' Yennefer snorted. 'And rumour has it that it was the sorcerers who got Viraxas crowned. That they organised and financed his return. And helped him to seize power.'

'Rumour knows what it's talking about. Viraxas will be paying the Chapter generously, and in order to do that he's raising duty and hopes to confiscate non-humans' property. The edict affects me personally; no other sorcerer has a house in Kerack. It's Ildiko Breckl's revenge. And retribution for the medical help I gave to the local women, which Viraxas' counsellors consider immoral. The Chapter could put pressure on my behalf, but won't. They're not satisfied with the commercial privileges, shares in the shipyard and maritime companies acquired from Viraxas. They're negotiating further ones and have no inention of weakening their position. Thus – now regarded as *persona non grata* – I shall have to emigrate to search for pastures new.'

'Which I nonetheless imagine you will do without undue regret. I'd have thought that under the present government, Kerack wouldn't have a great chance in a competition for the most pleasant place under the sun. You'll sell this villa and buy another. In the mountains in Lyria, for instance. The Lyrian mountains are fashionable now. Plenty of sorcerers have moved there, because it's pretty and the taxes are reasonable.'

'I don't like mountains. I prefer the sea. Never fear, I shall find a safe haven without much difficulty, considering my specialty.

Women are everywhere and they all need me. Drink, Yennefer. Your good health.'

'You urge me to drink, but barely moisten your lips yourself. Are you perhaps ill? You don't look very well.'

Lytta sighed theatrically.

'The last few days have been hard. The palace coup, that dreadful storm, ah . . . On top of that, morning sickness . . . I know, it'll pass after the first trimester. But that's not for another two months . . .'

It was possible to discern the buzzing of a wasp circling above an apple in the silence that fell.

'Ha, ha,' said Coral, breaking the silence. 'I was joking. Pity you can't see your face. I took you in! Ha, ha.'

Yennefer looked upwards at the ivy-covered top of the wall. For a long time.

'I took you in,' Lytta continued. 'And I'll bet your imagination was working hard at once. Admit it, you immediately linked my delicate condition with . . . Don't make faces, don't make faces. The news must have reached you, for rumours spread like ripples on the water. But relax, there isn't a scrap of truth in them. My chances of getting pregnant are no greater than yours, nothing has changed in that regard. And all that linked me to your Witcher was business. Professional matters. Nothing else.'

'Ah.'

'You know what the common folk are like, they love gossip. They see a woman with a man and at once turn it into an affair. The Witcher, I admit, visited me quite often. And indeed, we were seen together in town. But, I repeat, it only concerned business.'

Yennefer put down her goblet, rested her elbows on the table and put her fingertips together, creating a steeple. And looked the red-haired sorceress in the eyes.

'*Primo*,' Lytta coughed slightly, but didn't look down, 'I've never done anything like that to a close friend. *Secundo*, your Witcher wasn't interested in me at all.'

'Wasn't he?' Yennefer raised her eyebrows. 'Indeed? How can that be explained?'

'Perhaps mature women have stopped interesting him? Regardless of their current looks. Perhaps he prefers the genuinely young?

Mozaïk! Come here please. Just look, Yennefer. Youth in bloom. And innocence. Until recently.'

'She?' said Yennefer, irritated. 'He with her? With your pupil?'

'Well, Mozaïk. Come closer. Tell us about your amorous adventure. We're curious to listen. We love affairs. Stories about unhappy love. The unhappier, the better.'

'Madame Lytta . . .' The girl, rather than blushing, paled like a corpse. 'Please . . . You've already punished me for it, after all . . . How many times can I be punished for the same offence. Don't make me—'

'Tell us!'

'Let her be, Coral,' said Yennefer, waving a hand. 'Don't torment her. Furthermore, I'm not at all curious.'

'I surely don't believe that,' said Lytta Neyd, smiling spitefully. 'But very well, I'll forgive the girl, indeed I've already punished her, forgiven her and allowed her to continue her studies. And her mumbled confessions have stopped entertaining me. To summarise: she became infatuated with the Witcher and ran away with him. And he – once he'd become bored with her – simply abandoned her. She woke up alone one morning. All he left were cooled sheets and not a single trace. He left because he had to. He vanished into thin air. Gone with the wind.'

Although it seemed impossible, Mozaïk paled even more. Her hands trembled.

'He left some flowers,' said Yennefer softly. 'A little nosegay of flowers. Right?'

Mozaïk raised her head. But didn't answer.

'Flowers and a letter,' repeated Yennefer.

Mozaïk said nothing. But the colour slowly began to return to her cheeks.

'A letter,' said Lytta Neyd, looking closely at the girl. 'You didn't tell me about a letter. You didn't mention one.'

Mozaïk pursed her lips.

'So that's why,' Lytta finished, apparently calmly. 'So that's why you returned, although you could expect a stiff punishment, much stiffer than you consequently received. He ordered you to return. Were it not for that you wouldn't have.'

Mozaïk didn't reply. Yennefer also said nothing and twisted a lock of black hair around a finger. She suddenly raised her head and looked the girl in the eyes. And smiled.

'He ordered you to return to me,' said Lytta Neyd. 'He ordered you to return, although he could imagine what might be awaiting you. I must admit I'd have never expected that of him.'

The fountain splashed, the basin smelled of wet stone. There was a scent of flowers and ivy.

'I find it astonishing,' Lytta repeated. 'I'd never have expected it of him.'

'Because you didn't know him, Coral,' Yennefer replied calmly. 'You didn't know him at all.'

CHAPTER TWENTY

The stable boy had been given half a crown the evening before and the horses were waiting saddled. Dandelion yawned and scratched the back of his neck.

'Ye gods, Geralt . . . Do we really have to start this early? I mean it's still dark . . .'

'It isn't dark. It's just right. The sun will rise in an hour at the latest.'

'Not for another hour,' said Dandelion, clambering onto the saddle of his gelding. 'So I could have slept another one . . .'

Geralt leaped into the saddle and after a moment's thought handed the stable boy another half-crown.

'It's August,' he said. 'There are some fourteen hours between sunrise to sunset. I'd like to ride as far as possible in that time.'

Dandelion yawned. And only then seemed to see the unsaddled dapple-grey mare standing in the next stall. The mare shook its head as though wanting to attract their attention.

'Just a minute,' the poet wondered. 'And her? Mozaïk?'

'She's not riding any further with us. We're parting.'

'What? I don't understand . . . Would you be so kind as to explain . . .?'

'No I wouldn't. Not now. Let's ride, Dandelion.'

'Do you really know what you're doing? Are you fully aware?'

'No. Not fully. Not another word, I don't want to talk about it. Let's go.'

Dandelion sighed. And spurred on the gelding. He looked back. And sighed again. He was a poet so he could sigh as much as he liked.

The Secret and Whisper inn looked quite pretty against the daybreak, in the misty glow of the dawn. For all the world like a fairy castle, a sylvan temple of secret love drowning in hollyhocks, cloaked in bindweed and ivy. The poet fell into a reverie.

He sighed, yawned, hawked, spat, wrapped himself in his cloak and spurred on his horse. Owing to those few moments of reflection he fell behind. Geralt was barely visible in the fog.

The Witcher rode hard. And didn't look back.

*

'Here's the wine,' said the innkeeper, putting an earthenware jug on the table. 'Apple wine from Rivia, as requested. My wife asked me to ask you how you're finding the pork.'

'We're finding it among the kasha,' replied Dandelion. 'From time to time. Not as often as we'd like to.'

The tavern they had reached at the end of the day was, as the colourful sign announced, The Wild Boar and Stag. But the sign was the only game offered by the establishment; you wouldn't find it on the menu. The local speciality was kasha with pieces of fatty pork in thick onion sauce. Largely on principle, Dandelion turned his nose up a little at the – in his opinion – excessively plebeian vittals. Geralt didn't complain. You couldn't find much fault with the pork, the sauce was tolerable and the kasha *al dente* – in few roadside inns did the cooks prepare the latter well. They might have done worse, particularly since the choice was limited. Geralt insisted that during the day they cover the greatest distance possible and he hadn't wanted to stop in the inns they had previously passed.

Not only for them, it turned out, did The Wild Boar and Stag turn out to be the end of the last stage of the daily trek. One of the benches against the wall was occupied by travelling merchants. Modern-thinking merchants, who – unlike traditional ones – didn't disdain their servants and didn't consider it dishonourable to sit down to meals with them. The modern thinking and tolerance had their limits, naturally; the merchants occupied one end of the table and the servants the other, so the demarcation line was easy to observe. As it was among the dishes. The servants were eating pork and kasha – the speciality of the local cuisine – and were drinking watery ale. The gentlemen merchants had each received a roast chicken and several flagons of wine.

At the opposite table, beneath a stuffed wild boar's head, dined a couple: a fair-haired girl and an older man. The girl was dressed richly, very solemnly, not like a girl at all. The man looked like a clerk and by no means a high-ranking one. The couple were dining together, having quite an animated conversation, but it was a recent and fairly accidental acquaintance, which could be concluded unequivocally from the behaviour of the official, who was importunately dancing attendance on the girl in the clear hope of something more, which the girl received with courteous, although clearly ironic reserve.

Four priestesses occupied one of the shorter benches. They were wandering healers, which could easily be seen by the grey gowns and tight hoods covering their hair. The meal they were consuming was – Geralt noticed – more than modest, something like pearl barley without even meat dripping. Priestesses never demanded payment for healing, they treated everyone for nothing and custom dictated that in return for that they be given board and lodging on request. The innkeeper at The Wild Boar and Stag was evidently familiar with the custom, but was clearly rather observing the letter than the spirit of it.

Three local men were lounging on the next bench beneath a stag's antlers, busy with a bottle of rye vodka, clearly not their first. Since they had tolerably satisfied their evening's requirements, they were looking around for entertainment. They found it swiftly, of course. The priestesses were out of luck. Although they were probably accustomed to such things.

There was a single customer at the table in the corner. Shrouded, like the table, in shadow. The customer, Geralt noticed, was neither eating nor drinking. He sat motionless, leaning back against the wall.

The three locals weren't letting up, their taunts and jests directed at the priestesses becoming more and more vulgar and obscene. The priestesses kept stoically calm and didn't pay any attention at all. The fury of the locals was increasing in inverse relation to the level of the rye vodka in the bottle. Geralt began to work more quickly with his spoon. He had decided to give the boozers a hiding and didn't want his kasha to go cold because of it.

'The Witcher Geralt of Rivia.'

A flame suddenly flared up in the gloomy corner.

The lone man sitting at the table raised a hand. Flickering tongues of flame were shooting from his fingers. The man brought his hand closer to a candlestick on the table and lit all three candles one after the other. He let them illuminate him well.

His hair was as grey as ash with snow-white streaks at the temples. A deathly pale face. A hooked nose. And yellow-green eyes with vertical pupils.

The silver medallion around his neck that he had pulled out from his shirt flashed in the candlelight.

The head of a cat baring its fangs.

'The Witcher Geralt of Rivia,' repeated the man in the silence that had fallen in the inn. 'Travelling to Vizima, I presume? For the reward promised by King Foltest? Of two thousand orens? Do I guess right?'

Geralt did not reply. He didn't even twitch.

'I won't ask if you know who I am. Because you probably do.'

'Few of you remain,' replied Geralt calmly. 'Which makes things easier. You're Brehen. Also known as the Cat of Iello.'

'Well, I prithee,' snorted the man with the feline medallion. 'The famous White Wolf deigns to know my moniker. A veritable honour. Am I also to consider it an honour that you mean to steal the reward from me? Ought I to give you priority, bow to you and apologise? As in a wolf pack, step back from the quarry and wait, wagging my tail until the pack leader has eaten his fill? Until he graciously condescends to leave some scraps?'

Geralt said nothing.

'I won't give you the best,' continued Brehen, known as the Cat of Iello. 'And I won't share. You won't go to Vizima, White Wolf. You won't snatch the reward from me. Rumour has it that Vesemir has passed sentence on me. You have the opportunity to carry it out. Let's leave the inn. Out into the yard.'

'I won't fight you.'

The man with the cat medallion leaped up from behind the table with a movement so fast it was blurred. A sword snatched up from the table flashed. The man caught one of the priestesses by the hood, dragged her from the bench, threw her down on her knees and put the blade to her throat.

'You *will* fight with me,' he said coldly, looking at Geralt.

340

'You'll go out into the courtyard before I count to three. Otherwise the priestess's blood will bespatter the walls, ceiling and furniture. And then I'll slit the others' throats. One after the other. Nobody is to move! Not an inch!'

Silence fell in the inn, a dead silence, an absolute silence. Everybody stopped in their tracks. And stared open-mouthed.

'I won't fight you,' Geralt repeated calmly. 'But if you harm that woman you will die.'

'One of us will die, that's certain. Outside in the yard. But it isn't going to be me. Your famous swords have been stolen, rumour has it. And you've neglected to equip yourself with new ones, I see. Great conceit indeed is needed to go and steal somebody's bounty, not having armed oneself first. Or perhaps the famous White Wolf is so adept he doesn't need steel?'

A chair scraped as it was moved. The fair-haired girl stood up. She picked up a long package from under the table. She placed it in front of Geralt and returned to her place, sitting down beside the clerk.

He knew what it was. Before he had even unfastened the strap or unwrapped the felt.

A sword of siderite steel, total length forty and one half inches, the blade twenty-seven and one quarter inches long. Weight: thirty-seven ounces. The hilt and cross guard simple, but elegant.

The second sword, of a similar length and weight: silver. Partially, of course, for pure silver is too soft to take a good edge. Magical glyphs on the cross guard, runic signs along the entire length of the blade.

Pyral Pratt's expert had been unable to decipher them, demonstrating his poor expertise in so doing. The ancient runes formed an inscription. *Dubhenn haern am glândeal, morc'h am fhean aiesin. My gleam penetrates the darkness, my brightness disperses the gloom.*

Geralt stood up. And drew the steel sword. With a slow and measured movement. He didn't look at Brehen. But at the blade.

'Release the woman,' he said calmly. 'At once. Otherwise you'll perish.'

Brehen's hand twitched and a trickle of blood ran down the priestess's neck. The priestess didn't even groan.

341

'I'm in need,' hissed the Cat of Iello. 'That bounty must be mine!'

'Release the woman, I said. Otherwise I'll kill you. Not in the yard, but here, on the spot.'

Brehen hunched forward. He was breathing heavily. His eyes shone malevolently and his mouth was hideously contorted. His knuckles – tightened on the hilt – were white. He suddenly released the priestess and shoved her away. The people in the inn shuddered, as though awoken from a nightmare. There were gasps and sighs.

'Winter is coming,' Brehen said with effort. 'And I, unlike some, have nowhere to lodge. Warm, cosy Kaer Morhen is not for me!'

'No,' stated Geralt. 'It is not. And well you know the reason.'

'Kaer Morhen's only for you, the good, righteous and just, is it? Fucking hypocrites. You're just as much murderers as we are, nothing distinguishes you from us!'

'Get out,' said Geralt. 'Leave this place and get on your way.'

Brehen sheathed his sword. He straightened up. As he walked through the chamber his eyes changed. His pupils filled his entire irises.

'It's a lie to say that Vesemir passed sentence on you,' said Geralt as Brehen passed him. 'Witchers don't fight with witchers, they don't cross swords. But if what happened in Iello occurs again, if I hear word of anything like that . . . Then I'll make an exception. I'll find you and kill you. Treat the warning seriously.'

A dull silence reigned in the inn chamber for a good few moments after Brehen had closed the door behind him. Dandelion's sigh of relief seemed quite loud in the silence. Soon after, people began moving again. The local drunks stole out stealthily, not even finishing off the vodka. The merchants remained, although they fell silent and went pale, but they ordered their servants to leave the table, clearly with the task of urgently securing the wagons and the horses, now at risk with such shady company nearby. The priestesses bandaged the cut neck of their companion, thanked Geralt with silent bows and headed off to bed, probably to the barn, since it was doubtful that the innkeeper had offered them beds in a sleeping chamber.

Geralt bowed and gestured over to his table the fair-haired

young woman thanks to whom he had recovered his swords. She took advantage of the invitation most readily, abandoning her erstwhile companion, the clerk, quite without regret, leaving him with a sour expression.

'I am Tiziana Frevi,' she introduced herself, shaking Geralt's hand as a man would. 'Pleased to meet you.'

'The pleasure's all mine.'

'It was a bit hairy, wasn't it? Evenings in roadside inns can be boring, today it was interesting. At a certain moment, I even began to be afraid. But, it seems to me, wasn't it just a male competition? A testosterone-fuelled duel? Or mutual comparison of whose is longer? There wasn't really a threat?'

'No, there wasn't,' he lied. 'Mainly thanks to the swords I recovered because of you. Thank you for them. But I'm racking my brains trying to figure out how they ended up in your possession.'

'It was meant to remain a secret,' she explained freely. 'I was charged with handing over the swords noiselessly and secretly and then vanishing. But circumstances suddenly changed. I had to give you the swords openly, with upraised visor, so to speak, because the situation demanded it. It would be impolite to decline any explanations now. For which reason, I shall not decline to explain, assuming the responsibility for betraying the secret. I received the swords from Yennefer of Vengerberg. It occurred two weeks ago in Novigrad. I'm a dwimveandra. I met Yennefer by accident, at a master sorceress's where I was just finishing an apprenticeship. When she learned that I was heading south and my master could vouch for me, Madam Yennefer commissioned me. And gave me a letter of recommendation to a sorceress acquaintance of hers I was planning to do an apprenticeship with.'

'How . . .' said Geralt, swallowing. 'How is she? Yennefer? In good health?'

'Excellent, I think,' said Tiziana Frevi, peering at him from under her eyelashes. 'She's doing splendidly, she looks enviably well. And to be frank I do envy her.'

Geralt stood up. He went over to the innkeeper, who had almost fainted in fear.

'You shouldn't have . . .' said Tiziana modestly, when a moment later the innkeeper placed a flagon of Est Est, the most expensive white wine from Toussaint, in front of them. And several add-itional candles stuck into the necks of old bottles.

'You're going to too much trouble, really,' she added, when a moment later some dishes arrived on the table, one with slices of raw, dried ham, another with smoked trout, and a third with a selection of cheeses. 'You're spending too much, Witcher.'

'It's a special occasion. And the company is splendid.'

She thanked him with a nod. And a smile. A pretty smile.

On graduating from magic school every sorceress faced a choice. She could stay on at the school as an assistant to the master-preceptresses. She could ask one of the independent sorceress-masters to take her on as a permanent apprentice. Or she could choose the way of the dwimveandra.

The system had been borrowed from the guilds. In many of them an apprentice who had qualified as a journeyman would embark on a trek, during which he would take on casual work in various workshops with various masters, here and there, and finally return after several years to apply to take the final exam and be promoted to master. But there were differences. Forced to travel, journeymen who couldn't find work were often stared in the face by hunger, and the journey became aimless wandering. One became a dwimveandra through one's own will and desire, and the Chapter of sorcerers created for the journeymen witches a special endowment fund, which was quite sizeable, from what Geralt heard.

'That horrifying character was wearing a medallion similar to yours,' the poet said, joining the conversation. 'He was one of the Cats, wasn't he?'

'He was. I don't want to talk about it, Dandelion.'

'The notorious Cats,' said the poet, addressing the sorceress. 'Witchers – but failures. Unsuccessful mutations. Madmen, psychopaths and sadists. They nicknamed themselves "Cats", because they really are like cats: aggressive, cruel, unpredictable and impulsive. And Geralt, as usual, is making light of it in order not to worry us. Because there *was* a threat and a significant one. It's a miracle it went off without a fight, blood or corpses. There would have been a massacre, like there was in Iello four years ago. I was expecting at any moment—'

344

'Geralt asked you not to talk about it,' interrupted Tiziana Frevi, politely but firmly. 'Let's respect that.'

Geralt looked at her affectionately. She seemed pleasant to him. And pretty. Very pretty, even.

Sorceresses, he knew, improved their looks, since the prestige of their profession demanded that they should arouse admiration. But the beautification was never perfect, something always remained. Tiziana Frevi was no exception. Her forehead, just beneath the hairline, was marked by several barely perceptible scars from the chicken pox that she had probably experienced during childhood before she became immune. The shape of her pretty mouth was slightly marred by a wavy scar above her upper lip. Geralt, yet again, felt anger, anger at his eyesight, his eyes, forcing him to notice such insignificant details, which after all were nothing in view of the fact that Tiziana was sitting at a table with him, drinking Est Est, eating smoked trout and smiling at him. The Witcher had rarely seen or known women whose beauty could be considered flawless, but the chances that one of them might smile at him could be calculated at precisely nil.

'He talked about some reward . . .' said Dandelion, who, when he got onto a subject was difficult to be dislodged from it. 'Do any of you know what it was about? Geralt?'

'I have no idea.'

'But I do,' boasted Tiziana Frevi. 'And I'm astonished you haven't heard, because it was a well-known case. As Foltest, the King of Temeria, offered a reward. For removing a spell from his daughter who had been enchanted. She had been pricked by a spindle and consigned to eternal sleep. The poor thing, so the rumour goes, is lying in a coffin in a castle overrun with hawthorn. According to another rumour the coffin is made of glass and was placed at the top of a glass mountain. According to yet another the princess was turned into a swan. According to still one more into an awful monster, a striga. As a result of a curse, because the princess was the fruit of an incestuous union. Apparently, the rumours are being invented and spread by Vizimir, the King of Redania, who has territorial disputes with Foltest, is seriously at variance with him and will do anything to annoy him.'

'It indeed sounds like fabrication,' judged Geralt. 'Based on a fairy tale or fable. An accursed and transformed princess, the curse as a punishment for incest, a reward for removing a spell. Hackneyed and banal. The person who came up with it didn't make much of an effort.'

'The issue,' the dwimveandra added, 'has a clear political subtext, which is why the Chapter forbade sorcerers from getting involved in it.'

'Whether it's a fairy tale or not, that damned Cat believed it,' pronounced Dandelion. 'He was clearly hurrying to that enchanted princess in Vizima to remove the spell and claim the reward promised by King Foltest. He had acquired the suspicion that Geralt was also heading there and wanted to beat him to it.'

'He was mistaken,' Geralt responded dryly. 'I'm not going to Vizima. I don't intend to stick my fingers in that political cauldron. It's perfect work for somebody like Brehen who's in need, as he said himself. I'm not in need. I've recovered my swords, so I don't have to pay out for new ones. I have funds to support myself. Thanks to the sorcerers from Rissberg . . .'

'The Witcher Geralt of Rivia?'

'Indeed,' said Geralt, eyeing up and down the clerk, who was standing alongside looking sulky. 'Who wants to know?'

'That is inconsequential,' said the clerk, putting on airs and pouting, trying hard to make himself look important. 'What's consequential is the summons. Which I hereby give you. In front of witnesses. In accordance with the law.'

The clerk handed the Witcher a roll of paper. And then sat down, not failing to cast Tiziana Frevi a contemptuous glance.

Geralt broke the seal and unfurled the roll.

'"*Datum ex Castello Rissberg, die 20 mens. Jul. anno 1245 post Resurrectionem,*' he read. 'To the Magistrates' Court in Gors Velen. Plaintiff: The Rissberg Complex civil partnership. Defendant: Geralt of Rivia, witcher. Claim: the return of the sum of one thousand Novigradian crowns. We hereby petition, *primo*: a demand to the defendant Geralt of Rivia for the return of the sum of one thousand Novigradian crowns with due interest. *Secundo*, a demand to the defendant for the court costs to the plaintiff according to prescribed norms. *Tertio*: to lend the verdict the status of immediately enforceability. Grounds: the defendant swindled from the Rissberg Complex civil partnership the sum of one thousand Novigradian crowns. Proof: copies of bank orders. The sum constituted an advance fee for a service that the defendant never executed and in ill will never intended to execute . . . Witnesses: Biruta Anna Marquette Icarti, Axel Miguel Esparza, Igo Tarvix Sandoval . . ." The bastards.'

'I returned your swords to you,' said Tiziana, lowering her gaze. 'And at the same time saddled you with problems. That beadle tricked me. He overheard me this morning asking for you at the ferry port. And then immediately stuck to me like a leech. Now I know why. That summons is all my fault.'

'You'll be needing a lawyer,' stated Dandelion gloomily. 'But I don't recommend the one from Kerack. She only performs well outside the courtroom.'

'I can skip the lawyer. Did you notice the date of the claim? I'll wager the case has already been heard and the verdict read out *in absentia*. And that they've seized my account.'

'I am sorry,' said Tiziana. 'It's my fault. Forgive me.'

'There's nothing to forgive, you aren't to blame for anything. And Rissberg and the courts can go to hell. Master innkeeper! Another flagon of Est Est, if you would.'

*

They were soon the only guests left in the chamber. The innkeeper soon let them know – with an ostentatious yawn – that it was time to finish. Tiziana was first to go to her room and Dandelion followed suit to his soon after.

Geralt didn't go to the bedchamber he was sharing with the poet. Instead of that he knocked very softly at Tiziana Frevi's door. It opened at once.

'I've been waiting,' she murmured, pulling him inside. 'I knew you'd come. And if you hadn't I would have gone looking for you.'

*

She must have put him to sleep magically, otherwise she would certainly have woken him as she was leaving. And she must have left before dawn, while it was still dark. Her scent lingered after her. The delicate perfume of irises and bergamot. And something else. Roses?

A flower lay on the table by his swords. A rose. One of the white roses from the flowerpot standing outside the inn.

*

No one remembered what the place was, who had built it and whom and what it served. The ruins of an ancient edifice, once a large and probably prosperous complex, had survived in the valley beyond the inn. Practically nothing remained of the buildings apart from what was left of the foundations, some overgrown hollows and some stone blocks dotted about. The rest had been demolished and plundered. Building materials were precious, nothing went to waste.

They walked in beneath the ruins of a shattered portal, once an impressive arch, now resembling a gibbet; the impression of which was enhanced by ivy hanging like a severed noose. They walked along a path between the trees. Dead, crippled and misshapen trees, bent over as though by the weight of a curse hanging over the place. The path led towards a garden. Or rather towards something that had once been a garden. Beds of berberis, juniper shrubs, rambling roses, probably once decoratively pruned, were now a disordered and chaotic tangle of branches, prickly climbers and dried stalks. Peeping out of the tangle were the remains of statues and sculptures, mainly full-length. The remains were so vestigial that there was no way of even approximately determining who – or what – the statues had once portrayed. In any case, it wasn't especially important. The statues were the past. They hadn't survived and so they had stopped mattering. All that remained was a ruin and one – it seemed – that would survive a long time, since ruins are eternal.

A ruin. A monument to a devastated world.

'Dandelion.'

'Yes?'

'Lately everything that could have gone wrong has gone wrong.

And it seems to me that I've fucked everything up. Whatever I've touched lately I've botched.'

'Do you think so?'

'Yes, I do.'

'It must be so, then. Don't expect a comment. I'm tired of commenting. And now go and feel sorry for yourself in silence, if you would. I'm composing at the moment and your laments are distracting me.'

Dandelion sat down on a fallen column, pushed his bonnet back on his head, crossed his legs and adjusted the pegs on the lute.

A flickering candle, the fire went out,
A cold wind blew perceptibly . . .

A wind had indeed blown up, suddenly and violently. And Dandelion stopped playing. And sighed loudly.

The Witcher turned around.

She was standing at the entrance to the path, between the cracked plinth of an unrecognisable statue and the tangled thicket of a dead whipple-tree. She was tall and wore a clinging dress. With a head of greyish colouring, more typical of a corsac than a silver fox. Pointed ears and an elongated face.

Geralt didn't move.

'I warned you I would come.' Rows of teeth glistened in the she-fox's mouth. 'One day. Today is that day.'

Geralt didn't move. On his back, he felt the familiar weight of his two swords, a weight he had been missing for a month. Which usually gave him peace and certainty. That day, at that moment, the weight was just a burden.

'I have come . . .' said the aguara, flashing her fangs. 'I don't know why I came myself. In order to say goodbye, perhaps. Perhaps to let her say goodbye to you.'

A slender girl in a tight dress emerged from behind the vixen. Her pale and unnaturally unmoving face was still half human. But probably now more vulpine than human. The changes were occurring quickly.

The Witcher shook his head.

'You cured her . . . You brought her back to life? No, that's impossible. So, she was alive on the ship. Alive. But pretending to be dead.'

The aguara barked loudly. He needed a moment before realising it was laughter. That the vixen was laughing.

'Once we had great powers! Illusions of magical islands, dragons dancing in the sky, visions of a mighty army approaching city walls . . . Once, long ago. Now the world has changed and our abilities have dwindled . . . And we have grown smaller. There is more vixen in us than aguara. But still, even the smallest, even the youngest she-fox, is capable of deceiving your primitive human senses with an illusion.'

'For the first time in my life,' he said a moment later, 'I'm glad to have been tricked.'

'It's not true that you did everything wrong. And as a reward you may touch my face.'

He cleared his throat, looking at her great pointed teeth.

'Hmm . . .'

'Illusions are what you think about. What you fear. And what you dream of.'

'I beg your pardon?'

The vixen barked softly. And metamorphosed.

Dark, violet eyes, blazing in a pale, triangular face. A tornado of jet-black locks falling onto her shoulders, gleaming, reflecting light like peacock's feathers, curling and rippling with every movement. The mouth, marvellously thin and pale under her lipstick. A black velvet ribbon on her neck, on the ribbon an obsidian star, sparkling and sending thousands of reflections around . . .

Yennefer smiled. And the Witcher touched her cheek.

And then the dead dogwood bloomed.

And afterwards the wind blew and shook the bush. The world vanished behind a veil of tiny white whirling petals.

'Illusion.' He heard the aguara's voice. 'Everything is illusion.'

*

Dandelion stopped singing. But he didn't put down his lute. He was sitting on a chunk of overturned column. Looking up at the sky.

Geralt sat beside him. Weighing up various things. Arranging various things in his head. Or rather trying to. Making plans. In the main, wholly unfeasible. He promised himself various things. Seriously doubting if he was capable of keeping any of the promises.

'You know, you never congratulate me on my ballads,' Dandelion suddenly spoke up. 'I've composed and sung so many of them in your company. But you've never said: "That was nice. I'd like you to play that again." You've never said that.'

'You're right. I haven't. Do you want to know why?'

'Yes?'

'Because I've never wanted to.'

'Would it be such a sacrifice?' asked the bard, not giving up. 'Such a hardship? To say: "Play that again, Dandelion. Play *As Time Passes*".'

'Play it again, Dandelion. Play "As Time Passes".'

'You said that quite without conviction.'

'So what? You'll play it anyway.'

'You'd better believe it.

A flickering candle, the fire went out
A cold wind blew perceptibly
And the days pass
And time passes
In silence and imperceptibly
You're with me endlessly and endlessly
Something joins us, but not perfectly
For the days pass
For time passes
In silence and imperceptibly
The memory of travelled paths and roads
Remain in us irrevocably
Although the days pass
Although time passes
In silence and imperceptibly
So, my love, one more time
Let's repeat the chorus triumphantly
So do the days pass
So does time pass
In silence and imperceptibly

Geralt stood up.

'Time to ride, Dandelion.'
'Oh, yes? Where to?'
'Isn't it all the same?'
'Yes, by and large. Let's go.'

EPILOGUE

On the hillock, the remains of buildings shone white, fallen into ruin so long ago they were now completely overgrown. Ivy had enveloped the walls and young trees had grown through the cracked flagstones. It had once been – Nimue could not have known that – a temple, the seat of the priests of some forgotten deity. For Nimue it was just a ruin. A pile of stones. And a signpost. A sign that she was going the right way.

For just beyond the hillock and the ruins the highway forked. One path led west, over a moor. The other one, heading north, vanished into a thick, dense forest. It went deep into the black undergrowth, vanished into gloomy darkness, dissolving into it.

And that was her route. Northwards. Through the infamous Magpie Forest.

Nimue wasn't especially perturbed by the stories they had tried to frighten her with in Ivalo, since during her trek she had coped over and over with similar things. Each place had its own grim folklore, local dangers and horrors, serving to give travellers a scare. Nimue had already been threatened by drowners in lakes, bereginias in streams, wights at crossroads and ghosts in cemeteries. Every second footbridge was supposed to be a troll's lair, every second brake of crooked willows a striga's haunt. Nimue finally became accustomed to it and the commonplace horrors ceased to be fearful. But there was no way of mastering the strange anxiety that spread through her before she entered a dark forest, walked along a path between fog-bound burial mounds or a track among mist-shrouded swamps.

She also felt that anxiety now – as she stood before the dark wall of forest – creeping in tingles over the back of her neck and drying her lips.

The road is well travelled, she repeated to herself, *quite rutted by wagons, trodden down by the hooves of horses and oxen. So what if the forest looks frightful? It's no desolate backwoods, it's a busy track to Dorian, leading through the last patch of forest to escape the axes and saws. Many people ride through here, many walk through here. I'll also pass through it. I'm not afraid.*

I'm Nimue verch Wledyr ap Gwyn.

Vyrva, Guado, Sibell, Brugge, Casterfurt, Mortara, Ivalo, Dorian, Anchor, Gors Velen.

She looked back to see if anybody was approaching. *It would be more pleasant to have company*, she thought. But the highway, to make matters worse, had chosen not to be well-frequented. It was quite simply deserted.

There was no choice. Nimue cleared her throat, adjusted the bundle on her shoulder and gripped her stick tightly. And strode into the forest.

Oaks, elms and ancient hornbeams interwoven together predominated and there were also pines and larches. Lower down there was dense undergrowth, hawthorns, filberts, bird cherries and honeysuckle entangled together. You would have expected it to teem with bird life, but a malevolent silence reigned there. Nimue walked with her eyes fixed on the ground. She sighed with relief when all of a sudden, a woodpecker drummed somewhere deep in the forest. *So, something does live here*, she thought, *I'm not completely alone.*

She stopped and suddenly turned around. She didn't see anybody or anything, but for a moment was certain that someone was following her. She sensed she was being watched. Secretly stalked. Fear constricted her throat and shivers ran down her back.

She speeded up. The forest, or so it seemed, had begun to thin out, had become lighter and greener, for birches began to predominate. *One more bend, then two more*, she thought feverishly, *a little more and the forest will* finish. *I'll put this forest behind me, along with whatever's prowling there. And I'll keep going.*

Vyrva, Guado, Sibell, Brugge . . .

She didn't even hear a rustle, but caught sight of a movement out of the corner of her eye. A grey, many-limbed and incredibly fast shape shot out of the thicket of ferns. Nimue screamed, seeing the snapping pincers as large as scythes. Legs covered in spines and bristles. Many eyes, surrounding the head like a crown.

She felt a sharp tug, which picked her up and threw her aside. She tumbled down on her back onto the springy branches of a filbert shrub, caught hold of them, ready to leap up and flee. She froze, looking at the wild dance taking place on the track.

The many-legged creature was hopping and whirling around incredibly quickly, brandishing its limbs and clanking its dreadful mandibles. And around it, even quicker, so quick that he was blurred, danced a man. Armed with two swords.

First one, then a second and finally a third limb was hacked off and flew into the air in front of Nimue, who was watching petrified with fear. The blows of the swords fell on the flat body, from which a green sticky substance was squirting. The monster struggled and flailed around, finally making a desperate leap and fleeing into the forest, bolting. It didn't get far. The man with the swords caught up with it, stepped on it and pinned it to the ground with simultaneous, powerful thrusts of both blades. The creature threshed the ground with its limbs, then finally lay still.

Nimue pressed her hands to her chest, trying hard to calm her pounding heart. She saw her rescuer kneel over the dead monster and use a knife to lever something from its carapace. Saw him wipe the two blades and sheath the swords into the scabbards on his back.

'Everything in order?'

Some time passed before Nimue realised he was talking to her. But in any case, she couldn't utter a word or get up from the hazel thicket. Her rescuer was in no hurry to pull her out of the bush, so she finally had to get out herself. Her legs were trembling so much she had difficulty standing. The dryness in her mouth persisted stubbornly.

'It was a rotten idea, trekking alone through the forest,' said her rescuer, coming over.

He pulled back his hood and his snow-white hair positively shone in the sylvan twilight. Nimue almost cried out, bringing her fists to her mouth in an involuntary movement. *It's impossible*, she thought, *it's absolutely impossible. I must be dreaming.*

'But from this moment,' continued the white-haired man, examining a blackened and tarnished metal plate in his hand. 'From this moment, it will be possible to travel this way in safety. And what do we have here? IDR UL Ex IX 0008 BETA. Ha! This one was missing from my collection. Number eight. But now I've settled the score. How are you feeling, girl? Oh, forgive me. Parched mouth, eh? Tongue as dry as a board? I know it, I know it. Have a sip.'

She took the canteen he handed her in trembling hands.

'Where are we going?'

'To Do . . . To Dor . . .'

'Dor?'

'Dor . . . Dorian. What was that? That thing . . . over there?'

'A work of art. Masterpiece number eight. It's actually not important what it was. What's important is that it's no more. But who are you? Where are you making for?'

She nodded her head and swallowed. And spoke. Astonished by her own courage.

'I am . . . I'm Nimue verch Wledyr ap Gwyn. From Dorian I'm going to Anchor and from there to Gors Velen. And Aretuza, the school of sorceresses on the Isle of Thanedd.'

'Oho. And where did you come from?'

'From the village of Vyrva. Via Guado, Sibell, Brugge, Casterfurt—'

'I know that route,' he interrupted her. 'You've truly trekked through half the world, O Nimue, daughter of Wledyr. They ought to give you credit for that during the entry examination in Aretuza. But they're unlikely to. You've set yourself an ambitious route, O girl from the village of Vyrva. Very ambitious. Come with me.'

'Very well . . .' Nimue was still walking stiffly. 'Good sir . . .?'

'Yes?'

'Thank you for saving me.'

'The thanks are due to you. For a good few days I've been looking out for someone like you. For any travellers coming this way were in large groups, proud and armed, and our work-of-art number eight didn't dare to attack anyone like that, it didn't venture from its hideout. You lured it out. It was able to spot some easy meat, even at a great distance. Somebody travelling alone. And not very big. No offence meant.'

The edge of the forest was, as it turned out, just around the corner. The white-haired man's horse – a bay mare – was waiting a little way further, beside a lone clump of trees.

'It's some forty miles from here to Dorian,' said the white-haired man. 'Three days' march for you. Three and a half, including the rest of today. Are you aware of that?'

Nimue felt a sudden euphoria, eliminating the torpor and the other effects of terror. *It's a dream*, she thought. *I must be dreaming. Because I can't be awake.*

'What's the matter? Are you feeling well?'

Nimue plucked up her courage.

'That mare . . .' she said, so excited she was barely able to enunciate her words. 'That mare is called Roach. Because all your horses bear that name. For you are Geralt of Rivia. The Witcher Geralt of Rivia.'

He looked long at her. And said nothing. Nimue also said nothing, eyes fixed on the ground.

'What year is it?'

'One thousand three hundred . . .' she said, raising her astonished eyes. 'One thousand three hundred and seventy-three after the Revival.'

'If so—' the white-haired man wiped his face with his hand in his sleeve '—Geralt of Rivia has been dead for many years. He died a hundred and five years ago. But I think he would be happy, if . . . He'd be happy if people remembered him after all those hundred and five years. If they remembered who he was. Why, even if they remembered the name of his horse. Yes, I think, he would be happy . . . If he could know it. Come. I'll see you off.'

They walked on. Nimue bit her lip. Embarrassed, she decided not to say anything more.

'Ahead of us is a crossroads and the highway,' the white-haired man said, breaking the tense silence. 'The road to Dorian. You'll get there safely—'

'The Witcher Geralt didn't die!' Nimue blurted out. 'He only went away, went away to the Land of the Apple Trees. But he'll return . . . He'll return, because the legend says he will.'

'Legends. Fables. Fairy tales. Stories and romances. I might have guessed, Nimue from the village of Vyrva, who's going to the school for sorceresses on the Isle of Thanedd. You wouldn't have dared undertake such an insane quest had it not been for the legends and fairy tales you grew up on. But they're just fairy tales, Nimue. Just fairy tales. You've come too far from home not to understand that.'

'The Witcher will return from the beyond!' Nimue wasn't giving up. 'He'll return to protect people, so that Evil will never hold sway again. As long as darkness exists, witchers will be necessary. And darkness still exists!'

He said nothing, looking away. He finally turned towards her. And smiled.

'Darkness still exists,' he agreed. 'In spite of the progress being made which we're told to believe will light up the gloom, eliminate threats and drive away fears. Until now, progress hasn't achieved great success in that field. Until now, all progress has done is to persuade us that darkness is only a glimmering superstition, that there's nothing to be afraid of. But it's not true. There *are* things to be afraid of. Because darkness will always, always exist. And Evil will always rampage in the darkness, there will always be fangs and claws, killing and blood in the darkness. And witchers will always be necessary. And let's hope they'll always appear exactly where they're needed. Answering the call for help. Rushing to where they are summoned. May they appear with sword in hand. A sword whose gleam will penetrate the darkness, a sword whose brightness disperses the gloom. A pretty fairy tale, isn't it? And it ends well, as every fairy tale should.'

'But . . .' she stammered. 'But it's a hundred years . . . How is it possible for . . . ? How is it possible—?'

'A future novice of Aretuza may not ask questions like that,' he interrupted, still smiling. 'A novice of a school where they teach that nothing is impossible. Because everything that's impossible today may become possible tomorrow. A slogan like that should hang above the entrance to the school. Which will soon become your school. Fare you well, Nimue. Farewell. Here we part.'

'But . . .' She felt sudden relief, and her words gushed forth. 'But I'd like to know . . . Know more. About Yennefer. About Ciri. About how that story really ended. I've read it . . . I know the legend. I know everything. About witchers. About Kaer Morhen. I even know the names of all the witcher Signs! Please, tell me—'

'Here we part,' he interrupted her gently. 'The road to your